IN HONOR BOUND

IN HONOR BOUND

DeAnna Julie Dodson

CROSSWAY BOOKS • WHEATON, ILLINOIS
A DIVISION OF GOOD NEWS PUBLISHERS

In Honor Bound

Published by Crossway Books
a division of Good News Publishers
1300 Crescent Street
Wheaton, Illinois 60187

Cover design: Cindy Kiple

Cover illustration: Laura Lakey

First printing, 1997

Printed in the United States of America

Library of Congress Cataloging-in-Publication Data
Dodson, DeAnna Julie 1961-
In Honor Bound / DeAnna Julie Dodson.
p. cm.
ISBN 0-89107-909-2
I. Title.
PS3554.03414I5 1997
813'.54—dc21 96-47327

05 04 03 02 01 00 99 98 97
15 14 13 12 11 10 9 8 7 6 5 4 3 2 1

DEDICATION

To my Undefeated Champion
Fairest of Ten Thousand
Sweet Lover of my soul
My Jesus Christ—
I love You

ACKNOWLEDGMENTS

To my very first reader, Diana Norris,
who never let me quit—

To my very first editors, Jacky Chappell and Shawnita Lusk,
who read and reread and reread—

To Wayne Chappell and everyone at "Wayne's World"
who prayed so faithfully for so very, very long—

To my pastor, Dr. Dwayne Lusk,
who preaches the unadulterated Word of God
and practices what he preaches—

To my friend and mentor, Robin Hardy,
who was so generous with her wisdom and experience—

To my father, Julian Ray Dodson,
who has always been a wonderful daddy—

To all those who prayed and believed this book could be—

Your patience, encouragement, and loving support, like all gifts from God, are undeserved and impossible to repay.

PROLOGUE

FROM THE WINDOW OF HER TOWER ROOM, ROSALYNDE WATCHED a noisy, spirited cluster of men and boys on horseback sweep through the early snow into the courtyard, followed by an ornate carriage. Horses and riders both carried all the trappings of nobility, and the white saint's rose was emblazoned on every banner. Only those with the royal blood of Chastelayne were allowed to display it. This would have to be the Duke of Afton and his family at last.

"That one, Ankarette," Rosalynde said, picking out the leader of the party. He was tall and dark of hair and eye and sat his horse with all the handsome majesty of a king. "That must be Duke Robert." She saw him pull up and speak to the young copy of himself who rode at his side. "And that is, doubtless, his eldest, Richard of Bradford."

Her nursemaid glanced out the window and then went on weaving pink ribbon into Rosalynde's dark hair. "The boy looks of an age with your sister, my lady, and a fair match to her, if rumor proves true."

"Oh, that's been tattled about for months now," Rosalynde said, twisting around to look at her. "Ever since Duke Robert went to fight in the Riverlands."

"Your sister is near twenty," the tall, spare woman said, and she turned Rosalynde's head straight again. "She might have been married these five years and more—keep still now—unless my lord of Afton and my lord your father have had other plans for her."

"Father would never betroth them—not without the king's consent."

"Then why have they come here, the duke and his lady and their sons, with winter coming on and all? You mustn't turn your head about, my lady. You can hear me without seeing me. Anyway, Westered can hardly be on their way to anywhere but wilderness, unless they mean to put out to sea."

"They come out of friendship, Father says."

"Well, I'll not doubt his lordship's word after so long, even if it does strike me odd. Almost done now. Still, mayhap he means to match your sister with Prince Stephen."

"I daresay that would suit Margaret well enough, whatever the prince is like, but they say King Edward will have no less than a princess for his only son. Besides, I hear the prince is horribly ill-tempered."

Ankarette tucked in the ribbon's end. "Any proud-blooded man might be cross to have his command taken from himself, being a prince, and given over to a duke."

"I heard it told that the king put Duke Robert in his place because all Prince Stephen did was spoil the land with killings and burnings and never gained a foot of ground."

"Mayhap Lady Margaret would not be so set to be a princess if she heard of this."

"She has heard but says she cares not. I think she would never care if he were old enough to be her grandsire and as ugly as Vulcan either, so long as she could be queen."

Ankarette laughed. "I doubt he is little more than thirty." She drew Rosalynde back into the chamber and sat her down so she could put on her shoes. "And handsome enough, I suppose, with the king's Chastelayne blood in him. All the Chastelaynes are long famed for beauty as well as valor." She stood Rosalynde up again, checking to see that everything was properly done and then patted her cheek. "And I somehow doubt it is the tales of their valor that makes you so eager to see Afton's sons today."

Blushing, Rosalynde scurried back to the window, glad when Ankarette finally went to see if her father was ready for her to come down.

Afton had three more sons, Rosalynde knew—Philip of Caladen, then Thomas of Brenden, then John of Rounchaux—each a duke in his own right and, as Ankarette had said, all famed for beauty. She searched further through the band of riders down in the courtyard, dismissing several by their garments and deference to the others as servants, but she spied two among them who could be nothing less than sons to such a man as Robert Chastelayne.

The two were so close in age she could not decide which was Philip and which was Thomas. John, the youngest, was but ten or twelve, she had been told, and these two looked to be a year or perhaps two years older than herself. Even from a distance, she could see that they were much alike, tall and dark-haired and handsome like their father.

Hearing the two laugh between themselves at something she did not catch, she moved closer to the window. Then one of them chanced to look up at her, the smile still on his face, his blue eyes still warm with laughter. She froze where she stood, a surprised little sigh escaping her lips. Then she stepped swiftly back into the chamber.

Eyes like heaven, she thought, feeling an unaccustomed fluttering in her breast. *Which is he?*

"You're to go to your father now, my lady," Ankarette said, coming back into the room. Rosalynde went to her looking glass to see if there was still too much guilty pink in her cheeks.

"Am I fit to meet them?"

Ankarette adjusted one dark curl and tugged at the lace in Rosalynde's sleeve.

"You make a pretty picture, lamb."

Rosalynde looked at herself again and frowned. She was fifteen and looked plumply twelve, but she did make a pretty picture with her bountiful hair loosely bound down her back and her thick-lashed green eyes wide with excitement. Her frown deepened.

"You always say so."

"Because it always is so," Ankarette said calmly. "Now come along to your father. Your sister is down there already."

"You honor us, my lady," her father was saying to the exquisite woman standing at the Duke of Afton's side. Lady Elaine was tall, up to her tall husband's ear, and slenderly built, with flawless white skin, a wealth of fair hair, and eyes like twin sapphires. Rosalynde watched as her father kissed the lady's hand with the utmost reverence, as if he dared touch a goddess. Lady Elaine made a regal curtsey.

"You are most gracious to open your home to us, my lord of Westered," she said, her mellifluous voice in perfect accord with her golden beauty.

"You are welcome, my lady," Westered said, "and my young lords as well."

Rosalynde hesitated at the foot of the stairs, but he caught sight of her and reached one brawny hand toward her with a smile.

"And this is my younger daughter, Rosalynde."

She made a deep curtsey and took a better look at Duke Robert. He looked at most to be in his middle thirties, younger than she had expected to have a son grown and two others nearly so. He was a handsome man—she had seen that already. But now she saw there was something more in him that gave him such favor with the nobility in Lynaleigh and with the people, even above the king himself.

"Two such fair ones, my lord of Westered," Robert said, looking from Rosalynde to Margaret. "For the first time, I regret having had only sons. Still, such as they are, allow me to present them to you. This is Richard, my heir."

Margaret dropped a practiced curtsey, smiling boldly at Afton's eldest, and Rosalynde saw the young man's obvious appreciation of her sister's beauty. Then she looked at the comely fair-haired boy at his side.

"And my youngest, John," Robert said.

The boy was as finely golden as his mother, bearing out, as did they all, the truth behind the reputed grace of the royal Chastelaynes.

Rosalynde was keenly aware that there were yet two more to be presented—Afton's middle sons. Still not knowing which was which, she glanced furtively at them. They both had their mother's fair skin and her more-than-commonly-handsome features, but they also had inherited their father's strength and the stubborn Chastelayne jaw line. Their knightly training had left them lithe and gracefully well muscled, every inch the noble warriors they were born to be.

"This is my next youngest, Thomas," Robert said, and one of them stepped forward with an engaging smile. She let the warmth in his brown-velvet eyes coax a smile from her, but he was not the one who had caught her attention from the courtyard.

She looked up at the last of Afton's sons and forgot to breathe. The laughter was gone from his expression now, replaced with polite reserve, but she had never in all her life seen such eyes. They were like the sea that stretched along the west side of the castle, like the smooth summer sea touched with moonlight. Even his exquisite mother's eyes were not so blue, hadn't such lights in them or such feeling. Rosalynde imagined that if she could look hard enough, she would be able to see clear through their crystal depths into his very soul.

"This is my son Philip," Robert said, a hint of amusement in his tone, and Rosalynde realized she had been staring. The others laughed, and her lashes swept to her burning cheeks.

"You honor me, my lady," Philip said as he bent to kiss her hand. His voice was kind, and she glanced up again, surprised to see gentleness in those wondrous eyes and not annoyance or embarrassment. She knew nothing of young men and had expected these, from Margaret's estimation of the breed in general, to be spoiled and coarse and vain. She was glad it was not so.

That night the Duke of Westered held a great feast in honor of his guests. Richard quickly established himself as Margaret's escort, and Rosalynde found herself seated at the long, bountifully laden table between Philip and Thomas, listening to the quick banter that flew from one to the other. Their jesting made her laugh and eased her self-consciousness.

"Will you be with us long, my lords?" she ventured as the servants set out the honeyed quince that ended the meal. "My father did not say."

"A few days only," Philip replied, the soft, caressing tones of his northern-born voice falling pleasingly on her ears. "We're to winter at home in Treghatours. Then Father is to return south to the war come spring."

The war touched them little here in Westered, but Rosalynde knew of it well enough. Lynaleigh and her enemy, Grenaver, had been one kingdom until a long-ago king had decreed that upon his death his twin sons should each have a kingdom of his own. The realm was split in half—Lynaleigh in the north and Grenaver in the south—divided by the river that flowed from the western mountains to the sea.

For generations the two kingdoms had lived together in peace. Then one of the Grenaven scribes, looking into the old king's will, suggested that perhaps it was the northern branch of the river, a good distance into Lynaleighan territory, that the decree intended as the dividing line. The king of Grenaver, already chafing over a trade dispute, demanded the immediate return of his lands.

In response, the king of Lynaleigh claimed that the river's southern branch, winding almost as far into Grenaven territory, was the border. Both sides rejected as border marker the main river that divided the lands evenly. The dispute boiled between the two kings and their emissaries for a time and eventually flared into the war that had been raging off and on now for years. As long as Rosalynde could remember, there had been fighting in the Riverlands.

"They say your father will win the Riverlands back for King Edward in time," she said.

A fervent light sparked into Philip's eyes.

"The king'll not find a stouter champion nor a more loyal one. There's not a worthier man in Lynaleigh."

"Worthier than the king himself," Richard put in. "By blood if nothing else."

Rosalynde's eyes widened. She knew, as did the whole kingdom, the story of Robert of Afton, how he had once been heir to the throne. Now Edward of Ellenshaw, his uncle, his father's younger brother, was king and had been for almost thirty years. It was near treason to even speak of Robert's claims.

"Do not listen to his ramblings, my lady," Tom said lightly. "My father would likely box his ears for such talk, and he knows it."

Philip pushed his empty plate away and frowned at Richard. "Edward was anointed king in the sight of God. Father would never challenge that sanctity. It would hardly be honorable."

Richard dismissed him with a wave of his hand. "I never said he would make good his claim—just that by right he is more king than Edward."

There was a challenge in Margaret's eyes. "I think if I were rightly king and had an army at my back, I'd not let another keep my right from me."

"Meg!" Rosalynde cried, and Richard laughed.

"There, you see! And should it not be so, the right being on our side? Lady Margaret, you've won my very heart."

Rosalynde thought again of the rumored alliance between Margaret and Richard, between Westered and Afton, an alliance that would make Duke Robert strong enough to revive his claim if he desired. There was also the royal blood that flowed in the veins of his sons. Because of the direct lineage of both their father and mother, the blood they bore was more purely Chastelayne than any in Lynaleigh.

Right and might both together, she thought. Still, as Philip had said, there was not a more loyal man in the kingdom than Robert of Afton.

"Doubtless you know your own mind, Lady Margaret," Philip said with a polite nod. "For myself, I had sooner keep my dukedom and my honor."

"My brother has a very fine sense of honor on every point, my lady," Richard said, pouring himself more wine. "He'll not leave a dog in the cold or beat a lazy page or trifle with a woman's honesty."

Margaret gave Philip an insolent appraising glance. "Will he not?"

"No, faith," Richard said. "He's a very maid for chastity, but I have hope he will outgrow it."

The color rose in Philip's face, as if he were ashamed of his own innocence and angry that his brother had been able to make him ashamed of it. His eyes narrowed, but he said nothing.

"As you have outgrown it, my lord?" Margaret asked, looking with perfect innocence into Richard's face. This time it was Philip who laughed.

"I am as honest as any nobleman need be," Richard said with a touch of pique. "One day when I am too old for roistering, I shall mend my life and be as pious and dull as my brothers there. They are near Heretics for strictness."

"Pious and dull?" Tom popped a slice of fruit into his mouth with a smiling shake of his head. "You say it as if the two must go together perforce. Pious, I hope, but dull? May God spare me that. It was never His way."

"Nor the way of the Heretics," Philip added. "Nor mine either, I hope."

There were those they called Heretics, Rosalynde knew, even as far as Westered. Outside the established church, they claimed a simpler, purer faith than was fashionable. The belief was strongest in the north, near Afton, but she had not thought it would reach so high among the nobility.

"Are you a Heretic, my lord of Caladen?" Margaret asked.

"I'd not call it so, my lady," Philip said, an easy certainty in his tone. "Is it heresy to live as pleases God without hiding behind the rituals and the hypocrisy of the church?"

"Best be glad you are here and not in the king's court, my lord," Margaret said, "when you speak so boldly."

"I am not ashamed of my life, my lady. I would face whatever may come of it rather than deny what I believe to be true."

Richard smugly took a drink of wine. "As I said, my lady, he will outgrow it."

There was haughty amusement in Margaret's face, and

Rosalynde's eyes flashed. They had no right to make sport of this young man for holding to his principles, as if two or three years more of life had made the two of them all-wise.

"I'll not believe it of him!" she said, and Margaret laughed.

"I yield to your champion, Philip," Richard said. Then he made a mocking toast. "Lady Rosalynde."

Rosalynde felt her face turn hot, but Philip smiled at her and also raised his cup.

"Again you honor me, my lady. I pray I prove worthy of your faith in me."

She knew he said it impersonally, as any gentleman might in a chivalrous moment, but she could not help that odd quickening of her pulse when he turned that smile upon her.

"But you mustn't heed my brother too much," he added, a little mischief in his eyes. "We give him scope when he's had more than two cups of wine all of an evening."

"Faith, Philip, you are too good to me," Richard said, grinning. "I could never hope to deserve it of such a nonpareil."

He gouged Philip with his elbow. Then the jugglers began their tricks, and treason, for the moment, was forgotten.

❧

"My Rosalynde is quite taken with him," Westered said when he and the Duke of Afton spoke alone a few days later. "But she is young yet, I think, for such things."

"I was married at fifteen myself," Robert said, "and I have had nothing but pleasure in it. She and Philip would match as well as Margaret and Richard, I think."

Westered smiled. "A double bond never hurt a friendship, eh? That is, if there is to be any bond at all."

"Of course, you know there are more than a few young ladies *quite taken* with my boy," Robert reminded him, and Westered's smile widened.

"Come, my lord, shall we speak freely? Did you not come here to dangle him and the other one, Thomas, in front of my Rosalynde's eyes to see which she'd prefer? I'll admit your boys are all—in breeding, manners, and looks—the very pattern of what a young man ought be, but Westered will not be easily bought."

"Do you count your daughters as negotiable merchandise, my lord?"

"As much as you do your sons. Come, we both want to see our children well matched and our dukedoms enriched, but you must confess there is some danger in marriage between our households. Especially between your heir and mine. The king will see nothing but rebellion in it."

"He would have no cause to care if he knew he held true title to the throne. He knows I am no longer a boy of seven, to be bullied into relinquishing what is rightly mine." The tautness in his face turned again into affability. "Still, I did not come to talk of such perplexities but of both our futures."

"I have no quarrel with your title, my lord. There was no justice in your being set aside, regardless of your youth."

"You are not alone in that belief."

"I thought I might not be the only one you have spoken to of this," Westered said. "Yet there is danger even in support of a just cause."

"True," Robert said, "and much gain to those willing to risk much." He smiled. "A kingdom for risk of a dukedom?"

"Or a chopping block," Westered observed.

The next day the snow melted, and Rosalynde watched their guests sweep out of the courtyard as boisterously as they had come. It seemed such a short while ago. The days of riding and dancing, of long walks along the wintery beach and longer talks, of all Philip's chivalrous attentions—they were over.

There had been much ceremony in the parting between the two

noble families, formal embraces and flattering farewells. Rosalynde had felt her blood rush when Philip kissed her hand and shocked herself with the wish that he would kiss her lips instead. She had never desired such a thing before, had never understood that longing in anyone else.

Philip had smiled at her again as he mounted his horse and then had to lean down to catch her breathless "God speed." Now he was gone, his horse's tracks mixed in with all the others in the mud. She stared out toward the northeast where she imagined Treghatours must lie and wished he had never come just to leave again.

"You'll not die of it, goose," Margaret said.

Rosalynde did not turn around, knowing her whole heart was in her eyes.

"Still," Margaret continued, "he is a pretty piece of flesh. Now if you had been merely a serving wench and not his host's daughter . . ."

Margaret stopped with an insinuating smirk, and Rosalynde made her no reply, knowing anything she said would be mocked and twisted out of all recognition. But she did not believe it—not of the fervent-eyed boy who had spoken time and again with such passion of his honor and his God. Not of her Philip.

A year passed, and Margaret and Richard did marry. In two years more, King Edward's displeasure at their alliance was of no consequence. He was dead, and Robert of Afton was king.

Philip was a prince, but Rosalynde heard little more of him. She knew he and Tom had been brought to court right after their older brother's marriage and held in polite captivity as guarantee of their father's loyalty. Then Robert had returned from the war in victory and, in one swift, bloodless move, had used the threat of his army to take the throne. King Edward was imprisoned. Shortly afterward the announcement came that he had died in his cell.

Although the war in the Riverlands was over, a new war broke out in the south and in the east as the former Prince Stephen tried to retake the crown he had been raised to believe was his. Rosalynde sometimes wept at the thought of her Philip being slaughtered on the field of battle, defending a crown she knew he believed did not rightly belong to his father. But it pleased her, too, to think of him as a prince, to imagine him in the king's council standing for God's truth, certain he was one who would swear to his own hurt and not change.

There was still talk between his father and hers of a second alliance between Westered and Afton, but time passed and, despite her hopeful prayers, nothing came of it. She prayed for him anyway.

CHAPTER

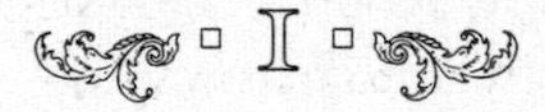

THE GREAT HALL OF THE KING'S PALACE IN WINTON WAS FILLED with lights and music, trimmed with ribbons and garlands of summer and the white saint's rose everywhere. The banqueting tables groaned under their burden of roast peacock and swan, huge platters of roast beef and wine to tempt every palate. Robert of Afton had been king for a year now, and he had invited all of his highborn subjects to celebrate the anniversary with him. That was not, however, the only reason for this gathering.

Stern and unwelcoming, Philip stood beside his father as, one after another, the eligible daughters of the nobility, fetched from throughout the kingdom, were presented to him. His presence here was not by invitation but by command.

"I have set the day for the great feast," Robert had informed him a few weeks before. "I will announce Tom's betrothal then."

"He is betrothed?" Philip had asked, surprised.

"I have contracted him to Lord Aberwain's daughter, Lady Elizabeth."

"And Tom is agreed?"

"He will be. I've not told him yet. My lord Aberwain and I have just concluded our terms, but he will be. She is reported fair and pliant and most truly virtuous. Tom can find no fault in the choice."

"Except if he does not love her."

"If not, he will grow to it in time, as you will when you marry. In faith, I never once saw your mother until we were at the altar, but from that moment I loved her as deeply and sweetly as even your stubborn heart could wish. Tom may easily find it so for him."

"And if she does not love him?"

Robert had laughed. "Not love Tom? I defy the girl to do it! Besides, he knows where his duty lies, as I trust you do. I wish to have your betrothal concluded soon, too."

"My lord, you pledged me I should have until spring," Philip had said stiffly. Robert had often pressed him to choose a wife, but Philip had reasons of his own to put him off and had wrested from him a pledge to keep his freedom for yet a while.

"You shall not marry until spring. I shall keep my word to you, but now is to promise. We have asked to the feast all the lovely maids whose fathers we wish to have bound to Afton. They are to be presented at court. Look among them, choose one, and I shall set my approval upon her."

"I cannot choose a wife as I would a horse or a pair of gloves—from stock on hand. I can tell you now already, there is none of them I could love."

Robert had taken a calm sip of wine, recognizing the stubborn set to his son's jaw and realizing that force would not move him now.

"It is that girl you've taken to sport with, is it not? This creature that waits on Richard's Lady Margaret—Katherine Fletcher. Surely you cannot mean to set aside your sacred duty and your honor, too, for your pleasure."

"I love her." Philip's stubbornness had melted into entreaty. "You said I might choose for myself now. Please, Father, let it be Kate. For that deep, sweet love you've known so long, the love I've only yet tasted, let it be Kate."

"It cannot be," Robert had answered. "I almost wish for your sake, son, I might say yes, but even if we were at peace, it cannot be. Have you forgotten the blood you bear? The very noblest, the most royal, and yet you would mix it so carelessly in marriage? With a serving wench? It cannot be."

"Forgive me, my lord, and do not think I mean you disrespect, but I cannot choose among your nobly bred maids. I cannot forsake the one I love. You know I have tried to please you since you betrayed the king—"

"I am the king."

Philip had rubbed his cheek, remembering the first time they had had this quarrel. "I know it. Please, Father, I do not mean to anger you. Ask me any other service, and I swear I will be Mercury to do it, but do not ask this of me, I beg you."

"You know it must be so, but it need not fret you. Marry one of these girls, help me keep Afton strong, and you need not give up your Kate. I will see her safely to some secret place, away from the tongues at court, and there you may keep her so long as it pleases you. Meanwhile, your noble lady and her kinsmen need never take offense at what they do not know. Just spare me the knowledge of any half-blooded whelps she gives you."

Philip had looked at him in disgust, his dark brows drawn into a hard line. "You dare call yourself a king and my father and urge me to willful adultery?"

"You make fine distinction between adulterer and whoremaster."

Philip's whole body had tightened with the desire to strike the cynical smirk from his father's face. He had made a curt bow instead.

"I ask your leave to withdraw, my lord, before I am no longer master of my tongue."

"Go on then, but make yourself ready to choose a wife come the feast day."

"I have told you my choice."

"And I have told you, that cannot be. Do you think this is some boys' game we play now? You are a Chastelayne prince. Your marriage is a matter of state. When you have tired of this wench, you will thank me that I have not let you tie yourself forever to one so far beneath you."

"Do what you will," Philip had said, a defiant light in his eyes. "I'll not be threatened or cajoled or ordered into marrying anyone."

"See here, proud boy—"

"No, my lord, I do not and will not see. Pardon me or let me not be pardoned, but do not force me in this. It can never be."

"It must be," Robert had said gravely. "Please you or no, it will be."

So now Philip stood watching the seemingly endless line of gentlewomen, some little more than children, some older even than his own mother. Their simpering chatter stung his already-nettled temper, and it would not have pleased him had he overheard them say among themselves that his frowns were as becoming as most men's smiles.

He could not have said afterwards which of them were fair and which were plain, which seemed well spoken, which quiet and shy. Many of their names he knew already, having heard them bandied about for several months now along with a catalog of their virtues and possessions.

He wondered vaguely why Lady Rosalynde was not present. He remembered her as modest and gentle, and it had pleased him to do as his father had asked and show her a little gallantry. Robert had asked it of him many times before and since, with the daughters and cousins and nieces of other noblemen, but it was only later that he realized his father had had more than courtesy in mind. Philip suspected now that Robert thought Margaret was alliance enough with Westered. There was a multitude of ladies among whom Philip might choose and other noblemen who might be bound to Afton with a well-considered marriage.

After all the others, the lord high chamberlain, Lord Dunois, Baron of Paxton, presented his daughter Marian—a timid girl of fourteen, as pale of hair and skin as her father was dark. Philip kissed her thin hand and said something grudgingly pleasant, word for word what he had spoken to each of the others.

Dunois looked with fondness upon her. "I shall be glad to have her at court with me now. I have missed having her gentleness always about me."

He neglected to mention that he had seen her but once since she was eight years old.

"She will be an ornament to our court," Robert said. "Will she not, Philip?"

"Of course, my lord," Philip said dutifully.

"She has been most eager to dance with you, my prince," Dunois said, giving the girl an almost imperceptible push forward.

"Please, no," she whispered, her eyes pleading against her father's subtle urging. She pulled back, catching Philip's glance, and the tears started into her eyes. Philip let an encouraging smile soften his expression.

"Please, my lady," he said, offering his hand. "You would do me much honor."

Dunois signaled the music to begin, and Philip took the girl into his arms, ignoring the satisfied expression on her father's face.

"You needn't dance the whole measure with me, my lord," she said gratefully as he whirled her across the floor. "My father would have me to dance with you, but I would never presume—"

"You, my lady, do not presume, and for that I count you my friend."

"He's taken to her," Robert said, watching her flush with pleasure at his son's careful attentions, and Dunois could hardly manage a serene reply.

"She'll do well enough for such a little chit of a girl. Her mother, you know, was the Duke of Ellison's niece."

"Was she, in faith? Then there is a touch of the blood in her. It speaks well, my lord. It speaks well."

The king and queen danced frequently that night and between times sat close together, sharing a cup and a plate, their glances full of deep secret meaning, their eyes sparkling more brightly than the jewels in their heavy crowns.

Richard, too, danced awhile with his own wife, making great show of his affection toward her and hers for him. He knew what a pretty sight they made together, him with his solid dark handsomeness and her with her honey locks and eyes of green. Margaret would make him a fine, fair queen, and if he found her tedious company already, well, the people needn't see that.

As the night wore on, many of those less inclined to merrymaking retired to the comfort of their bedchambers. Even John had been hustled off to bed by one of the servants. The rest of the nobility, well heated with wine, sang and danced and drank yet more, growing louder with each passing hour. The dancing went faster and faster, and the room swirled with color, sparkled with the silver and gold of rich jewelry.

Richard led the revels, downing a flagon of wine with each of his numerous changes of partner. Tom joined in, too, dancing with this lady and that, blind to their admiring glances, evading their too-possessive embraces, making them laugh with his humorous refusals of their attentions and winning them the more because of it.

Philip danced with one potential bride and then another, but always he returned to little Marian, setting her at ease in this vast world of strangers, finally coaxing a smile from her. He pitied greatly to see her used so for her father's advancement.

"It seems you have chosen after all," Robert said late in the evening after he had called Philip to a quiet corner of the hall.

"My lord?"

Dunois bowed. "I am honored, my prince, but I dare not hope that you have chosen to grace my poor house—"

"You mistake, my lord," Philip said, turning stern eyes on him, "if you think I mean to marry your daughter. You spoke truly of her gentleness, and I believe of herself she is a most worthy lady, but I'll not marry her."

"Philip!"

Seeing his father's indignation, Philip made his tone more gentle. "I do truly ask your pardon, my lord Dunois, for I am sure in time Lady Marian would bless any man with her heart and hand, but I cannot marry her. I know you have done good service for my father, but I cannot do this to please you or him. Not and be true to my heart."

Robert's lip curled into a sneer. "True to your heart! As if the base-born slut you've chosen could mean more than sport to a royal prince. Go back to the ladies, boy. Choose the one you best like and bring her to me. I've no more patience for this."

For a moment Philip stood glaring. Then he bowed. "At your pleasure, my liege."

The two men watched as he stalked across the room, Dunois noting with growing satisfaction that he was going toward Marian. But Philip turned aside before he reached her and instead pulled one of the waiting women out from among Margaret's astonished attendants—a plain fair-haired girl not yet twenty.

She struggled, bewildered, against him.

"Please, my lord, not before your father and the court—"

He did not answer her as he pulled her back to where the king stood. He did not change his flinty expression.

"Here, my liege, is my choice." He turned in fierce triumph to the crowded hall. "Come! Music for the queen of my heart!"

The musicians struck up a jarring, merry tune, and Philip spun the fearful girl a few defiant turns around the room. Then he halted at the foot of the stairs, a wicked smile marring his handsome face.

"Good night, my liege, my noble ladies all! Come, Kate, it's long past time we were to bed."

He pulled her up the steps after him, and the room began to buzz. Robert's face was a deep red.

"Before God and all the saints, dare he shame me before my court? I will have the strumpet whipped out of my kingdom!"

"Softly, my liege," came Dunois's calm counsel. "Do that and he will likely follow after her. He is proud, and the more you belittle his choice, the more his honor demands he hold to it. Let him have until spring as you promised, and by then, considering the changeable nature of young men, he will be pleased to be rid of the girl."

"And what of his betrothal?"

"The more you urge him, the more his pride will resist you. Leave it for now. Speak gently to him when next you meet, and we will find a way to put all right. Let him consider the fair ladies he might have, the great wealth and honor that comes with each of them, and this worn dishrag of a serving wench will be quickly shaken off."

"You speak wisely," Robert said, mollified. There was a touch of humor on his face. "I've half a mind to simply give him to your daughter in payment for all you've done."

"Too much honor for my poor house," Dunois said, the glint in his black eyes belying his words. "What could my humble service have meant, in truth, to your nobility? Any man would have done as much."

"Not so, Edmund. I remain your debtor still, and if my insolent boy braves me so once again, I may use him in paying that debt."

The next morning Philip went to his father's chamber and requested a private audience.

"His Majesty is not yet risen, my lord," Dunois informed him. "If it shall please you, I will take him your request and return you his answer."

Philip thanked him and set himself to wait. He did not expect that the space of one night would be enough to cool his father's anger, and he steeled himself to meet the full force of it. He would be humble and ask pardon for his rashness the night before. Surely peace with his father was worth that much pride. Surely Katherine was.

"Have you puzzled out all the mysteries of the ages yet?"

Philip lifted his head and saw Tom grinning down on him.

"Do I look so perplexed?"

Tom sat next to him, looking not for the first time at the fine sapphire cross that hung around Philip's neck, only half concealed by his shirt. Doubtless he had noticed that it was the same one Katherine Fletcher had worn but wore no longer, just as Philip no longer wore the ruby ring that marked him as a Chastelayne prince.

"I suppose you've been summoned to answer for last night."

"I was a fool," Philip said. "That was no way to win his liking for Kate. All I did was shame her and make him the angrier. I came to make it right with him if he will let me, but, no, I was not summoned. Were you?"

Tom nodded. "I expect it will be more upon this favorite theme of his—marriage."

"Can you do it, Tom? Marry for policy?"

"I would I had freedom in the choice, as much as you do, but even before Father was king, we knew it would not be so. They say Lady Elizabeth is fair and virtuous. I shall make it all my study to love her as it was meant a wife should be loved, and I daresay we shall be happy enough. I cannot believe God will let it be otherwise."

"What if you loved already? Would you let them marry you to someone else?"

"If I loved a woman truly and knew I could love no other, I suppose I would have to marry my beloved, no matter the cost." Looking steadily into his eyes, Tom tucked the cross back inside Philip's shirt. "Then I would tell Father I'd done it."

"Tom—"

"You might have told me. I've kept your counsel before."

"How could you know?"

"I know you."

There was a telltale light in Philip's eyes. "I love her, Tom."

"I know that, too."

"I know what I've given up in marrying her," Philip said. "I'd pay that price and a dozen times over for the love she has given me."

"Father might not think it such a bargain after what you've doubtless cost him in some alliance or other."

"He needn't know for some while yet, I hope."

"Well, now you've done it, tell him. He will be vexed, but not so much as if you were his heir."

Philip shook his head. "Not yet. Let the country be more at peace than it is now. He will be angry enough as it is. If he knows she is truly my wife, I fear what he might do. Now he pleases to think I am a stubborn, wanton boy. He thinks I will tire of her soon and make one of his precious alliances. Our best safety lies in that."

"Good morning, my sons."

Philip and Tom leapt to their feet and bowed deeply as their mother came from the king's private chamber. She was dressed in a robe of sky blue velvet with the rich lace of her shift peeping out at her wrists and throat and her hair falling in golden ringlets down her back. She looked as fresh and fair as a bride. It was little wonder that their father found arranged marriages nothing to fear.

"Madam my mother," Tom murmured.

"Madam," Philip echoed, and she looked at him as if they shared a secret.

"You were indiscreet last night, Philip."

"I do beg your pardon, madam," he said with another bow. "I know you think me intemperate and disgraceful, and for that I am heartily sorry."

"I merely said you were indiscreet." There was a sly smile on her full lips. "A true gentleman is always discreet with his mistresses."

A true gentleman has none, Philip thought, his eyes turning cold. Before he could reply, another voice interrupted. "Elaine, my love, not gone yet?"

The boys bowed once more, and their mother curtseyed as the king came from his chamber. He pulled his wife to him and said something low in her ear to make her giggle. Then he put her hand in Tom's.

"See your mother back to her ladies, Tom, while I talk to this rascal here. Then I shall wish to speak to you."

Philip looked at his brother, surprised at the king's affability, but Tom merely gave him a quizzical smile and led his mother away.

"Now, my son, you wished to see me?"

Philip drew a deep breath. "Yes, my lord. My behavior last night was most unbecoming, and I wish to apologize for it. It ill suits the son of Lynaleigh's king to make such common display before the court, and I crave your pardon."

"Bravely spoken," Robert said, clasping his shoulder. "We were both of us too hot in speaking last night. Let us say no more of it, and it will soon be forgotten. I have perhaps pushed too hard in this matter of marriages. You shall have until spring as I promised."

"I shall?" A brilliant smile broke through Philip's incredulity. "Tell me what service I may do you now to prove my obedience."

Robert ruffled his son's thick hair. "Go to your brothers. Tell them to put on their royal white. We are to make procession through the streets this afternoon in further celebration of my reign. The lord mayor has asked it at the people's request, and I can grant them no less. Show bravely for Afton today, and I can wish no more."

"I will!"

At the appointed time, Philip and his brothers met in the courtyard, dressed as their father had requested. Their horses were also decked in the immaculate luster of royal white, ready for them to mount. Beside them, the king's groomsman was calming a skittish Barbary roan, one the princes had never seen before.

"Whose horse is that, Hawkins?" Richard asked, impressed by the beast's fiery temper.

"His Majesty's, my lord. A gift from the lord mayor."

Richard held out his hand. "Let me try him."

"I cannot, my lord. Not until His Majesty says I might."

Richard frowned, and Philip tried to stroke the roan's nose.

"Have a care!" Hawkins warned as the horse snapped at him. "He's hardly tamed."

"Father will let me ride him," Philip said lightly. "I shall see he is gentled down."

Tom laid his hand on the roan's flank and was nearly kicked for it. "Best have a care, Philip. This one will throw you, like as not."

"Nonsense. I've never been thrown yet."

"Not true," Richard said laughing. "I remember once you walked home bloodied and bruised because old Samson had tossed you off in the forest."

"He did not!"

"He did!" Richard insisted, looking to Tom and John for confirmation. "You were no more than twelve, as I remember, but I thought it odd that you'd been thrown. You never had been before and not since."

"I remember that day," John said before Philip could protest again. "You must have fallen hard, you were so battered."

Tom laughed. "You were so mortified you did not even speak when Nathaniel was searching you over for broken bones."

"Odd I don't remember it," Philip said with a puzzled grin, "but it'll not likely happen again." He swung up onto his horse, a long-legged black, and patted its silken mane. "Not likely, my Alethia."

"This one is not so fierce as Hawkins says," John said, feeding the roan a handful of fresh straw. The horse showed no hint of skittishness.

"What's this, boys?" the king asked when he came into the courtyard with his dazzling queen on his arm, both of them also in white.

"A gift from the lord mayor, Father," Richard said eagerly. "May I ride him?"

"Sometime. Today I shall."

"You ought not, Your Majesty. Pardon me," Hawkins said. "He is very skittish."

"Let me decide on that, Hawkins. Give me the reins, man."

Hawkins obeyed, and the king swung up into the saddle. The roan's only protest was a whinny and a little pawing of the ground. Robert smiled.

"There. No need to fear now. Come, let us go among the people. I would have the lord mayor see how fitting his gift is for a king."

Hawkins helped the queen up onto her palfrey and, bowing, handed her the reins.

"But where is your lady, Richard?" she asked.

Richard's mouth turned down in annoyance. "She asks your pardon, madam, and yours, Father, but she is ill with the coming child and cannot ride today."

"They say that happens often," Elaine said gaily, "though I have not found it so. Not once in four times."

"Have patience, Richard," Robert advised, smiling upon his own wife. "You will find yourself well rewarded the first time you hold your heir. Let your lady have her rest now. You mustn't risk the child."

"As you say, Father. Shall we go on?"

Preceded by banners and trumpets and drums, followed by richly attired nobility, the royal family rode out into the streets of Winton, a brisk wind at their backs. As always, the peasantry crowded around them, cheering and whistling and covering them with blessings and rose petals. The king had his hands full with acknowledging their favors and keeping his horse from bolting. Once he made his speech, promising justice and prosperity to his people and thanking the lord mayor for his fine gift, he turned gladly toward home. The roan wanted more gentling before he could be ridden again among the people.

The wind was in their faces on the way back, tugging at cloaks and snatching caps and popping the rich gilt-edged banners.

"I shall have my hair down about my knees before we've reached the palace," Elaine said, holding one hand to the heavy golden mass twisted at the back of her head. Just then one of the streaming banners snapped loose and flew into the roan's face. With a shrill, terrified neigh, he reared up and struck out blindly with his hooves, beating the queen from her own mount.

"Elaine!"

Robert jerked at his reins, wrenching the beast's head to one side. Wild-eyed, the roan continued to plunge, and Robert could only watch in horror as his wife's soft body was trampled into the cobbled street.

Braving the flashing hooves, Philip and Richard seized hold of the panicked animal's bridle on either side and pulled him away from their mother. Robert leapt to the ground and took his wife's battered body out of Tom's lap, pulled her crushed hand out of John's fearful grasp.

"Elaine."

He kissed her bloodied lips and then lifted her up in his arms, echoing her cry of agony.

Several of the nobles took charge of the roan, and Richard and Philip went to their mother's side.

"Let me help you, Father," Richard offered, but Robert only crushed his wife tighter against himself, making her cry out again.

"Let him alone," Tom said in a low voice, and Richard stepped back, his face marked with disbelief.

"It was over before it could be stopped."

"It could not be stopped," Philip said, his breath coming hard and unevenly.

John's eyes were wide, bewildered. "Mother?"

Tom put one arm around his shoulders. "Come on, John."

Robert carried his wife in his arms the short distance back to the castle, speaking soft, loving words with every step. Their sons and all the others came in grim, silent procession after them. The physicians were sent for, every comfort was thought of, but no one seeing the crushed remains of so delicate flesh could believe there was any hope for more than a few brief hours of pain before death.

Somber and restless, the princes stood outside the chamber where their mother lay dying. They watched the evening fade into night and, after eternity, watched the lazy sunrise bring in the everlasting morning. They heard her call sometimes for John, always John, but he was forbidden to go to her. Only her tormented husband was allowed at her side as the physicians labored against hope to save her.

Philip found himself burdened with a sorrow that surprised him. There was no mother heart in this woman for him, never had been, and he thought he had made himself proof against the pain that brought him. She had never taken much notice of any of her sons. Even John, her youngest, the one most like her, had only held her momentary interest. Her gowns, her jewels, her entourage of admirers—these had been much dearer to her. But Philip felt deep pain at her passing.

More than that, it was his father's sudden, cruel loss of the woman that meant more than the world to him that drew Philip's pity and remorse. Having so recently found such a deep love himself, he felt his father's pain as if it were his own. He knew if he should have Katherine only twenty or thirty years, it would not be half enough. To have her so brutally torn away from him would be beyond bearing.

He could hear the priests now on the other side of the door

intoning an ave, muffled and indistinct, and knew his mother was making confession. Soon she would be absolved, and her spirit would be put into the hands of God. Then the priests would be silent.

The silence came, and the princes crossed themselves and waited for word to be brought. Finally the door swung open, and Robert came out of the chamber, pale and trembling, the bloody stamp of Elaine's wounds still on his white doublet. The brothers were startled at his expression. He looked furious, not grieved.

"You," he snapped, pointing at John. "I will have you from my sight and from my court. You are not to stay even for the burying." He took rough hold of John's wrist and stripped the Chastelayne ring from his finger. "Go where it pleases you, but go now and do not let me see your face again."

John flinched as if he had been struck, and Robert turned to his other sons. "I will not have a word from the three of you. Keep silent, or before God Himself, you go with him!"

He stalked into the room opposite the one where their mother's broken body lay and slammed the door. A look of rage crossed Philip's face, and he started after his father.

"No," John said, pale and shaken. "I will go if he wishes me to."

"You'll not!" Richard said, and, swearing a terrible oath, he flung open the door his father had just slammed and slammed it again behind him. Immediately the sounds of quarreling filtered out, the words unintelligible but the tone unmistakable.

"He is hurting, John," Tom said. "I am sorry he has hurt you."

"How could he say such a thing?" Philip fumed, pained by the shattered expression on his youngest brother's face. "He cannot mean really for you to go. By my life, John, you've always loved him better than any of us have!"

The three of them stood silent, listening to Richard's voice battling his father's, back and forth, ever louder and more vicious. The door flew open again, and Richard stormed out with the king close behind him.

"Richard!"

Richard halted and turned back to his father. "Rumor is a strong tool in the right hands, my lord king," he warned. "Take care what you speak before the court. Once told, it cannot be again unsaid."

Robert considered for a moment. Then as he looked again at John, his eyes turned steely. "Very well. I will say nothing to my nobles of this, but he is banished. I'll not be swayed from that."

John had not wept at the news of his mother's death, but now he did, the quiet tears slipping down cheeks that had not quite lost their childish roundness.

"If you banish him, banish me as well," Richard warned. "I'll not stay at your court if you do this to him."

"I'll not be threatened by you or anyone," Robert returned. "He is banished, and you may do as pleases you."

Richard looked at him, fury coloring his face. Then he grabbed John by the arm. "Come on."

"I have sons yet to do my bidding, my lord of Bradford!" Robert shouted after him. "Your loss will not be keenly felt!"

"Stop them, Father," Philip insisted. "Mercy and grace, what has John done?"

"This does not concern you."

"Does it not? John is—"

"Father, please—," Tom began at the same time.

"Enough, Philip. Tom, not another word. Will you both rebel against me, too?"

"No, Father." Tom put a restraining hand on his brother's arm. "Come, Philip, I think we all of us would do well to consider for a moment before we say anything more."

"As you say," Philip agreed. With a taut bow he left the room.

Robert sat down abruptly. The light from the window above him was unkind to his haggard face and made the wounded rage in his eyes all the clearer to see.

"May I get something for you, Father?" Tom asked.

"Bring me some wine. Then leave me."

Tom overlooked the sharpness of his tone. "Shall I have Dunois tell the court of the queen's passing? They will be waiting."

Robert drew a harsh breath as if he were going to swear. Then he checked himself. "Tell him. And tell Richard he is to go to Tanglewood, if he must leave, and take—take my lord of Rounchaux with him. I will make it known that I have sent them there to lead the army at the border."

"Please, Father. John would never—"

"Not another word, Tom. Not one. Do as I bade you and leave me in peace."

Tom bowed. "Yes, my lord."

Little more than a week later news came that dealt an even heavier blow to a court already devastated.

"'Richard should never have gone out to them,'" Tom read from the letter John had sent.

> *"They came to the wall and challenged us, and even though they had twice our strength, he went out to them. He swore he'd never send to the king for more men, that we were easily worth their number and so many more besides, and he went out to them as merrily as if he were going to a May morris dance. I would God had made him more wise and less proud, but I think he's in heaven. I went to him when the fighting was over. He'd been three times thrust through and could scarcely speak, but he said, 'Mercy, Lord Jesus, pardon . . . sinful soul,' and more I could not understand, but surely God heard him."*

"I know He did," Tom said, and Philip nodded, but Robert only looked through them.

"Richard." The king put his head in his hands. Then he took a deep drink of the wine that had been his constant companion in the days since the queen's death.

Richard was dead. The son he had groomed for kingship, the one he had meant for greatness, was gone. All that was left of his hopes was Richard's battered body, the child Margaret carried, and the echo of his own acrid words. *Your loss will not be keenly felt*.

"I am sorry about Richard, Father," Philip murmured, only now daring to speak. "I know John is sorry, too."

"And well he should be," Robert returned, his grief now cold contempt. "Were it not for him, Richard would not have been there in Tanglewood to die. What more is in the letter? I suppose the city is lost, too."

"No," Tom said. "He writes that he sent to Eastbrook for help, and it is firmly ours again."

"Let him see better to his duties then," Robert said, "or, before God, I will have him driven from my kingdom altogether."

"Let him return to us," Tom asked, not for the first time.

"Show him your mercy, Father," Philip pled, "as you would have God show Richard His."

"Yes, faith, he shall have mercy," Robert replied. "All the mercy Ellenshaw can afford him down in Tanglewood. I'll not have him in my court. Do not plead for him again."

CHAPTER

2

WINTON HAD ALREADY BEEN IN SOLEMN MOURNING FOR THE queen, and the loss of the crown prince only darkened the city's mood. The peasants crowded the streets, each of them with at least a scrap of black tied on sleeve or hat, watching as Richard's coffin was borne into the city. The silence was oppressive. Only in low murmurs out of public hearing did they reason among themselves on how swiftly these deep blows had been dealt the king at blind fortune's hand. Or as they thought back on deposed King Edward's death, was it the hand of righteous heaven?

The two funerals followed swiftly afterwards, separated by only a few days, the grim necessity of the war forbidding prolonged ceremony. As he watched his older brother's body being entombed in the splendor of Winterbrooke Cathedral, Philip felt a quick wringing pain deep inside himself.

He and Richard had not been close, not since they had begun to grow into men and Richard had gone on to be marred by war and willfulness. Often they had been at odds, both stubborn and fiercely proud, but now that Richard was gone, Philip could only remember him as he had always known him, bluff and soldierly, reckless and mocking, but with a touch of pity and possessed of a brave heart, too. Glancing at the austere, dry-eyed widow, Philip realized that Richard had never known what it was to be loved, not as Philip knew even now with Katherine's anxious, pitying eyes on him from the other side of her mistress.

Well, Richard knew perfect love now, a better love, Philip was certain, than even his own precious Kate could give. He was glad that Richard had at the last been granted those final brief moments and had time to call for God's mercy. He was thankful, too, that John had been witness to Richard's last prayer and knew that the boy took comfort in the knowledge that his impetuous brother was at last safe forever.

At least I have Kate, Philip thought. *John has no one*.

Still, he knew his father was grieving. John was the youngest, Robert's pet. The king could not be angry forever.

A month passed. In the midst of the continued mourning, Tom was married to Elizabeth Briesionne, daughter to the Duke of Aberwain. At her father's insistence, the betrothal agreement stipulated that she would stay only a week with her bridegroom, just long enough for the contract to be irrevocably consummated before she was returned to her home. There she would remain until, with the aid of her father's men and money, peace was achieved. She was his heir and only child, and he would have her kept safe.

So at the altar, Tom looked for the first time into his bride's face. It was a good face, fresh and young, saved from plainness by a sweet mouth and large, expressive eyes as velvet-brown as his own. She stood there for all the world like a scared little girl dressed in a lady's borrowed finery, not daring to look at him, not daring to respond when he squeezed her hand and gave her a welcoming smile.

Watching them, Philip hoped that Tom's smile was from his heart and wondered how he could bear to take this stranger to his bed that very night as the marriage contract required. He was glad he had himself been spared that awkwardness.

He watched the newlyweds part a week later and wondered how the girl could still have that fearful expression after Tom's tireless efforts to put her at ease. She would still not lift her eyes to her husband's face, but Philip saw her cast furtive, wistful, half-ashamed glances in Tom's direction whenever she thought she would not be seen. He smiled to himself and imagined that one day, when they were reunited, Tom's kindness and gentle patience would calm her fears and win her love. He prayed it would be so. Tom deserved it to be so.

Eventually the news came to Westered of an alliance between the royal family and the Duke of Aberwain. Hearing it, Rosalynde felt her heart crash against her breastbone. Had so many of her prayers gone for nothing? Did her Philip belong to someone else now?

She remembered every moment of their time together, every word, every smile. She could still smell the winter in the breeze that blew off the sea, remembering how she had ridden out into the snow beside him with Ankarette as reluctant chaperone. He had been dressed only in his shirt sleeves, without even his doublet, his shirt not even laced, and she had asked him if he did not need his cloak, but he had only smiled at her concern.

"Nonsense. There is nothing so wholesome as a fresh snow and a brisk wind to bank it everywhere."

"But you shall freeze dressed so."

"This is nothing, my lady. If we were in Treghatours, we would be to our knees, at the very least, in snow."

"I should like one day to see it."

"I'd not trade it for the king's palace," he had said. "They say Winton is fairer than any place in Lynaleigh, but I cannot believe it could match Treghatours for beauty. Faith, it has less of a winter than even Westered—and no saint's rose."

She had reached over and touched the emblem that adorned his horse's bridle. "Why is it they call it that, my lord? It looks to be no more than a little field flower."

"You mustn't judge its worth by its humble outside, my lady. Have you never seen one growing? Or better, smelled one? But, no, I suppose they rarely grow so far west. Treghatours is always white with them come spring. They used to be called chastelayne. One of my ancestors took our name from it because it is always the first to come up each year, even before the crocus, and it means hope. Still, that was long ago. The peasants have called the flower saint's rose since. They say the prayers of the saints make such a fragrance in God's throne room." He had grinned at her then. She remembered it still. "Though why they call them roses I've yet to fathom."

"And there are none in Winton?"

"Not many, I do not think."

"Perhaps Winton has other beauties, my lord."

"Perhaps it does," he had allowed, "but I'd not live at court. There is no place there for an honest man."

"Perhaps if more honest men went to court, they could make it into an honest place."

He had smiled again at her earnest suggestion. "It is more likely the court would corrupt their honesty, but still it may be a pleasant enough place. Now in Treghatours we have a meadow that would come near to take your breath away for beauty this time of year. There you might say you have had snow. I never take a cloak out in it there, no matter how Joan scolds."

"Joan?"

"Joan was set to look after me and my brothers from before I was born. She and her husband Nathaniel fairly raised us all. If we are Heretics, it was they who taught us."

"I heard the Heretics' teaching once," she had said, dropping her voice. "I saw no harm in it."

"I am not ashamed to count myself one of them. Far rather than follow after the priests who sell God's pardon or the bishops who play politics better than the nobility. I would not trust my soul to one of them, but only to God Himself, face to face. Has He not, by even the smallest act of His grace, earned our allegiance?"

She could see still the deep, fervent light in his eyes and hear the intense feeling in his words.

Beauty, nobility, grace, wit, and faith, too, she had thought then and thought still. *What is there more to ask in a man?*

"I suppose there might be something not so grave to speak of on a morning's ride," he had said when she made him no answer. "Perhaps we should go back. You are cold."

"Oh, no, my lord," she had assured him. "Ankarette's come near to suffocate me in all these wraps."

"Take some of them off, my lady, and truly feel the winter."

She had looked back again to see Ankarette even farther behind. "It is stifling," she had admitted. Then she had untied her cloak and dropped it back across her saddle.

"Now breathe deeply," he had suggested. She remembered the rush of the cold into her lungs and the way he smiled at her pleasure in it.

"Now, my lady, let your horse have his head."

Forgetting Ankarette altogether, they had both let their horses go, and Rosalynde felt the bracing tingle of the winter air in her face. Philip had pulled ahead of her, and his laughter came back to her on the wind as he jumped a shallow stream. Before he could caution her, she had galloped toward the stream also.

"Lady Rosalynde!"

Rosalynde had turned at her nursemaid's horrified voice and at once found herself dumped on her backside in the middle of the water, gasping at the icy wetness. Looking back on it, she had found her dousing well worth it, for Philip waded out to her and, asking anxiously if she were hurt, scooped her up in his arms.

"You will pardon me, my lord," Ankarette had scolded as Philip carried her, dripping, to the bank, "and saving your reverence, I'll have you know my lord of Westered will hear of this. She might have been killed for your foolishness. By your leave, my lord, you should know better than to teach a young girl such tricks. She has no business riding like some common wench. And jumping, God save us!"

Trying to soothe Ankarette's indignant objections, he had pushed the sodden little scrap of satin and ribbon that was Rosalynde's shoe back onto her foot, wrapped her in his cloak, and ridden away with her before him in his saddle, leaving Ankarette behind them again.

Rosalynde remembered resting contentedly against him, hearing the rumble of his apologetic words in his chest, glad to be there in the warm security of his arms. But too soon they were back in the courtyard and then before both of their fathers in the great hall.

"What's this, young man?" Westered had asked.

"Philip, explain yourself," Robert had demanded. Westered had immediately taken Rosalynde from Philip's arms.

"By my faith, she is drenched!"

"I am sorry, my lord," Philip had said. "You must forgive me for not taking better care of you, my lady." Again he had pushed her shoe back onto her foot, this time deftly tightening the ribbon.

"I thank you for the morning, my lady," he had called after her as her father carried her up the stairs. She remembered him looking up at her as he had in the courtyard the first time she saw him, that same smile on his face. That time he had taken her fancy. This time he had taken her heart. He had it still—she knew it deep inside herself, and now she could hardly bear the thought of him married to another.

"Which of them was it?" Rosalynde asked when she could trust her voice, and her father smiled at the anxiousness in her eyes.

"The younger one—Thomas of Brenden."

"Oh," she sighed. "Not that it is anything to me," she added quickly, and Westered turned her face up to his.

"Is it still young Philip, sweetheart? After four years?"

She nodded her head, and the tears filled her eyes.

"Is there no one else who would please you, child? There are more than a few who have asked me for you."

"Oh, no, Father, please." She clung to his arm and hid her face against his sleeve. "None of them is worth one of Philip's boot straps. Not five of them together."

Over her head, Westered smiled. "Well, then they could hardly be worth my Rosalynde." He lifted her face again and kissed her nose. Then he hugged her tight. "You shall have him then, your Philip, if by any means I can get the king's consent."

Once his bride was gone, Tom had been sent to Chrisdale to the army there, and Philip found himself virtually alone. His heart was with Katherine, always with her, but he saw little of her except in times and places where they could not openly speak. She was busy with the endless complications of the official mourning, and he had his own duties as well. There was frequently no more than an eloquent glance between them, a quick, fervent clasp of hands, sometimes a stolen kiss, before they were again forced apart.

Then late one night, she came to him, her face stained with tears, her body trembling with fear and weariness. He did his best to soothe her into calmness. Then he tucked her into his bed and went immediately to wake his father with the news she had brought.

"No. I cannot think it." Robert drew his dressing gown more closely around his shoulders and looked, bewildered, from his son to his lord high chamberlain. "Why should Lady Margaret destroy her own child? What could she possibly gain?"

"I do not know why," Philip insisted, "only that she is guilty. She had her waiting woman, Merryn, prepare her some potion that brought the child too soon. Murder, if ever there was such a crime."

"How is it that you know this, my lord?" Dunois asked with his usual calm.

"I had it from one who knows, one who overheard the plotting."

"I will speak to Lady Margaret of this," Robert said. "Dunois, send to her to come."

"You cannot," Philip said. "She is by far too ill just now, but I know she was deliberate in this."

Robert sighed. "So Richard's child is dead, too."

Philip nodded, his eyes full of sorrow. He knew his father had hoped to have another Richard in Richard's son.

"This is a serious matter, my lord," Dunois said. "Who is this 'one who knows' you speak of?"

"One of Margaret's maids," Philip admitted, not wanting to say more.

"Her name?"

"Philip?" Robert prompted.

"Katherine," Philip said half under his breath. Then he looked at the two older men with resolution. "Katherine Fletcher."

Dunois raised one insinuating eyebrow.

"I believe her, Father," Philip said glowering. Then he knit his brow, remembering her grief. "She put the child in the shroud herself and wept as she told me of it. Why should she lie?"

His father looked more past him than at him. "Was it a boy?"

Philip nodded.

"A boy," Robert repeated almost inaudibly.

"Speak to the princess, Your Majesty, before passing judgment," Dunois suggested. "It may be that this girl was mistaken."

"Very true," Robert said, recovering himself. "I will speak to her. This thing will be sounded to the very bottom, and we shall have justice."

❧

At dawn the king went to Margaret's bedside, ready to answer with a vengeance the murder of his dead son's child. He almost wavered at the sight of her before him, her eyes sunken and ringed with black, her thin lips colorless and chapped. It was difficult for him to discern the much-toasted beauty in the haggard woman who had to be supported even to sit up.

"Madam, there have been grievous wrongs laid to your charge."

"Wrongs, my lord?" Weary puzzlement was on her face, and she leaned more heavily upon her ladies. "In what have I offended Your Majesty?"

"Come, come, lady. Taking the innocent life of a babe unborn is offense enough, but to kill the next king of Lynaleigh, my Richard's only child—"

Margaret seemed to wilt at the harsh words, and her tears flowed freely. "Kill? My lord, you cannot think I purposed to lose my child. It is too cruel to say so to me now."

"I was told you had engineered the babe's death. Is it not so?"

"Who could so abuse Your Majesty and me to make you believe such a lie? I have just lost my lord and husband. Could you truly believe that I would kill all that was left of him, my only consolation in his death? The child was mine as well as his, made from my flesh, nurtured with my blood. What could make me destroy it?" The tears welled up again. "Yet it may be that I am to blame. I did so grieve for Richard that it may be I caused the child to be born too soon."

"Let us speak plainly, lady, for I am not so easily trifled with as I have been. I know there was no great love between you and my son, unless it was love for the throne he would have had."

"Perhaps that is so," she said, growing suddenly cool, "but if my love was all for the throne, why would I destroy my only link to it, the child that had next claim? Put my motives at their basest, and you will see I had every reason to safeguard the child. What gain has its loss brought me?"

"None," he said finally.

She lay back against her pillows. "I am tired, my lord."

His face was still stern, but there was resignation in it now. "You must forgive me, lady. It was sorrow and not reason that spoke in me before."

He left her to her women and returned wearily to his chamber, grateful for the cup of wine Dunois brought him.

"How do we punish ill fortune for her crimes?"

He did not expect an answer, but the chamberlain came closer.

"When ill fortune effects her own designs, we can do nothing, but when she sets them to another's doing, then it is in our power to punish."

Robert shook his head. "There was no murder here. The child simply miscarried. This Fletcher woman was merely mistaken, hysterical with the suddenness of it all."

"Or had a greater purpose in making such an accusation."

"How do you mean?"

"Suppose it was Katherine Fletcher who gave her the potion that killed the child, not Merryn, as my lord Philip was told."

"But what cause could she have for it?"

There was a knowing significance in Dunois's glance. "An ambitious woman may use any means to gain power."

"But what could she hope to gain by this?"

Dunois hesitated for a moment. "I know, my liege, that she has been Lord Philip's mistress for some time now. The child's death makes him your heir."

"Then you accuse Philip—"

"Of nothing, Majesty, except perhaps of being deceived. He is smitten with the wench and will not even spare a glance to any of the others. She has beguiled him soundly. Many a mistress aspires to be wife and, if wife to him, then queen."

"Philip would never stoop so low as to marry one of these common wenches!" Robert said, shocked more at the idea of such a marriage than at such a murder.

"He has refused all the others. I hardly dare to speak it, but might he not set this girl up one day as Lynaleigh's queen? I fear even the thought, but it seems he'll never take a noble wife as long as this base wench is alive."

"No."

"He is your heir now. If you should die before his marriage, he would be free to choose a wife for himself. He thinks he loves this drab."

"But he'd not marry her!"

"If I know him, my liege, as no doubt you do, he'll have no other so long as she lives."

"Would you have me take her life?"

"Would you have her common blood forever pollute the line of Lynaleighan kings?"

Robert was galled by the thought. "He says he loves her, calls her fair and virtuous and most loving to him. He has braved me again and again for her sake. Can I condemn her and keep my son?"

"Is she truly all these things, my lord, or does she merely seem so to him?" Dunois lowered his voice. "I have heard that a man might be—" He paused and almost imperceptibly stressed the word. "—*bewitched* by such a woman."

For a moment Robert looked as if he might laugh at the suggestion. Then understanding flashed into his eyes, and he crossed himself. "God defend us—do you think her a witch?"

The two exchanged telling looks.

"It could explain to the satisfaction of any who might raise questions his sudden infatuation with her and his disobedience to you and why she must not live. A young prince of such promise would be especially prized by the evil one. Doubtless the girl has been empowered by Satan expressly to draw him into destruction. Still, we must not act rashly in so grave a matter. This should be tried in court."

"The girl is nothing, but Philip would never forgive me such a trial."

"Send him away, my liege. When he returns, she will be gone, and he will quickly forget her. Such light wenches are easily replaced in a boy's fancy."

"Where?"

"To Amberly, so please you. The unrest there has too long been neglected, and we both well know how apt my young lord is to win a people's loyalty with just a few brave words."

Robert looked at his counselor, an awed, admiring fascination in his eyes. "What will you have, my lord, to pay you for saving my kingdom yet again?"

"I only wish your happiness, Your Majesty, and my lord Philip's, of course. I wish him happy in his marriage, too. Of all the ladies that might be suitable for him, I noted but one that seemed to win his favor."

"Your Marian."

Dunois's answer was a self-deprecating shrug, but the king's expression turned thoughtful.

"Your lady was of the Chastelaynes, I know, Dunois, and Marian is heir to your lands. More importantly, Philip did seem to favor her most of all the nobility."

"Perhaps he will take the Fletcher girl's loss the better if Marian above all the others is chosen."

Robert thought for a moment. Then a kind of remorse shadowed his face. "For Philip's sake, I cannot on so slight evidence take the girl's life."

"Not even if it was she who made away with the poor, innocent child of the son you lost?"

"There is no proof of that."

"I spoke to Princess Margaret earlier this morning, my liege. She remembered taking a potion to ease her discomfort shortly before her pains started."

"So Philip said, and it was given her by Merryn."

"It was given her by Katherine Fletcher."

"Dunois—"

"Who is to say it was not? The child is dead, my lord, whether by chance or by design. If this charge was proved against Katherine Fletcher, could you not then, in law, rid yourself of her and remove this dangerous hindrance to your son's reign? Surely, my lord Philip would not sanction murder just for the benefit of his lust."

"Let it be so," Robert said after long consideration. "Rid me of this low-blooded Katherine, and your daughter shall be Lynaleigh's next queen."

"Your Majesty overwhelms me with this honor."

"It will be well worth it if you can do what you have said and keep me my son."

"One day he will thank you, my liege, for sparing him the

ignominy he now seems bent upon," Dunois assured him. "Bring the witch to trial."

The king nodded. "There my nobles can see and tell the people she is fairly dealt with, and none can call it unjust."

"Of course," Dunois agreed. "Of course."

Before noon Philip was again in his father's private chamber.

"Have you spoken yet to Margaret, Father? Heaven and earth, what she has done is an offense to God Himself!"

"She is very ill yet," Robert said placidly, "but do not fear. This matter shall be brought before the court, and the guilty shall not go unpunished. So let that rest. I have need of you now in another cause. You must go to Amberly."

"Why?"

"There has been a dispute and near rebellion in the town over our levies for war. The mayor has asked me to send someone to settle the matter, and I think it only right you should be my representative."

"But the trial, my lord. I cannot go now."

"That must wait until Margaret is well. It is important now that you be seen governing the people. You will be king next in Lynaleigh."

Philip's eyes widened. He would be king. He had not deeply considered what the death of Richard's child would mean to him. He would be king, and Kate would be queen. He could never tell his father about her now. There was no knowing what Robert might do to keep the royal line pure.

"No."

"Of course you will, Philip. You are my heir."

"No, please, Father, I have no right. I cannot."

"You can, boy, you can! By the mass, have I strived so long for this kingdom to have you balk now? No right? Your ancestors have been the kings of Lynaleigh time out of mind. You are now my eldest son. I was my father's eldest, and he was firstborn to an anointed king. No right? By law and before God, you have every right to the crown after me. Do you think that butcher Stephen would better fit the place?"

"No."

"Well then, do as you are bidden. I would have you leave tomorrow early. Settle matters in Amberly, and then, if you please to, you have my leave to visit Tom awhile in Chrisdale. It is not so much farther on."

Philip left Katherine sleeping, pausing only long enough to press the image of her indelibly into his memory. When he was very old, he wanted still to see her as she was just then with her hands clasped together under her blooming cheek and the fair cascade of her hair caressing her skin. He wanted so much to wake her for a last kiss, a last embrace, a last farewell, but he dared not. This swift, silent parting was kinder, and he would only be a few days away.

"Good-bye, sweeting," he murmured, promising himself he would make all the haste he could in returning to her. And then he was gone.

He and his men had ridden little more than half a day before they came upon a rider from Chrisdale. Philip recognized him as one of Tom's serving men, the one who openly numbered himself with the Heretics, the one Tom had recently made a captain in his army, much to their father's disapproval. Tom had taken a liking to his easygoing ways, and despite the ten or fifteen years difference in their ages, the two had become fast friends. Philip himself found much to like in the man and smiled at the sight of him.

"Palmer!"

"You are very well met, my lord. I have letters to you."

"From my brother?"

"Yes, my lord, to you and to the king such as should please."

"Yes?"

Palmer tossed a thick handful of his long hair back out of his face and nodded. "There was some trouble in Amberly, and my lord Tom, hearing of it, went to see what was the matter. The grievance was more to the old tune, but he told them again of your father's descent and right to the crown and how these levies they balked at are meant more for their own protection, being so near Ellenshaw as they are, and more such until they swore faith again to the king. I am sent to tell His Majesty that it is settled now, and he need not worry any further."

"Better and better, thank God. Your news spares me a task I was loath to do. Let us go back to Winton. I know your duty requires you there, and mine no longer requires me away."

It was very late when they again came to Winton, but Philip would not hear of stopping anywhere else for the night. He was disappointed to find his chamber empty of Katherine, though it was bright and warm as if it had only just been left.

He was searching the palace for her when he heard the sound of voices in the council chamber and saw a flicker of light under the door. He had never known the council to meet so late, and he stopped for a moment to listen.

"Confess that you took the life of our late Prince Richard's child!"

Philip recognized the lord chief justice's clipped tones. Could it be that they had brought Margaret to trial already? And at this hour?

"Will none of you take the part of right and innocency?"

That was Katherine's voice!

"If not for mercy's sake, my lords, then for the love you bear Prince Philip? I beg you, call him here. He will witness the truth of what I say. Please, my lords, I am innocent!"

Philip flung open the door.

"She is innocent, Your Majesty!"

Robert drew back from the white-lipped fury on his son's face.

"Philip, son, I thought you would be by now in Amberly."

"Tom settled that matter before I could get there. I met his messenger along the way. What is this?"

"My lord of Caladen," the justice said over the rumblings of the others, "you are not required at this trial."

Philip turned to the haughty, gray-faced old man. "I believe, if you will pardon me, my lord Chief Justice, that I am most required." His voice was taut. "Mistress Fletcher is innocent, and you will be guilty of gross misjustice if you find her anything less. Question me, if it please you. You know I always speak the truth."

"That's so," one of the courtiers said, and a murmur of assent rippled through the onlookers. Dunois frowned.

"My lord, it is not your honor that is in question here. We all know it to be beyond reproach. Your judgment, however . . . " He faltered there, as if he were reluctant to continue.

Philip turned cold eyes on him. "Say what it is you have to say, my lord. There is no argument you can make that will stand up to plain truth."

Dunois only looked uncomfortably at the king, but the lord chief justice did not hesitate to speak what was on his mind. "I say, my lord, Your Majesty, and all peers here, that my lord of Caladen cannot speak truth because he has been blinded from it. This witch has charmed his tongue so he cannot speak truth. Having seduced him with her body, she has gained control of his spirit and thinks to rule Lynaleigh through him when he is one day king."

"That's a lie!" Philip protested. "If Lynaleigh is abused by witches, then it is that witch from Westered, Margaret, and her serving woman that abuse us! Katherine is innocent. I know it."

"How is it that you know this, might I ask?"

"She told me."

A ripple of nervous laughter passed through the court.

"She spoke the truth!" Philip insisted.

"This is no evidence, Your Majesty," the lord chief justice said. "It has already been proven that she has bewitched our unfortunate Prince Philip to say anything she chooses."

"Already been proven?" Philip protested. "How proven? I've not been questioned. Try me and see if I am master of my own spirit."

"She has confessed to sympathy with the Heretics already, my lord, and will not recant. It is but one small step from blasphemy to witchcraft."

"Then condemn me along with her," Philip said. "I am as guilty in that as she."

"Your words only prove your enslavement to her black arts, Your Highness, as much as it pains me to say so," the justice told him, his voice gentle.

Desperate, Philip turned to the lord high chamberlain. "Dunois, this is madness. How can they say this? Can you not see that this is Margaret's doing?"

Dunois only shook his head sadly and turned back to the king. "I grieve with you, Your Majesty."

"What proof?" Philip cried, wondering if he were indeed mad or bewitched or if the entire court were. "What have I done, I beseech you, my lords, tell me, that has convinced you of this?"

"If you are your own master, as you say, then renounce the heresy this woman has led you into."

Philip looked at Katherine. Her eyes pled with him, and for a moment he wavered. Then she dropped her head and shook it, a slow, decisive gesture.

Philip looked up hopelessly. "I cannot."

Every face in the court was turned to him, every expression grieved and sympathetic.

"Come away, my lord," Dunois suggested. "You should not be here now. It will only pain you to—"

Philip shoved him aside and went to his father. "You'll not do this to her. Did you think to bring her here in the night and make away with her without my knowing? You'll not do this to her. You'll not do this to me."

Robert was careful to keep his voice gentle. "Please, son, go with Dunois. Once you have been freed from her, you will understand why it must be so."

"I shall never understand."

Robert stood and tried to calm him. "Go with Dunois. Let us do what must be done."

With a speed born of desperation, Philip threw his father aside and grabbed the girl's arm. He pulled her toward the door, but he was not halfway there before he was overpowered by the king's guard.

"Philip!" she shrieked as she was dragged away from him. "Philip, no!"

"Kate! Do not touch her!" Philip's struggles became more violent, wild. "Let me go!"

"Take him to the north tower," Robert commanded over his protests. "We need see no more of this to prove the witch guilty, and the sooner my son is away from her, the better."

"Philip! Philip, please!" the girl cried. "Speak them fair! Your ravings condemn me!"

Abruptly Philip stopped his struggling, and only the heaving in his chest remained to testify to his earlier outburst. "I beg your pardon, Your Majesty, my lord Chief Justice, my lords all," he said with a controlled expression and a still-trembling voice, "but I cannot let such a terrible punishment be meted out to the innocent. Mistress Fletcher is—"

"See how he calms at her command," the lord chief justice said in an awed half-whisper, crossing himself, and the king was quick to press his sudden advantage.

"Need you further proof?" he said into the court's dead silence. Then he signaled the guard. "Do as I have bidden you."

"Please, Philip," Katherine cried, "tell them. Tell them!"

"I cannot. If you are to have any hope of mercy, I cannot." Philip turned desperate eyes to his father. "Please." Then he felt the strong hands on him tighten as he was pulled toward the door. "No, Your Majesty. My lord! Father! Please do not do this! Please! Kate! Kate, forgive me!"

Suddenly her arms were around his neck, her lips on his. Moving to prevent her, the guards were forced to loosen their grasp on him, and that was enough to allow him to hold her close one last time.

"Kate, Kate," he sobbed.

"Part them!" the king barked, and one of the guards pulled

Katherine from Philip's arms. Philip lunged at him, but could not break his captors' hold.

"Father," he pled again, the words choked out, hardly intelligible. "I beg you, oh, God! Father, on my knees. Don't. You take my life in taking hers."

He tried to kneel, to give force to his plea, but he was denied even that.

"The witch's power over him is strong," the justice said gravely. "Speak true, witch! Have you given him some token to bind him to you? Or taken aught of his?"

The girl clutched her hands against her breast.

"Nothing in sorcery, my lord."

"See. She lies again." The justice pulled her hands away and seized the treasure she had sought to conceal against her heart. "Do you know this ring, my sovereign?"

Robert snatched it from him. "My son's! A token by which she might rule him. God defend us!"

"God defend us from false accusations!" Philip spat.

"He is likely to have some talisman of hers as well, Your Majesty." The justice flicked open Philip's shirt and lifted up the fine sapphire cross that hung against his chest. "This."

"No." Philip struggled again. "A holy cross, my lords. It speaks for her innocence. Would a witch give such a token?"

Robert came to him and examined the cross. "Whenever did evil shun to put on seeming grace to disguise itself?"

He snapped the fine chain and dropped it to the floor. Philip watched in horror as he ground the delicate cross under his heel.

"Take the prince away. I shall not bid you again."

Philip howled curses at them all, struggling once more to free himself until it felt as if his sinews would snap.

"God will judge all of you for this!"

It took four of them to drag him backwards out the door, and he fought them wildly, straining every muscle, using every ounce of strength he had, screaming all the while.

The silence that followed was sullied by the echoes of his cries and by the girl's desolate sobs.

"What say my lords now?" Robert said finally. "The witch seems guilty to me. I trust you will find her so."

"What can we say, Your Majesty, in the face of such evidence?" asked Dunois. Then he turned to the other lords. "We have seen his bewitchment with our own eyes. Can we find, in our love for the poor, oppressed boy, any verdict but guilty?"

Philip sat numbly in the corner of his cell, oblivious to the dawn light that filtered into his bleak surroundings. His mind was fixed on his last sight of his young wife, looking scared and small, flanked by soldiers, forbidden to speak to him. He knew it would likely be the last time he ever saw her.

It still astounded him that he was even here in his father's prison, forbidden to communicate with anyone. His father thought him mad or bewitched and would not hear him. Katherine was doomed. He could feel it in the cold dread that sat heavily in the pit of his stomach, and he could do nothing.

He knew Margaret had somehow engineered this mockery of a trial to cover her own infanticide, but he could not understand why. He believed Katherine's story, knew her tender heart incapable of such a monstrous deed, but even she had no explanation for what Margaret had done. What could Margaret have gained by it?

The low noise of a crowd broke into his thoughts and drew him to the window. The people thronged the streets, pressing against the soldiers who were holding open a pathway through them. The rumble grew until it seemed loud even high up in Philip's prison tower, and then he saw what he most feared.

There was Katherine being brought along in a cart, tied to a post, barefoot, wearing only her shift. Her face was pale, and there was a look of terror on her face that Philip could not bear. And her hair!

The long, glorious locks that had hung like spun gold past her knees were gone, shorn as a sign of her excommunication and disgrace. She was truly condemned, and he could do nothing.

"No!" He struggled with the bars on the window. "Do not do this! Kate! Kate!"

His voice was drowned out by the jeering crowd.

"Burn, witch!" they taunted. "Die, and be damned!"

Even from where he was, Philip could see she was covered with cuts and bruises from the stones they threw. As he watched, they spit on her, taking pleasure in her suffering.

"You'll not practice your damned arts on our Prince Philip after today!"

"Kate!" Philip howled, cursing their misdirected loyalty to him, still grappling uselessly with the bars. "Kate! Kate!"

He did not know if she actually heard him over the din, but she looked up just then, and their eyes met.

"Kate!" he cried again, and he stretched his hand down toward her. Her mouth formed his name, but he could not hear her. Then a stone caught her in the face, and she flinched and turned away. A moment later the cart passed out of his sight, and he saw her no more.

He turned from the window and slid numbly down to sit on the floor. All of this was incomprehensible to him. How could it be that he, the son and heir to the reigning king, could have his life torn apart, his heart ripped from him and cut to pieces before his eyes? He was the crown prince of Lynaleigh, yet he was made to sit helplessly by and let his beloved face fiery death alone.

"Why?" he moaned, his voice worn ragged from a night of raging pleas.

The wind shifted and brought into the prison the dank, foul stench that was too familiar to his soldier's senses. He blanched at the malodorous cloud. There was no mistaking the smell of burnt flesh.

At first he did not notice that the door to his prison had been opened or that he had a visitor.

"My lord, I have brought you your breakfast."

Philip looked up listlessly, but then leapt to his feet.

"Palmer? Palmer! Have they burned her, Palmer? Tell me!"

Palmer's grim expression offered no hope. "I am sorry."

Philip closed his eyes, and Palmer quickly set down the tray he carried and went to him.

"Take comfort, sir," he said, lowering his voice. "She gave me a message for you."

"A message?" Philip repeated as if the word were foreign to him.

"I have friends among your father's men. I managed to see her for a moment before they took her away. She said for you to remember her love and forget all the rest. She wanted me to give you this, too, because it was all she had." Glancing furtively toward the door, he opened the pouch that hung over his shoulder. "I'll be hanged if they find out I took this."

He pulled out a long, thick braid of fair hair, hair that shone like spun gold, and laid it in Philip's hands. "I had to steal it away from the hag who cut it off."

Philip stared down at it, bewildered. After a moment Palmer began setting out the food he had brought as a pretense to deliver Katherine's message—food Philip would never touch.

"I must go now, my lord," he said.

But Philip still stood staring and made no reply.

Hearing once more the clank of the key in the lock, Philip let the braid slide slowly through his hands to fall in a coil at his feet. The stench of the burning had saturated the air, and, looking at the rich food Palmer had brought, Philip felt a rising wave of nausea that made his head spin.

With an inarticulate cry, he pounded his fists on the little table until the dishes rattled and the pitcher was upset. In helpless fury, he raked everything to the floor and overturned the table on top of it. For a moment he stared at the destruction he had made. Then he dug frantically through the shattered crockery, but Palmer had been wise enough not to give him a knife.

CHAPTER

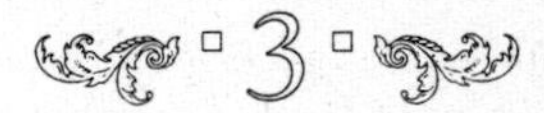

KATHERINE HAD BEEN DEAD TWO DAYS BEFORE TOM, HEARING THE news, returned to Winton.

"I want to see Philip," he said, ignoring the king's welcome.

"Listen to me, Tom. You do not know what has happened here—"

"I've heard. I want to see him."

Robert looked uncomfortably at his lord high chamberlain.

"My lord of Brenden," Dunois said with a faintly contemptuous bow, "if you have heard, then you know my lord of Caladen has been under the evil influence of a witch. He is liable to rave yet. Thus far he has refused to speak to anyone, even the archbishop himself. He'll not even take food."

Tom did not spare him a glance. "The girl was burned two days ago, Father. If she did have some sort of spell over him, she can hardly have it anymore, and even if she did, what harm can there be in my seeing him?"

Robert could say nothing that would stand in the face of Tom's cool resolution. He had not yet had the courage to see Philip himself. Sending Tom now might be easier.

"Go on, then, and take his release to the lieutenant of the prison," he said, ignoring Dunois's frown, "but try to understand, son."

"I always try to understand," Tom said. Now he did look at Dunois. "And sometimes I actually manage to do it."

As soon as the secretary had written Philip's release and the king had signed it, Tom took it to the prison. The guard was quick to open the door to Philip's cell, and Tom bounded in.

"Philip—oh, Philip!"

Philip lay gagged and glassy-eyed on the narrow bed, bound in strips of sheeting, his hands and face cut and bruised. Tom went to him and gently removed the bloodied cloth from his mouth.

Philip worked his stiff jaw and moistened his lips. "I am not mad, Tom," he said, his voice hoarse. "Do not let them tell you so."

Tom unknotted his brother's bonds, his hands trembling with anger, and then helped him sit up.

"Drink some of this," he said, taking a dipper full of water from the bucket beside the bed. Philip took it in numb obedience.

"Get in here!" Tom ordered, and the soldier on guard came hesitantly into the room. "What do you mean to use a Lynaleighan prince like this?"

"My lord, it was for his own good."

"His own good?"

"Please, my lord, he was a danger to himself. He beat his fists against the wall and his head, too. We had no choice but to tie him, but we used cloth instead of rope. It was gentler."

Tom glanced sadly at his brother. "Very well. Go back to your commander and tell him you have been relieved of your charge."

The soldier was quick to obey, and Tom sat down on the bed.

"Philip."

Philip shook his head. "They've burned her, Tom," he whispered, his eyes great wells of pain. "They've burned my Kate."

"I know."

Tom put his arms around him and let him cry.

Rafe Bonnechamp was waiting when they returned to the palace. For two days he had wondered when his young master would be released. He had inwardly cursed the king for forbidding him to go to the prison to watch over Philip himself. He did so again now, seeing the Philip that Tom brought back to him—faint shadow of the spirited young prince he had served since the boy had grown too old for a nursemaid.

"Come, my lord, I've made ready your bed."

"No. Not sleep."

Rafe knit his bushy brows and looked at Tom, his sturdy, brown-bearded commoner's face anxious and unsettled.

"Then I will bring you something to eat, my lord."

Philip shook his head and pulled away from him.

"Is there anything you want?" he asked.

Philip once more shook his head. "What I want is beyond your power or any man's to get back." He covered his grief-marked face with his hands, and Rafe said nothing.

Tom, too, was silent, knowing nothing he could say to be of help. He merely stayed close, hoping Philip would draw comfort from that, comfort at least that he would not be left in this sudden darkness alone.

Even that reassurance was soon denied. The next day Robert ordered Tom to return to his post, and no amount of persuading on Tom's part could change his mind. The place was too important to the defense of the kingdom.

"I am sent back to Chrisdale," Tom said sadly to his brother.

"No, Tom," Philip pled, "do not go. Have pity. Do not leave me just yet."

"I must. Father will have it so."

"He will have it so! He will have it so! Must the sun rise in the west because he will have it so? Kate is dead because he would have it so!"

"I'll not defend him, Philip. I cannot. But he is our king, and we must obey him. He alone must answer for the things he has done."

"And on that day, come what judgment there will, Kate will still be dead." Philip faced the narrow window and looked out onto the lush forest, not seeing it. "Stay with me, Tom. I need someone with me now."

"I cannot stay, but you will not be alone. Let God be your refuge. Take strength from Him."

"Not now," Philip said in a hard voice Tom hardly recognized. "Not anymore. I stood for Him at her trial, for what I believed was His own truth, and He did nothing. I'll not seek His help again."

"You will not always think thus," Tom said softly.

Breathing a sigh of desolation that would not be comforted, Philip bowed his head. Tom put one hand on his sagging shoulder and was gone.

The next day the king sent a message to Philip's chamber, borne by the lord high chamberlain himself. Rafe would not let him in.

"I am come of commission from the king," Dunois said. "I charge you in his name to let me pass."

"I cannot do it, my lord. My lord of Caladen gave me express charge that I not admit anyone to him. If you have a message, I will give it to him, but I can in obedience do no more."

Dunois paused for a moment of incensed consideration. "Very well. Tell the prince that His Majesty requires his presence in his private chamber this afternoon."

"I will tell him so."

Rafe bowed stiffly and went into Philip's room, shutting the door behind him. Philip was sitting on the bed, clutching a pillow in his arms, looking raw-nerved and easily set off.

"I have a message from your father," Rafe said, keeping his voice low. "He has summoned you to him this afternoon."

"No."

"A direct summons from the king, my lord," Rafe said, startled at the flat rejection. "You cannot refuse it."

"I do and I have. Tell him so, or else do not. I do not care."

"My lord—"

"I cannot see him now, Rafe. Not now."

Bonnechamp argued the matter no further. "I will tell him."

Not an hour later, the king himself came to Philip's chamber. The room was black, for Philip had made Rafe close up the shutters and take away the candles. Even the hearth fire was unlit.

"Philip?"

The candle Robert brought cast only a faint glow as he held it before him to search the darkness.

"Philip, son?"

"Do not ever call me son, butcher!" Philip hissed in his ear, low and fierce, startlingly close.

Robert turned and saw little more than his son's half-wild eyes, circled with black. "You left me little choice," Robert pled, reaching out to him.

Philip stiffened and drew back. "Keep those hands away from me. They reek of her blood."

"For you, Philip. I did this for you. I could not leave you prey to her sorcery, leave my kingdom's heir pawn to Satan."

Philip shook his head warily. "I believe that no more than you do. It was for policy, not for witchcraft, that you burned her. If ever anyone was Satan's pawn, it is you."

"No, son, believe me—"

"You've killed my Kate! Killed her! Are you my father that you could kill what I best love in all the world?" Philip lowered his head under the weight of his grief. "Never say it was for me."

"She was condemned by law."

"Your law!"

"She killed your brother's child! Are you so eager to be king that you would sanction that?"

"The crown is accursed. I hate it. Kate knew that. And even if I had begged it of her, she never would have done so horrible a thing as kill an innocent child, not for me or all this world. You may lay that infamy at Margaret's door."

"Why, Philip? You have yet to tell me why Margaret would do

such a thing? She carried the next heir of Lynaleigh. What could she hope to gain by that child's loss?"

Philip sat on the edge of the bed and rested his arms and his head on his knees. "I do not know. I have reasoned on that again and again, until my mind is sick with it, but I do not know."

"Because she had no reason. This Fletcher woman did it. How else could such a lowborn creature hope to advance herself except through you? It is time you face the truth now, Philip. I know you were fond of her, but—"

"Fond of her?" Philip stood up, his hands tightening into fists. "Fond? She was a woman, not a puppy! Merciful heaven, fond of her? I loved her—heart and soul, I loved her, and you killed her!" His voice broke, and the acid tears coursed down his face. "Murderer! Murderer!"

He struck out blindly at his father, raining blows on his chest, arms, face. Robert grabbed his wrists and held them bruisingly tight until, weakened with grief, Philip could fight no more. Abruptly, his struggling stopped, and he looked beseechingly into his father's eyes. His sobs came again without warning, uncontrollable, tearing through his worn body until he felt his lungs would burst.

"Shh. Shh." Robert pulled him close into a soothing, comforting embrace. "I would have spared you this if only you had listened to me. I had no choice but to condemn her. Understand me in that, but, believe me, Philip, what I must needs do as king has no bearing on the love I have for you."

Philip sagged against him until his sobs quieted. Then he fell to his knees. "Send me away." His broken plea stabbed deeply into his father's heart. "If there is any mercy left in you, Father, send me away from here."

"I cannot, Philip. You are the crown prince. I need you with me here in the council."

"Please, Father, for a month. A week. Even a day, I beg you! Do not make me stay here."

Pity in his eyes, Robert made his son lie down.

"I am sorry, but I must. You know it is so." He swept away a tear on his son's sunken cheek, and his voice grew more tender. "This will please you. I have decided that we'll not speak of marriage for you for yet awhile. Let your mind be easy in that regard until you are more ready to think on it. You have my promise. As for this deal of sorrow, time will heal it. You are young yet. In time you will realize that these fancies pass. You will see, boy. Now go to sleep."

For several days Philip did not sleep. He did nothing but sit in silent grief by day and walk the dark corridors at night. Rafe wore himself out worrying over his young master. Philip still would not eat the food brought to him, hardly drank even water, and sternly forbade Rafe to follow him in his restless wanderings. Nearly a week passed before Rafe could persuade him to talk with him.

There was scarcely a trace of the famed Chastelayne beauty in him now. He was worn and pale, his white lips pressed tight in a struggle to keep his raging grief in check. His eyes seemed larger for the black smudges beneath them, and they held such pain that it tore Rafe's heart to look into them.

"My lord," he said as he watched Philip's bruised hands fitfully clenching and unclenching the arms of his chair. "Please, my lord, this cannot go on."

One side of Philip's mouth twitched into a wrenching mockery of a smile. "The church, I understand, does not look favorably upon suicide, so I suppose it must go on."

"My lord!"

Before Rafe could say more, there was a sharp rap on the chamber door. Without waiting for an invitation, the lord high chamberlain swept into the room. "If you would grant me a moment, Your Highness."

Rafe turned. "My lord Dunois—"

"Leave here, my lord," Philip warned.

The chamberlain's face turned all concerned sorrow. "I know you are grieved, Your Highness—"

"I'll not hear sympathy from you. You had none for her."

"Please, my prince, I tried as best I might to spare you this. Ask your father's men if I did not go to her during the trial to see what plea she might make to save her life, even in the face of such strong proof against her." Dunois held up one hand in pledge of truth. "God knows I begged the king not to act hastily in this, but you know His Majesty when he's set his mind to a thing."

He ended with an apologetic shake of his head, and Philip squeezed his eyes shut and drew a painful breath. "I know."

"I hope, then, you do not believe me disloyal to Your Highness."

"You are loyal to Afton, my lord," Philip said, looking as if he wished he could choke the sycophantic voice into silence. "I suppose that is loyal enough."

"I thank you, Your Highness."

Dunois made a flourishing bow, and Philip shifted in his chair. "Well? I trust there is more to what you have in charge."

"Oh, yes, my lord. I am commanded by His Majesty the king to read to you the accounts of the last council meetings at which you have not been in attendance." Dunois held out the massive book the scribes used for such records. "I will do so now if you have your leisure."

"I am not an idiot or a child, my lord, that I must be read to," Philip snapped.

Rafe moved closer to him, almost putting himself between the two of them. "My lord chamberlain," he interposed, "if you will pardon me, my lord of Caladen has not been well. Such a reading would overtire him, and I feel—"

"It is an order direct from your father, my lord," Dunois said, ignoring Rafe's protest.

Philip slumped down into his chair. "By all means, let the royal will be carried out."

"My lord," Dunois said with a bow and an unctuous smile, and he began to read of the cost of the crystal goblets given to the archbishop at his investiture, how many pairs of boots were needed for the army on the southern border, of the importance of strict control over the supply of silks brought into the country, and how many of these new ministers were spreading their heresy here in the south. Before he could finish his explanation of why a tax should be imposed on beeswax, Rafe noticed that Philip had fallen into an uneasy sleep.

"My lord," he whispered to Dunois, "please, you can see he has not slept well since the trial. Another time, I beg you."

Dunois closed the book. "The king will not be pleased," he warned. He turned on his heel and left, slamming the door shut.

Looking down at Philip, Rafe shook his head. "No. I do not imagine he will."

He lifted Philip like a child in his arms and laid him down on the bed, drawing the coverlet over him. He dared not remove his boots for fear of waking him, but the boy looked so worn out that Rafe doubted he would have felt even that.

"Rest now, boy. Life'll not seem so cruel after a little sleep."

He gently loosened Philip's fingers from the tight fists they had formed. Then he sat down in the chair and went to sleep himself.

The blackness of Philip's exhaustion dissolved into dreams. He saw Katherine as she had been the morning after they were married, with the dawn light shining on her, making a halo of her long, fair hair. Her lips were curved into a sweet smile, and she bent down, as she had then, to stir the fire.

Then the dream turned nightmare. A tendril of blonde hair caught fire, and in an instant the flames consumed her. With a shriek, she fell into ashes, and the well-remembered acrid smell of burnt hair and flesh filled Philip's nose.

Gasping, he bolted upright in bed. For a long while he did not move. He forced himself to breathe slowly, reminded himself that it was only a dream. Still, the memory nauseated him. He'd been spared the sight but not the smell of her execution. It seemed he would carry that to his grave.

It was dark. He did not know how long he had slept, but he was determined not to let it happen again. Sleep now held for him a terror he could not control. He would have gotten up and roamed the passageways as had become his habit, but he knew he would never be able to get past Rafe unseen. Instead, he gathered up the pillows and propped himself up, prepared to spend the hours until dawn battling this new enemy—sleep.

The following day Philip received another royal summons. This one he obeyed.

"Sit down, son," Robert said. "I trust today finds you well."

Philip felt no inclination toward idle talking. "What would you have of me?"

"I must command something of you, something I would not ask yet, except it has become necessity. Please, sit down."

"I would rather stand. What would you have of me?"

"I must require your marriage now. It cannot wait any longer."

Philip turned even paler. "You promised me."

"As I before told you, this is no boys' game—this playing for kingdoms. Your safety and mine, Tom's, the whole realm's, could depend upon the alliance you make."

Anger brought sudden color to Philip's cheeks. "Is this alliance so dear that you would lie and murder for it?"

"It could mean the whole kingdom to Afton," Robert said, pricked by his son's frank accusation. "Our link with Westered could bring us victory. Without it we can hope for nothing but defeat."

"Westered? But Margaret—"

"Not Margaret, but Lady Rosalynde, her sister. The grieving widow Margaret seeks yet to be queen. I've had word that she's gone to Stephen of Ellenshaw, and he's married her."

The color again dropped out of Philip's face. "Then that was her reason." He felt a knot pull tight inside his heart. "You must see now that Kate was innocent."

"It may well be so," Robert said gravely.

"You know it is so!"

"I did not know it when she was condemned. What was I to think in the face of the evidence? But that is past. We must think of the future now, and to keep that safe, we need Westered. I must have you marry Lady Rosalynde at once. If her father throws his support to Margaret and Ellenshaw, we are lost." He picked up a ring from the table, the one that Philip had not worn since he had hung it around Katherine's neck, a token of the vows they had exchanged. "Put this on. It is time you remembered that you are a royal prince."

The crystal eyes flashed fury. "I'll not wear your cursed ring anymore!"

"Be reasonable."

Philip snatched the ring out of his hand and hurled it at him. "You and your Rosalynde be hanged together! Yes, and I with you if ever I marry her!"

The bright metal made a ringing bounce off the stone wall and landed at Robert's feet.

"Philip—"

"Murderer!"

Robert's face turned hard. "You've used that word to me enough, boy."

"Truth speaks best in plain terms," Philip spat.

"Very well, my young lord, if we are to speak in plain terms—who was I to believe? My son's widow or my son's harlot?"

"Before God you'll not speak so of her."

"Who shall say I may not? Do you think just because you dared shame me with flaunting your trull before my court that you may now tell me what I may and may not do? I suppose with Richard's child gone, I was to accept her first brat as heir to the throne after you and see you stand insolently by, having put so much of your pure Chastelayne blood into such a bastard that you'd not have enough left yourself to color a blush of shame."

"Kate would never have shamed our name. She was the only pure thing I ever found in this place. But I'll not defend her to you.

You deserve your ignorance. God grant you may die in it." Tears came back into his eyes, and his father sought to console him.

"Philip, son—"

Philip wrenched away from him, unable to endure his touch, unable to endure the pain that wracked him again and still.

"Send me away from here," he pled once more, his voice ragged and grating. "Send me away."

"Where would you go?" Robert asked, a touch of hollow regret in his tone.

"Someplace where there is much work to be done. I care not where."

"You know with Ellenshaw's rebellion, Grenaver thinks that now is the time to reopen the dispute over the Riverlands. We must make ready for them."

"Where?"

"Maughn has yet to be garrisoned and fortified. It will take a winter of hard labor. Would you go there?"

"If I may go at once."

"Believe me, son, I am sorry for your grief, but for my kingdom's sake, you left me no choice."

Robert tried to reach out to him, but again Philip backed away. "Do not force me," the prince warned, his voice as taut as his strained nerves. "Let me away from here. I cannot bear any more from you."

Robert took a step back himself, a little afraid of what he saw in his son's eyes. "Go then. But withhold your judgment of me until you have yourself lived awhile as king."

"God grant that that day will never come."

It was a weary, slow ride to Maughn, and Philip was relieved when the colorless little town finally came into sight. Perhaps here in a place that held none of Katherine's memories, he could escape some of the pain and maybe even sleep without fear. There was little more to hope for now. She was gone, not to be resurrected until that final day when even the sea would give up its dead. There was not even a grave at which he could mourn—only a handful of ashes lost to the wind and a charred pyre that had seen and would see other such executions.

The long golden rope of her hair was all he had left of her, all he had to bind his memories together. He blessed and cursed Palmer for bringing it to him. It drove an iron spike of pain through him to look on it, yet he clung to it as if it were the hope of his salvation. He had nothing else.

The chamber that had been prepared for him here in Maughn was smaller than the one he had had at Winton, the bed narrower and harder. Everything here seemed that way. Maughn was not a pretty place, nor was it a place of ease. He was glad. He had just now no eye for beauty, no taste for comfort. He wanted only work to busy his hands and dull his mind until God in His mercy ended the life remaining to him.

Worn after the long journey, he gave in to Rafe's urging for him to lie down. Surely his body was too overtaxed, his brain too numbed with effort, to admit anything but oblivion tonight. A moment later, he was wrapped in sleep.

The oblivion did not last long. Philip found himself thrust into a nightmare more felt than seen. Without warning, a wicked blade stabbed deep into his chest, plunged again and again into his heart, but it did not leave clean, merciful wounds that would kill at a stroke. Rather it made a jagged, gaping hole that widened with each hacking blow.

At first he fought wildly for his life, struggling and clawing at his obscure assailant, but finally he lay still, hardly flinching at each clumsy, grating thrust. The agony went on and on even when he had no strength left to fight.

"Why don't you die?" he heard his own voice saying. "Why don't you die?"

He woke sobbing with pain, his fist over his heart, twisted into his sweat-sodden shirt.

The next morning before dawn he arose and began his work. For more than a month he buried himself in hard labor, working each day shoulder to shoulder with his men until darkness and exhaustion demanded that the day should end. Soon his body refused to mourn any longer, and he was forced to satisfy its demands for food and sleep. His nightmares grew less vivid and less frequent and finally ceased. He looked almost once more the dashing, valiant prince he had been. Almost.

Anyone who saw him now, anyone who had seen him before the trial, could tell something had gone from him. He was all soldier now, rough and hard, with not a moment to give to ease or pleasure or even thoughts of God. He lived only to do the work for which he had been sent, to acquit himself honorably in the only task he saw before him. By April Maughn was an impressive stronghold against the enemy.

He looked on it and tried to feel some pride in his work, but all he felt was grief and bewilderment that sometimes it was his father that he mourned more than Katherine. He had laughed at her fears and told her that the king would not harm her any more than he would his own son. He could not laugh now. He had assured King Edward, too, of his father's honorable intentions. How foolish he had been.

Philip knew how sacred the Chastelayne bloodline was to his father. Perhaps, in truth, it was inconceivable to him that Lynaleigh's crown prince should mix his proud blood with a serving wench's and bring ignoble stock to the throne. Perhaps he had even believed her guilty of murder.

He could not have known how deeply I loved her.

Philip had just dismissed his men for the evening when a messenger came riding in from the southeast, from Tanglewood. John's message was brief:

We've had intelligence of an attack from Grenaver set to come at any time. They are said to be five thousand strong against the fifteen hundred I have here. I've sent word every day to Winton for aid from the king, but he gives me no reply. I beg you, if I have any sway in your heart, and if you have any sway in his, send to him. I am already so out of favor with him now that if I lose Tanglewood, I could never again face him. If you cannot persuade him, do not let it fret you or make any division between you and him. I am not afraid to do my duty.

John

Philip immediately ordered his men to ready themselves for battle. Tanglewood was not far, and they could be there in ample time to back John's army.

"Go at once to my brother in Chrisdale," he told the messenger. "Tell Tom we're needed in Tanglewood."

"What of your reply to my lord John, Your Highness?"

"My army will be his answer."

"And your father, my lord?" Rafe asked once the messenger had gone. "It will not please him to know you have left the post he has entrusted to you."

"I will send to him about it."

"He gave you orders specifically that you were to keep Maughn. What will he say if you disobey him?"

"If John's messages have gotten through to Winton at all, then he must not realize how grave John's position is. He would not let whatever grievance he has been holding against John risk his son's life and the kingdom. We shall keep Tanglewood, and he will applaud my boldness. Come on."

CHAPTER

ROSALYNDE'S EYES FLEW OPEN, AND SHE PULLED HER COVERlet up to her chin. The night was moonless, starless, and she could see nothing as she lay there shivering, waiting for her heart to slow and her nightmare to fade. She was in Westered in her own bed, not on a battlefield, and Philip was not lying dead at her feet.

How vividly she had seen him, though, stumbling toward her, soaked with his own blood, both hands stretched out to her, pleading. He had fallen to his knees before her and then collapsed altogether, his cheek resting on her wet satin-shod foot. She had reached down to him, but he was cold, and his wondrous eyes were empty.

She had forced herself awake at that, afraid to see more, but the fear would not leave her. The reports of the war were worse than ever now. Might not such a thing happen? Perhaps it had already.

"Oh, my Philip," she whispered into the darkness. "Be merciful to him, Lord God."

It was dawn when she finished her prayers and finally slept again.

Tom sat near Philip's bedside listening to his ragged breathing. He had shown no other sign of life since the battle, and Tom had worn the meaning out of the single prayer that had been all night on his lips.

"Please, God, mercy."

He murmured the words again, hardly knowing that he did. Philip was so pale and still. He had been grazed by an arrow high up on his left cheek, leaving that side of his face swollen and angrily red, but that wound was slight. One arm was splinted and bandaged, broken in two places, but that, too, would mend. It was the ugly, black-stitched gash down Philip's side that worried Tom the most.

Three of Philip's ribs had been broken in the battle, and one of them had stabbed into his lung. Tom remembered having to hold him down while Livrette cut him open. Then the physician had reached blood-slicked fingers into his side to pull the rib back into place. Tom remembered Philip weakly struggling against the pain that had clawed its way through his unconsciousness, and he remembered, too, the grim look on Livrette's face as he had sewed the incision shut.

"It is of little use even closing this up, my lord. His lung is pierced. He'll likely drown in his own blood."

Tom had prayed then as he had never prayed before, and now hours later Philip still breathed. Tom still prayed.

"Please, God, mercy."

Tom and his army had come to Tanglewood as soon as he received Philip's message, but they found that the battle had already ended. The influx of Philip's men had brought Afton triumph, but the victory was grim.

Shortly after dawn Philip asked hoarsely for water, and Tom held the cup to his lips.

"Give John some, too," Philip insisted. "He is hurt."

"John is not here," Tom told him carefully. His heart lurched when Philip moaned and for a moment seemed not to breathe.

Tom watched him lying there, the ashen touch of death on his face. "Philip," he begged. "Philip, please."

Philip's lashes fluttered, but his eyes did not open. "John," he murmured. "Where's John?"

Tom glanced back at Rafe, who was hovering at the foot of the bed, and then went to him. "What do I answer him, Rafe?" Tom asked softly. "I am afraid to tell him now."

"Tell him Lord John is too badly hurt to come."

Tom shook his head. "I could never lie to him. He would know."

"You know as well as I do how he's grieved since the trial. He's hurt badly and bound to mourn again once he knows about your brother. I know he's had little enough cause to love this world of late. All this at once may be too much for him to bear. He may merely let go. I've seen it before."

"Rafe, I—"

"John," Philip moaned again.

Rafe looked urgently to Tom. "Have I your permission, my lord?"

Tom nodded, and Rafe went to Philip's side. "My lord, hear me."

Philip managed to open his eyes. "John?"

"No, Highness. Prince John lies in his own bed, wounded, too. His physician says that the news of your loss would finish him as well. You must not disappoint him."

Tom took a deep breath and then went to his brother. "Philip, try." He took Philip's hand in both of his own. "Please, try."

Philip looked at him unsteadily. "Hurts."

"You must try," Tom said, squeezing his hand tighter. "You must."

Rafe leaned closer to him. "For Lord John's sake, my lord. For your brother."

Philip took a rasping breath. "I'll not—" He stopped, gritting his teeth, but determination shone through the pain in his eyes. "I'll not disappoint him."

"I will get Livrette," Rafe said.

After the physician examined Philip, he looked at Tom. "I will tell you plain, my lord, I am surprised to see him still alive. He still is very ill, but he may make it through this yet. He seems determined today to live."

"We will see he stays in that mind," Bonnechamp said. Tom nodded in half-hearted agreement.

"What am I to say to him when he finds out?" Tom asked as he and Rafe sat near the fire that night.

The servant merely shook his head and drained his cup. "He will be well enough to bear it then, my lord, and it'll not matter so much."

"It will break his heart," Tom said, glancing toward the still figure on the bed.

"Well, whatever they say, sir, there's never a man died yet of that."

For two days Philip struggled with death, and Rafe was constantly at his side, reminding him that John's survival depended heavily on his own. Tom, biting his lip, watched and said nothing, but wept in his prayers for help and forgiveness.

On the third day, while the soldiers were still trying to identify the dead, Philip regained full consciousness and asked for John.

"I am sorry—," Tom began.

Rafe interrupted him smoothly, "You cannot see him yet, my lord. Not until you are strong enough to walk there yourself."

Philip shifted impatiently and laid his warm face on a cooler part of his pillow. "I need to know for certain he is safe. Tom, you tell me. He looked very bad when last I saw him."

Tom looked with sudden panic at Rafe. Then, steeling himself, he came close to his brother. "John is fine."

"You are sure?"

Tom covered the hand that plucked his sleeve, hating himself. "You know I never lie to you, Philip. John is safe and well."

Philip smiled faintly and fell asleep.

For the next few days, Rafe fed Philip on porridge, fresh broth, and stories of John's slow recovery. Philip was soon able to stand and even walk shakily across the room.

"I am going to see John," he announced.

Tom felt a guilty tightening in his stomach. "Philip—"

"You said when I could walk there on my own, I could see him. Well, I can now."

Tom shook his head helplessly. "Philip—"

"He is not worse, is he? You told me yesterday—"

"Philip—"

"Will you sit down, my lord," Rafe said quietly, urging Philip back to his bed, but Philip shook him off.

"Tom?"

Tom wanted desperately to tear his gaze away from the bewildered, fearful expression on Philip's face, but he forced himself to hold his head up. "John died the day of the battle."

Rafe took Philip's arm, a look of concern on his face. Weak as Philip was, this news might yet be too much for him. Again Philip shook him off, never taking his eyes from Tom's face.

"Tom?"

"I am sorry, Philip, truly."

"Tom, you lied to me? John is dead?"

"You were so badly hurt, we were afraid you'd not survive the news. We had to tell you—"

"You lied to me, Tom. To me."

Tom could not meet the look of stunned anguish in Philip's eyes.

"Merciful heaven," Philip murmured, "is there no one who'll not betray me?"

"The lie was mine, my lord," Rafe said finally. "Lord Tom told you nothing that is untrue. He told you Lord John is safe and well, and so he is. If there's but one soul in heaven, it is that boy."

Philip swayed suddenly, and Tom and Rafe both rushed to support him, but Philip shrugged off his brother's hand. He refused even to look Tom in the face.

"Philip—" Tom began, but Rafe gave him a warning look over Philip's head. With another useless apology, Tom left.

Rafe settled his master back into the bed he had not left for over a week and realized from the stricken look on his face that he was likely to be there awhile longer.

It was a long tedious afternoon. That night Philip's fever rose again, but he would not allow Rafe to send for the physician.

"Trust no one," he confided half-deliriously after a restless silence. Rafe replaced the cloth on his forehead with a cool one and said nothing.

"'I never lie to you, Philip,'" Philip continued sarcastically. "Good, trusty Tom."

He pushed aside the water Rafe was urging him to drink and tried to sit up, but Rafe held him down. "No, my lord. Dawn is a long way off."

"I want to see John. He promised." The words turned into a half-choked sob. "He promised and he lied."

"I lied to you, my lord. You seem to have forgiven me."

"Everyone lies, Rafe," Philip said, and his voice was bitter. "It is the way of the world. But not Tom. Not to me."

"He did not want to lose you, my lord. He tried to spare you because he knew it would break your heart. Can you not see you are breaking his?"

Philip looked at him unsteadily.

"He loved the boy, my lord, fully as much as you did. Can you not understand that and comfort his grief instead of heaping on more?"

Two great tears welled up in Philip's eyes, and Rafe knew he hurt so badly, body and spirit, that he needed Tom now not as enemy but as brother.

"Shall I send for him?" he asked gently.

Philip nodded. With an abrupt release, Philip let the air out of his lungs, easing the pressure on his battered ribs. Rafe deftly wiped the sudden sweat from his brow.

"I'll tell the physician your fever's broken," Rafe said. Then he left the room, fighting to keep the enormity of his relief from showing on his face.

For a long while Philip lay there, his memories of the battle too vivid yet. He had found John in the middle of the field, down on one knee, bare-headed, surrounded by the dead of both armies, the Chastelayne banner trampled and bloodied beneath him. John had looked pale and shaken, but he had insisted that he was not hurt, that the blood that covered him belonged to their enemies.

I should have known, Philip thought, but he had been so badly hurt himself that all he could think of was getting to Livrette and having his wounds seen to. It pained him now to think of John trying to help him from the field when his own life was trickling away.

They had not reached the town yet when he had heard John hoarsely whisper his name. When he had turned, John's face was gray and lined with pain, and he was trailing blood with every step. Then John had stumbled, pulling Philip down with him. Philip flinched at the memory, feeling again the jarring pain of his already-cracked rib snapping and stabbing its way into his lung.

"I swear I never felt it," John had said, bright bubbles of blood showing at his white lips, "not till just now. I was jostled between two of their soldiers, but I fought them off, killed them both. I thought truly I was just bruised."

Philip had tried to drag himself to where John was, to somehow stop the blood welling from the gap down John's side where his armor was joined, but unconsciousness had taken him.

John's soft voice was the last sound to pierce the blackness. "I am sorry, Philip."

"I am sorry, too, John," Philip murmured now. "If I had only . . . "

He let the words trail into nothing. There were no words, no promises, kept or broken, that could change it. John was dead.

Philip tried to swallow, but his mouth was too dry. He reached for the pitcher beside his bed. It was full and heavy, and before he could pour anything out, it slipped from his tenuous grip and shattered into hopeless fragments on the stone floor. His head fell limply back onto the pillows. Then he turned over and put his bandaged arm across his face to muffle his sobs.

"Oh, John."

It was long past dawn when the physician woke him in order to dress his wounds. There was no trace left of the broken pitcher.

"Where is Tom?" Philip asked groggily. Livrette gave his shoulder a soothing pat.

"Never you mind that, my lord. Since you were asleep when I came in last night, I told your man to let you and Lord Tom both have your rest. I think he's had none since the battle."

"Where is Rafe? I must speak with Tom," Philip said, but all that got him was another pat and a patronizing smile.

"Soon enough, my lord, soon enough. First we must tend these wounds of yours and bind them up again. There will be time enough and to spare for your talk later on."

Philip submitted, knowing even a direct command was unlikely to shake the methodical physician out of caring for his patient.

"You are doing well, my lord," Livrette said once he had rebandaged Philip's ribs and forearm. "Is there much pain today?"

"Not so much as last night," Philip told him, looking away. The dull throb he felt now was insignificant to him. Like the cruel truth of John's death, the pain remained unchanged, and he told himself he could learn to live with them both.

"It may not even scar," Livrette remarked once he had removed the bandage from Philip's cheek, but a rapid knock on the door drew their attention before Philip could answer. It was Rafe.

"My lord, the king has come in from Winton. He had some news of the battle from a messenger, but I do not know how much he's been told. It's likely he already knows, but do you wish for me to tell him—"

"No. I shall do it."

"Perhaps Lord Tom—"

"I said I would do it, Rafe."

Seeing his determination, Rafe bowed and left the room.

Livrette did his work silently for a while. "I could tell him, my lord, if you wish it," he ventured at last.

"It is my place. I do not know why he was angry with John, but he will be sorry for it now, I know that much. He always loved John. He truly did. He has to know now how wrong he was to banish him. Whatever it was, it could not have been any more than a trifle if John was at fault in it. John was ever so—" The words choked down in his throat, and he stopped himself. He needed to be strong for his father's sake. "When my father comes—"

"Your father is here, my lord," Livrette told him.

Philip looked up to see the king standing in the doorway, his expression as incomprehensibly harsh as it had been on the day he had sent John away. There was no sign of grief, no fatherly concern, nothing on his face but angry displeasure.

"Your Majesty," the physician murmured as he quickly knelt, but Robert scarcely noticed him.

"We have no further need of you at present," he said to dismiss Livrette, but he never took his stern gaze from his son's face. Philip could only stare back at him, bewildered into dumbness. Perhaps he truly had not yet heard.

"I await your obedience, Philip," Robert said. "I'll not have your stiff-necked insolence today."

Still Philip stared.

"My liege," Livrette objected, "surely he is too ill—"

"You are dismissed. When we need you, we shall send for you."

Livrette dared protest no further. Leaving his work unfinished, he left the room and shut the heavy door behind him.

"Now, boy, shall I await your pleasure?"

"Please listen," Philip said, finally finding his voice. "I have to tell you, John is—"

"Is dead," Robert said flatly. "I have had that news already. What I came for now is to know why my orders were disobeyed and why you are not on your knees before your king."

"But he is dead. Your son—"

"Immediately, my lord of Caladen!"

He did not care. The realization struck Philip harder than the weapons of the enemy had. John was dead, and his father did not care. He did not care.

His eyes flashing accusation, Philip took a deep breath. Then he pushed the bedclothes from him and got shakily to his feet. Steadying himself on the edge of the bed, he dropped heavily to his knees.

"You have been disobedient to me," Robert said, "against the duty you owe me as your king and as your father. There can be no excuse for it. None. Nothing that has happened here justifies your rebelliousness. This might have ended in a disaster for Afton because of your willfulness."

Philip fixed his gaze on the floor and set his mouth in a tight line. "You know full well why I disobeyed. The power here was not by half strong enough to meet the attack, and we knew of it before they struck—well before. Yet you sent no help, not so much as a word in answer to John's pleas. I could not choose but to disobey you. We might have lost this town and many others along with it had I stayed in Maughn as you ordered." He glanced up, and again there was reproach in his eyes. "The casualties were heavy enough."

"You had no right to question my command," Robert said. "If Tanglewood had fallen, the next stronghold would have been Maughn. Maughn has been left defenseless for over a week now!"

"If I had not come, Tanglewood would have surely been taken, and Maughn would be under siege. You know that as well as I."

"I will not be disobeyed again. There's punishment for treason, boy, even for princes."

Robert turned to go, but Philip's next question stopped him. "Why?" Philip choked back a sob and then asked again, "Why?"

The anger had gone out of his tone, the reproach and defiance, too. All that was left was wounded pleading that tugged at Robert's guilty heart, making him turn back around.

"Why did you let this happen to John, Father?"

"I? Any man may die in a battle. I'm for certain not to blame for it."

"You wanted him to die," Philip said, still hardly able to believe it himself. "Even if you had to lose Tanglewood with him, you wanted him to die. Why? What did he do that made you stop loving him?"

"If it had not been for him, Richard would never have come here. Richard would be alive yet."

"That was your pride and Richard's. You cannot lay the blame of that on John."

"It is not for you to question me, Philip," Robert said, avoiding his son's eyes.

But Philip refused to leave it at that. "Just tell me why. Please, Father, I have to know. I know why you took Kate's life." Somehow his voice held steady. "Whatever she was to me, she was nothing to you. But John—I have to know what could make a man hate his own son."

"John was not my son!"

Philip stared at his father, stunned by the fierce words. "That's a lie," he said finally, his voice low. "Whoever told you that was lying. He had to be." His voice was desperate now, but nothing in his father's expression left any room for hope.

"I heard your mother's confession," Robert said flatly. "You heard her calling for John before she died, again and again for John. It was John Albright, my seneschal, she meant. John was Albright's bastard. She confessed it. I should have seen all along that he was never any of my blood."

For a moment Philip considered in silence. Then he broke into his father's dark thoughts. "If this is true—"

"If! Do you doubt me? I heard her confession!"

Philip closed his eyes against the venom in the words. "Given that it is true then, how can you blame John for it? He had no part in their faithlessness." Grief filled his voice. "He was worthier to be a king's son than any of us. He always tried to do what best pleased you. He was loyal to you even through all of this travesty."

Robert grabbed Philip fiercely by the shoulders and pulled him to his feet, ignoring his groan of pain. Philip fought dizziness, but his indignation sustained him. "He never once objected to what you have done, though I know the shame of it weighed heavily on him. He actually defended you to us. He said you were our sovereign and our father, and we owed you our love, our service, and our very lives. He gave you all that, and still you hated him."

"Would you have me keep a bastard as Lord of Rounchaux? Perhaps to sit one day on the throne of Lynaleigh?"

"You should have denounced him then, if you could not let the truth die with the guilty. Even bastards are still allowed to keep their lives in Lynaleigh."

"And have my nobles know that I had been deceived these sixteen years and more? That I had claimed a squire's by-blow as son and prince of the blood? That my dear wife was a common strumpet?" Robert shook his head. "Never."

"He was your son," Philip insisted over his father's protests. "He was raised your son and loved you as his father. No matter what you did, he loved you. You could not break that love, though you know you broke his heart." Agonizing pain racked Philip's body, but he was determined to finish what he had to say. "I am glad to know he was not yours. Arrogance and selfish pride could never have lived in him. That's all the legacy you pass on to your sons, that and unforgiveness." He looked coldly into his father's eyes. "I think you will find that I am true-bred Chastelayne."

His icy expression a match for his son's, Robert slowly removed his gloves. "We will speak no more of this, my lord of Caladen," he said, a forced evenness in his tone. "What I have done I have done, and it is not for you to question me. You are my son, and from here on I expect you to obey me without pause."

He turned to go.

"Before God," Philip flung after him, "would I had been born a bastard and not tainted with the blood of a murderer!"

Spinning around, Robert gave him a vicious slap across the face. Philip dropped leadenly to the floor and did not stir.

Robert's eyes widened in horror. He stared at his son lying crumpled at his feet, then stiffly turned his gaze to his own stinging hand. He gasped to see it smeared with blood. The blow had torn open the wound on Philip's cheek, and now it was bleeding more than it had on the battlefield.

"Philip," Robert breathed, unstrung by what he had done. Sitting on the floor, he took Philip's limp body into his arms and pressed his pale cheek against his son's bloody one. "Philip, Philip," he murmured over and over again. There was no response.

CHAPTER

PALMER STOOD WITH HIS BACK TO TOM'S DOOR, HIS ARMS OBDURATELY crossed. "I do not know what was said between them, but it's weighed heavy on him. He's had no rest since he came from Prince Philip's rooms—not till just now, and I'll not have him disturbed."

Rafe was equally adamant. "Lord Philip would speak with him, and I know what he has to say will be better for Lord Tom than a fortnight's sleep. Livrette will have done with his work by now, and I told the prince I'd fetch his brother for him straightaway. You must at least tell him—"

"Tell me what?" Tom asked leaning in the doorway, too sleepy to stand unsupported. He still had on the clothes he had worn the day before, and his face was pale under the dark late-morning stubble of beard. "How is Philip?"

"Much improved, my lord," Rafe said, with an encouraging smile that did not acknowledge Palmer's scowl. "Forgive me for disturbing your rest, but he sent me for you."

Tom's expression brightened. "He wants to see me?"

"He does. Go to him, my lord, please. Your father is with him now. After the death of Lord John, they will both need you."

"My father, too?" Tom looked reproachfully at Palmer. "When did he arrive?"

"Not an hour ago, my lord," Palmer said. Then he frowned again. "My lord, you've not slept well in days. You'd only just dropped off when the news came that the king was here. I could not bring myself to—"

"Never mind now. Just come in here. I need some fresh clothes and to be shaved." He sighed heavily and then turned to Rafe. "I will be there shortly."

Just then Livrette rushed into the corridor. "My lord, forgive me disturbing your rest, but the king has dismissed me, and he was in such a temper I fear he will endanger my lord Philip's recovery."

Tom rubbed his eyes with the back of his hand and yawned. "I shall go now then. Never mind the shave. You had best come along, Rafe, to see to Philip. And you, too, Palmer. I know you will anyway."

Tom shook his head sorrowfully as they hurried to Philip's chamber, fully expecting to find his father and brother at each other's throats. Even John's death, it seemed, could not soften the tension between them.

He pushed open the door and came to an abrupt halt, shocked by the sight before him. Philip lay unconscious in his father's arms, his face deathly pale and bloody. Robert's face, too, was pale and bloody, but the pallor came from fear, and the blood was not his own.

The king was rambling on wildly, filling Philip's insensible ears with excuses and calling on every saint he could name to revive him. Tom came up behind him and put one hand on his shoulder.

"Father."

Robert's head jerked up.

"I've killed him," he said, his ghostly voice sending a chill through Tom's heart.

Tom dropped to one knee and put two fingers on the side of Philip's throat. Then he breathed a little easier for the steady throbbing he felt there.

"Philip," Tom said, shaking him sharply, but there was no response.

"I've killed him," Robert repeated, displaying his blood-smeared hand as proof.

"Let us take him, my liege," Livrette coaxed, sliding one arm under Philip's shoulders, but Robert only held him more tightly.

"You must let them tend to him," Tom told him. With Palmer's help, Tom pried his father's fingers away. Rafe and Livrette lifted Philip up onto the bed, and the physician began to wash the blood from his patient's face, wise enough to keep his indignation to himself.

Tom helped his father stand, intending to lead him from the room, but Robert struggled again to go to Philip's side. "Philip—"

"No," Tom insisted, and he and Palmer held the king back. "You must leave him alone, or he truly will die."

"He lives yet?" Robert asked, seizing Tom by the upper arms. "I did not kill him?"

Tom squirmed under the viselike pressure. "No. He is alive still."

It took a moment for the words to sink in. Then the king dropped his hands helplessly to his sides.

Tom urged him toward the door. "Let us leave them to their work."

"Tom, you must understand—"

"It does not matter now, Father," Tom told him, sudden weariness in his voice. "If you will, I think it would be best if you rested from your journey. No doubt you are tired. I know I am."

Robert looked at him as if seeing him for the first time. "You look as if you've not slept." He brushed his fingers across Tom's rough cheek. "Or been shaved."

"I will, Father, as soon as I take you to your rooms."

"You will see that he is well as soon as possible?" Robert asked, abruptly recovering his authoritative tone.

Livrette managed a deferential nod. "Everything will be done to speed his recovery, my liege."

"See that it is then. You shall be well rewarded," Robert said. Then, with another glance at Philip, he followed Tom out of the room.

Once he had left his father, Tom returned to his own room with Palmer, as usual, dogging his heels.

"That is all, Palmer. Go amuse yourself. Go ride or hunt or what you will. I am going to bed."

"I will wait upon you, my lord," Palmer said.

"I will not need anything till nightfall but sleep, and that is something I must get for myself."

Palmer nodded. "True enough. Sleep well then."

Tom watched the man walk reluctantly down the corridor. Then he went into his chamber and sagged against the door he had shut behind him, his arms crossed over his eyes. *This "glory" Father has chosen and for which he has fought so hard has become such a hell of death and rage and hate! How will there ever be peace now, in the land or in our family?* he wondered. *Can there be peace between Father and Philip after this? With already so much between them that Philip has not forgiven? So much that to all mortal concept is unforgivable?*

"Lord God," Tom began, knowing that only the Almighty could heal these wounds. But he felt a relentless wave of sleep pass over him, and he realized he was too tired even to pray. "Forgive me, Lord," he murmured half-intelligibly. Then he stumbled to the bed and fell across it, immediately asleep.

When he awoke, he found that his boots had been removed, and he was no longer lying across the bed but under the coverlet with his head on the pillows—Palmer's handiwork.

"What time is it?"

"It's not yet noon, my lord. You've slept no more than two hours."

Tom sat up. "Is there any news of Philip? I want to be with him when he wakes. I know he'll be stewing over this."

"I've heard nothing yet, my lord," Palmer said. "I made inquiries while I was out, but all Livrette would say was that there was no change. I've been here since."

"Well, so long as you are here, I want you to shave me and get me something to wear."

"My lord, can you not rest awhile more? It may be some time before Lord Philip wakes. He is well tended, I know. You needn't worry on that account."

Tom threw off the covers. "I have to be there when he wakes. Come, my razor. I shall feel much better once I get this stubble off my face and these stale clothes off my back."

The late afternoon sun was slanting through the narrow windows when Philip again opened his eyes. His head felt heavy, as if it were packed with sand, and the gash in his cheek throbbed in rhythm with the pounding in his skull. There was another pain, too, different from the hurts he had awakened to for so many days now, and this pain, like all the others, could not be remedied. He did not fight it.

He turned his head and found that he was not alone. Tom was there, kneeling beside the bed, his cheek resting on his prayer-clasped hands, his eyes closed in exhausted sleep.

Philip quickly dismissed the thought of prayer and stared up at the ceiling, forcing himself to concentrate on nothingness. *When the pain is gone*, he considered, *nothingness is all I will have left*.

Feeling stiff, he tried to roll over, but the movement wrenched something inside him and stabbed him through with pain. A surprised gasp escaped him, and Tom woke with a start.

"Philip?" Tom studied his brother's impassive face, waiting for an answer, receiving none. "Philip, shall I get Livrette?"

Philip answered him with an indifferent shake of his head, and Tom's expression grew more anxious. "How do you feel?"

"Well enough."

"But you sounded as if—"

"It is nothing."

Tom put one hand on Philip's forehead and found it surprisingly cool. "Tell me what happened this morning. Father is beside himself."

Philip fingered the thick bandage on his face. "I spoke to him more roundly than I should have—that is all."

"Philip, whatever is between you, he is sorry. You know that he—"

"Leave it, Tom. It does not matter." Philip's voice was empty and brittle.

Tom looked at him for another moment, helpless to know what to say. Finally, he stood up. "Rafe said you asked for me last night."

"I suppose I was still in a fever then and knew not what I said, but I am certain it was nothing. Rafe can see to all my needs."

"Will you forgive me?" Tom asked, his dark eyes pleading. "Losing John as we did, I was desperate not to lose you, too, but it was wrong of me to let you be misled. You know I am sorry."

"You need speak no more of it. It is forgotten."

"Philip, I know it hurts." Bewildered tears came into Tom's eyes. "It hurts me as well. Please do not turn me off coldly now. We can better bear our grief if we bear it together."

Philip's face remained expressionless. "I have no grief. John is safe and well, just as you said, and I've no need to mourn for that."

"Philip, please. Please."

"I am only hungry and a bit stiff."

Tom took a slow, deep breath. "I will send for Livrette."

"I do not need him."

"Very well. Shall I send Rafe to you?"

Philip nodded. "I should be most grateful."

There was still pleading in Tom's eyes.

"Truly, Tom, I need nothing but some food to give me back my strength. And you need not look at me as if I've lost my senses. I know full well where I am and what has happened." Philip smiled an empty little smile that Tom could not bear. "I am fine, Tom. Truly."

Tom sent for Rafe. Then he went at once to his father's chamber and dismissed the attendants. There were two empty bottles overturned on the table and another, still half full, beside them. Robert was sitting on the edge of the bed, his head cradled in his hands. He winced when Tom shut the door. Then he lifted his head and looked blearily at his son, red-eyed and slack-jawed.

"What of Philip?"

Tom had to force himself not to draw back from the stale stench of strong liquor. "He is awake and seems to have little fever. He's asked for something to eat."

"Thanks be to God! I must speak to him."

Robert could hardly stand, and Tom tried to push him back onto the bed. "Sleep awhile first, Father."

"I have slept." Robert scrubbed his face with both hands and then squinted painfully into the fading sunset. "A long while." He groaned as he leaned down to retrieve his goblet from the floor and frowned to find it empty. "Bring me that bottle."

His lips pressed into a straight, disapproving line, Tom obeyed. "Forgive me, Father, but you would be wise to wait yet to see Philip. Give him time to sort through his grief and cool his anger. If you but step amiss with him now, you shall truly lose him."

"He is my son. I must make peace with him. Faith, I know he'll rage at me, but I've withstood his temper before."

Tom shook his head. "He was very quiet when I left him. Unnaturally so. Please, Father, let him alone awhile."

Robert did not miss the uneasiness in Tom's expression, and it struck fear into his own heart. "I cannot let this fester between us, Tom. If I go to him now, I can make him understand. He came to understand about the Fletcher girl."

"Did he?" Tom asked, wondering how a man could know his own son so imperfectly. "Truly?"

Robert took a deep drink. "I must win him back to me."

He staggered to his basin and splashed his haggard face in the stale water. Then he drew himself back up straight, back into the majestic kingliness that had brought him the admiration of the whole kingdom.

"I will win him back to me."

Philip got to his feet and then in jerky stages went to his knees before his father, visible pain in every stiff motion.

"You honor me, my liege. It would have been more proper had you sent for me to come to you."

"I did not mean for you to leave your bed, son," Robert said, fearful of the gleam of sweat that had broken out on Philip's blank face. "You endanger yourself."

"I am well, Your Majesty, or will be very soon."

Robert found his utter composure unsettling. "I'll not have you kneel, Philip. Not today."

"As pleases you, my liege."

Not daring to offer his help, Robert watched him as he fought to stand. He knew his son must be in pain, knew he must be angry and hurt as well, but Philip's face betrayed none of that. Once Philip gained his feet, he merely waited for his father to speak, infinitely patient, completely motionless. He could have been carved from marble.

"You nearly stopped my poor heart this morning, son."

Robert's eyes reflected the terror he had felt, seeing his son still as death at his feet. Philip yet was still.

"You need not have feared, my liege. I am not easily hurt."

Robert began to pace. "Now curse this evil temper of mine, Philip. I was wrong to strike you."

"I had forgotten the respect I owe the royal lord of Lynaleigh. Your Majesty merely put me in mind of it."

Philip's voice was steady, soft, without emotion.

Be angry! Robert pled silently. *Weep! Rage! Strike at me! Spit at me!*

Philip was only still, and Robert looked at him for a long moment. Then he put his hands on his son's shoulders, gently this time, and his eyes filled with remorse. "Please, can you never forgive me?"

Philip did not resist his touch, did not try to free himself. "I am not your judge."

Robert was chilled by the words, coming with such hollowness from such empty eyes and chilled by the thought that pierced him. *I have killed him.*

He dropped his hands in frustration. Then his restraint broke. "Before God, Philip, what would you have me to say? I swear I would lose this right hand of mine before I would have it deal you another blow. If any other man dared strike my son, I would have his head in that instant. Sweet heavens, tell me what penance will buy your forgiveness!"

It was more than he had meant to say, but surely the boy would relent now.

"I am your vassal, my liege. It is I who am answerable to you, not you to me."

Robert stared at him, bewildered. He could not fight where there was no resistance, and he could not win where there was no fight. He put the back of his hand to the unbandaged side of Philip's face.

"You are not so feverish tonight. I am glad of it." The touch turned into a caress. "Philip, you are my son. I would have peace between us."

"We have no quarrel, my liege."

"Well." Robert nodded his head rapidly. "Well, I am glad of it. Rest now, son, and let us speak no more of this."

Philip bowed his head in acknowledgment and watched stoically as his father left the room. Then, trembling with fatigue, he stumbled back to his bed. Almost immediately, he was asleep.

John was buried in Tanglewood with all the ceremony befitting a prince of the blood royal, his bier escorted by a company of knights, attended by the mournful chants of an entire monastery, followed by the king and all the nobility, their faces appropriately grave.

Philip had been forbidden to accompany the procession as it wound for miles through the streets. The physician had pronounced him too weak for such a strain, so he watched from the window as they carried John's body to the church.

John was robed in purple and ermine and arrayed in fine armor, burnished to rival the sun. His battle-scarred sword lay upon his breast, testament to his youthful valor, his slender fingers clasped around it as if he were ready at a moment's notice to serve again the king he had loved. His fair hair, gleaming like his armor, curled thickly around his head. Philip wondered who could have lifted a blade to kill such bright innocence.

Earlier Philip had asked the date and found that John still lacked eleven days to be sixteen. Not yet sixteen, and he was being borne to his tomb. Even now the procession was passing from Philip's sight, and he realized more concretely than he had before that this was a journey from which John would never return. It was too soon. Too soon for him to be gone forever.

Philip crept down the steps that led into the servants' quarters and made his way quietly into the street. A pale shadow, noticed only by the murmuring crowds, he fell into step with the procession, kept painful pace behind his father and brother until they had covered the short distance remaining and went into the church.

He watched his father kneel and pray, distantly curious to know how Robert managed that look of startled remorse and those tears that slipped, seemingly unbidden, down his lank cheeks. He watched Tom, too, standing drawn and numb-looking beside the bier—Tom who bore everyone's griefs if he could not ease them, Tom who hurt for John and for their father, as if one could pity a murderer's guilt as easily as the victim's innocence.

Philip waited until the ceremony ended and the last requiem ceased to echo in the chapel. Then he stole up to the bier to look one last time on his brother's ashen face. He caught his breath. A heavy band of gold set with a deep ruby was on the stiff right hand, copy to the ring that had been buried with Richard, the one Tom still wore, and the one that had once graced Philip's own hand. Only the king himself could have set this one on John's finger now.

Too little, too late, Philip thought, remembering John's wounded eyes when Robert had without explanation stripped it from him.

"You were fitter for that heaven you've gone to than this hell we've made here," he whispered. Then he leaned down and kissed John's cold cheek.

Looking startled to see him there, Robert rushed up to him and took his arm. Tom was quickly beside him, too.

"Surely it is too soon yet, son," Robert said. "You should have kept to your bed."

Philip did not reply. He merely dipped one knee perfunctorily before the altar and then made his way back through the hushed assembly and into the still-crowded street. His father and brother followed close behind him, fearing he would not have strength enough to make it back to the castle, but he took no notice of them.

When he reached his chamber, he did not respond to Bonnechamp's overanxious questioning, did not explain how he had managed to slip away unnoticed. He merely fell into bed and once more took refuge in sleep. Sleep that had been cruel adversary to him after Katherine's death was now his dearest friend, his comforter and most welcome companion. Only in sleep could he escape the deathlike stillness in his heart. Only in sleep could he forget.

Soon after the funeral, Robert sent for more men to garrison Tanglewood under the Duke of Ellison's authority. Philip's men and Tom's were sent back to their posts in Maughn and Chrisdale with Lord Darlington and Lord Eastbrook to command them. Philip was to stay in Tanglewood until he was well enough to return to Winton, and Tom was to stay with him.

"Will that please you, son?" Robert asked hopefully.

"If it pleases you, my liege."

The king took little joy in the aloof response. It was with a subdued train and a somber heaviness that he took leave of his sons and returned to his palace in Winton.

Philip's body healed quickly afterwards. He had willed it to, just as he had willed his heart to feel no more pain. As soon as Livrette declared him fit to go, he went back to Winton. The ride wore on him, but he refused to show it. Tom and Rafe, for all their concern, could not persuade him to take a slower pace.

When he reached his father's city, he was received like a conquering hero, the savior of Tanglewood. Robert had told of Philip's unsanctioned sweep into the battle as the bold stroke of a man who would one day make them a bold king, and the people loved their crown prince the more for it. Philip took no notice of their adoration or of the praises heaped on him by the nobility. Accounted as becoming modesty, it made him the more popular.

His father greeted him heartily before the court, gave public thanks to God for his rapid recovery, and praised his valor in the hearing of his subjects. In private Robert said little. Despite his clumsy attempts, and they were many, he could find no way to reach his son's heart or break through his aloofness.

Days passed with no change, and Robert had all but given up when a post came to him from Westered. Reading the message, he was certain his intractable son would not be indifferent to its contents. He summoned Philip.

"Your Majesty," Philip said with a graceful bow.

"I've received a letter that directly concerns you, and I think it best you hear it in part before I make answer. It was sent from the Duke of Westered."

"Yes, my liege?"

Robert looked at him, into the blue depths of his eyes, and still found nothing. He gripped the paper more tightly and began to read:

> "*What Margaret has done was without my knowledge or consent, and I fear her faithless alliance with Ellenshaw will cause Your High Majesty doubt regarding the loyalty of Westered and her lord. In defense of this, I have disinherited the traitress, and I swear again my allegiance to you, my only king and most royal lord. My younger daughter Rosalynde is now heir to all that is Westered, and I gladly offer her as wife to your son Philip of Caladen. I pray that such a marriage will weld Afton and Westered inseparably together and forever silence any doubts Your Majesty may have regarding my constancy. It is an alliance of which Your Majesty and I have often spoken and for which all Westered is eager.*"

Robert looked over the top of the page at his son, but Philip's dispassionate expression had not changed.

"What say you to this, Philip?"

"Let it be as pleases Your Majesty."

"Did you hear?" Robert shook the stiff paper in his son's face. "This is the same Lady Rosalynde you have refused again and again, and will you have her now?"

"I will do as Your Majesty commands."

"You know we must have Westered now more than ever," Robert said as he tensely refolded the letter. As much as he needed this alliance, he had hoped the mere mention of it would spark some emotion in his son—anger, defiance, anything but this blankness.

"I know."

Robert flung the paper onto the table and pounded it with his fist. "He was a bastard, Philip! No son of mine!"

Philip did not flinch. "Yes, my lord. So you said."

"You could not expect me to—" A look almost of pleading crossed Robert's face. "He was a bastard. I could not leave him as a prince and sully the royal line with Albright's common blood. But I left him his honors, Philip. You saw his funeral procession. Before God, Richard was not buried so well!"

Philip made him no answer, and Robert knit his brow. "This is more than John, I see. This is Edward and that Fletcher girl and only God Himself knows what else. What I have done is done, Philip, and there is nothing more than that. I cannot undo what's past!"

Still Philip looked at him, nothing in his expression but faint indifference.

"I have been made to deal harshly sometimes," Robert said, his tone reasonable now, more persuasive, "but it is my sacred trust to keep the name and blood of Chastelayne above reproach. Surely you can find no fault in that."

"I have told you before, my liege, we have no quarrel."

"And you have no objection now to Lady Rosalynde?"

"I will marry her if that is what you wish."

The king drew something out of the pouch at his waist and held it out to his son. "And you will wear this?"

He opened his hand. A ruby ring lay sparkling in it—Philip's ring. He watched his son's eyes, but there was no fury there now. Philip merely took the ring and slipped it onto his finger and waited for his father's next command.

"Very well," Robert said, grim resolution making his face look hard. "I will send to Westered to bring his daughter here within this month. You and she will be married the day following her arrival."

It was the first day of spring.

CHAPTER

THREE WEEKS LATER JAMES OF WESTERED AND HIS DAUGHTER arrived at the palace and were immediately granted an audience with the king.

"All health to Your Majesty," Westered said, sweeping the hat from his head as he knelt.

Robert came down from his throne and formally embraced him. "And to your lordship and to your fair daughter."

Rosalynde curtseyed. Robert of Afton still carried an air of indisputable majesty, she saw, but there was something in the lines on his face—the fine, furtive lines around his eyes—that somehow tarnished the image. He kissed her hand.

"My lady, you grace us with your sweet beauty."

As she murmured her thanks, she noticed one of the king's councillors staring at her, a short man with sharp, dark eyes and a narrow, swarthy face.

"This is my lord high chamberlain, Baron of Paxton, Edmund Dunois," Robert said in introduction.

Again Rosalynde curtseyed. "My lord."

Dunois bowed. "Lady Rosalynde. My lord of Westered."

"You have been of great assistance to His Majesty, my lord

Dunois," Westered observed. "Your accomplishments are spoken of even in my own lands."

He did not mention that the people of Westered also spoke of the thirty years of faithful service to old King Edward that had won Dunois titles, lands, and a nobly born wife—and of the betrayal of that same king that had made Dunois the second most powerful man in Lynaleigh. King Robert did nothing now without consulting his lord high chamberlain.

"Your lordship honors me," Dunois replied with a bow. "I am surely the least of all of His Majesty's servants."

Robert smiled. "He could teach the saints humility, but I swear, my lord of Westered, a wiser, more industrious, more loyal man you'll not find in a thousand. But we mustn't neglect the rest of the court. My lady, you remember my son, Thomas of Brenden?"

Tom stepped forward and kissed her hand. "Now that you are to be my sister, Lady Rosalynde, I pray you will also be my friend."

She thanked him, taking comfort from the steadying squeeze of his hand on hers and the understanding warmth of his smile. He had grown up fine and gentle and handsome. What would her Philip be like?

"I had thought the bridegroom would be here, Your Majesty," Westered said after half a dozen more introductions.

The king smiled with faint uneasiness. "He will be, my lord, at any moment now."

He turned and spoke to one of the pages, keeping his voice low. The boy darted from the room and returned a moment later to whisper a message to him.

"Tell him he *will* come and at this instant!" Robert's voice rang through the suddenly silent court, and the page scurried to obey him. Rosalynde paled and moved closer to her father.

"He is strong-willed, my son is," Robert said, forcing a smile. "He will make Lynaleigh a strong king one day."

"We will still have a wedding tomorrow, I trust, Your Majesty," Westered said with concern.

"Of course. Of course. You have my pledge already. Philip is something of a boy yet, my lord, with some wildness left in him, but do not fear for tomorrow. He's never failed to keep an oath."

"Forgive me my tardiness, Your Majesty."

Rosalynde looked up and was unable to do anything but stare as Philip strode from the back of the great hall, wearing only breeches and an unlaced shirt, barefoot and soaking wet.

For a long time she had imagined this meeting, expecting to see him in all his princely finery, his father's chief courtier, the pride of the kingdom. Yet here he was, half-dressed and dripping, his hair slicked carelessly back from his face, channeling rivulets of water down his bare chest. The raw beauty of the sight made her heart jerk painfully in her breast.

He was still tall and lithe, but he had a man's body now, broad-shouldered and hard-muscled. There was something different about his face, too—something more than just maturity, but she could not precisely define it. Even with the fine scar high up on his left cheek, he was as handsome as before—even more so, but he was not the same.

"Philip, what do you mean by coming into my court this way?" Robert demanded.

"I have been hunting and thought I should wash before I met with your guests. I did not think they would find it pleasant to be in the company of a man with blood on his hands." Philip let his gaze rest for only an instant on his father's heavily jeweled fingers. Then he looked the king calmly in the face. "I know I would not."

Robert tensed. "Then you should not have come until you were properly dressed."

"I was told Your Majesty required my presence at once," Philip replied impassively. "I did not intend to displease you with my obedience."

With a quick glance at his guests, Robert went to Philip's side and clasped his wet shoulder, all gracious smiles again. "Of course you did not, son. I did not realize you were preening for your bride. Still, give her your greetings now that you've come."

Rosalynde curtseyed as her bridegroom turned dutifully to her.

Their eyes met, and he froze for a moment where he stood, the air rushing from his lungs. She noticed the unsteadiness in his hand as he lifted her velvet-gloved fingers to his lips.

"You are welcome to Winton, Lady Rosalynde. You must forgive me coming to you so ill-kept."

"I am always pleased to see you, my lord," she said, her hopeful smile growing uncertain.

She realized that the difference in him was somewhere in his eyes. They were still as deeply blue as she remembered, still beckoning, fathomless oceans that drew her helplessly into them, but the light that had been in them was gone, leaving him as coldly beautiful as the marble angels in the cathedral at Westered.

"You must be pleased, too, son, to see what a lovely creature she's become," the king prompted. "I know how eager you have been to see her again."

"Yes, Your Majesty," Philip said. "You know how I look forward to tomorrow."

There was nothing in his tone or expression that indicated anything but gracious sincerity, but something in his ambiguous choice of words, something in the concealing depths of his eyes, made Rosalynde apprehensive.

Tom gave her a small encouraging smile, but she could not overcome her bewildered disappointment and face him. He was the Tom she remembered, still the same open-hearted, smiling Tom. Where was Philip? Her Philip?

She had always thought of Philip as hers. Ever since he had come to Westered, she had called him hers and built her unspoken romantic dreams around him. Now at last the time had come for her to see him again, but where was he? Her Philip had had gentle eyes and a warm, easy smile. She wondered if the man standing before her now ever smiled at all.

She wanted desperately to escape the scrutiny of the courtiers around her, the expectant glances of his father and hers, and speak to him alone. Surely somewhere behind this cold facade was the boy she had known in Westered. If she could be alone with him, away from the court, surely he would prove to be the gallant, passionate hero-prince she had so long entertained in her fancy. He had to be.

"His Majesty is right, Lady Rosalynde," he said with a bow. "You are very beautiful."

Her smile brightened, then faded when she saw that even as he acknowledged it, her beauty brought him no pleasure.

"You are too kind, my lord," she murmured, looking down, pained to see that he spoke only for the sake of courtesy, to please the king.

"I am happy to see you well, my lord," he said to her father. Westered bowed slightly.

"I thank you, Your Highness. I am pleased to see you so, too, and to see you safe. I know these wars have cost dearly in Afton blood. I pray the blood of Westered will strengthen it."

Philip took a deep breath and did not reply.

"I say amen to that," Robert answered for him.

Philip bowed once more, his expression more blank than ever. "If you will pardon me, Your Majesty, my lord, my lady, I must make myself presentable for supper."

"And I, Father," Tom added as Philip left the hall. He nodded to the visitors. "My lord. Lady Rosalynde."

"I'll not have the both of you coming tardy for supper, Thomas, mind you," Robert said, spoiling his stern tone with an indulgent smile.

"We'll not, Father."

Westered smiled, too, as he watched Tom follow after his brother.

"I've always envied you your fine sons, Your Majesty. I was sorry to lose a son in Richard, but I am glad to have another in Philip." He gave Rosalynde's cheek a playful pinch. "I know one little heart that's pleased. I believe I lost her to him five years ago."

She blushed furiously.

"Philip and I have spoken often of you as well, Lady Rosalynde," the king told her.

Westered nodded toward the doorway through which Philip had just gone. "He'll truly make a fine king one day, Your Majesty. The quality shines from him even without his finery."

"You must pardon him coming to you as he did, my lord. Please take no offense, my lady."

"Faith, no, let it pass," Westered said. "It is good to see a boy quick to be obedient to his father in everything."

"He is that, my lord, indeed," Robert replied, but the fact did not seem to please him.

❧

Tom caught up to his brother on the winding stairway that led to their chambers.

"She's quite changed, is she not?" Tom observed. He could read Philip better than anyone could, and he had seen the quickly hidden fire in Philip's eyes when he had first looked on the girl. He had also seen the unmistakable pain and guilt that had followed it.

"She'd hardly be fifteen anymore," Philip snapped.

"But you could never have expected—"

"It makes no difference what I expected or what she is like. I've given my word—I shall marry her."

"Philip, if you feel it is too soon—"

"Let it be, Tom. We cannot change things now. Besides, I do not feel it is too soon. I do not feel anything at all."

With that, Philip went into his chamber and shut the door, leaving Tom outside.

❧

Supper was an eternity of empty pleasantries, and it was very late when Philip was at last allowed to retire. He was quick to dismiss all of his servants. Then, careless of his fine clothes, he sprawled on the bed and closed his eyes. He knew this kind of exhaustion, though—exhaustion of the mind and of the emotions. He knew it would likely deny him the charitable sleep that had sheltered him in Tanglewood.

His body was strong enough now to withstand the assault of his memories and the tightening bands of duty placed upon him.

What had he pledged himself to? There was hardly anything of the little girl he was expecting in the delicate oval face that had looked up at him at supper. Only the shy green eyes under perfectly arched fine brows and the thick, dark hair were the same. Her childish plumpness had melted into slender-waisted voluptuousness, into tantalizing, maddening curves.

He had agreed to marry the timid, round-faced child he had left in Westered, not this enticing Eve who tempted and smiled as she damned. But he had agreed. He had agreed, and now it was too late.

He flung himself restlessly onto his side and tried to pillow his head on his arms, but something hard and sharp pressed into his cheek. He knew what it was.

He turned again to his back and let his ring catch the wan firelight. It felt heavy on his hand, as it had when it had been placed there the first time, at his father's coronation, hallowed and blessed by the archbishop himself. Four times, once for Philip and once for each of his brothers, the austere cleric had made his solemn recitation. "Be you, young prince, as pure as this gold, as truly set as this precious stone, and, honor binding all, serve your king."

Four times a proud-blooded young prince had knelt and then made grave answer. "So, before God and His angels, I do swear."

Four times the heavy seal had been set on a strong, young hand, and four times the gathered nobility had answered a reverent "amen." *Let it be so.*

Philip turned the ring on his finger, as if it chafed him, and almost permitted himself a jaded smile at the single word engraved upon it—*honor*. Honor. It had seen little enough of that, even from the first day he wore it at his father's stolen coronation. Later he had himself given it as a pledge. He had thought then never to wear it again. Yet here it was on his hand. So much for honor.

It belongs with you, Kate.

He could see her still as he had at the very first, standing with Margaret's waiting women, looking all innocence among their worldliness. He had not thought her beautiful then, not the cold, perfect way his mother had been beautiful. But then Katherine's soft sweetness had begun to work its way into his heart deeper and deeper, until he could see no beauty but hers.

Perhaps it was because she was the only woman at court who dared go out to Brenning where the Heretics met. He saw her there whenever he went anonymously to hear their words of life, and in time he was certain that a man could safely trust his heart to such a woman.

If God Himself had no respect for wealth, title, or nobility of birth, as they preached, how could a man? Why should any man, slave or prince, desire more in a wife than a true, loving heart? He had convinced himself their words were all true, but he had been very young then.

"Marry me, Kate," he had begged her when he could bear no more to be without her. "Love me."

She had drawn a startled breath and then rushed into his embrace. "I do. Oh, I will."

Then came that first hesitant kiss between them, a kiss that grew in intensity until it left them clinging, trembling together.

"Now," he had murmured, his mouth very close to hers. "Marry me now."

"My lord—"

"It will have to be in secret." The words had spilled out of him, as if they feared they would be seized and silenced. "And you know what will be said of you."

"My lord, your father—"

"I will keep you safe." He had kissed her then, kissed her until he was afraid she would swoon. Then he had wrapped his arms tight around her. "Will you have me, Kate?"

He could still see her sweet eyes filled with sudden tears. "You know I would die if I did not."

The ride to Brenning had seemed swift, the simple ceremony even swifter. It was then that he had given her his ring in exchange for her fine sapphire cross, the only jewelry she had.

"I will wear it always near my heart," he had sworn once they had been proclaimed man and wife.

"I shall have to wear this near my heart as well," she had said, looking at the ring that was clearly too large for her slender finger. "It would never do for anyone to see it on my hand."

He closed his eyes and saw Katherine again as she had been their first night together, nestled in his scented sheets, clad only in her shift, with his ring hanging from a ribbon around her neck and her fair hair falling loose and lush onto his pillows.

He could still feel the racing in his heart, remembering how he had gone to her and knelt beside the bed, clutching both of her hands. "Kate—"

He felt once more the softness of those hands against his lips and pressed tenderly to his face. He remembered his own breathless words: "Oh, Kate, I've waited so long for you, my own precious—"

"Do you mean to talk until morning, my lord?"

Her voice was still velvet in his ear. Almost he could feel her sweet breath, almost taste that first deep, hungry kiss. She had slid her arms around his neck then, pressing closer to him, twining her fingers into his hair.

"Oh, my lord."

"Do not call me that, Kate," he had murmured against her soft skin. "Not here, not now."

She had turned his face up to her and kissed him again. Then she lay back on the bed, drawing him with her. "Then come to me, Philip."

"Come to me," he whispered, an invocation to the torturous memory of her not to leave him. Not yet. Not while this last night was his. His and hers.

Come to me.

He pulled one cold pillow into his arms and hid his face in it, remembering the words and the sweet exchange of innocence that had followed, that wondrous rush of pure love.

Never again. Never again.

He ached with the remembrance. She was gone, but the memories would not stop. He imagined her there in his arms and remembered how she had admired the way that first dawn had gilded them both and how she had called him beautiful.

"So very beautiful."

He had laughed then, low and full of wonder, and pulled her closer to his side.

"If I could find words to tell you how much I love you, Kate, you never would believe me."

"That you could love me?"

"No. That I could love you so much and not die of the pure joy of it."

She had moved closer still and pressed her face to his shoulder. He remembered the warm wetness of her tears on his skin.

"I would have died to see you marry one of those noblewomen your father wants for you. I would have died to know someone else might hold you and kiss you and love you like this." She had looked up at him with those guileless brown eyes, those eyes that had from the first drawn him with their sweet purity. She had urgently clutched his arm. "You would never play me false?"

"Kate, by my honor—"

"Oh, do not swear." She had caressed his cheek and relaxed against him again. "You know you needn't swear to me. It's not in you ever to deceive me. I just cannot believe it all yet. There must be great evil ahead for me. I've had too much happiness all at once."

Again he had laughed and put both arms snugly around her. "Never be afraid, Kate. I will take care of you."

He had sworn it, but the oath mocked him now.

Kate, by my honor—

He grappled the pillow more tightly against himself.

"Must I remember? Please, God, no more. No more."

Sleep came to him at last, and it was mercy.

Rafe came early the next morning to prepare him for the wedding. Before long Philip was standing at his looking glass while Rafe searched for the tiniest flaw in the image it reflected. There was none.

Philip's doublet was exactly the deep blue of his eyes and had been styled to compliment the elegant lines of his body. Like the doublet, his boots were newly made—soft as glove leather and cut to cling snugly to his long legs, all the way up to the middle of his hard-muscled thighs. He showed no trace of the sleeplessness of the night before. From the dark sleekness of his hair to the burnished gleam of the ruby ring on his finger, everything about him was perfection.

The young lady will not be able to take her eyes off him, Rafe considered. *No, nor none of the court.*

Rafe had been wont to take pride in the comeliness of his young master, as if he had had a hand in creating it, but now he could not. It was his duty to see that Philip was properly dressed for the great occasion, but it seemed like betrayal now to do it.

Still, he does look magnificent, Rafe thought. *He would have been too thin and worn before to cut such a fine figure.*

Rafe had hoped that one day Philip would be able to put aside the deep grief that had shadowed his expressive eyes. That was before the king had come to Tanglewood, when Philip's eyes still held some expression.

"What more?" Philip asked, and Rafe was startled back into the present.

"Uh, forgive me, my lord. Nothing more. The young lady cannot choose but be pleased."

Rafe wondered for a moment if that was the wrong thing to say, but Philip's face told him nothing. Rafe dared say no more.

The ceremony proceeded without a flaw. The bride was radiant in cloth of gold that had been slashed and inset with pearl-white silk.

Her dress and her dark hair both were liberally sprinkled with seed pearls, and heavy ropes of pearl hung at her wrists and throat. On her finger was a ruby ring, the very image of the one Philip wore but made smaller to fit her hand. He had been told it was his wedding gift to her.

He did not look at her during the ceremony. He fixed his gaze on the iron lock that secured the gate to the catacombs behind the altar and let the archbishop's words slide past him, making unintelligible singsong in his ears. Only his bride's responses, soft and hesitant beside him, refused to be muted into meaninglessness. He was to be cherished and obeyed and cleaved to, whether he would have it so or no.

Then he heard his own name spoken and his own oath asked. Would he cherish this woman who had been chosen for his father's security? Would he give himself for a woman he did not know, who did not know him? Would he cleave to such a woman, knowing the one he loved had been swept aside to make place for her?

There was absolute silence in the cathedral as everyone awaited Philip's answer. His eyes met his father's. Then he looked abruptly back at the archbishop. When he spoke, his voice was as clear and as cold as crystal. "I will."

The wedding guests smiled their satisfaction, and Philip knew there must be triumph on his father's face, long-awaited triumph.

I have obeyed you now, Your Majesty, Philip thought darkly. *I hope you are pleased.*

The archbishop blessed the new couple in the name of the Father, the Son, and the Holy Spirit. Philip moved his lips to say the amen with everyone else, but his throat tightened around the word and would not let it pass.

That done, he turned with Rosalynde to bow low to the king and then to James of Westered, who sat beaming at his renewed alliance. Only one thing remained.

All color gone from his face, Philip turned to his bride and, taking her hands, coldly brushed her lips with his own. A great cheer rose from the crowd, and the cathedral bells began to peal in celebration.

Rosalynde blinked back tears and pressed her trembling lips together. Then she lifted her chin and smiled a wide, stiff smile, acknowledging the people, her people now. Philip, too, was smiling, smiling the dazzling smile his people loved, and they cheered the louder because of it. Only Rosalynde was near enough to see that the smile did not reach his eyes.

He offered her his arm, and she took it apprehensively, looking as if she might swoon from the claustrophobic press of people around them. Her attendants took up her long train, and the halberdiers opened a path through the crowd to let the new couple pass. The wedding guests flooded out behind them, eager to begin the feasting and celebration that would last well into the night.

For the next few hours, Philip never left Rosalynde's side, playing to perfection the role of the attentive bridegroom. She watched as he graciously accepted the congratulations and good wishes of the guests and tactfully passed over the drunken, ribald comments some of them made. When they raised a toast to her, he chivalrously kissed her hand and said something pretty about her beauty and his good fortune. He even filled her plate from the banquet table himself and poured her wine. All in all, he flawlessly kept the promise he had given. The king could have no complaint regarding his obedience now.

She, too, kept up the pretense, smiling and clinging to his arm. For almost five years she had dreamed of him, made him her passion's idol. Often she had prayed for this very night to come, the night when she could give herself to him, but now she realized she was in truth not so bold as in her imagination. This man she had been given to, this beautiful man with eyes of ice, was not her Philip at all. Whoever he was, though, he was her husband, and she was his wife.

"Will you have more wine?"

Startled from her musings, she turned to him. "My lord?"

"Will you have more—" A flicker of concern touched his face. "There are tears in your eyes, my lady. I hope I have not put them there."

She dashed the telltale drops away. "I was just thinking how swiftly life changes."

"You miss Westered, no doubt," he said.

"It holds all my sweetest memories."

He nodded, looking as if he pitied her being stolen from her home and thrust into a life not of her own choosing, as if he were familiar with that pain.

"Westered is not so far that you will never see it again."

"That's so, my lord, but my duty is here now."

A hint of sympathy softened his expression. "And duty is rarely easy. Still, I had thought your Ankarette would have come to attend you here, if only to keep you company."

She managed a tiny smile. "I would she could have, my lord, but she died two months ago."

Again he looked as if he pitied her, as if this pain, too, were a familiar one. "I am sorry, my lady. I know she cared for you a long while."

"Since I was born. I never knew my mother."

"Nor I mine."

She looked at him puzzled. The queen had died little more than a year ago.

"I thought—" She dropped her eyes. "I am sorry, my lord."

The day dragged tediously into night, and finally the king announced that the bride and groom would retire. That set off a round of suggestive toasts and raucous laughter. Rosalynde looked at the floor, red-faced, unable to meet Philip's eyes.

"Come, my lady," he said, putting his arm protectively around her, his stern disapproval dampening the guests' high spirits. He led her to where his father and hers stood talking.

"Good night, Your Majesty. My lord."

Philip bowed formally to each of them, and Rosalynde curtseyed.

"Good night, Your Majesty," she said.

Robert took her hand to kiss. "Faith, son, she's a tempting wench," he said heartily, his voice unsteady with wine. "A man might envy you tonight."

"He might, Your Majesty," Philip replied, his expression unchanging.

"And, fair daughter, good night," Robert said. Then he leaned even closer to her. "My son allows himself little pleasure, girl. I trust you will please him."

"I pray I shall," she said softly, her blush deepening. Then she turned quickly to her father. "Good night, Father."

She kissed him on the cheek, and he held her close for a moment. Darting a glance at Philip, he murmured something in her ear, but she shook her head. "It will be all right."

Westered turned then to his son-in-law. "Your Highness, I have entrusted to you the dearest thing I have, and I would have her kept safe. I'll not remind you of the vows you made this morning. I know you in all honor will keep them, but I know, too, that these are uncertain times."

He took off his ring marked with the Westered lions and pressed it into Philip's hand, holding it there, holding Philip's eyes with his intense gaze. "If ever, as ever need may come, you find you want my aid, send me this, and I and my army will come to you."

He caught Rosalynde's hand and put it into Philip's, the ring between them and his own large hands around both of theirs.

"You were good to my girl before, son. Be so now."

Philip briefly bowed his head. "I will defend her with my life."

Westered kissed his daughter once more. "God bless you, sweetheart."

"Good night, Father," she said, just the slightest tremor in her voice. "I pray He will bless us all."

Philip escorted her to the bridal chamber and left her in the care of her ladies-in-waiting, the same ones who had waited upon her sister Margaret before her defection. They carefully removed her crumpled gown and the delicate undergarments beneath. Then they unbound her hair. It fell in heavy coils down her back, and she shook her head, glad to be free of the painful pull of the clasps. As they combed the tresses into dark, shimmering waves, she studied herself in the mirror and wondered if her husband would be pleased.

She got under the coverlet and considered again what it could have been that had taken the light from his eyes and the warmth from his heart. Whatever it was, she determined to love him so purely, so deeply, so fiercely that he could not choose but love her in return.

Her resolve evaporated when there was a knock at the door. The room flooded with light as a brace of courtiers entered, followed by her father and the archbishop. Last of all was her new-made husband, flanked by his father and brother. Philip got gingerly into bed beside her and handed his dressing gown to Rafe Bonnechamp.

"Pity he did not remove it before he got into the bed," one noblewoman murmured to another. Rosalynde colored as the other stifled a giggle.

She glanced at Philip to see if he, too, had overheard, but he was still sitting up, staring fixedly at the archbishop, seemingly oblivious to anything but the blessing of their marriage bed. Rosalynde let the holy words slip by her until finally the ceremony was over and the courtiers left, taking the bright lights with them.

Philip sat still as he had been, looking straight ahead, knowing she was watching the flickering hearth light play over his skin, watching as it defined the muscles in his arms and shoulders, watching as if she wished she dared touch him. After a moment, he turned to her, his face carefully blank. She lay there with the coverlet pulled to her chin, only the barest hint of white shoulders visible beneath, her eyes holding an odd mixture of hope and fear and desire.

"I am sorry there was not time for us to become better acquainted before now, my lady."

"We are not wholly strangers." She laid her hand on his arm, and the touch burned. "I remember you were very kind to me in Westered."

"That was a long time ago," he said unsteadily. He had not touched a woman, not since Katherine and not before.

"There has not been a day of the time since, my lord, that you have not been in my heart or my prayers."

He looked abruptly into her eyes. "Not a day?"

"No."

He focused on her full wine-colored lips as they formed the word and realized that his body was eager to keep the vow he had made, though his heart rebelled at it still.

"I want to be a good wife to you, my lord," she said, her voice trembling and the color rising to her cheeks. "I want to please you."

Nervously moistening his lips, he leaned over her and kissed her mouth, and she clasped her arms around him.

"Oh, my lord," she sighed.

Her breath was sweetly warm in his ear, and for a moment he clung to her, hiding his face against her shoulder. Her soft words brought him back to the sweet, innocent fire of that first night with Katherine, left him longing to rekindle it, longing to feel something besides pain.

Let it be more than this, he pled silently, for himself and for this gentle girl who had kept him so long in her prayers. It was meant to be more, he knew from his few nights with Katherine. He had no experience of passion without love.

"Philip," Rosalynde whispered, pressing her lips to his temple. He closed his eyes and kissed her again.

He lay with his back against the pillows, motionless. She rested yet against his heart, warm and content, her dark hair flowing over them both. He had been careful to be gentle, knowing from his brief time with Katherine that the hopeful innocence this girl had just given him was something fragile, something he should hold dear, something he should cherish. She was such a soft little thing.

It's not in you ever to deceive me. Katherine's trusting words scourged him again, and he took his guilty arms from around Rosalynde's waist.

I would have died to know someone else might hold you and kiss you and love you like this.

Rosalynde leaned up to nuzzle his ear, and he had to fight the urge to shove her away.

I should have died, Kate, he thought, *before I let it come to this. Forgive me. Forgive me.*

You would never play me false?

Kate, by my honor—

She'll never have my heart, Kate, he swore silently. *Never. I'll not be false in that.*

Rosalynde looked with adoration into his eyes. Then she drew back, bewildered. He knew any tenderness, any passion she had seen in him a few moments ago was gone. She could not possibly know that the disgust she saw on his face now was directed not at her but at himself.

She burst into tears and moved away from him to the edge of the bed, hiding under the coverlet again. He felt a twinge of guilt at those tears, but he shoved it to the back of his mind and reminded himself that he had never once spoken of love to her. She had no right to expect it.

Still, he considered the intimacy they had just shared. *A mixing of bodies, not hearts,* he told himself sternly. Perhaps it meant more to a woman. He refused to care. Making love to her satisfied the vows he had made. If she wanted more than that, she would just have to be disappointed.

With a quivering sob, her weeping stopped, and she lay there beside him, wrapped in deepest humiliation. She had bared her heart and soul to him, offered him her innocence like a shower of precious jewels, and he had taken it from her with no more thought than when he took his falcon's hard-won prey. He clenched his jaw. *Her choice, not mine.*

She sobbed again, the sound cutting through the static silence, then augmented by the rustle of sheets as he turned toward her.

"My lady, have I hurt you?"

More than you know, her brief glance told him, turning his twinge of guilt into a steady ache that was a little harder to push aside.

"No," she said thickly, but she could not hold back a few more tears. Her gentle lover was gone, and all that was left to her was a cold-eyed, cold-hearted stranger.

"Lady Rosalynde," he began formally. Then his voice softened into weary resignation. "Please, my lady, do not cry anymore. If I have caused you any pain, please forgive me. They've done you cruelly wrong, marrying you to me. You should have been given to a man with a heart, one who could love you as you deserve."

She turned toward him again, fervent longing on her tear-stained face. "I would not want anyone else, my lord. I love you."

That startled a bitter laugh out of him, one that was cruel in its mirthlessness. "You do not love me. You do not even know me."

"But when you were in Westered—"

"That boy is dead. Let him have his peace."

"But, Philip, I love you."

"Never say that again. Not ever."

"But—"

"Hear me," he said with cold finality. "I promise you three things, Lady Rosalynde, and you will find me true to my word. I will not lie to you, I will not be unfaithful to you, and I will not love you. My heart is pledged already, and I am not a man to break an oath."

For a long moment she looked at him, wounded pleading in her emerald eyes. Then she hid her face in the pillow. He could tell from the silent tremors that she was crying again.

He rolled onto his back and waited until he was sure she was asleep. Then he let the pent-up air seep out of his lungs, let it out so slowly that it seemed he did not breathe at all.

Well, it was done. He had betrayed Katherine, prostituted himself, taken this girl's innocence and broken her trusting heart in doing it, all for his father's ambition. He felt irredeemably soiled. Where was the sweet purity he had felt after that first night with Katherine?

He brushed the back of his hand across his temple where Rosalynde had kissed him and noticed her father's ring on his finger.

Be good to her, the duke had requested, and Philip had had to turn away from the gruff, pleading tenderness in his father-in-law's eyes.

I will defend her with my life.

It was not the pledge Westered had desired, but it was as much as Philip could swear to. He had given his word to Katherine, to take care of her. He would not again promise what he could not keep.

He pulled the ring off and set it on the table near the bed, but he could still feel the weight of it, binding him, pressing him. Nothing was changed. Only death could free him now.

Soundly asleep, Rosalynde took a deep, sobbing breath and rolled over against him, her cheek pressed to his shoulder. Longing to atone, he put his arms around her and buried his face in her sweet-smelling hair, unable to tell by the dying firelight that it was dark and not fair.

CHAPTER

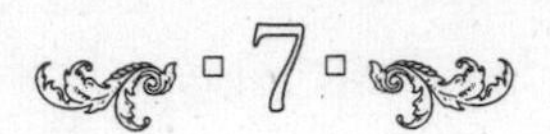

PHILIP WENT TO HIS WIFE THE NEXT NIGHT BECAUSE HE KNEW IT was expected of him. There were several unwritten rules for royal newlyweds, he was discovering, and among them was the undefined period of time during which they were supposed to spend every night together. He knew tonight would be awkward for both of them after the wounding words of the night before and the strained politeness of this morning, but it could not be helped.

He found her sitting alone before her looking glass, pensively combing her long, dark tresses. She watched his reflection as he came up beside her, but she did not turn around.

"Good evening, my lady."

"My lord."

There was a long silence. Then he took the comb from her and began running it through her hair.

"There is no need for that, my lord. I am ready."

He looked into the glass, into the reflection of her eyes, and was strangely reminded of John as he lay on the ground at Tanglewood bleeding inwardly.

"I want to do it, my lady. Your hair is lovely." He stroked it with his hand. "You are lovely."

She dropped her head, and he saw big tears fall silently into her lap.

"It will not take you long to find I am not worth one of those tears," he said gently. Then he stroked her hair again. "I would never willingly hurt you, but you must face the truth and not expect more from me than is in me to give."

She nodded, her delicate lips trembling, and he brushed a stray tear from her cheek.

"Shall we go to bed?"

Again she nodded, as if she were unable to trust her voice. He led her to the bedside and turned down the coverlet, then took the robe from her white shoulders, leaving only her thin shift. Desire tore at him, but he checked it, refusing to use her any more than her vows and his required.

He knew, despite her claims of love, that their marriage was no more her choice than it was his own. Regardless of her feelings, she would have been given to him for the sake of their fathers' alliance. He determined that the next time he touched her it would be because she wanted him to, not because he must.

Giving her only a chaste kiss on the cheek, he tucked the coverlet over her and put out the candles. Then he undressed himself and lay down next to her. He knew at once that he would find it difficult to sleep with her so close. Her presence was too tangible. Her scent, her very warmth beside him, was enough to keep the intoxicating memory of last night relentlessly in his mind.

It seemed the more he fought the remembrance, the more it hounded him. Just when he thought he had it mastered, he heard a plaintive whisper out of the darkness.

"Hold me, Philip."

Steeling himself, he put his arms carefully around her, and she nestled close to him. She wanted tender comforting and nothing more, he was sure of it. He felt he owed her that much without taking anything for himself. But her cheek was pressed to his chest, his heart pounding against it, and he could feel his restraint weakening with every breathless beat.

"Hold me, Philip," she whispered again, bringing her lips close to his.

With no more thought of resistance, he let her sweet softness fill his senses and dull the everlasting pain.

He was gone when she woke the next morning, but she did not mind that. The memory of him was still with her, the quick fire of his kisses and the burning sweetness of his touch and, more than that, his arms strong around her afterwards, cuddling her close until she fell asleep.

She hummed to herself as she ate her breakfast and thought of him. He did not love her yet—she decided it was too soon for that, but she was sure she had brought him closer to it. Now it was only a question of time. She was confident she could make him forget whatever it was that had hurt him so badly and the pledge that had a strangling hold on his heart. All she had to do now was love him, and love him better than he had ever been loved before.

She had her ladies dress her quickly. Then she rushed down into the great hall to find him. He was not there. After several inquiries, she learned that he was in a council meeting and would likely be thus engaged for most of the day.

Disappointed, she wandered back to her chamber and tried to occupy herself with her needlework, but finally she put it aside to watch one of her waiting women setting a hem in a new dress. Rosalynde always thought of hummingbirds when she was near this girl's bright busyness, and she thought of them now as she followed the darting flash of the needle.

"What time is it, Julia?" she asked.

The girl looked up, deftly pulling a knot in her thread as she finished the stitch. "It must be near ten, my lady."

"I can see the clock tower. It has struck," another of her ladies said from near the window. Then Ursula stood and stretched her long limbs. "Might we go into the garden this morning, my lady? My eyes ache at this work. Or we could practice that new dance Lady Ellison brought back from abroad."

"You mean the one that made Lord Ellison so angry?" Julia asked, giggling.

Ursula nodded. "All the court was scandalized, my lady. 'I'll not have my wife flung about so wantonly!'" she mimicked, and then she laughed, too. "I saw no harm in it. It seemed like flying to be swung so high into the air!"

"It was not the dancing my lord Ellison objected to," Julia commented, "but his wife's partner."

The two waiting women began to exchange some of the juicier tidbits of court gossip, and Rosalynde went back to her sewing wishing the night was come, wishing for Philip.

It did not seem fair to her that they made him attend their tedious meetings all day. He had just been married. Surely there was nothing more important for him now than to spend time with his bride. Let the other men, the old ones, the ones who did not need so much to be cared for, let them plan this foolish war. She wanted her husband with her.

She had already gone to bed when he finally came to her chamber. He did not strike a light, no doubt in consideration of her, so she lit the candle herself. When she did, she saw he had already removed his doublet, and his shirt was halfway over his head. He looked surprised to find her awake.

"I did not mean to disturb you, my lady."

"I was waiting for you," she said with a shy, inviting smile. "I missed you today."

He turned away. "This war makes many demands upon me. I have time for little else."

The war. She noticed the scar that ran for several inches down his left side and wondered how he had gotten it. Like the one on his cheek, this one was well healed but not very old. She hated the war for daring to put such marks on him.

"I had hoped we might at least have supper together," she said, trying to make it sound like an invitation and not a complaint.

"I am sorry. It could not be helped."

Her forehead wrinkled in bewildered disappointment. After last night she had been sure that he would be eager to come back to her, that he would be much less distant. She was sure she had all but won him. Now he was no closer than when she was still in Westered.

Bidding her good night, he put out the light and got into bed. She tried to cuddle up next to him, but he turned his back to her.

"I am very tired, my lady," he said stiffly. "Good night."

Her father and the other guests left the following day. The bridal celebration was over. She learned over the next few weeks that this was to be the pattern of her marriage. When they made love, and even afterwards, he always held her close to him, expressing gentle tenderness with his hands and lips but never, never with words. And every moment of closeness, every embrace, every caress was purchased at the cost of his coolness toward her the next day or, worse, his absence from her altogether.

He was usually gone before she woke each morning, and if she saw him at all during the day, he treated her as if there had never been any intimacy between them. He was unfailingly polite and showed her every gentlemanly consideration, but he made sure to keep a careful distance. He would not allow her to forget his merciless promise never to love her.

It puzzled her still, the change in him since Westered. She knew he had lost his mother not so long ago and two of his brothers, one after the other, and thought that must pain him deeply. But that could have nothing to do with the oath that bound his heart. That did not explain why he was so fiercely cold to his father, the same father he had once so obviously worshiped. She decided she would have to be bold and ask him about it, if ever he seemed willing to speak of the past, if ever she found the right time.

Several days later when she heard that a troupe of acrobats and jugglers would be coming to the palace, she hoped she had found her opportunity.

Weary of war and knowing his nobles were too, the king had sent for some entertainment. Great excitement stirred the court when it arrived. All the nobility flocked into the great hall, eager to see if this troupe could live up to its reputation as the finest in all the kingdom, and Rosalynde was as eager as they. She remembered how the actors and clowns had delighted Philip in Westered. Now, sitting on the cushions between him and Tom, she hoped they still would. It helped her cause that the king and his lord high chamberlain were too occupied with court matters to attend the fete.

"They say they have a man who can breathe fire," she said as the first act was being prepared, "and swallow the whole length of a rapier."

"All at once?" Philip asked dryly.

"While speaking verse," Tom assured them with a grin.

Philip did not smile, not really, but there was a glint of amusement in his eyes, a hint of laughter in the set of his mouth that gave Rosalynde hope. As the performance got underway, she saw him watching each demonstration of skill and daring, every inexplicable feat of sleight of hand, and she was sure she saw just a trace of the eager, boyish amazement she remembered.

"They are very good," she said, watching his face as the acrobats finished their tricks.

He nodded. "They well deserve the fame they have."

"I wonder if they would teach me that last trick," Tom mused. Then in one lithe motion, he stood up and flipped backwards to stand on his hands. "Or perhaps they would make me one of the company."

Rosalynde clapped her hands in delight, and Philip merely looked at him speculatively. "I shouldn't wonder, Tom," he conceded. "Surely they are in need of more trained apes."

"Then they should have place for you," Tom countered.

Rosalynde laughed to see her husband casually tug at one of the cushions and topple Tom back to the floor. The two scuffled briefly until Tom yielded and sprawled back onto the cushions, breathless and laughing.

Rosalynde caught a glimpse of Philip's rare smile—not the polite, stiff twist of his mouth that had passed for a smile since their marriage, but a real one, however brief. She had to force herself not to stare. Tom caught her glance, looking pleased himself to see his brother relaxing his guard just a little, and she smiled at him.

"Have you seen enough for one night, my lady?" Philip asked as the clock struck half past one, but Tom shushed him. Rosalynde was soundly asleep with her head on Philip's shoulder, her hand tucked in his. He shifted her into his arms to carry her up to her chamber, and he was suddenly aware of her dainty softness. He was aware, too, of the scent that seemed always to surround her. It was saint's rose, he knew, in honor of Afton, but the delicate fragrance seemed especially suited to her.

She must perfume her bath with it.

The thought stirred him, and he drew her closer. She was so soft.

"'Night, Tom," he said, standing.

Tom looked up. "Sleep well," he replied. Then he put one hand up to Philip's arm. "Be good to her."

It was what her father had asked. Not love her. Not make her happy. Just be good to her.

Poor gentle thing. Surely she deserves kindness if nothing more.

When he pushed open her door, he saw that her ladies had retired, but the coverlet was turned down, and a clean shift was warming at the hearth. He had meant only to bring her to her chamber and leave her there on the bed, but he realized that would hardly be comfortable for her. He could at least take down her hair and loosen the lacings of her bodice. That was little enough.

He sat on the bed and, holding her against him, undid the clasp at the nape of her neck. Her hair fell down her back and over his hands, and the smell of saint's rose filled his nose. He breathed it in, drawn by the memories it brought. Then, reluctantly, he remembered the task he had set himself. Freeing his hands, he laid her back on the bed, and her arms went around his neck in a tender, sleepy embrace.

"Stay with me," she murmured, lifting her mouth to his, and he kissed her softly.

"It is late, my lady," he whispered as he slipped her shoes off her feet. "You will want your sleep."

She watched him fumbling with the lacings at her waist, the languor in her eyes kindling into desire, firing the light in his.

"Stay," she said again as she feathered her fingers through his hair, and he let her pull him down beside her.

Sometime later he was still trailing soft kisses across her cheeks and nose and chin as she lay drowsing in his embrace. She stroked her hand along his side, wondering again about the long scar she felt there.

"How did you get that?" she asked sleepily, thinking the question innocent enough to begin with. The kisses stopped.

"Battle."

"And this one?"

She traced the mark on his cheek, and he jerked back as if her touch had scalded him.

"By not knowing when to speak and when to keep silent."

Shoving himself away from her, he rolled to the side of the bed and lay with his back turned.

"My lord."

"You've had what you wanted of me. Now go to sleep."

She was stunned by his harsh tone. "Philip—"

"Never ask me about the past. It cannot be changed, and it cannot be helped."

Hesitantly she touched his arm, but he shook her off.

"Go to sleep."

Philip lay there feeling again the heavy blow that had scarred him and the deeper wounds that had left only invisible marks. Was there not even a moment that would let him forget? But he told himself he had no right to forget, no right to drown his memories with Rosalynde as his father drowned his guilt with wine.

I will remember, he pledged silently, and the fierce pain turned cold inside him. *I will remember*.

She did not see him at all the next day, and she wondered if he would even come back to her that night. If he did, she knew she would have nothing but cold indifference for her bedfellow.

"Is there something wrong, my lady?" Julia asked as she finished unlacing her dress. "You look so sad."

"I do not think I would be sad if Prince Philip were coming to my bed tonight," Ursula said, sitting on a footstool at Rosalynde's feet to remove her shoes. But Rosalynde was too preoccupied to scold her for her saucy tongue.

"What do you know of my husband, Julia?"

"Only what all Winton knows, my lady. He is a true gentleman and a handsome one and of the finest blood. What more need I know of him?"

"I know there is little at court, great or small, that misses your eye. Tell me, do you know how he came to get the scar on his cheek?"

"He took an arrow in the face. My, that was a battle, they say. For many days after, it was feared my lord Philip would die."

"From so shallow a wound?"

"Oh, no, my lady. He was grievously hurt in the side as well."

"The left side?"

"I do not know, my lady."

"But what battle was it?"

"It was in Tanglewood, not three or four months ago. When young Prince John was killed."

"I did not know," Rosalynde said, thinking it was no wonder he did not wish to discuss those wounds. She had unwittingly brought him pain. "Philip loved him well, did he not?"

"Yes, my lady, very dearly."

"My poor love—he's lost much these past months."

The two waiting women exchanged glances.

"Yes, my lady," Julia said. "More than is commonly asked of anyone to bear all at once."

"But tell me more. I want to know everything about him."

"You should ask of him, my lady," Julia said, looking uncomfortable. "He best can tell you."

Rosalynde sighed. "I do not think he will. Please. You must know more. Who are his friends at court?" She picked a loose thread from her shift and avoided the other girls' eyes. "I suppose he has been much sought after by the ladies."

"They used to call him Ice-Heart, my lady, because he would not play at love, not even a little bit," Ursula said. Then her expression changed. "You needn't worry that you will one day come face to face with a cast-off mistress of his."

"Not anymore," Julia agreed. Then she bit her lip as Rosalynde turned to face her.

"Then there was someone once."

"Oh, my lady, I seem to be forever saying more than I should. Please. We are not to speak of her."

"Of whom?"

"Please, my lady, the king has forbidden—"

"Katherine," Ursula whispered. She pulled her footstool closer. "They say she bewitched Prince Philip and stole the heart right out of his breast."

Julia crossed herself. "They burned her out in Bakersfield."

"Burned her?" Rosalynde gasped.

"For sorcery and for what she did to my lady Margaret's unborn child."

"Margaret was with child?"

Julia nodded. "By Prince Richard, but she lost it. It was witchcraft, they said. Did you not know, my lady? I suppose news is slow to come so far as Westered, but it's a wonder you've not heard."

"Tell me," Rosalynde whispered, feeling sick. "Did she truly make Margaret lose her child?"

"Katherine attended Lady Margaret with us, but I never saw

proof that her ladyship did not lose her child naturally. Her woman Merryn could tell you better. She looked after her ladyship more closely than any of us."

Rosalynde remembered Merryn—meddlesome and superstitious and fiercely devoted to Margaret. "She went with my sister to Ellenshaw, I suppose. But what of this Katherine? What did she do?"

"They say she gave Lady Margaret something she claimed was to ease her pains, but it made the child miscarry, and Lady Margaret almost died as well."

"So they burned Katherine for it. Was she a witch, do you think? What was she like?"

"She was never my lord Philip's match in looks or breeding. Not as you are, my lady," Ursula said. "She was nearly as straight as any boy, and she was such a meek little thing, too. It had to be witchcraft that won him to her. Even the noblest, fairest ladies at court could coax him into no more than a dance or two."

"She had a sweet face," Julia protested. "I never believed she was a witch. She seemed too gentle and more truly pious than anyone I ever saw."

"Not too pious to go to his bed!"

Rosalynde's heart contracted violently.

"You should not say such things, Ursula," Julia scolded. "Not in our lady's hearing."

"She'd have heard of it anyway, like as not," Ursula said. "He made brazen enough show of it. Ice-Heart, indeed! He was hot enough with that pious-tongued Katherine!"

"You are wicked to say such things!" Julia cried. "Just because he favored her and never tossed you so much as a smile! She is jealous, my lady."

Rosalynde sat there with the tears welling up in her eyes. Her Philip, her honorable, stainless knight, and this base-born—

"Forgive me, my lady," Ursula said quickly. "I meant no harm in what I said. I would not be a woman had I never sighed after him, but it is true he would never look at me nor any of the others, noble or not—only Katherine. I swear I'll not speak of her again."

"No," Rosalynde insisted. "I must know everything. Did—did she love him?"

Ursula laughed. "Who would not?"

Indeed, who would not? Rosalynde thought miserably, and the tears fell to her cheeks. "And did he—did he—"

"Do not torture yourself, my lady," Julia said gently. "She is gone. Whatever love he may have had for her is gone with her."

No. Not gone, Rosalynde told herself with agonizing certainty. *That love is not gone*. She took a painful breath. "How long ago?"

"Not a year yet, I think," Ursula considered.

Julia agreed. "Less than a year since she was burned."

"They kept him locked away until it was done, and he was free of her," Ursula added. "They say burning breaks any spell."

Rosalynde felt a chill thread through her veins. She quickly crossed herself. "I pray that is so."

Could it be that this Katherine's sorcery had truly stolen his heart from him? That she yet somehow had a hold on him that would not allow him to love again? Or was it only grief for this girl and for his mother and brothers, too, that weighed upon him? Rosalynde vowed to pray for him, to pray that God would send him peace and break any bonds that fettered him still.

A little hope struggled up inside her. His grief would pass. It had to. She would treat him tenderly until it did, despite his determined coldness, and win him with patience. She managed to smile at the thought.

CHAPTER

SHE DID NOT SEE HIM THAT NIGHT, AND THE NEXT MORNING A messenger arrived bringing her word that he had been sent away on some unnamed business for his father and would not return for a fortnight at the least.

Her mouth turned down in disappointment. A fortnight. To her longing heart, a fortnight was an eternity of separation from him. She was grieved that he should go away without even a farewell, after their last moments together had left them both wounded. She determined to make his homecoming the sweeter for it.

Since he had forbidden her to speak of her love, she decided that she would give him some fine token of it, something rich and exquisite that would speak for her. But what could it be? He had no lack of possessions, of jewels and finery with which to deck himself, and what could she give him that was not purchased out of his own bounty to her?

The solution came to her while she was sitting in the large window of her chamber sewing. What better demonstration of her affection than something she made herself? She remembered hearing it said that work of the hand was the work of the heart, and she determined that hers truly would be. The ladies at court always commented upon the fineness of her needlework. It would make the time alone pass more quickly if she spent it making something that she could give to him as a peace offering when he returned.

She worked carefully, painstakingly, often for long stretches at a time. The night before he was to return, she stayed up until dawn had nearly come again, straining in the flickering candlelight to finish her task. When she woke later, she was dismayed to find that it was past noon, and he had returned some hours before. She made her ladies hurry in dressing her. Then, with his gift carefully wrapped up in plain cloth, she went down to him.

Finding him talking to his father near the council chamber, she stood off from them to wait until they had finished. Philip could not have missed the eager welcome in her expression, and for an instant she thought he might answer her in kind. But then the king summoned her to them.

"I daresay, son, you had rather have the greeting of this fair creature than stand here talking matters of state."

At the king's self-satisfied smile, as if he'd just bestowed upon his son a great gift, Philip's face lost its animation. "My lady." He kissed her hand formally. "I trust you have been well in my absence."

"Yes, my lord," she said, wondering if he was never to forgive the innocent injury she had inflicted before he had gone away. "I—I am glad you are returned safely."

Robert quickly broke the thick silence that followed. "Well, I see the two of you are newly married enough to be shy yet in company. I will leave you then, Philip, so you may greet your little mouse as you are no doubt eager to do." He pushed her a step toward his son. "A little more feelingly, eh?"

Rosalynde felt her face burn and knew without looking that her husband's eyes had turned to ice. His voice was chillingly even. "If you will pardon me, Your Majesty, my lady, Alethia came up lame as I rode in this morning. I should go see if Hawkins has found the cause of it."

Robert frowned. "Philip—"

"I am sure the lady understands."

They both looked to Rosalynde, and she lowered her eyes. "Of course, my lord. We will have time at supper."

Philip looked back at his father with a slight lift of one eyebrow.

"Go on then," Robert reluctantly conceded.

Philip bowed. "Your Majesty. My lady."

A moment later he was gone. Watching him, Robert shook his head. "He will not take his leisure until he has seen to his duty," he said, his tone thinly cheerful. "A good quality in any man and a better one in a prince."

"Yes, my lord," Rosalynde said, tightly clutching the gift she had had no chance to give. With a look of pained understanding, Robert gave her shoulder an awkward pat and left her.

Supper that night was a strained affair, and afterward, claiming further business to attend, Philip sent her to bed alone. Still she had no opportunity to bring him her offering, her token of love. Again she forced down the hurt and told herself there would be tomorrow.

She rose early and, taking her gift with her, went down to the council chamber. It was empty. Hearing a clamor of voices outside, she went to the window and saw her husband down in the courtyard with his dogs and his servants. Tom was with him, his falcon on his arm.

The sight pleased her. The prospect of a day of leisure seemed to have lightened Philip's expression. If anyone could cheer his spirits, it was his brother Tom. Well, her gift would keep until this afternoon and be all the better for the waiting.

"Good morning, Lady Rosalynde. You are early up."

She turned and made a deep curtsey. "Good morning, Your Majesty. I had meant to speak to my lord Philip this morning before he was again mewed up in council, but I see he is going hunting."

Robert smiled. "He did me good service this past fortnight. I thought I would reward him with a day's pleasure. Is your business with him urgent?"

"Oh, no, my lord. It will keep until tonight."

"Nonsense. I will send for him."

Despite her protests, Philip was standing before his father a moment later. "You wished something of me, Your Majesty?"

"I would have you hear what your lady would say to you. A light enough task, I think."

Philip turned to her, only a slight twitch in his jaw to betray his annoyance. "My lady?"

"I—I have something for you, my lord, but I see His Majesty has already given you a gift, a day of freedom."

Philip smiled politely. "He gives me my freedom on a very short leash."

Robert's benign expression did not change. "Go ahead, my lady."

"My lady?" Philip asked again.

"This will wait, my lord," she said with an uncomfortable glance at his father, "until you have your leisure."

There was a hint of triumph in Philip's calm expression, a little twist of pride in his mouth as he, too, glanced at his father. "I thank you, my lady." He bowed. "If you will excuse me, Your Majesty."

"No, Philip, I will not." Robert frowned. "I wish you to hear your lady out."

Philip turned dutifully to her once more. "My lady?"

"I made you this while you were away," she said, fingering the package, wishing she had never said anything. Her nervousness made her hurry to fill in the silence that followed. "Your father says you did him good service. Where did you go?"

Philip looked askance at his father and Robert nodded.

"You may tell her."

"I went to Westered. To your father."

Rosalynde's face lit. "Oh, tell me how he fares. Is he well?"

"Very well, my lady. He asked of you and sent you his love."

"I trust you gave him mine."

"I thought you would wish me to."

"Were you with him long?"

"Only long enough to do what I was sent for."

"My lord your father says you did well," she said, hoping to please him with his father's praise.

"I am gratified to hear it," Philip said coolly, glancing again at the king. "I feared at first that I would fail. I was never trained in beggary."

"The war has wasted my treasury, Lady Rosalynde," Robert was quick to explain. "I merely sent him to ask your father's aid, for the love your father bears you and for the love you have in my son. I daresay it is well worth it to my lord of Westered to do his part to see you are kept safe."

"My father is loyal to Afton, my lord king," Rosalynde said, unconsciously twisting her gift in her hands. "I know he was pleased to do it. Was he not?"

Philip shrugged. "I told him what he wanted to hear, and he gave me the money."

Rosalynde hung her head, realizing how abased her proud-spirited husband must have felt at such a task. She put her wadded-up bundle behind her back, hoping it had been forgotten. She did not want her gift soiled with the unpleasantness between Philip and his father.

"Well, my lady," Robert said lightly, "you said you had something for my son?"

Her heart sank. "No, please, my lord, it will keep."

"Come, girl."

Reluctantly, she took the wrapping from the bundle and handed Philip a pair of gloves, white velvet embroidered with his cognizance, the saint's rose, the white chastelayne. She had wanted in the days of work she had put into them for them to be the finest, most beautiful pair he had, and indeed they were. Hundreds of tiny white stitches, each carefully placed, showed a quality of work well worthy of a prince, well worthy of a king.

He accepted them with his usual cool grace. "I thank you, my lady."

Immediately, she knew her pains had been wasted. She wished fervently that she had said nothing until they were alone.

"I believe your lady made those with her own hands, Philip," the king prompted.

Philip inclined his head. "They are excellently well done, my lady," he said with a polite smile. "I thank you."

"I took some of your old ones as a pattern. Do they fit?"

He pulled the gloves snugly onto his hands, all icy patience. "I could not ask better."

"I had hoped they would please you," she said miserably.

"That was most gracious. Is there anything more, Your Majesty?"

"No," Robert said with a frown. "That is quite enough."

Philip bowed. "Pardon me, my lady, but I am stayed for."

Rosalynde made curtsey and watched him walk away. She wanted desperately to run after him but knew that would not improve his estimation of her. She reminded herself to be patient. Perhaps he would come to her that night. He often did after a hunt, when he was relaxed and had burned off some of his restless energy. Perhaps then, away from his father, he would show more appreciation for the gift she had given him.

Her eyes filled with tears, and Robert turned her face up to him. "Has he been cruel to you? I'll not have it."

"No. No, Your Majesty. He has never lifted a hand to me in anger or his voice."

"He would hardly have need," Robert said ruefully. "He knows he can cut deeper by far with one cold look or one soft, scathing word. But you mustn't cry, girl. His arrows were aimed at me today, not you." He rubbed his forehead. "I've surely earned them."

Rosalynde accompanied the king out into the courtyard when the hunting party returned late that afternoon with a deer and several partridges.

"Philip took the deer himself," Tom bragged to his father, and Robert looked pleased.

"You were always the finest hunter of us all, son," he said proudly as they went into the library.

Philip returned his gaze with no betrayal of emotion. "I thank you for allowing me that pleasure still."

Robert looked uncomfortable, and Tom glowered at his brother, but Philip only stripped off his gloves and tossed them crumpled onto a small table.

Rosalynde cried as she snatched them up, the gloves she had so painstakingly made for him. The stag's blood had dyed the fine white stitches red, and the costly velvet was matted with gore. She shook the gloves in his face, wanting him to see them ruined.

With a quick glance at his father, Philip shrugged negligently. "I forgot I had them on."

"Do you weigh my gift so lightly, Your Highness?" she snapped, the words tart on her tongue. "Are they too fine perhaps? I've heard you have a taste for commoner things."

Philip turned his icy eyes on her. "If common things held any charm for me, madam, your behavior at this moment would have me entranced."

Catching her breath with a sob, she walked swiftly out of the room before she made an even greater fool of herself.

"Well, go after her, boy!" Robert demanded.

"What would Your Majesty have me say to her?" Philip asked, his complaisance more insolent than docile.

"Apologize for ruining her gloves! Pretend, if you must, that there is more than ice in that bosom of yours! She's not done you wrong. I have, and, before God, I'll not crawl after you the rest of my life begging forgiveness. You go to her as I told you, and do not let me hear any more of this."

"At once," Philip replied, the only expression on his face faint, arrogant contempt. Then he stepped into the corridor. "My lady."

Rosalynde whirled to face him. "I suppose I cannot compare to all your other women."

He was not prepared for that. "All what other women?"

"All the mistresses you've had and have still for aught I know," she said, her tone defiant.

"I have never had a mistress."

He said it coldly, steadily, his eyes on hers so unwaveringly that she would have sworn he spoke truth had she not known.

"You were no novice on our wedding night," she said with a contemptuous toss of her chin.

His eyes grew even colder. "And upon what experience do you base that observation?"

The color flamed into her face, but she did not look away. "Well, were you?"

"I was what your father bought for you," he said haughtily. "Take your complaints to him."

He stalked back into the library, and she flew after him, still clutching the gloves. "I am your wife, my lord, and I mean no more to you than your harlot!"

"Far less, madam," he said with almost inhuman calm. "Far less."

"Philip!" Robert reproved. "You will not speak so to her! Apologize!"

Philip bowed to him, rigidly submissive, and turned obediently back to his wife. "I ask your pardon."

She stiffened her spine at the lack of contrition in his too-proud expression and struck him hard across the face with the bloody gloves and then threw them down at his feet. "Do not think to come to me tonight!" she cried, shaking with helpless fury. "Do not think to come to me ever again!"

"As you wish it," he said, a hint of triumph in his chilling nod. She ran from the room blinded with tears.

"Philip, have you no shame?" Robert demanded, grabbing his son roughly by the shoulders. The muscles under his hands quivered, taut as whipcord, but Philip made no attempt to pull free of him. Philip just looked steadily at him, then turned his face, patiently offering his cheek for another slap.

"Oh, Philip," Robert murmured, releasing him and then quickly reaching out to wipe away the smear of blood the gloves had left behind. Involuntarily, Philip flinched, and Robert dropped his hand.

"Philip, son, can we never heal this hurt between us?"

His impassioned plea answered only with stony silence, the High Majesty of Lynaleigh slunk from the room like a whipped cur.

"That was unworthy of you, Philip," Tom said gravely. "I've never known you to be so careless of whom you hurt."

"No more than he," Philip answered with another shrug of his shoulders.

"And when did you begin to let the behavior of others dictate to you yours? Besides, I did not mean him. I meant your lady. Whatever he has done, surely she is innocent."

"Innocent?" Philip lashed back, taking deep, indignant breaths. "You heard what she said about Kate! Common things! My harlot!" He rubbed his cheek where it still stung, and his hand shook. "And dare she strike me!"

His anger was as sudden as it was fierce, and just as suddenly it was gone. Tom watched in amazement as Philip forced his body to relax, forced his doubled fists to unclench, and banished his emotions once more into imprisonment. The calm emptiness in his eyes and the blood that marked a crimson line across his scarred cheek brought back too vividly that awful day in Tanglewood when Philip had first sought refuge behind this mask of indifference.

"She was hurt," Tom said, feeling the same powerlessness he had felt then. "She does not know how deeply she hurt you. How could she? Please, Philip, do not—"

"I know I made her angry with me," Philip said dispassionately, "but I cannot help that. She has told me I am not to come to her, and naturally I will respect her wishes. If she should change her mind, I am content to let things be as they have been between us. If not, I am content as much to let them be as they are now." He looked calmly at the stag's blood on his hand, the blood he had wiped from his face. "I had best wash before supper."

Rosalynde cried herself to sleep that night and several nights afterward, angry and humiliated and hurting. She had told Philip never to come to her again, and he was taking cold pleasure in honoring her wishes. She felt like a fool, wearing out her heart over such a man and wished she could be as he was—needing nothing and no one.

He was in the wrong, her wounded pride told her. Let him ask pardon. He was cruel and thoughtless and must be taught to treat her as his wife and as a princess. He should beg for forgiveness, on his knees, before he expected her favor again.

Then when the night deepened around her and her bed was wide and cold and lonely, her heart brought to her remembrance the love she had claimed to have for him. Was this the whole depth of her love, so easily tossed away for a pair of spoilt gloves?

It was not just the gloves, her pride flung back.

Her heart quietly reminded her that she had hurt him, too, that she had meant to cut him deeply with her sharp words, and the tears came again.

She knew she could stay here alone, match him pride for pride, and be miserable in her self-righteousness. Or she could go to him and teach him that her love truly was the love Saint Paul had written of, love that would bear, believe, hope, and endure all things.

Still, if she did dare to go to him, she knew he was likely to accept her apology as coolly as he had accepted her gloves, thank her politely, and send her back to her bed alone. She could not bear the thought of that, not quite yet.

"Dear Lord God, help me," she wept in anguish. "Help me to love him as You love him. Oh, God, he needs to be loved." She sobbed and hiccoughed. Then she buried her face in her pillows, weeping for the love she so desperately needed herself and did not have. Her tears finally run dry, she fell into a heavy, restless sleep.

Suddenly she awoke to find him standing over her, barely visible in the dim light, his shirt only half tucked into his breeches, his sleeves pushed carelessly to his elbows, one mislaced boot bunched around his ankle. She had never expected him to come to her, not until she had humbled herself, but he was truly here. Her pride forgotten, she held out her arms to him.

"Oh, Philip—"

He put his hand swiftly over her mouth. "Be quiet, my lady. I already woke your gentlewomen to get you dressed. Be sure they do not make a sound."

"My lord—"

"Shh. You must be quiet. Stephen's soldiers have somehow gotten inside the walls and are coming here. They mean to take us by surprise, but we caught wind of them. Still, we haven't enough men here to fight them, so we must creep away before they know we have found them out."

"Oh, holy God, save us!"

"Shh! Get up, get dressed. We have only a moment."

Her ladies came in then, their own clothes pulled quickly over their shifts, and scurried to dress her. Fear and sleepiness made them clumsy and slow at their tasks. Rosalynde's heart pounded harder and harder at the thought of the enemy stealing upon them, at the thought of what would happen if they did not make it away in time.

She could see Philip waiting in the doorway, watching the dark corridor for movement. Silver moonlight edged his drawn sword, and she could tell by the lift of his head and his wary stance that he was ready to spring at the first sign of the enemy. There was no one yet.

Finally dressed, Rosalynde pulled her cloak around her and came to his side. "We are ready, my lord."

He nodded and, with another cautious look, led the women into the corridor. Tom met them coming from the other way, bringing another half-dozen waiting women with him.

"They may be in the castle already," he said as he padded lightly up to Philip.

"I sent Rafe and a few of the men down to the stables to ready some horses," Philip said. "We can trust the women to him until we have made sure there is no use in fighting here."

"I sent Palmer down there as well."

Philip nodded. "Take the lead. I will see we are not taken from behind."

Tom gave the women a reassuring wink and led them to the end of the corridor toward the winding stairs that ended down in the kitchen. Trailing after them all, Rosalynde wished for her husband's comforting touch, but he merely pushed her ahead of him and kept his attention on the darkness behind.

Most of them had made it to the stairway when there was a sudden light at the end of the corridor and the sound of soldiers.

"Down there!"

Philip whirled to face them. "Tom, they've found us!"

The women on the narrow stairs began to scream and push each other, frantic to escape. Rosalynde grabbed Philip's arm. "Oh, run, my lord!"

"Get down there!" he thundered, shoving her away. Terrified, she obeyed.

Philip watched the small group of Stephen's men, six or eight at most, stop a few yards down the corridor. Though he was alone, he had reputation enough with a broadsword to earn their respectful distance. He held the weapon now with both hands, battle ready, and one of them stepped cautiously forward.

"Surrender, my lord."

"Not until I've seen these ladies safe and even then not until I've seen the man who can take my sword from me."

Stephen's men started toward him, and he glanced backwards. "Are they down, Tom? Tom?"

Hearing nothing but the fearful squealing of the waiting women, he backed swiftly down the stairs, glad at least that the narrow passageway prevented the enemy from coming at him more than one at a time. The first soldier charged at him with a shout, swinging his sword. Philip dodged as the heavy steel blade whooshed past his ear, and then he answered with his own blade, dispatching his opponent easily. He gained some distance as they wrestled the body to one side to get past it.

He knew it could be only a few more steps until he reached the kitchen. He could hear the women still and then something more—the clanging of metal on metal.

"Tom! Tom, can you hear me?"

"They're down here, too," Tom shouted up to him. "Hurry!"

Philip made a clean thrust through the man above him and then, swift as thought, through the next one. He turned and ran, knowing there was a door made of stout oak at the bottom of the stairs.

"Tom, the door!"

He stumbled into the kitchen, and Tom shoved the door shut

behind him and swiftly turned the key. Then they both swung back toward the two soldiers Tom had kept at bay.

"They've sent for more men," Tom panted.

"We have your king already, my lord," Philip's opponent said. "Afton is lost. Give yourselves up."

The soldier lunged forward, and the women shrieked as Philip shoved him back and thrust him through.

"They will be here any moment now," the other one blurted as Tom forced him into a corner, his sword at the man's throat. "You cannot hope to escape them."

Philip shifted his weapon into his left hand and smashed his fist into the soldier's jaw. The man fell into a heap on the stone floor.

Tom lifted his head and turned toward the passageway that led into the great hall. "They are here. I can hear them."

"Get the women away," Philip said. "I will bar that door."

"Come, my lady," Tom said, taking his sister-in-law's arm. "Be quiet and quick."

He paused to scoop a few provisions into a basket, and Rosalynde slipped out of his grasp, running to her husband. "Hurry! Oh, hurry, please!"

"Take her out, Tom!" Philip ordered as he lifted the door's heavy bar.

She tugged at his shirt. "Please, my lord!"

Philip swore softly, dropped the bar into place, and then grabbed her by the arm and dragged her out into the darkness. The others were quick to follow.

When they reached the stables, he shoved her onto her horse's back, then swung into his own saddle, and spurred away, pulling her horse behind him.

They rode out through Cook's Gate and through the forest as swiftly as the darkness would allow, even though the scouts Philip sent behind them and ahead of them saw nothing of the enemy. By dawn the refugees were well away from the fallen city and could afford to let their horses slow to a lulling walk.

The women sagged sleepily in their saddles, and one of the soldiers finally put one of them, obviously his sweetheart, up in front of him so she could sleep resting against him. Philip saw Rosalynde take one longing look at them, but she dropped her eyes when they met his. Irritably, he touched his horse's flanks with his spurs and came up alongside his brother.

"We are not pursued, but I cannot see how that could be. Or why they posted no guards outside the palace to keep us in."

"I do not know," Tom said. "No doubt they meant to take us in our beds and leave us no room to escape. I think it is a thorough miracle that we got past them or had warning of them at all. Palmer is never so late coming in as he was last night, and I thank God for those sharp eyes of his."

Philip's expression blackened. "Would to God I knew the name of the villain who opened that gate to Stephen's men. He could have never taken us by force, even with as few soldiers as we had there."

"We will run the traitor to ground eventually," Tom said with a shake of his head, "but what we must consider now is how best to free our father."

Philip frowned, but he nodded in agreement. "Once the women are safe in Bridgewater, we will go to Eastbrook's forces for help. Dunois is doubtless with him." He looked back at the weary party behind them. "We should stop awhile and let them eat and take a moment's rest."

Rosalynde was relieved when he dropped back alongside her and led them all to a cold, rushing brook. He spread out his cloak on the grass and settled her on it. Then he gave her some of the food Tom had brought along, but took none for himself.

"I will watch the road," he said to his brother. "Be swift."

Tom nodded and went to sit beside Rosalynde, apart from the others.

"Are you comfortable, my lady?"

"I am afraid. What will we do?"

"Do not let that fret you. We will soon have you in a safe place."

"Then you will go take back the city?" she asked.

"As soon as we can get men enough to do it, yes."

She nodded and picked for a moment at the bread she had been given. Then she flung it into the grass.

"What am I to do, my lord? I can say nothing, do nothing, but it is wrong!" She looked pleadingly at him. "I could cut my tongue from my mouth for speaking to him as I did. I never have said such things to anyone before."

"I know it's not been easy for you, my lady. He can put an angel out of patience if he cares to, but you mustn't take it too much to heart. Most of his barbs are not meant for you."

"So your father said. Please, my lord, what has happened between them?"

"It's not been right with them since Father took the crown. We were two years in King Edward's court, and the king treated us more like sons than prisoners. All that while, Philip told him that our father was loyal. He swore to it, and you know what an oath means to Philip. He said if our father proved traitor, Edward could take his life, that he would deliver the blade to him himself. He was so sure of Father's trustworthiness that he made Edward believe it as well. Then Father came to court, and Edward received him, not in chains as he might have done, but in triumph and in honor. He praised Father as hero of the Riverlands, and, in answer, Father stole his crown."

"I know from what Philip said in Westered that that could not have pleased him."

Tom frowned. "We were none of us prepared for it, except for Richard, but Philip took it the worst. He had engaged his own honor in certainty of our father's, and Father had made him false to his word. He went to King Edward in the prison, he told me, to pay his pledge, but Edward would not take his life. He merely let the dagger Philip brought him fall to the floor. Then he told Philip he did not hold him to fault for what our father had done, that he prayed Philip and all of us would not have to pay for our father's wrongs."

"Poor man," Rosalynde murmured.

"Philip went back to the court afterwards to plead for Edward's release. I remember that day. Father came in, and all the nobles knelt, all except Philip. 'Have you no knee for your king, boy?' Father demanded, and Philip looked at him, you know the way he does, proud and immovable, and said, 'Yes, my lord. Bring me before him, and he shall have it.' Father slapped him for it there before the court. He'd never struck any of us before. Then he said, 'Is this the love and allegiance I have due me as your father and as your king?' Philip was too stunned for a moment to answer him. Then he said, 'As you are my father, I tender you my love. As you are my king, I tender you my allegiance. Which would you have?'"

Rosalynde could imagine him as he must have looked, that determination on his face and the hurt pleading, too.

"What did he answer him?"

"Before Father could reply, Darlington came in with the news that Edward was dead. Faith, I hope I am never the object of such a look as Philip gave our father then. He dropped to his knee and said, 'Long live King Robert,' with such condemnation in his voice that it was judge, jury, and executioner all at once."

"Then your father—he did order King Edward's death, as they say."

"No. It was not so, though it might have been easier if he had. Darlington said he did not know how, but Edward had somehow gotten hold of a dagger and turned it on himself."

"Oh, not Philip's!"

Tom nodded. "Edward cut his own throat with it. Philip has not forgiven himself yet for leaving it behind in his cell."

"Then it was King Edward's death that came between him and your father."

"Partly," Tom said. "That was only the first betrayal he lays to our father's charge. John was the last."

"Your brother John? He was killed in battle. How could that be a betrayal?"

"It was given out that John was sent to the army in Tanglewood when our mother died. In truth, Father banished him there. He died there because Father would not send him enough men to defend the place. Philip pled with Father to send soldiers and quarreled with him, too, over it."

"But what had the boy done?" Rosalynde asked, wondering how much more was left to be told and how Philip, and Tom, too, had borne it all.

"Nothing Father would say. Nothing reason could fault John for. Then after John died, they quarreled again, over John doubtless, and over other things, I know not what. Father slapped him that time, too." Tom put his hand up to his cheek. "There where the arrow hit him, with no mind of Philip's wounds or his grief. Philip's not been the same since."

"And I struck him there, too," Rosalynde murmured, putting her hand over her mouth. "Oh, my Philip."

"It was as if he'd given up after that," Tom said, "on love and trust and anything else but his honor and his memories."

"His memories of Katherine."

"Do not fault him for loving her," Tom said slowly, seeing the pain that caused her. "She was not nobly born, but she had a true heart, and she loved him well. He told me once she was the only one who loved him for nothing but himself alone, past his titles and noble blood and all the rest. And you remember him how he was. He would never have loved her at all if he had loved her lightly."

"I would he had," she said, struggling to keep the tears out of her eyes.

"No," Tom corrected, his voice gentle, "you would not. He would not be the Philip you love if he had used her so."

"He is not the Philip I love!" She briefly pressed her lips together. "No, I mean to say I love him still, but he is not what he was."

"That's true," Tom agreed, "but he could be again in time, if you will have patience with him. He is wounded yet. Inside." Sadness shadowed his face. "It would have broken your heart to see him after her trial. I feared he would die when she did, he loved her so."

"But she was a witch!" Rosalynde protested. "She killed my sister's child!"

"I never believed those charges, my lady. She was as Christian as any I know."

"But she was his mistress!"

"My lady, I know he would never speak to you of this, but—"

"We must needs be gone from here," Philip called from the road. Tom stood up quickly.

"It is not precisely as you have been told," Tom said softly as he helped her to her feet. Then Philip came up beside them, and Tom said no more.

Rosalynde watched her husband as he shook the grass from his cloak, rolled it up, and packed it in the pouch on his saddle, the usual taut expression on his face.

He is wounded yet. Inside.

She could tell that was so and that somewhere past the scars and the memories, he truly was the Philip she loved. She determined to find a way to his heart if love and patience could find it.

"Are you ready, my lady?" Philip asked as he put his hands around her waist, meaning to lift her back onto her horse, but something stopped him there. "I suppose the last time I put you up here I was not very gentle. You must forgive me if I sometimes am forced to be rough with you."

He did not see the reproach he expected to see in her expression, the reproach he knew he deserved. Instead there was only uncertain hope and a desire to trust, just as there had been when she had told him that she had always kept him in her prayers. From that first night, he had done nothing to earn her trust. How could she still have that look now, even mixed with remorse as it was?

"I was so afraid," she said, shyly toying with the lacing on his shirt. "I am sorry."

"What—for being afraid?"

She nodded.

"You need not have feared, my lady. I am sworn to protect you, and they would have had to take my life before I would have let them hurt you."

"I know. That was what I feared, that they would kill you. You are too careless of your life, and I am so afraid that one day you will go to fight and never return to me."

Surprised, he searched her face for any hint of pretense but found none. How could he have been so reckless with such a tender heart?

"I suppose you are tired, my lady," he said awkwardly. "Would you care to ride with me awhile?"

A hesitant smile touched her lips. "If it would not weary you too much."

He turned her horse over to one of his men and swung her up in front of him on Alethia's back. Soon her head sank to his chest in trusting sleep, and he held her a little more snugly to be sure she did not fall.

It was dark again when they reached Bridgewater and sanctuary. The village was small and secluded, centered around Lord Darlington's country house, a secure little fortified manor that could withstand an army, if need be, manned by only a handful of soldiers. The women would be safe here until Winton was retaken.

Darlington's steward was quick to make the royal visitors welcome. As soon as they were fed, he showed them to the guest quarters.

When they made their way to the chamber that had been given them, Rosalynde slipped her hand into Philip's, another gesture of the loving trust he knew he did not deserve. Her hand was small in his, white and soft and meant to be protected, as was her whole self. And still that expression was on her face. After they had quarreled, he was sure that he had finally killed that look in her, that glow of love, but it was still there.

"Will this room suit you, my lady?" he asked once they were alone. She nodded, and he clasped her hand a little tighter. "I fear I must leave you here until my father and Winton are both freed. I cannot say when I will be back for you."

She looked up at him, her tear-filled eyes like emeralds in seawater. He wondered how she could be sorry to see him go when he had brought her nothing but heartache. She put her free hand over their clasped ones, and he took a quick breath.

"And I am sorry about your gloves. They were finer than I deserved."

The tears spilled onto her cheeks. "Oh, my lord, will you forgive me the wicked things I said that day? I was willful and cruel."

"God forgive me," he murmured as he gathered her to him. Willful and cruel. Could she have described him any better?

"I never wished to add hurt to that you already carry," she sobbed against his chest. He wrapped his arms around her, her pity and forgiveness heaping coals of fire on his heart.

"I know. I know. And I never truly meant to hurt you. If things had fallen out differently, I could have loved you." He pressed his lips against her hair. "I could have loved you the way you were meant to be loved."

"Oh, Philip—"

"Let me go," he said even as he held her closer, his voice low and husky. "Tom and I must leave at first light."

"Not yet," she breathed, the soft curve of her mouth and the unabashed tenderness in her eyes begging him to love her. "It's hours till dawn."

She wept to find him gone when she woke. Only one thing consoled her, and she was not sure if that was half-conscious reality or just a tangible dream, but she could still feel his lips soft and warm on hers as he left her and could hear his hurried whispered words.

I could have loved you.

CHAPTER

PHILIP RODE AWAY FROM BRIDGEWATER UNABLE TO ESCAPE THE memory of the night's warm darkness. Now in the sober light of day, he felt the familiar guilty pain overtake him. There was an exquisite torture in this unrelenting duty that required him to take Rosalynde to his bed but demanded, too, that he have no tender feelings toward her lest he break his oath to Katherine.

Even in that he knew he was failing. Despite his best efforts, he could not divorce his emotions from his duty, not with those soft, loving hands touching him, that tender mouth on his, the limitless depth of those eyes nearly drowning him with love. With Katherine, he had known nothing but love in lovemaking. He could not take Rosalynde's body and then just leave her. Not right away. Not when she gave herself so completely.

"We shall part here," Tom said, drawing his brother out of his deep thoughts. "If you can bring Eastbrook's men to join those I will bring from Chrisdale and meet us outside of Winton, we shall, by God's grace, have our city and our father back again."

Philip's face was grim. "Stephen must know we have no course but to mass our armies and come back to Winton. We shall buy our victories dearly, if we are to have them at all."

"Be faithful, and we shall have them. We shall have good success and a godly peace."

Tom held out his hand, and Philip took it in a strong clasp.

"Pray God it will be soon," Philip said. Then he held out his hand to Palmer. "See to your master well. I shall be much bounden to you for that and for some old debts I have neglected to show my thanks in."

A little surprised at the frankness of the gesture, Palmer grasped his hand. "God keep you, sir. You owe me nothing. What little service I may have once done you was no more than my duty to your house and to my God. It pleased me to see them both satisfied, though I sorrowed at the need for such service."

"It is enough," Philip said curtly. "Tom, be wary."

He spurred away with his men trailing after, a stiff, hard expression on his face.

"God, give him peace," Tom breathed as he watched him fading into the distance. Then he turned to his own men and ordered them to move on.

Tom's army joined up with Ellison's forces and began the arduous push back west toward Winton. Stephen's chief supporter, Hubert of Weatherford, had his soldiers ready to meet them in Amberly, and for weeks they fought back and forth, but, to Tom's satisfaction, the battles always moved westward.

The news he had of Philip was sketchy, sometimes no more than rumor, often nothing at all. He gathered that Philip's battles farther north went much like his own. As they had planned, Philip had met up with the Duke of Eastbrook's men in Falkness. Eventually the two armies, Tom's and Philip's, would band together and defeat the enemy. Tom believed that firmly. He believed it until his men were driven suddenly southward toward Stephen's stronghold in Cold Spring, and his forces faced Weatherford's near a place called Grant.

The enemy had reached the town first, and when Tom's men arrived, the place had been burned to the ground. Weatherford's men were drawn up in battle lines, well prepared to meet them. Tom ordered his men to pull back until the odds were more equal, but Weatherford would not allow it. Flanking his opponent, the enemy forced Tom to stand and fight.

The slaughter was immense, and Tom saw his men fall like so many stalks of ripe wheat before the scythe. Still he fought on, aching with weariness, nerve alone powering his arm, until Palmer rode up beside him.

"Come, my lord," he gasped. "My lord Ellison has been slain; our ranks are broken through. We cannot stand here."

"We must pull back then!"

"They'll never allow it. The men are already running, those who are able. There's no more to be done."

"Palmer—"

"Come, my lord!" Palmer cried, galloping away from the battlefield. Tom looked back at the battle scene. Truly there was no hope. He spurred his horse after Palmer.

They stopped for only a moment in a secluded grove to shed the armor that would slow their flight and make capture almost certain. When they returned to the road, Stephen's men were close behind them.

"Give yourselves up!" Weatherford ordered.

Tom and Palmer veered away from him and from the horsemen pursuing them and tried to plunge into the woods.

Tom tore ahead of his servant, seeing a path through the dense thicket. "Come on!" he shouted. Then he saw Palmer slow down long enough to pull his crossbow . "No, not now! Come on, man! We can never beat them in a fight!"

"Go on, my lord! I will hold them here!"

Even as he said it, one of the soldiers took aim and shot. Palmer fell from his saddle.

"Palmer!"

Tom leapt from his saddle and took one long stride toward his friend's still form.

"Get him!" Weatherford ordered, pointing at Tom. "Hurry before he goes back into the forest! And take him alive!"

Tom bounded toward his horse, but the animal shied away from him and disappeared into the trees. Tom followed on foot, knowing he had no other hope of escape.

The soldiers were no more than twenty yards behind him, but their horses slowed them down, forced them to pick the wider paths and more open spaces. Tom wriggled between the dense trees and sometimes climbed them, using their branches to swing over obstacles. Soon his pursuers could no longer see him, but he could still hear them calling to one another, searching for him, cursing his deft escape.

He moved stealthily forward, hearing their voices grow more and more faint behind him. It was not long before he saw an open meadow ahead and, some ways off, a town.

"Please, God," he whispered, "show me a place of refuge."

He stepped cautiously out into the clearing and, seeing no one, began to lope across it. He had not gone fifty feet before he heard horses crash through the undergrowth to his left.

"There he is! Come on!"

Tom spun and lunged back into the woods with three of the riders hotly behind him. In desperation he scrambled up into a tree and drew his dagger, wishing furiously for the broadsword that was still strapped to his saddle.

"Jesus, help," he panted. "Please, God."

With a flash of inspiration, he resheathed his dagger and grasped a dead branch that had broken off from above and fallen onto the limb where he stood. Soon two of his pursuers lay motionless on the damp ground, and the third was backing his mount warily away, spewing curses.

"Leave me, friend," Tom warned from above the man's head. "We neither of us want to die today."

"Come down, boy. I've orders not to hurt you."

Tom smiled, a dangerous glint in his eyes. "You were one of those who killed my friend. I would say you've hurt me already."

"Come down, curse you!"

Tom raised his makeshift weapon, still smiling. "You may discuss the matter with my companion here. Your friends have already been introduced."

"I'll not tell you again! Come down!"

Tom shook his head.

The man pulled his crossbow and fitted a bolt into it. "Come on, boy. Drop that cudgel and come down."

He was close now. A shot from that distance would not miss. Tom lowered his head in surrender and dropped the branch to the ground.

Watching it fall, the soldier never saw Tom's booted feet flying toward him until they came in contact with his head and sent him sprawling. In the same fluid motion, Tom straddled the soldier's horse and burst once more onto the meadow. Quick to recover, the soldier scrambled up on one of his companions' abandoned mounts and dashed after him.

As they galloped across the wide meadow, Tom could feel the tired horse faltering beneath him. There was no chance of outrunning his pursuer. He drew the soldier's stout broadsword from its scabbard and turned his mount toward the man.

"I see there is a blade on your saddle. Pull it and let us be quit of this chase. I'll face any man in a fair fight."

The soldier reined in, too. "Very well, my lord. A fair fight."

He reached back as if to draw the sword, but snatched up a crossbow instead. Laying an arrow into the slot, he turned and shot all in an instant. Reflexively, Tom dodged and swung the flat of his sword against the man's treacherous head. That made quick end to the fair fight.

Tom looked toward the town and then at the still heap on the ground. He knew that, once they came to, this man and the two in the forest would join with the others and search for him again.

"If I were much of a soldier, I'd finish you where you lie, but then I guess I'd not be much of a man."

He swatted the riderless horse on the rump and watched it bolt away. Then he turned again toward the town. The soldiers would look for him there first, and soon, too. Regretfully, he spurred his horse and circled southeast, pushing thoughts of food and rest to the back of his mind. Speed now was his priority.

He forced his weary mount onward, riding through more dense woodland, seeing no one all the while but not sure if he was being followed. Finally he came upon a shallow stream and stopped for water for himself and his horse.

It was not until he allowed himself to rest that he realized how exhausted he was. He was used to the fighting, used to endless bloody battles, to forcing arms and legs long numb to continue on. The fight was his life. He had been raised in it and trained in it and now, regardless of his own will, he lived in it. Even so, he was wearied beyond belief. And grieved.

He managed to keep his feet when he slid to the ground, but he clung for support to his horse's neck, panting. It was only due to the narrowly spaced trees and God's own mercy that the villains had not ridden him down. And Palmer—

He pushed himself away from his heaving, lathered mount, pitying the poor beast as it stood there, head drooping almost to the ground, legs locked wide apart, eyes half-closed. It scarcely looked as if it could walk a mile farther but, thinking of the soldiers who were surely searching for him, Tom knew he had to go on.

He took a long drink and splashed his face. Then he gripped the saddle to mount again. When he did, the horse took a wheezing breath and collapsed at his feet. He saw at once that there was no use in trying to get the beast back up. Instead, he took off the saddle and bridle and left them on the ground. The broadsword he strapped around his waist.

"I cannot bring myself to destroy you," Tom told the animal, stroking its nose. "I give you your freedom instead, when you are ready to take it. You've helped me to keep mine."

He took one last drink and then started out again toward the southeast. He walked briskly, but he had gone less than a mile before it was too dark to see. He huddled under a tree for the night.

Rain came with the morning, adding damp to the cold and hunger he felt already. Still he pushed onward. All day he stumbled down the sodden path, footsore and leg-weary, soaked to the skin with rain, wondering how close Weatherford's soldiers were now. The one he had left on the meadow had been very determined. Stephen had doubtless promised a great reward to anyone who captured one of the Afton princes. His men would not give the search up easily.

Just as he was about to resign himself to sleeping again in the wet, he saw a tiny cottage almost hidden in the trees. With a grateful sigh, he loped up to the door. His knock was answered by a sharp-eyed, rawboned man dressed in little more than rags.

"I pray you," Tom asked hopefully, despite the man's scowl, "might I warm myself at your fire and shelter under your roof tonight?"

The man's frown deepened. "You'll find little cheer here," he snapped. Then he looked more closely at Tom's clothes, no longer fresh but obviously expensive. His scowl changed to a deferential smile. "But what we have here is yours to command."

Tom, too weary to wonder at his host's change of heart, thanked the man and went in. The cottage was dark inside, despite the struggling fire, and musty from the rain.

"Molly," the man called out as Tom began to warm himself, "bring the gentleman something to drink. Sit, sir, sit."

A girl of no more than fifteen came from out of the darkness at the back of the hovel. She was as thin and ragged-looking as the man, with a hungry look haunting her dark eyes. She looked Tom over appraisingly and then handed him a wooden cup full of strong, stale beer. He grimaced as he tasted it, but drank it down anyway. It had been some time since he had last eaten.

She took the cup, filled it again, and handed it back to him. He smiled gratefully and lifted the drink in a silent toast to her.

"Ah, Molly girl, you're a sweet creature," her father said almost too heartily as she brought him a cup as well. "Is she not, in faith?"

Tom nodded, feeling uncomfortable under their scrutiny.

"You've come a long way then, have you?" the man asked when Tom did not speak. "It seems you've fallen on some ill luck."

"It changes," Tom allowed, holding his hands up again to warm.

His ring caught the firelight, and the man leaned closer, squinting to study it more carefully. His eyes widened, and the girl looked at him questioningly behind Tom's back. He urged her toward the young man with a forceful nod.

"Will you have more, sir?" she asked with a bold smile. "I see your cup is empty."

"Pardon me, but is there no food?" Tom asked, aching for something to fill his empty stomach.

The man cleared his throat. "I was about to go into the village to try to sell the wood I have cut and bring home what I may from that. For now, you share in all we have."

"God shall bless your kindness," Tom told him earnestly, wishing he had not been forced to beg from those who had so little. "And in better times, I shall repay it as well."

The man nodded. "It may be late before I come back, girl. See the gentleman is well cared for."

Once he had gone, Tom moved closer to the hearth and felt the warmth of the fire and the liquor spreading through his cold bones, relaxing his tired muscles. The girl put the cup back into his hands, full again, and sat down on the bench next to him. Once more he drank deeply and then handed the cup back to her.

"Come, drink," she coaxed. "It holds off the hunger, and maybe it will help you forget whatever it is that makes you so sad."

Sudden tears filled his eyes, and he wiped them wearily away. He knew too much of Palmer's unshakable faith to doubt that he was anywhere but in heaven, and how could he truly mourn for him being there? Still, he felt the pain of irreparable loss. He should have surrendered, but it had happened so fast. So fast.

He took the cup again and emptied it. Once more she filled it and sat down next to him, nearer than before.

"I am sorry for it, whatever it is," she said, putting her hand over his, "but do not be sad anymore."

His fingers closed on hers, and he took comfort from the warm nearness of her and the tender sympathy he felt in her touch. He looked up at her, and she smiled sweetly upon him and caressed his cheek, leaning against him.

He felt a sudden heat rise in his blood and mix with the drink to muddy his thinking. "I, uh, I lost a friend yesterday."

The girl traced her finger down his jawline. "Then we should drink to his memory."

Holding his eyes with her own, she drank from his cup and then held it to his mouth. He drank more, but when he reached up to take the cup from her, she set it down on the floor and put his unprotesting arms around her.

"More?" she breathed, bringing her mouth provocatively close to his.

He leaned forward and touched his lips to hers. Her arms tightened around him, and he began to kiss her in earnest, the drink robbing him of his habitual restraint.

"I'll have that ring first," she murmured in his ear.

He froze as her words seeped into his muddled brain. The ring. The ring that had been entrusted to him as a Chastelayne prince. She'd have the ring and all that it meant. She'd have his honor, his faith, the last bit of his pride. She'd have the ring first.

With one sobering shake of his head, he could see clearly again—the wretchedness of the hovel, the miserable inadequacy of the fire, the hungry desperation in the eyes of the girl. There was no comfort here. He took one quick breath as if he had been stung and then swiftly unclasped her hands from behind his neck.

"What is the matter?" she asked, a tinge of fear in her eyes.

He wiped his mouth with the back of his hand and stood up unsteadily. The memory of his Elizabeth, his wife—standing in the cathedral, her dark eyes pleading behind their fear, hardly hoping yet desperately needing him to be the honest, faithful lover he had pledged to be—rose before him, shaming him with her defenseless reliance on the pledge he had made. Now exhaustion and grief and hunger and loneliness had all conspired against him, had come near to besting him in one moment of laxness, almost before he had realized. *Oh, Bess—*

"I have presumed too much."

"I am willing," Molly protested, standing and putting her arms around his waist.

"No." He pulled back, but she would not let him go. He grabbed her wrists and sat her down roughly, holding her away from him. "I cannot—"

Seeing her frightened expression, he softened his own, feeling a sudden compassion for her. She was so young, younger than Elizabeth. Whatever she was, whatever she had done, she was still just a girl. He sat down and forced his breathing to slow, his pulse to beat temperately.

"It was wrong of me to repay your father's hospitality with such ungentlemanly coin," he said, chivalrously overlooking the part she had played. "Forgive me."

Her lip quivered. "Please. He will beat me if I let you leave here and have nothing from you."

"Your father?"

She nodded. "He wants that ring especially, I could tell. We rarely see anything so fine."

Tom swallowed down a sudden hatred for the man. "You do not know what you ask. This ring was given me in trust and is not mine to give. Besides, I would not want to dishonor you. You deserve better than to be used so."

"Me?"

"Do not fear. I will speak to your father when he returns. I promise you I will repay your hospitality ten times this ring's worth the very hour I am able. I will tell him so. Surely he'll not beat you then."

"And you are not angry with me?"

"No. Only with myself perhaps and with this miserable world. Maybe when we have peace again, we can find you a better means of earning your living."

Her expression told him plainly that this was the closest to kindness she had ever been shown. Without warning, she pressed herself to him again and tried to kiss him. He put her firmly away.

"I told you the ring is not mine to give."

"I would ask nothing in payment," she insisted. He saw that his refusal had hurt her.

"My body is not mine to give either," he told her gently. "It belongs first to God, then to the sweetest lady in Christendom. I have already betrayed them both tonight. I'll not compound my fault any further."

"I wanted only to thank you," she said, confused and ashamed.

"Show me where I may lay my head for the night." He kissed her hand as if she were a fine lady. "That will be thanks and plenty."

The gnawing hunger woke him the next morning very early, and try as he might, he could not seem to fall asleep again. He lay on the thin pallet of straw trying to stretch the soreness out of his stiff limbs and stop the merciless hammering inside his head, wondering if he dared stay until the man returned with the food he had promised. Two days since the battle now, two days since Palmer had died, and no word of Stephen or of Philip.

He got up when the girl came to put more wood on the fire.

"Good morning."

"I hope I've not awakened you, sir."

"No. I was just debating whether I ought to wait any longer for your father to return. I should leave here before sunrise."

"But you were going to speak to him for me," she reminded him, looking very worried. "About the ring."

"Yes, and I will, to be sure. And do not worry. Have faith, and God will help you."

"He helps them that helps themselves."

Startled, the two spun around and saw the girl's father standing in the darkness near the door.

"It behooves a man to make shift for himself," the man went on. "One king or another makes us little difference. It is if we shall eat today concerns us most." He tossed up a small heavy bag, and it made chinking noises as he caught it again. "I thank you, my lord, for this."

He flung open the door, and soldiers poured into the tiny room, their swords drawn, Weatherford at their head.

"No," the girl wailed.

Tom turned grimly to the smug-faced lord.

"At last," Weatherford said. "I should have expected to find you with some strumpet. Well, look once more on him, girl. You'll not find him so comely if you see him after the king's justice." He kicked over the bench that stood between them and put the point of his sword to Tom's throat. "Bind him," he ordered, and two of his soldiers wrenched Tom's arms behind his back.

"Comfortable, my lord of Brenden?" he asked once they had finished.

Tom nodded. "More so than you could be, my lord, with so much death on your conscience, supporting a man like Ellenshaw."

"Keep still," Weatherford commanded, striking him across the mouth, drawing blood.

"Oh, forgive me, my lord prince!" Molly sobbed, realizing whom she had helped betray. "Forgive me. I did not know!"

"No fault of yours," Tom said, looking with tight-lipped accusation at her father.

The man merely tossed the heavy bag once more into the air and caught it, watching emotionlessly as Tom was taken from the hovel out to where the horses and the other soldiers were. Molly followed after, her eyes wide and full of remorse.

"Put a halter on him like the gallows meat he is!" Weatherford ordered. One of the soldiers forced Tom to his knees and knotted a rope around his neck.

"Now comes *your* turn to walk," the soldier said with a gloating sneer. It was the man Tom had left in the meadow two days before. A long, narrow bruise ran down the side of his face.

"I spared your life when I could just as easily have taken it," Tom reminded him coolly.

The soldier pulled him roughly to his feet. "The more fool you."

"Move on!" Weatherford commanded. Tying the rope to his saddle, he urged his horse forward.

The soldiers kept up a brisk pace, Weatherford riding just fast enough to keep Tom at a half-running trot. When finally they halted, Tom dropped exhausted to the ground, his parched tongue clinging to the roof of his mouth, his heart pounding like a rabbit's. He swallowed painfully and twisted his neck to shift the rope away from the raw places it was rubbing on his skin. Then he noticed Weatherford watching him.

"I trust you are enjoying your walk."

Tom licked his dry lips and dredged up an unconquered grin. "It is a fine day for it."

"Savor it, my lord. It's likely to be your last."

They soon set off again. By nightfall Tom was standing before his cousin's makeshift throne in the great hall at Cold Spring Castle.

CHAPTER

STEPHEN WAS JUST AS TOM REMEMBERED HIM. IT OCCURRED TO Tom, as it had at their first meeting, that this supposed heir to the Lynaleigh throne did not look much like Chastelayne nobility. His limbs were thick and heavily muscled, and he lacked the lithe agility that graced his Afton cousins. His blond hair hung limply around his dough-complected face, a face that might have been handsome but for the marks of reckless cruelty on it. He was King Edward's son—there was enough Chastelayne in him to attest to that, but only just.

"I am quite pleased to see you here, cousin," Stephen said, the look in his pale eyes frighteningly sincere. "Really quite pleased."

Tom made an elaborate bow. "I am gratified, my lord of Ellenshaw, and honored by your kind attentions. May I ask what you intend for me now?"

"I mean you no harm, cousin. You and your father and your brother, too, are guilty of treason and murder. My duty as your king is to see the law satisfied in these matters. Nothing more."

"Nothing more than hanging, drawing, and quartering. Again I am gratified. May I be allowed to see my father?"

"If that pleases you. I for one am loath to see families parted. Even now I wish with all my heart that your brother were here with us."

"Yes," Tom replied, "I am certain you do."

"Yes. Well, perhaps that can be remedied soon. I hear he has his army at Lindfors and is stubbornly refusing to yield to my forces. Still, there will be time enough, I'll warrant, to teach him the folly of false pride. Come, I will send you to your father now. Pity you've come so late though. You've just missed supper." His mouth twisted into a sardonic grin when he saw Tom swallow hungrily. "But you'll be all the keener for breakfast in the morning."

Tom bowed once again. "Most considerate, my lord."

Bidding his host good night, Tom followed his guards through a maze of corridors and finally down into the depths of Stephen's dungeon. In the deepest passageway, posted with guards every few feet, was the captive king's cell. The silent soldiers opened the door and stepped aside to let Tom enter. Once they had freed his hands, they locked the door on him.

"Father?"

The prisoner stopped pacing and lifted his head, a suspicious, searching look on his face. Tom came closer, dismayed by the toll captivity had taken on his father. Robert was not old, scarcely forty, yet he looked older by far and as ravaged by grief and care as King Edward had when Tom had last seen him.

"Father?" Tom repeated.

Robert's expression turned to one of astonished recognition. "Tom? Oh, Tom, have they taken you, too?" He pulled his son into a crushing embrace. "It's a selfish thing, boy, but I am glad you are here."

Tom returned the hug, understanding.

"You are well, son?" Robert asked, eyeing Tom's swollen lip and his many bruises.

"I am hungrier than I would like but well enough. Are you well treated?"

"Better than I deserve."

Tom looked at him, puzzled. "Father—"

"Have you had news of Philip?" Robert asked anxiously.

"Rarely, and that I've had I can hardly trust. I heard he was in

Deerfield, but Stephen told me just a moment ago that he was at Lindfors and likely to be taken. I cannot tell which is true, if either, but you mustn't worry for him. God is watching over him, better than you or I could."

"How can I not worry for him?" Robert sat down on the bed and dropped his head into his hands, his whole aspect deeply engraved with grief. "When I think of what I have made him to endure for my sake. What grief I've brought all of you boys for my ambition! Dear God, I would not lay upon my greatest enemy such a burden of sorrow, much less upon my own sons. It is a bitter thing for a man to know he destroys everything he touches."

"You mustn't think that."

"I've had a long while to think, Tom. If nothing else, Stephen has given me time to reflect upon my life. I see now what I am, but it is not what I had meant to be. I knew it would not come cheaply, this throne, but I thought I could quickly regain what I gave up to get it. Now I see I paid for it with things that I can never buy back." He rubbed his furrowed brow. "I knew I could win the people as hero of the Riverlands, so I paid for my warrior reputation with your mother's love. My long absences from home told her plainly which I valued more highly, although I cannot say now whether I ever truly had her love at all. I paid with my sons, too. Richard is dead, Philip is as lost to me as if he were dead, and even you, Tom . . ." He looked up for a moment, searching for something. "That trusting admiration that once burned in your eyes is gone."

Tom looked down and said nothing, knowing he could not deny his father's words.

"I lost my sons' respect and my own," Robert mourned, covering his face again. "And the lives I've thrown away. God forgive me—that unborn child of Philip's. I knew it was his."

"Unborn child?"

"And the Fletcher girl pled so for it. I can hear her still."

"Katherine was to have a child?" Tom felt a sting of pain. "Does Philip know?"

Robert's head drooped lower. "She said she'd not told him yet. I never could tell him. It would only be cruelty for him to know now. But I know. That sin of mine hangs hard and heavy in my heart, more than all the rest. That and one other."

"John."

"John." Slow, hot tears ran down Robert's cheeks. "I told myself I had done what I must, but seeing him lying there in Tanglewood—he was such a boy yet. Lying there, he did not belong to the sins of his faithless mother anymore. He was not even Albright's bastard. He was just John. My John. The little boy I had held in my arms. Oh, Tom. Tom. So many wrongs. So many wrongs I can never make right. I did what pleased me to get the crown, thinking I could get forgiveness later. Now I've gone too far to even ask."

"Ask, Father. God always forgives a repentant heart."

"He sees me for what I am. He knows all of my iniquities. How can He ever forgive me? I know Philip never will."

"Philip must forgive you. The hate will kill him if he does not."

"I've done him wrong, Tom. I've done all of you so much wrong, but I never meant not to love you. I thought I could make everything right again once I had the crown. Now I've lost it all."

"You must believe that God will forgive you if you ask Him."

"No. I am beyond forgiveness, even from Him. I'll not ask the impossible."

"No, Father, please. Never give up hope. God's mercy goes beyond what we can ever hope to know. He will—"

"Stop, Tom." Robert looked up, his face drawn and weary and resigned to hopelessness. "Sit here by me, son, but let's not talk anymore. I cannot think about this anymore tonight."

Tom sat down on the bed, resting his tired shoulders against the damp wall, hardly able to stay awake any longer.

Despite his own request, Robert could not bear the silence for very long. "What happened to your men, Tom?"

"I lost them. At Grant two days ago. Every one of them." He fought to stay awake, but his eyelashes fluttered and came to rest on his cheeks. "Sorry."

Seeing he was asleep, Robert stood up and laid him down gently on the bed. Then he covered him with the musty blanket and began pacing again.

The rustle of footsteps on the rush-strewn floor was the first sound Tom heard when he woke several hours later. He struggled with his sluggish muscles and then managed to sit up.

"You should not have given me your bed," he said, groggily rubbing his eyes.

"I sleep very little these days. Here, eat."

Robert offered him a piece of black bread, and Tom wolfed it down, wincing as it scratched its way down his raw throat.

"They're taking us to Winton today. I've just been told."

"Winton?" Tom asked, the word muffled by food.

"We're to be tried for treason. Stephen will have us brought openly before his nobility, before the people. He wants them all to see that he is just in making away with us. There's little doubt what verdict Stephen's court will bring."

Robert looked puzzled to see his son's quick grin.

"Do you not see, Father? If they kept us here for trial, there would be no hope at all that we might escape. But outside these walls, who can say what might happen? It is a long way to Winton."

"Philip is in Deerfield or Lindfors, you said. We cannot hope that he will be able to rescue us. We cannot hope at all."

Stephen had realized too late that it was a mistake to bring his prisoners openly through the streets, even in such an insignificant town as this Breebonne was. Tom could see that he ruled now only by the force of his army. In the people's eyes, Robert of Afton was still king.

The usurper rode at the center of a band of soldiers, rough Alensbrook men scarcely tamed by the gold with which he purchased their protection. They obeyed him without question, even seemed to take pleasure in the show of force, but it was obvious that their only loyalty was to his purse.

Tom and his father rode just behind their captor on jaded nags that could barely manage to keep plodding forward. Both of them were dressed in rags, unshaven, bound at the wrists, but only Robert looked defeated. Tom rode easily, as if he were still astride his fine thoroughbred, looking out over the people who lined the street, wordlessly conveying to them the fragment of hope he kept always in his heart.

Hearing the ominous murmur of the crowd, Stephen looked back fearfully at his prisoners. He could not afford to lose them now.

"Poor bonny boy," a peasant woman said, looking at Tom. He gave her a brave smile, and she began to weep openly.

Her husband, a vigorous-looking old man, put his arm around her. "Bloody usurper!" he shouted, shaking his fist at Stephen.

The self-styled king turned eyes of fury on the crowd, and they began to cry out, "God save King Robert! Down with the usurper!"

Stephen pulled his horse closer to the captain of his bodyguard, a swarthy-faced man, broad-backed and black-bearded. "Do not let my prisoners escape my hands, Cafton. See to it."

Cafton nodded his head and turned to one of his men. The word passed quickly to the others.

The crowd became louder and angrier as the troop passed through the center of town. Soon the press of bodies completely stopped the horses.

"I charge you in His Majesty's name, let us pass in peace!" Cafton's orders only made the crowd more hostile.

"Peasant slaves!" Stephen shouted over the noise. "We command that you let our royal person pass through with no further hindrance!"

"Release the king!" came the strident reply.

"Bloody tyrant!" another voice cried. "Give us our king!"

A stone whizzed from out of the crowd, thudding against Stephen's chest, causing his high-strung horse to rear up.

"Rescue the king! Save the king and the prince!"

Taking advantage of the sudden confusion, the townsmen swarmed around the usurper's bodyguard, and Tom felt himself lifted from his horse and dragged roughly over its back by many hands. They set him on his feet, protecting him with their own bodies, and he twisted around trying to see what was happening to Robert.

"My father!" he cried, struggling back toward the king. He stumbled over a body, but the press of men around him kept him on his feet.

"This way, my lord," one of them shouted, seeking to turn him back, but Tom fought their protective hold.

"The king! You must save the king!"

He saw Stephen shouting orders to his men but could not hear what he was saying. Then he watched in horror as three of them dragged Robert from his horse and the one called Cafton cut his throat. Blood spurted on the murderer, on the shrieking women who stood witness to the savage act, on the usurper himself. Stephen's fair hair was bright with it, and he tried to scrub it from his face while backing his skittish mount toward the city gate.

"No!" Tom screamed, frantically struggling with the ropes that still bound his wrists. The man guarding his back was killed by one of Stephen's men, who was killed in turn by another of the townsmen.

A tall blond man quickly took charge of the situation. "Come, it's too late, my lord!" he said as he filled the place at Tom's back.

They had to pull Tom off his feet and drag him away from the melee. His last sight of his father was of his blood-soaked corpse being slung over a horse as the Alensbrook men defended Stephen's escape.

The men of Breebonne took Tom to a peasant hut and sat him down before the fire. Kneeling before him, the tall man gently removed Tom's bonds. "You'll be safe, my lord. They'll not look for you here if they've a mind to come back for you."

Someone thrust a cup of bitter ale into Tom's numb hands, and he held tightly to it, trembling.

"Stephen has fled," one of the men said, "and his soldiers, too!"

"Yes," another answered, "but he shall be back and with more men. Breebonne will pay for this."

A murmur of agreement and fear went through the men, and their words sank finally into Tom's mind. Because of their efforts, he had been rescued from Stephen's hands and certain death. He could not let them suffer the sure-to-come revenge.

He drained his cup at a gulp and set it wearily on the rough table. "Do not fear. Afton does not forget her friends. My brother Philip will see you do not suffer for your loyalty."

"How can Afton protect us if she cannot keep her own safe?"

Before Tom could answer, a woman's voice came from the back of the room. "Peace, for shame! To badger the young prince so now!"

It was the woman who had wept for him earlier in the street. She pushed her way through the men and came to stand near Tom. "Go outside and do your plotting and worrying," she scolded. "There's nothing more can be done here. Let the prince have some rest now."

"Come, lads," the tall man agreed, bowing briefly to Tom. "We must see to our own safety."

Tom looked up at him, too spent to stand. "Send to my brother. He will not let you go unrewarded." He was finding it difficult now to concentrate on what he was saying.

The peasants filed silently out of the room. As he watched them go, exhaustion overcame Tom. He rubbed his eyes, and the woman put a motherly arm around him and pushed the hair from his forehead. Unable to stay brave in the face of her pity, he leaned against her and put his arms tightly around her thick waist, letting the tears flood from him.

"Oh, poor, poor boy," she clucked sympathetically as she sat next to him, hugging him closely, comforting him as she had her own children.

"My father, my father," he sobbed again and again, feeling the familiar pain in his chest, as if his heart were being squeezed by a strong hand.

She held him there for a long time, consoling and comforting, until he had calmed. Then she gently took his arms from around her and laid his head down in her lap. "Shh," she soothed, stroking his sweat-matted hair. Taking a handkerchief from her sleeve, she tenderly wiped his face. He was soon asleep. Only then did she dry her own tears.

When her husband came in, he saw her there, still tear-stained. He looked at Tom intently for a moment and then bent over and kissed the woman's cheek. She wiped her eyes again and smiled a little.

"Miserable business, this," he said gruffly, "murderin' a king."

She put a finger to her lips, eased Tom's head off her lap, and stood up, smoothing her rumpled skirt.

"Poor poppet," she whispered. "It breaks my very heart."

"The king himself and many a good man else killed today, and there's no telling how many when Stephen returns."

"Maybe we should have him away tonight," she said, darting a glance in Tom's direction.

"No, do not worry tonight. Stephen will make straight for Winton for his army there. He could never come back here before tomorrow night very late, but rest assured he'll be back sooner than we could wish."

The next morning a ragged, bloodied soldier rode into Chrisdale.

"Where is my lord of Caladen?" he panted as he dismounted.

"What are you doing here?" Dunois demanded.

The soldier gasped for breath. "My lord of Caladen," he asked again, "where is he?"

Dunois grabbed him by the shoulders. "Speak, dog!" he commanded, raising his hand to the man, but his arm was stopped short by a strong grip on his wrist.

"Let him go," Philip ordered, his soft voice steely. The soldier slid to his knees in relief.

"You must hear me, my lord."

"Palmer? By heavens, Palmer! Where is Tom? Tell me, man!"

"My lord, the king—," Palmer blurted. Then he ducked his head and began again more carefully. "My lord, His Majesty, your royal father, is dead. He was killed yesterday at Breebonne."

Philip felt the blood rush out of his face.

"Killed?" Dunois snapped, seizing Palmer by the front of his jerkin, but Philip pushed him away.

"Leave us!" he thundered. With a dogged nod of his head, Dunois obeyed.

"I am sorry, my lord," Palmer said, "to give you such news so bluntly, but Lord Tom being also captive to the usurper—"

"Oh, not Tom, too! He hasn't murdered Tom!"

"No, no, my lord," Palmer assured him. "He was there but rescued by the men of Breebonne."

Philip exhaled painfully. "Thank God."

"He was rescued, but, being alone and unprotected, he is easy prey for Ellenshaw if he should come once more against Breebonne for revenge. I beg you, bring your power to help them as soon as you are able."

"But Tom is safe, you say?"

"He is, my lord, for now."

"How is it that you were separated from him?"

"We were at Grant. Ellenshaw's men destroyed our army there, and Lord Tom and I tried to escape. I was wounded and left for dead, not of consequence enough to be made sure of, I expect. I thought Lord Tom had gotten clean away, and I went to Breebonne to take shelter. There I saw what happened, but I could not get to him before the people there spirited him off. I thought it best to let you hear of it as quickly as I could."

Philip pulled the exhausted man to his feet. "Go to the captain of my guard and tell him to be ready at his first speed to march to Breebonne. Quick!"

Returning to his chamber, Philip had his servants ready him for a swift departure. Dunois was quick to come to him. "My condolences on your gracious father's death, Your Majesty," he said smoothly.

Philip's mind was too full of Palmer's news to take the chamberlain's full meaning. "I thank you, my lord," he said automatically, pulling tight the strap on his boot.

Every moment he struggled to keep his expression calm and controlled. The gentlemen of his chamber, Rafe and the rest, were watching him closely. He could see on their faces the uncertainty and fear they felt at the death of a king, but Dunois seemed unruffled.

"I hope Your Majesty will remember those who served your father well and will take them also into your grace and favor," he said more pointedly.

"There's no time for this now, my lord," Philip told him, scooping up his gloves. "Stay here until I send for you. I shall need you in Winton once it is ours again."

He left the room calling for his horse. Dunois watched after him, a look of pure hatred in his eyes.

Philip walked quickly out to the square and then stopped short. There waiting for him were all of his nobles, his soldiers, and the people of the town. Seeing him, they knelt, and his eyes met theirs steadily. He would not allow them to see his reeling emotions.

Eastbrook stood, stepped forward, and knelt again at Philip's feet. "May I be the first, my lord, to swear my allegiance and pledge my sword to Your Majesty."

There was that word again, the one that put such fear into Philip's heart. *Majesty*. It was used only for kings, and he could no longer ignore it. He nodded, shaken.

"Do not grieve, lad," his old teacher said, standing and taking his arm. Then he released it quickly, as if he felt he had presumed too much, been too familiar with this new king. "Your father's murder shall be avenged, Your Majesty. Never doubt it."

Philip nodded again, glad to let them think grief and not fear was the cause of his pallor. The others followed Eastbrook's example, kneeling to him and swearing their loyalty, but he hardly saw them, barely heard them. He was thinking of the rest of the nobility, the rest of the people. Would they, too, swear? Or would they, fearing his youth and inexperience, turn to Stephen for their king? Surely they would if ever they saw into the tumult of emotion behind his stiff expression.

God, he thought, nodding automatically as they filed past him, *You have put more upon me than I can bear. I cannot accomplish what You have given me to do.*

You can, boy. You can.

It sent a shiver through him to remember his father's words, but then he realized that he had withstood all that had been laid upon him because he had had no choice. Now he was charged with the care of a country, not just an army, a country divided and in unrest. He did not feel equal to the task. Yet the nobility, it seemed, trusted him with their lives and their fortunes.

Following like sheep, he thought. Perhaps they could smell the slaughterhouse ahead but saw no way out but through it.

They were in duty bound to follow him, as he was bound to lead, but he could see in their eyes their despair and their fear. He must not show them his, or they would truly be lost to him. He could not afford to lose them now, not if he were to keep his crown and his head.

He had long been aware that, once his father died, he would have to fight to stay alive. He could resign his right to the throne for himself and for his heirs into perpetuity, leaving this burden on Tom's shoulders. If Tom were to do the same, leaving their cousin with the right to rule, Stephen would never allow it to end there, not so long as anyone with a higher claim was left alive. Even if he would, Philip knew he could never leave his people to struggle under Stephen's cruel reign. That was part of the weight of his charge. He must fight on.

Under close watch of the men who had rescued him, Tom knelt before the altar of the little church in Breebonne, praying earnestly for Elizabeth and Philip and Rosalynde, for his protectors, and for the dear woman who had comforted him.

"God, I do not even know her name, but You do. Bless her and her good husband." He prayed for his men and for peace to come soon, even at this blackest hour. "God, my father is dead," he whispered, as if the Omniscient One did not already know.

He felt his grief come down hard on him then. Unable to force the vision of his father's murder from his mind, he heard again the din of the crowd and the soldiers and felt the claustrophobic crush of the townspeople. Again he felt his breath come with difficulty and the blood beat jerkily in his veins. Again he saw the terror in his father's eyes and the sudden thick gush of crimson from his throat and his mouth.

He knew he must have cried out, because he felt a steadying hand on his shoulder. Wiping the sweat from his face, he opened his eyes and turned around.

"Philip! Oh, Philip, it's been a black, black day."

He got to his feet, and the brothers embraced.

"Palmer was in the town when it happened. He brought me word."

"Palmer? No, he is dead."

"Not so, my lord," Palmer said, coming out from among Philip's men.

"Palmer. Oh, thank God, Palmer." Tom clasped his friend's hand and then pulled him into his arms. "Thank God."

"I am sorry about your father, my lord."

"There will be justice," Philip said, his face unreadable. Tom wondered if he meant for Stephen or for Robert, but he did not ask.

Philip looked at Tom for a moment, as if satisfying himself that he was indeed all right. Then he clasped his brother's shoulder and turned him toward the door.

"Come on, Tom. Let's be gone from here before Stephen can come back against us."

"Did you not bring any soldiers to defend Breebonne?"

"Tom, I haven't the men to garrison this town and scarcely money enough to pay those soldiers I have."

"We cannot leave them so, Philip. They died in the streets to save me. One of them was killed at my back. I've pledged my word!"

"Tom, I know you do not give your word lightly, but I cannot make it good. I cannot!"

Tom bowed his head. Then he looked up quickly. "Then let us leave Breebonne."

The tall blond man came from the back of the chapel, almost indignant. "My lord of Brenden—"

Tom grinned. "Leave Breebonne, Philip, and take your men to Winton. Do not let Stephen catch his breath."

Palmer smiled, admiring Tom's unbowed spirit.

Philip was aghast. "Have you gone mad? Attack Winton with Stephen's greatest power there? With our king new-killed and the men with their hearts in their boots? Are you weary of your life that you say so?"

Tom's smile widened. "So Stephen will think as well, and he'll never look for us to attack yet. Besides, he was routed from this city, hardly escaping with his life and a few of his men." He looked with admiration at his protectors. "These men of Breebonne fight as if each of them were possessed of two score devils."

"We will gladly come with you, my lords," the blond man pledged. "We want payment for the slaughter of our townspeople and our king."

Philip could not resist a tight smile. "Tom, only you could convince me that this lunatic plan will prove good strategy for Afton."

CHAPTER

II

"WARD HIM ABOUT WITH YOUR ANGELS, DEAR GOD," ROSALYNDE prayed as she looked out toward the south, toward the war. More than two months had passed since Philip had left her. "Open a way for him, sweet Lord, and give him victory." She wandered back to the bed where they had last lain together and smoothed the coverlet, hardly conscious anymore of the petitions so constantly on her lips. "Show him Your mercy, Lord, and bring him safe home."

She wondered where he was. A late winter had allowed the war to continue on through October, and she had such uncertain reports of the battles, of victories and defeats, that she did not know whether to weep or rejoice at them.

"Oh, God, let it be Your will that he come back safe again to me."

"My lady, there is a messenger coming from the south!" Julia cried as she scurried into the chamber. The other waiting women crowded around, eager for the news. Rosalynde ran to her.

"Oh, from my lord?"

"The soldiers say it is very like."

Rosalynde fairly flew down the stairs, and the messenger dropped to one knee as she reached the front step. She stopped, panting, before him.

"God save you, Your Majesty," he said.

"Majesty?"

Rosalynde looked back bewildered at Darlington's steward, and he quickly took her arm. "Come, my lady, it is scarcely fit for you to stand out in the damp so to receive a messenger. Come in, fellow. Deliver yourself with more seemliness."

"No," Rosalynde said, recovering herself. "I would hear this news here and now. Why do you call me Majesty?"

The messenger bowed his head. "King Robert is dead, lady. My lord Philip is now king."

"King?" she breathed, her eyes blazing and her face deadly white. "Where is he?"

"Coming, my lady, with some few of his men to return Your Majesty to Winton."

"Then it belongs once more to Afton!"

"It does, my lady. When King Robert was killed, the usurper returned to the city, and all of us, from my lord Philip's army and from my lord Tom's, joined together to follow him there." Amusement flickered in the messenger's eyes. "It seems the people of Winton did not much relish his reign and were happy to give some stealthy aid from inside the walls to let us in. Lord Tom keeps the city now, and our king is in pursuit of Ellenshaw himself. The traitor fled northward and will likely try to escape us by moving east and then south to refuge in Cold Spring."

"But the king is coming here, you say?"

"He is, my lady, not a quarter of an hour behind. You are to send some of your ladies ahead to make ready for your return to Winton, and the king will set out with you in the morning under the protection of his army."

"We shall be ready," she said. She spied Julia peeking out the doorway. "Go tell the others, Julia. Tell Ursula and Helena they are to go with you to Winton now. The others will attend me until my lord and I can ourselves return. Tell them all to make ready. Hurry."

With a swift curtsey, Julia scurried away.

Rosalynde clutched the messenger's arm. "He is well? He is not wounded?"

"Oh, no, my lady. His Majesty is well and whole, God bless his grace, and longing for a sight of your ladyship, if we may judge by his haste."

He grinned as he said it, then coughed, and ducked his head again, but Rosalynde did not notice his embarrassment. She stood gazing into the mist that rose over the fields southward, remembering that last night, her beloved's sweet tenderness, and the words that still held hope in her heart.

I could have loved you.

Did he love her now?

She trembled and could not seem to draw her breath fully. Philip was coming at last, and he was eager to be with her again. Her heart began to sing within her.

Dear God, thank You! Thank You, sweet, sweet Lord! Oh, holy, merciful—

A group of riders appeared out of the misty forest, a proud warrior-king at their head. She ran toward him, ignoring the cold, wet grasses that dragged at her skirts and soaked her velvet shoes, holding out her arms to him even from far off, her whole being crying out a joyous welcome.

She saw him urge his horse forward at the sight of her. Reaching her side, he scooped her up into his arms. Clinging to him, she kissed him again and again and again. He moved his mouth to the corner of her jaw, and her heart fluttered at his nearness.

"My lady," he said softly in her ear, "bear yourself like a queen."

Stung by the stern rebuke, she sat up stiffly before him, holding to him just enough to stay in the saddle. Was this his eagerness?

When they reached the house, she let the steward help her down. Then she knelt with the others.

"God save Your Majesty."

Philip immediately dismounted and raised her up, touching her fingers with a formal kiss.

"My sovereign lady, will you come out of the damp? All of you, we've no time for ceremony. Come, we must away in the morning."

He studied her for a moment. Then he dismissed his men and escorted her to her chamber.

"Make ready, my lady," he said. "I told you I would return you to Winton when the city and my father were free. Winton is ours again, and my father is past helping, so it is time I made good my promise, but I must be brief. Stephen is free and at the head of an army."

"Perhaps you should send to my father." She pulled the ring from her finger, the one Westered had given to Philip the day of their wedding, the one Philip would not wear. The sight of it did not please him.

"I thought I had left that in Winton."

"You did, my lord, but I thought you might wish to send it now."

"That alliance was my father's, not mine," he said, refusing to take it from her. "I'll not go to Westered again to beg."

"It would not be begging, my lord. My father offered his help out of love and friendship."

"I did not ask it of him," he said. "Not then and not now."

"But the ring, my lord."

"Keep it," he snapped. "Or leave it or bury it, what you will. I shall never need it."

"Very well," she said. She put it back on her finger, covering it with her other hand, too aware of his disapproval.

"Good night then," he said finally. "I shall come for you at dawn."

"Philip."

He turned back to her as if the familiarity startled him.

"Will you not stay, my lord?" She faltered at the look almost of scorn in his eyes, but she pitied the burdened weariness she saw there, too. "You must rest sometime."

"There is more I must attend to, my lady. I'll not disturb you tonight."

"Oh, but you would not—"

He was gone.

She rode along with him the next day, too conscious that she was only another of his duties, so hungry to be more. She had so longed to have him with her last night, if just to watch over him as he slept and know he was beside her. He was beside her now, solemn with his responsibilities, seeing to each detail himself, never relaxing for an instant.

"We shall stop the night in Attlebrae, my lady," he told her. "My lord Kimberlin has offered us the use of his house, and your ladies shall go ahead to Abbey to make a place ready for your comfort there the next night. I am certain one of Kimberlin's maids can wait upon you tonight."

"Will my ladies be safe, my lord?"

"My army is in Attlebrae now. I'll send a few of my men ahead with your gentlewomen. Then we shall all come after them the next day. It is safe enough. Stephen has no cause to come so far north. Besides, a great many of my soldiers sent their families to refuge in Abbey when Winton was taken, and they are eager to go there."

The young king and queen were received with all courtesy in Attlebrae. Philip spoke briefly to his soldiers, commending their bravery and the justice of the Afton cause, reminding them of the loved ones that waited in Abbey and how their safety rested upon Stephen's defeat. Rosalynde spoke to them, too, a shy little echo of her husband's words, and their cheers nearly overwhelmed her. Weary as they were, they were not blind to her grace and beauty, and they felt sure this fair, sweet queen was well worthy the title.

It was only a short ride to Abbey the next morning. The soldiers strained forward as they marched, boisterous and high-spirited, hungry for a few days' peace. Philip had promised they might stay in Abbey until he took the queen back to Winton and returned to lead them again. They talked and laughed along the way, their chatter growing more and more excited as Abbey came into view. Then gradually their voices died into silence.

"Stay here," Philip commanded. He spurred his horse and dismounted in the midst of the smoking ruins. The town was burned. All the inhabitants lay slain in the streets. Women, children, young, old—all slain, all butchered. Not one was left alive.

Philip saw the bodies of two of his wife's waiting women in a pitiful heap under a scorched tree. This could have been done no earlier than yesterday, and there could be no reason for it but cruel revenge. Stephen had no need to come this way if his only motive had been escape. It was all Philip could do to keep his tongue from condemning his cousin to blackest hell.

Suddenly he realized he was no longer alone. All around him the weeping and wailing rose, mounting cry upon anguished cry, the clamor frequently punctuated by heart-rending howls as yet another of his soldiers found the body of one dear to him. He walked through the maze of butchery and grief, struck dumb by the horror of it.

"Alice! Alice!"

Hearing the broken words close beside him, Philip turned. Even warped with agony as it was, the voice was familiar to him.

Peter Hawkins, his groomsman, knelt there before the splintered door of a fire-blackened house, leaning his cheek against his dead wife's cold bosom. Her stiff arms yet clutched their little boy, both mother and child run through with the same single sword thrust.

Philip knew too well the ache of losing a dearly loved wife. The horror and pity he felt was plain on his face, but Hawkins was blind to all but grief and pain and rage. He turned on his master as a mad dog might. "This is your doing!" he accused.

Philip stared at him, speechless.

"Mind your tongue before the king!" Eastbrook reprimanded, but Hawkins was beyond restraint now.

"I'll speak!" he cried. "Though it cost me my tongue, I'll speak!" He surveyed the slaughter that surrounded them and then looked intently at Philip. "We fight because of our duty to the crown. How much does duty ask? Not only soldiers die, but wives and children, women and boys! Will the king not be satisfied until he has all? I'll fight no more."

The mourners around him began to murmur their agreement.

"It was you who promised us safety for our families," one said, pointing his finger at the young king, his voice shrill over all the others. "They are safe enough now. Now nothing can harm them."

Philip lowered his head in shame. He had promised. *Follow me*, he had said, *and Lynaleigh shall be safe for your loved ones*. Safe enough indeed.

"Why should we care who is king?" another asked angrily. "Afton or Ellenshaw, what's that to us? We fight the wars and make the bread and sow the fields and breed more subjects to serve the king, and then we die. Why should we kill ourselves and our own countrymen debating who shall be king when this one or that one makes us no difference? Can this," he asked, sweeping his arm around the square, "this sacrifice to your ambition ever be justified?"

Philip could not answer, could not meet the man's penetrating, accusing eyes.

"We'll fight no more," Hawkins repeated emptily. The soldiers began to drift silently away, defeat charactered in their every step.

"Wait! You must go on fighting!"

The tearful plea stopped them, and they turned, stubbornly prepared not to hear any more. Rosalynde stood at her husband's side, the body of a little girl, perhaps three or four years old, in her arms.

"You must go on fighting," she said again. She held the small body out beseechingly before her, and the child's white-blonde hair fell thickly over her arm. "Need you any more reason why Ellenshaw should not be king?"

Philip sensed an abrupt change in the men. *Before God,* he thought, *Stephen should not be king.*

"Hear her," he said, his words no longer failing him. "If you do not wish to fight for me, for my right, I'll not hold you. But if you do not fight, you give your voice alongside Ellenshaw's in the order of more such butchery."

He put his hand on Hawkins's thin shoulder, seeing the fierce hatred was gone, and only the grief and bewilderment remained. "I mourn with you, Peter," he said gently. Then he raised his voice for all to hear. "I mourn with you all. You have lost dear ones, but they were dear to me as well because they were dear to you." He gave Hawkins's shoulder a squeeze and then began to pass through the men, speaking sympathy and comfort as he viewed each private scene of grief.

"You men have given me all you have. A king could ask no more of his subjects nor a general of his soldiers. This," he said sorrowfully, "believe me, I would have renounced my true title to the crown to prevent or I would have given my heart's blood. But, my soldiers, we cannot make these sacrifices live again. We can only seek to prevent another such slaughter by driving Ellenshaw from this land. All of you, it is for you to decide what you will do next. I've no chains on you. God knows I've seen blood and death enough to last fifty lifetimes. Go, those of you who've a mind to. I cannot fault you for it."

He paused a moment, but not a man moved from his place; not a word disturbed the thick silence. "Shall we continue on then?" he asked finally, his soft voice carrying easily on the cold air.

Hawkins looked up at him, desperation in his red-rimmed eyes. "Yes."

The others echoed him, their common grief bonding them together more firmly than any question of state could have done. Philip let out a weary breath and told Darlington to see that the dead were buried. He took the little body from Rosalynde's arms and handed it to Eastbrook.

"Bury her," he ordered. "Then take the queen back to Attlebrae. She should never have come here."

"My lord, will you not come with me?" Rosalynde asked, taking his hand. "You've had no rest and—"

"They've had no rest," he reminded her sharply. Then he brought her hand to his lips. "Forgive me, my lady, but I must see them through this. I owe them that much." He paused. "I'll not forget I owe you, too."

"Philip—"

"Go," he said thickly. Then he turned again to Eastbrook. "Take her back. I'll come with the men."

It was very late before the signs of slaughter were covered by black Lynaleighan earth and Abbey was left to smolder into oblivion. The army limped back again toward Attlebrae, demoralized and defeated. Bone-weary, Philip led them, stumbling mechanically forward, always forward. How quickly their joy in victory had been drowned in grief.

He could see the deep despair on the faces that surrounded him, but he could not afford the luxury of showing his own desperation. He knew they all looked to him for guidance and encouragement. If he did not provide it, he would lose them. Everything depended on how well he could counterfeit wisdom and confidence, but he was weary of the game, weary of these men with their grimly frightened eyes who depended on him to know all the answers and make miracles where there was no hope. He needed a quiet place and some time, time to lick his wounds and catch his breath, time to rest both mind and body, time to unshoulder his burden, if only for a moment.

Is there no refuge? he wondered numbly as they reached Attlebrae, knowing here, too, they were vulnerable.

Let God be your refuge. Take strength from Him.

He heard the words again as clearly as if Tom had just spoken them, but he pushed them to the back of his mind and called together his lieutenants. "Have you secured the town?"

"It is deserted, Your Majesty," Eastbrook informed him. "The people heard what happened in Abbey and fear Ellenshaw will come here next in search of us."

"Do we have knowledge yet of where he is?"

"Not yet, my lord, but we should have some report soon."

"Well, my lords, I put the men in your charge. Have their comforts seen to. That is all for tonight."

"Will you not speak to them once more, Your Majesty?" Darlington pled. "They are weary and grieved. Some of them have the fever. I fear that many of them will yet go after today's business."

Philip refrained from telling him to let them all go. "I'll not try to hold any man with words tonight," he said instead. "They've done too much already. Tomorrow."

"But, sire—"

"No. Tomorrow is soon enough."

With that he left them and made his way through the solemn huddled soldiers, heading toward Kimberlin's house. The men looked at him strangely, startled to see their king walking alone and unheralded. He could hear the swell of murmuring voices as he passed and knew they spoke of him. One of the bolder ones, an archer, stepped out before him and made an awkward bow.

"Pardon me, my lord king, but where will we go now?"

Philip shook his head. "I do not know, friend. You men have a rest due you, God and Ellenshaw willing. Then we must see where we can engage them again. Leave that for now though. It will come soon enough."

"Not for me," the archer said with hate in his eyes. "That was my little one Her Majesty was holding today. I had three others, too, and a wife. It cannot come soon enough for me."

Philip stared at him, grief and pity and remorse tugging at his face. Abruptly he threw his arms around the surprised man, embracing him fiercely. "Dear God, I am sorry."

"Your Majesty, I—I—"

As startled as the soldier, Philip released him and backed away, shaking his head. Then he turned and broke into a run. By the time he reached Kimberlin's house, his limbs felt heavy and weak, and he was forced to slow to a walk. The pounding in his heart slowed to an almost painless throb.

Rosalynde looked up expectantly when he pushed open the door, relief and joy mingled in her face. "Oh, my lord—"

She broke off, seeing his strained expression, the discouragement in his eyes. He took three shuffling steps to the table and dropped into a chair, his back to her, his shoulders sagging. Before she could go to him, Bonnechamp came into the room.

"Your Majesty," he said with a hasty bow, "I am sent to beg you to return to the men. My lord Eastbrook has report that Ellenshaw is no farther away than Holyvale and may be making his way here even now."

Philip slowly nodded. "I will be there."

Rafe bowed once more, relieved. "I will tell him so."

Philip flinched when the door slammed, then buried his face in his hands with a moan. Swallowing her fear of rebuff, Rosalynde went to him and put her hands on his shoulders, massaging the tension-knotted muscles. He started at her first touch but did not resist it. She continued for several minutes, pleased to feel him relax, pleased to hear his breathing slow, pleased that he did not order her away.

"Rest," she urged gently, but she knew he would not stay long.

"I must go to them," he said, his tired voice muffled and indistinct, but she put one hand on his overwarm brow and drew his head back to rest against her bosom.

"Just another moment," she said, holding him there. He made a half-hearted attempt to pull away from her. Then with another low moan, he gave himself over to his exhaustion. She rubbed his temples with her soft fingers, and he leaned into her soothing caresses, gradually going limp against her. Gaining confidence from his yielding tractability, she decided to tell him the news she had hardly been able to contain. She let her hands travel down over his shoulders to rest on his chest.

"When you speak to your soldiers, cheer them with the tidings that there will soon be another Afton prince to lead them."

Her eyes sparkled as they sought his, for she felt sure he would take as much pleasure in the news as she did, but he was Philip still and never what she expected him to be.

"You are with child?" he asked woodenly. He did not look surprised. Doubtless he knew this was the natural course of things, but he seemed unprepared, unwilling to add this burden to those he already carried.

"I had thought you would be pleased," she said uncertainly.

He sat there unmoving, still entwined in her arms. She had felt his muscles tighten again at her announcement. Yet when he spoke, it was with a calm that belied the disquiet in his heart and mind.

"A king must have an heir," he said, disentangling himself from her, "and an heir must have an inheritance. There shall be no unrest in Lynaleigh when this child is born." With that he stood up and went out to his men.

She put her hand on her stomach and tried not to cry. "He will love you, my little one," she whispered. "You are not a reality to him yet, but he will come to love you. I know he will." She sat down and pillowed her head on her arms. "He will love me, too."

She had meant only to rest her eyes, but it was dawn when the door flew open and a blast of cold air woke her. Rafe stood in the doorway with Philip unconscious in his arms.

"Philip!" she cried.

Rafe carried him to the fire. "Quick, my lady, get blankets. As many as you can."

She closed the door and went to him. "Has he been wounded, Master Bonnechamp?" She smoothed the tangled hair back from Philip's forehead and caressed his face. He was much warmer than before.

"No, but he's taken this fever that's swept through the army. I can feel it through his cloak. Please, my lady, turn down the bed and get some blankets."

She managed to find four blankets and followed Rafe into the bedchamber with them.

"Warm them," he ordered brusquely. Then he turned back to his master. "Young fool," he muttered as he began to strip off Philip's damp clothes. "Not enough food, not enough sleep, taking this whole war on your shoulders. It's a wonder you've lasted this long! Spending the night in the chill and—"

He broke off, seeing Rosalynde watching him.

"Tell me what happened, Master Bonnechamp."

"My lords Eastbrook and Darlington think that Ellenshaw is likely to come against us again at any time." He struggled for a moment with one of the rawhide bindings on Philip's leggings and finally had to cut the moisture-tightened strip before he went on. "They and my lord Philip and some of the others were debating what was to be done when he went very pale and had to steady himself against a tree. Before I could get to him, he was flat on his face in a puddle and hot as new-forged iron. Bring one of those, please you, my lady."

She handed him a warmed blanket, and he quickly bundled his master in it and put him in the bed.

"Now the others."

Soon Philip was tucked under four blankets and the coverlet. He began to struggle weakly against the stifling heat, but Rafe held him still.

"Please, my lord, rest," Rosalynde begged, but Rafe merely shook his head.

"He cannot hear you, my lady, and would not understand you if he did. This fever's not taken him lightly. We must see that he stays warm."

They kept careful watch over him as he went from restless delirium to deathlike stillness and back again. About noon Rafe scrounged some dried beef from his pouch and shared it with Rosalynde. He even boiled some and tried to get Philip to drink the broth, but Philip turned his face stubbornly away.

"Sick or well, he will have his way," Rafe observed sourly.

Rosalynde managed a smile. "You are a good man, Master Bonnechamp, despite your grumbling. I hope I can find another like you to tend to my child as faithfully as you do his father."

"Does Your Majesty mean to say—"

"Yes," she said, the glow rekindling in her eyes. "This summer."

"So that was what he meant," Rafe said almost to himself. Then he smiled, too. "I am happy for you, my lady."

"What who meant?"

"He told us last night that we must fight on now. If not for him, for the Afton that is to be."

Just then a frantic pounding came on the chamber door, and Darlington entered. "Where is the king?"

"He is very ill," Rafe said.

"I must speak to him."

"Speak," Rafe told him, gesturing toward the bed, "but he'll not hear you."

"You must wake him, Bonnechamp! Ellenshaw's ordered his men to set the town afire!"

"Fire!" Rosalynde cried, and Philip stirred.

"What of the army, my lord Darlington?" Rafe asked, taking Rosalynde's arm to still her.

"Ellenshaw is driving us back north. We cannot stand against him, for all that we might want to. We must leave here and rally later on. Wake him up."

"My lord, I cannot. He is unconscious."

Darlington pushed past him and went to Philip's side. "Your Majesty, please, you must hear me. Ellenshaw is going to burn Attlebrae and us in it if we do nothing."

Philip's eyes did not open, but he began to breathe faster and struggled once more against the weight of blankets over him.

"Please, my lord," Rafe insisted, trying to pull Darlington away, "he is not well enough for this."

"He will be dead if we stay here and do nothing! Do you want him to burn?"

"No," Philip murmured, struggling harder, "do not let her burn. Please, not the fire. Oh, my God, Your Majesty, please, Father, not the fire!"

His brow furrowed with deep pain, and Rosalynde began to cry. "Shh, Philip," she whispered, stroking his hair. "Everything is well. She is safe."

"Please, my lord," Rafe said, "leave him now. This is too much."

"Are you ordering me, Master Bonnechamp?" Darlington asked indignantly.

Rosalynde turned on him fiercely. "I will, my lord! I think, being your queen, I may! Whatever men you have yet, you must go on defending the town as best you can. His Majesty cannot be disturbed any further."

She had never before given him a command, and, taken aback by her authoritative tone, he bowed. "Just as you say, Your Majesty. We will do what can be done." In another instant he was gone.

Philip thrashed against the confining blankets and managed to throw them off, but Rafe pulled them back over him.

"No, my lord. Lie still now."

Philip opened his eyes and stared wildly at him. "Rafe?"

"I am here. Lie still."

"They are going to burn her!" Philip cried deliriously, fighting to sit up. "Please, God, Rafe, stop them!"

Holding him down, Rafe turned to Rosalynde. "Bring some water, my lady. Quickly."

She snatched up the bucket and brought it to the bedside.

"What are we to do?" she asked as she held the dipper to Philip's mouth, but Philip shoved it and her away.

"Rafe, do not let them! Please, God, have mercy—not the fire!"

"Shh, my lord," Rafe said. "You must lie still. She will not be harmed."

Philip's breath was coming in gasping sobs now. "You do not speak true. They'll burn her sure."

Rafe grabbed Rosalynde's arm and pulled her close to his master. "Here, my lord. She is here." He lowered his voice. "Speak to him, girl."

"I am here, my lord," she said.

Philip stared at her without seeing. Then he smiled a little and put his hands on her face.

"My sweet love," he whispered. He drew her to him, against his hot skin. She nestled there, soothing him with gentle words and caresses, and soon his breathing slowed and became regular. Thinking he slept, she moved away from him. He immediately grew restless again. Rafe tried once more to get him to drink, but Philip threw up his arm, flinging water and dipper against the wall.

"Shh, my lord, I am here," Rosalynde assured him.

He grasped her hands tightly and drew her close, murmuring tender, garbled words against her hair until he fell into a heavy sleep. For a short while there was peace in the house. Then Darlington dashed back into the chamber, this time without knocking.

"Please, Your Majesty," he said to Rosalynde, "you must wake the king. If you cannot, then at least get him away from here. Ellenshaw will be coming very soon. The south side of the town is gone already. I do not know how much longer our men will last, and help is not likely to come before they are spent."

She looked up at Rafe. "What shall we do?"

Rafe shook his head. "We should not take him out into the cold unless, as my lord says, Ellenshaw is burning the town around us."

"You doubt me, man?" Darlington asked indignantly. "Look outside!"

Rosalynde looked anxiously at Rafe. "If it is so bad, we should leave now."

Rafe bowed. "I will see how the battle goes and be back to you in a moment. Stay near the king."

"I will."

Darlington bowed, too. "I will try to defend this house awhile longer, Your Majesty. Pray God, I can."

Once they had gone, Rosalynde got into bed next to her husband, thankful that he was resting quietly at least for now. Still holding him close, she prayed fervently for his recovery and for his safety, for Afton's success in the battle, and a merciful end to the war. She had no desire to look out into the streets to see how near the fighting was. It made no difference.

It was dark before Rafe returned. His nose was bloodied and bruised, and he smelled heavily of smoke. There was blood all down the front of his jerkin and on the sword in his hand.

"We must leave now, my lady," he said, his voice roughened by smoke. "Get him dressed, take a blanket, and I'll fetch horses for us. Ellenshaw's men will soon be here. Most of ours have retreated north."

Left alone, she managed to put Philip's clothes back on him, thankful that they were dry and warm. He never stirred, even when Rafe slung him over his shoulder and carried him out into the cold.

"I could get only one horse, my lady. I fear you shall have to walk. You would not be strong enough to hold him in the saddle."

"Where are we to go?"

"North is all I know. We surely will find someplace safe to shelter along the road. The few of our men still in Attlebrae will try to hold Ellenshaw back until we can make away. He will assume the king is with them and not think to look for us for a while."

He put Philip in the saddle and then climbed up behind him and settled him against his shoulder. Rosalynde took the reins and led the horse into the wind. She did not look back into the blaze that had once been Attlebrae.

CHAPTER

ROSALYNDE STUMBLED ALONG THE DARK, UNFAMILIAR ROAD until dawn came again. Her arms and shoulders ached from constantly tugging the tired, overburdened horse forward, and she stopped for a rest, burying her face against the poor beast's neck. Philip moaned and shifted sideways in the saddle. Rafe just managed to keep him from falling to the ground.

"We must rest awhile, my lady," Rafe said. "I'll drop him next time—my arms are that numb."

"They will find us by daylight!"

"Not if we leave the road. He needs rest, too, and water and warm shelter. Some food as well, if we can find any and get him to take it."

She reached up and put her hand on Philip's forehead. He was no cooler, and, even unconscious, there were tense lines in his face. Her touch turned into a pitying caress.

"Where can we take him, Master Bonnechamp, hunted as he is? I do not even know where we are."

"It is difficult to say now, my lady, but if we keep north, we shall come to Treghatours. There's safety there."

"And for now?"

"There is a village down in that valley," Rafe said, pointing east.

"Would they shelter us, do you think?"

"We dare not risk it. Ellenshaw's men will check every village on this road. We can stop near it though and perhaps find something to eat."

Rosalynde nodded and led them into the field and down to the valley. Soon they came upon a farm. They sheltered in the haystacks a short way off, concealing the horse in a nearby grove of trees.

Rafe could find nothing for them to eat but eggs, still hen-warm. Rosalynde nearly choked as the slimy warmth slid down her throat, but she was hungry and knew, for Philip's sake and their child's, she needed her strength. She cradled Philip's head against her, and Rafe cracked an egg into his mouth. Then Rafe massaged his throat and made him swallow. Still he did not stir.

"He's been asleep so long," Rosalynde said anxiously.

"Sleep is what he most needs."

Rafe swallowed down three eggs himself and fed another one to Philip. Then he burrowed out a place in the hay for them and put Philip inside.

"It is turning colder, my lady. Get in beside him and put your arms around him. If he takes a chill, he may not be able to survive it."

She did as he told her. He crawled in on Philip's other side.

"Now go to sleep. We can stay only until dark."

She pressed her lips to Philip's cheek and pulled him a little closer. Already she had begun to sweat with his feverish body against her and the stifling straw chafing her, but she was too tired to really notice. As soon as she closed her eyes, she was asleep.

At dusk they returned to the road and trudged on. An hour or two before daybreak the next morning it began to rain, penetrating drops only slightly warmer than ice. Philip huddled against Rafe, shaking with cold and breathing hard, rain running from his dark hair, making it look black.

"We shall kill him to keep him out in such weather," Rosalynde said. "There must be some shelter to be had."

"I saw another farm little more than a mile back, west of us. It is a risk, my lady, but better to risk destruction than do nothing and be certain of it."

Rosalynde led them back the way they had come. When they reached the farm, Rafe tied the horse in the forest behind the house and, with Philip once more over his shoulder, crept with Rosalynde into the barn.

Feeling their way through the darkness, they found an empty stall. Rosalynde quickly pushed some straw together, and Rafe put Philip down on it. Something in the movement pierced his unconsciousness.

"Rafe?"

"Shh, my lord," Rafe hissed, clamping his hand over his master's mouth, but it was too late. There was a rustling noise in the loft and then a light.

"Who's there?"

Rafe shifted Philip's head into Rosalynde's lap, putting her hand in place of the one he held over Philip's mouth. Then he crept toward the voice, drawing his sword.

"Who's there, I say!"

Rosalynde sank back into the shadows as the rustling came closer. Rafe tensed, waited, then sprang toward the light. The struggle was short.

"Move and I'll kill you." Rafe's voice was soft but very convincing.

"Mercy, for the good God's sake! Oh, please, my lord!"

Rosalynde could tell from the terrified cracking in his voice that their adversary was little more than a boy.

"I am not your lord," Rafe told him ill-humoredly, "and you will speak softly, or I'll cut out your tongue!"

"What is it you want?" The boy spoke so softly now Rosalynde could scarcely hear him. She did hear the stirring of straw as Rafe let him up.

"Shelter for the day. And perhaps something to eat."

"My master would beat me sure if he knew I let ruffians and cut-purses in his barn," the boy said, his voice indignant but still very soft.

"Then no need to tell him," Rafe reasoned. "If I meant you harm, you'd not be standing whole by now. Look at me. Do I look like a cut-purse?"

Rosalynde strained her ears but for a moment heard nothing. Then the boy's reluctant voice came again. "No. Perhaps not, but you've blood enough on you to be a highwayman." She heard another pause. "Or maybe a soldier. I've seen them coming north away from the battles."

"Whatever I am, boy, is it not enough that I need shelter until nightfall and a little food? I swear I mean you no harm."

"Well, I suppose, so long as my master—"

"Where are you, Rafe?"

Philip's voice was loud in the barn's tense stillness. Rosalynde pressed her hand over his mouth again, but she knew it was too late.

"There is someone with you!"

"No harm there, believe me," Rafe told the boy quickly. "Just a sick boy and his little wife, both wet through and cold and as hungry as Pharaoh's lean kine. God would put it down a good deed if you say nothing to your master and let them stay."

"Let me see them," the young voice insisted. A moment later Rosalynde found herself looking up at a gawky, sharp-featured boy of fifteen. He smiled a little at her, and she read pity in his gray eyes.

"Please, boy," she begged, and he brought his lantern closer, peering into Philip's flushed face. Philip stared back at him glassy-eyed. Then with a little sigh, he closed his eyes again.

"He does look done up. And you, too, mistress," the boy observed. He looked back at Rafe. "Will they keep quiet while they are here? My master—"

"I pledge it," Rafe said solemnly. "But for pity's sake, would you bring some food for us?"

The boy shook his head. "It will be an hour or more before cook is up and calls us in to eat." He considered for a moment. "I could creep in and hook a bit of something, I suppose," he said. Then his face curved into an elfin grin. "It would not be the first time."

He disappeared into the darkness, leaving the lantern with them.

Rosalynde sighed. "Thank God."

"Amen," Rafe agreed. "My lady, I have better thought what we should do. Instead of resting today and taking the king on at nightfall, I believe you would both do better to stay here and let me bring back some men from my lord of Darlington. He was to come to Treghatours as well, and he must be close on this road by now. I can bring him to you much faster than I can bring you both to him."

"Will you leave us unprotected?"

"Never fear, my lady. The boy's a good sort, and I think he will see you both safe. Here, I'll leave you my sword if you want defense."

Rosalynde laughed a little hysterically. "I could never heft it, Master Bonnechamp."

"Very well, my dagger then." He pressed the small blade into her hand. "Please, my lady, it is the best way for us all."

"Should you not rest awhile before you go?"

"No. If I am not away before dawn, I'll likely be seen. I will eat first though if that stripling is as proper a man of his hands as he claims."

He was. A few minutes later they were eating brown bread and cold boiled beef and drinking down the sweetest well water in Lynaleigh. It was all delicious.

Rosalynde softened a piece of the bread in water and managed to get Philip to eat it. Some of the furrows smoothed out of his brow, and he slept quietly again, his face buried in her lap.

She stroked his hair and smiled at the boy. "I thank you indeed."

He grinned at her again and tugged self-consciously at the dark blond curls clustered at the nape of his neck. "I would be little better than a heathen to turn you out to freeze or let you starve in my master's own barn. Despite your companion here," he said, indicating Rafe, "and with no respect to his threatenings, I would not have helped you except I do feel some pity for you, mistress, and your husband looks as if he'd not last a mile farther."

"I am grateful in any case," Rafe said gruffly. "As it stands though,

I'll push your kindness a bit more. Will you let them stay here until tomorrow night? I must go to our friends for help and will likely not be back until then."

"Until tomorrow night?" the boy exclaimed. Then he pointed at Philip. "My master will know sure, what with him thrashing about out here. Cook'll likely lock the pantry if she finds any more food gone."

Rosalynde looked up at him. "Please."

There was something so pitifully needy in her eyes that he could not refuse her. "Let it be so," he said with an air of tragic resignation. Rosalynde and Rafe both smiled.

"You shall have your reward for this, boy," Rafe said. "Trust me, you shall, but I cannot say whether it will be in this life or the next." He looked at Philip for a moment. Then he turned to Rosalynde. "Keep safe. I shall return soon."

She pressed his hand, and he stole quietly away.

"You have come from the battle, have you not?" the boy asked as he squatted near Rosalynde on the straw. She nodded guardedly.

"You belong to Afton, true?"

Again she nodded, and he seemed pleased with his powers of deduction.

"I could tell it. If you belonged to Ellenshaw, you'd have no need to hide now. My master has his lands of my lord of Weatherford and stands to lose all if Ellenshaw is defeated. He'd not look fondly upon you were he to find you here."

"Will you betray us?" she asked, pulling Philip closer.

The boy grinned again. "My master is a cruel man, and I have little cause to love him. I would have run away from my indenture long ago but for my honor," he said with a proud lift of his head. Then a wicked little spark lit his eyes. "Oh, it would chafe him to know someone had taken his shelter and eaten his food and all scarcely farther away than the end of his stingy nose. I'd not betray you, knowing that. Besides, if King Philip has good success, then my master will have nothing, and my indentures will be no more. I have far greater cause to love Afton than hate it. Do not fear. I will never betray you."

Her gratitude was plain on her face. "You must tell me your name for my prayers."

Just then a woman called from outside the barn, her voice as rough as tree bark. "Jerome!"

The boy leapt to his feet. "That is my name," he said with an ungainly bow. "At this very moment, I trust God is writing it again in His book of charitable deeds."

Rosalynde could not keep from smiling as he ran out of the barn calling to the cook.

All that day Rosalynde never left Philip's side, lavishing on him all the care and devotion he would not allow her to show him when he was well. She dared do no more than doze now and again, afraid Philip in his delirium might say something that could expose them to their enemies.

Late that night Philip's temperature rose alarmingly, throwing him into convulsions. Terrified, Rosalynde called Jerome down from the loft, and the two of them rubbed Philip down with cold water in an attempt to reduce the fever. As quickly as they had begun, the convulsions stopped, and Philip was still, only his uneven breathing giving proof of life.

"Dearest Lord God, spare him," she pled, afraid and exhausted almost beyond endurance. "Oh, please, God, do not let my child be born without a father."

Jerome gaped at her as she blotted the cold water from Philip's skin with her cloak. "A child, too? Oh, you should rest. You cannot spend so long tending him and not yourself and your child."

"He needs me."

"You must, or you will be of no use to him at all. Let me watch over him while you sleep."

"No, I cannot ask it of you. We're none of your worry."

She had seen the arduousness of the work he had done all that day, man's work, not boy's, and knew he must be weary.

"You did not ask it of me. I asked it of you. Let me play Samaritan, mistress. It could do no harm for me to have my good deeds written yet again in God's book. Please."

She nodded her head and felt a sudden release of hot, weary tears. "God surely has an entire book just for you, Jerome."

"Several volumes, else I'm mistaken," he said with his usual lop-sided grin.

He made a place in the straw for her next to her husband and then covered them both with the blanket.

"You will wake me if anything happens?"

"If he so much as sighs, you'll know of it," he assured her.

"God's blessing on you, Jerome," she said as she closed her eyes.

"And on you."

Jerome shook her awake a short time later.

"He's drenched in sweat of a sudden, mistress. I thought you should know."

"Poor love," Rosalynde murmured, her eyes all pity as she pressed her hand to Philip's cheek. Jerome looked more concerned when her expression suddenly changed.

"He is worse?"

"No. Oh, no, much better. His fever is broken at last." She smiled through her tears. "He is only sleeping now, good sweet sleep."

"I am very glad," Jerome said through a yawn. "Is there more I can do?"

"Only go back to your bed," she told him, giving his arm a squeeze. "You have been too kind already."

With a weary grin, the boy climbed back up to the loft. Rosalynde wiped the sweat from Philip's brow, grateful to see that the pain lines had smoothed out of his face. Then she curled up next to him again and laid her head on his chest, relieved to hear the steady pounding of his heart and the clear rush of air in his lungs. Her fervent, half-coherent thanks rose up to heaven until she, too, slept.

She woke at midmorning, and, careful not to disturb him, she went to the bucket to splash her face. The girl she saw reflected in the water was almost a stranger to her, so pinched and worn-looking as she was. She tried to push her snarled hair into place, but with a sigh she gave it up and spoiled her mirror by drinking from it. When she turned back around, he was awake.

He lay there in the straw, spent and shivering. His hollow eyes darted apprehensively around the shadowy barn until they lighted on the one thing he recognized.

"Rosalynde?"

She went to him, relieved at his lucidity, glad that he had called her by her name and not by any of the cold titles he usually used with her. He gulped down the water she brought, holding her wrist tightly with both hands as he did.

Breaking into a cold sweat from the effort, he slumped back into the straw. She took him into her arms. With the fever gone out of him, she knew he must feel the cold all the more. He huddled against her like a child, clinging the closer when she stroked the damp hair off his forehead.

"Where is this place?" he asked, his voice ragged and parched, his expression troubled.

"You have been so ill, my lord. This was the only refuge we could find, but Jerome the stableboy has been very kind. He's helped me tend you, though he does not know who you are. His master has no love for Afton, I fear. He must not find us here."

"But where is this? Are we yet in Attlebrae?"

"No. Stephen's men came the first night you were ill. Thursday it was. They routed our army and burned the whole town, attempting to take your life. We only just got away."

He looked about again, bewildered. "But where are the others?"

She was unable to cloak the fear in her eyes. "There are no others. We are alone."

"Rafe?"

"He went to my lord Darlington for help. Pray God, they will come for us soon."

"We should go to them."

"No. Please, my lord, do not think to leave yet. Jerome will see we are safe until help comes."

"Jerome?"

"The stableboy I told you of."

"Oh." He pushed his fingers through his hair, looking as if he was finding it difficult still to think clearly. "Uh, Attlebrae is burned, you say?"

"Yes."

"And all our men gone?"

"Yes."

He put his hand over his face. "Great God, have mercy on us all."

"It will be well," she soothed. "God will protect us, and I will be here to watch over you."

That made him laugh a little but not unkindly. "I think you would make a fierce warrior indeed."

She laughed a little, too.

CHAPTER

ROSALYNDE AND PHILIP BOTH SLEPT AGAIN, AND IT WAS HE WHO woke first a few hours later. He watched her for a moment as she slept, propped against the rough beam in the wall. She looked very tired, but there was a sweet purity in her face that he had not before allowed himself to see. He found himself drawn to her, and just now he was too weak to resist the feeling or even to tell himself he ought to. It did not occur to him to move away from her.

He felt oddly at peace here. He remembered most of what she had told him about where they were and why, but, lying in the warm circle of her arms, he felt only a comfortable weariness and a deep contentment that he did not quite understand. He was hungry and worn and pursued by a ruthless enemy, but here he felt nothing but peace.

She woke when he moved to stretch. He answered her inquiring look with a vague, sleepy smile.

"I feel I should say good morning, but I can tell it is almost night again."

Her smile was shy. "Do you feel better?"

"I feel hungry."

Her eyes warmed at that. "Shall I see if I can fetch the stableboy?"

"Jerome."

She smiled again. "Yes. Shall I fetch him?"

"Is it safe?"

"We mustn't be seen, I'll grant you. I shall just peep out the doorway there and get him."

The risk seemed inconsequential to her now, as if, seeing him awake and hungry, she was sure the danger was past. She slid his head off her lap and stood up.

"Have him bring a great lot of food," he said after she tucked the blanket over him. The words were scarcely out of his mouth before he was again asleep.

A thin, hard line of cold pressure woke him he did not know how long afterwards. He dared not move for fear that the long blade would cut his throat.

"Now there will be only one king."

"Dunois!"

"Good evening, my lord," Dunois said, his eyes glittering as coldly as his sword.

"Let me up. What do you mean by this?"

"I mean to serve my master and take your life, my lord."

Philip stared at him in disbelief. "Your master?"

"Stephen of Ellenshaw, my king and yours."

"You betrayed his father, my father, and now me, and will he trust you?"

"He has for some while now. I have been his silent ally since before your father died."

"So you were the traitor after all. It follows now how we lost Winton." Philip's expression held nothing but royal disdain. "I marvel you dare show your face to me without a pack of my cousin's soldiers to guard you."

"They are waiting for us outside. Ellenshaw thought surely you were with your army making for Treghatours, but I knew better. I knew you would try to lose yourself somewhere in this wretched wilderness. I brought these men to deal with any escort you might have with you, but the pleasure of taking your life I have reserved for myself. Have you made peace with your God, my lord?"

Philip's mouth was suddenly dry, and he made no answer.

"They tell me your father was whey-faced with fear, too," Dunois prodded, "before his throat was cut."

Philip did not allow himself to tremble. He had not seen his father die. He had not seen the unmistakable terror in Robert's eyes in that instant when he knew he was about to stand before God Almighty in the gross ripeness of his sin, unprepared for judgment. Philip had seen none of this, but he had drawn it over and over in his mind from Tom's description. He knew without doubt, with Dunois's knee digging into his chest and the sharp sting of the blade at his throat, that the same look was on his own face now.

"You betrayed him, did you not, my lord high traitor," Philip said, letting contempt mask his fear. "What honor did you lack at his hands or mine that makes you betray Afton now?"

"Your father offered me half his kingdom because I had made him king of it. It was my right to take it, too, but I asked only the half of that. One quarter of his greatest wealth was all I asked, and he promised I should have it. It was he who betrayed me. He did not make his promise good, after all I had done for him, so now I'll take what he offered and by force."

"If my father promised you a quarter of his wealth for helping him to the crown, it is only right I should make his word good. Then I will have you hanged for treason."

"Very generous of you, my lord," Dunois said with a sardonic grin. "Still, you cannot make it good unless you consent to renounce your queen and take my daughter Marian in her place."

"I do not understand you."

"I asked for one quarter of your father's greatest wealth but not an ounce of gold or a foot of land. I asked for one of his fine sons."

"You asked for—"

"He promised me that you, my lord, would marry my daughter and ally my house with the kings of Lynaleigh. He did not know it then, but it was to be my grandson on Lynaleigh's throne one day."

"But Richard was the next heir. Did you mean to kill him, too?"

"If need be. Your father and I knew we needed Westered's support if ever we were to overthrow Edward, and we knew that Westered would not back a rebellion for anything less than the crown prince for his daughter. Richard and Margaret had to marry. If Richard hadn't been killed when he was, I would have had to arrange something. I did convince his grieving widow to destroy his child. I thought my way was clear then, for I never thought Stephen would truly take her despite what I told her. Next I knew your father was begging my pardon and beseeching me to understand that he must have another alliance with Westered, and you must marry Lady Rosalynde and not my Marian. I hope there is a deep pit in hell for those who break faith."

"It will be your own soul howling there then."

"Not before I see the name Dunois in the line of Lynaleighan kings."

"Killing me will not give you what you want."

Dunois laughed. "Will it not, in faith? There is still Stephen. I tried for years to get King Edward to match his son and my daughter, but he only laughed at me and said he was determined to have a princess as wife for his heir. Now Ellenshaw needs me again, and I shall have what I want. Your loving cousin Stephen has pledged his word that he would himself marry Marian if I but bring him your head. I'll do it, too."

"He's married to Margaret already," Philip said, trying to sit up. Dunois only widened his smile and pressed the blade more firmly against the throbbing vein in his throat.

"She can be disposed of easily enough," Dunois said matter-of-factly. "I think my king found her a deal less desirable once her father disinherited her to keep his support with Afton. Stephen told me he will gladly replace her now. Your father and I managed at least an appearance of legality for your sake when that Fletcher woman was made away with. I think Stephen's requirements are not so precise."

Philip felt a sharp stab of old pain. "You knew Kate was innocent, and you consented to her death."

"I suggested it. I even convinced her to confess. I told her that if she did, they would not burn her for the sake of her child, and she condemned herself in doing it. It was masterly done," Dunois gloated, "even if I praise myself to say so."

Philip tried to speak, swallowed hard, and then tried again. "Her child?" he choked out finally.

Dunois looked down on him, savoring every nuance of torment in his face. "Her child. Your child, my lord—more's the pity. She and the child both would have been safe had they not been yours, had they not stood in my way." He pressed the blade deeper into Philip's skin. "Do you think I could let a low-born slut bear the legitimate heir to Lynaleigh while my own daughter is set aside? Do you think I would let an arrogant boy's petty passions confound my plans? No more than I will let you stop me now. Your father promised me his son to make my daughter queen. I take him at his word. Your death buys the throne for Dunois. Say your prayers if that comforts you."

Philip's heart skipped a beat as the sword suddenly jerked, and the edge bit into his throat. Dunois stiffened with a gasping groan and crumpled twitching on top of him. With a cry, Philip shoved him away. The would-be assassin lay in the straw perfectly still, stone dead.

Philip looked up jerkily. Rosalynde stood there with Rafe's dagger in her white hands, stained with Dunois's bright blood. Their eyes met, and they stared at each other, a mingling of horror and relief on their faces. She looked again where Dunois lay, then pleadingly back at Philip. Sobbing faintly, she let the bloodied weapon fall to the ground as if she were no longer capable of holding it.

Philip managed to stand and took her with awkward numbness into his arms. Instinctively, she clung to him, burying her face against him, soaking his shirt with tears.

"Do not cry," he said, and she looked up at him. He was pale and still as shaken as she, but there was warmth, no more than a flicker of warmth, in his trembling half-smile. "Do not cry. It is past now."

He held her by the upper arms, trying to steady himself as much as her with his words. She ducked her head against his chest once more.

"He tried to kill you."

She started to wipe the tears from her face, but seeing her hands covered with blood, she began to cry hysterically. He drew her closer, wrapping his arms tightly around her, and she held desperately to him, leaving bloody handprints on his back.

"It is done, it is done," he said, a low sturdiness to his tone that comforted her. "Shh, it is all done."

"He—he would have killed you," she sobbed. Then she noticed the slight cut across his throat. "Oh, he has hurt you!"

Philip wiped his hand across the stinging wound and drew it back stickily red. "A scratch, no more, thanks to you."

He scrubbed his hand against his sleeve. Then he pressed her close again. She was still sobbing.

"Shh. Listen to me, Rosalynde. We are yet surrounded by his men. If he does not return to them soon, no doubt they have orders to—"

They both gasped as the barn door swung open. In one swift motion, he thrust her behind him and wrested the sword out of Dunois's dead grip.

The soldiers in the doorway were no more than black silhouettes against the sunset's red blaze, their faces indistinguishable.

"Your master is dead," Philip said, holding the weapon defensively in both hands. "Leave here, or you shall follow him to hell."

"Our master is alive, praise God," one of the silhouettes replied.

Philip let the tip of the blade drop to the ground. "Rafe."

Rosalynde sighed, a relieved mixture of laughter and tears.

"I am glad you've come, Rafe," Philip said.

Rafe went to him and took the heavy broadsword from his hands. Without its support, Philip sagged forward, and Rafe had to take his arm to steady him.

"I fear we were too late coming, my lord," Rafe said, looking at

Dunois lying unmoving on the ground. "I wonder you had strength enough to defend yourself."

Philip shook his head. "I did not—" He stopped, seeing Rosalynde turn even more pale, seeing the silent pleading in her eyes. "I did not have any choice," he finished quietly. Then he pulled her to him, turning her away from the body. "Take him away from here."

"At once, my lord. And his soldiers?"

"They are captured?"

"My lord Darlington and his men have them. We took them by surprise, and there were too few of them to make much of a struggle."

"Good. Let them go."

"My lord?"

"They're likely mercenaries with no loyalty to Ellenshaw. Take their weapons and let them go."

"I will see to it, my lord," Rafe said, disapproval plain in his face. "Will you come into the house now? I told the squire of these lands that we would be here a few days, that he should have rooms made ready for you and Her Majesty. He is not pleased to be your host, I fear."

"A few days? Not even one. It could not be but a few hours to Treghatours."

"It will take all night by carriage."

"Then we shall ride."

"You cannot think it, my lord!"

Rosalynde clutched her husband's arm. "Please, my lord, it is almost dark, and it would be best if—"

"I am well enough to ride," he insisted, "and I want to go on."

"My lord, you'd not make two miles on horseback," Rafe said evenly, "and I am sure you would not want Her Majesty to make such a journey so soon after this ordeal, and she expecting a child."

A look of startled remembrance flashed across Philip's face, sweeping away the stubbornness.

"Go on, Rafe," he said softly. "Go tell them to make a room ready for us and something to eat."

"Let me help you to the house, my lord."

"No, go on. We will be there in just a moment."

"Very well." Rafe bowed and then motioned to his men. "Come on, lads. There's more to do."

Philip waited until they had all gone, carrying Dunois's body with them. Then he turned to Rosalynde, and she could see the uncertainty in his eyes.

"Rosalynde—" He faltered, as if the words had swelled in his throat and would not be easily spoken. "Rosalynde—" He put one hand hesitantly on her stomach. "When will it be?" he managed finally.

"Early in the summer, I think."

"In the summer," he repeated, and she knew he was thinking of the child that had been lost. Katherine's child. His child. *Legitimate heir to Lynaleigh*, Dunois had said. *Legitimate*. Then he had loved this Katherine enough to brave his father and all the conventions of royalty and truly marry her.

Rosalynde's heart ached for him. She could easily imagine him as he had been, that pure, trusting light in his eyes, and then to have his heart's dear love so cruelly torn away from him by the father he had loved.

But he had stayed true to what he had professed in Westered, she realized. He was her honorable, stainless knight after all, and his love for Katherine had been as pure as his faithfulness to her, as fair born as their child.

She and the child both would have been safe had they not been yours, Dunois had told him cruelly. Dunois.

Rosalynde shuddered, and Philip held her close to him.

"We are safe now."

"I am so very tired," she whispered, slipping her arms around his waist, and he nodded.

"Let's go into the house."

With one arm snugly around her, he led her out of the comparative warmth of the barn into the raw, fast-falling night. Darlington stopped him before he could cross the yard.

"Your pardon, my lord. Bonnechamp says I am to release our prisoners. Is that so?"

"It is," Philip said dully. "Do it now."

A ragged murmur of hope rose from the huddled captives. Then they slunk into the darkness with Darlington looking apprehensively after them.

"See my men are fed and have a warm place to sleep," Philip said. "We are all of us in need of that."

"Yes, my lord."

The house was warm and snug and filled with the tantalizing smell of roasting pork and stewed potatoes. The squire and his wife were standing sullenly near the stairs watching Rafe and several of the men rummaging through chests looking for clean linens and fresh clothes and whatever else they could find to make the king and queen comfortable.

Seeing Philip, Rafe clapped one hand firmly on the old man's shoulder and pushed him to his knees. "This is Squire Keller, Your Majesty."

"I thank you for your hospitality," Philip said, "however grudgingly given."

The woman managed a reluctant curtsey, but Keller only scowled. "I daresay your lordship'd not call it hospitality if he had his home ransacked by insolent ruffians."

"See they are paid for whatever you take, Rafe," Philip said wearily.

"Of course, my lord. Come, let me show you where you are to sleep."

Rafe led Philip and Rosalynde up the stairs into a cozy chamber dominated by a huge featherbed and a blazing fire. A tub of hot water sat near the hearth.

"There was little work for us to do. The squire and his lady had just finished their supper and were about to retire," Rafe explained. Then he opened the door to a smaller chamber off the first. "There is water for your bath in here, my lady. I am sorry there are none of your ladies to tend you. Shall I send the woman up?"

"No, just see to the king."

"There is a fresh shift for you, too, my lady. It belongs to the squire's wife, and I fear it will be a world too wide for you."

"It will do, Master Bonnechamp. Thank you."

Philip groaned as he stretched out on the bed, his long legs hanging over the side. "Are we to have something to eat, Rafe?"

"At once, my lord."

Rafe brought two platters piled high with roast pork and potatoes. Rosalynde had him leave hers on a small stool by her bath and then shut the door behind him. She was not used to undressing without the help of her maids, but it took her only a moment to wriggle out of her filthy clothes and slip gratefully into the bath.

The water was soon an unsettling reddish brown, and it seemed she could not scrub Dunois's blood away quickly enough. Philip was used to killing men in battle. He took no pleasure in it, she knew, but to him it was commonplace. Rosalynde had never even struck anyone before, except only Philip that once. She hugged herself tightly to stop the shaking and wished he were here to hold her now.

She had killed a man. She could still feel the dagger's handle in her hands and the jarring resistance when she had thrust the blade deep into Dunois's side. How she had the strength to do it she did not know, when now even the memory of it made her tremble. But seeing Philip lying there kitten-weak under Dunois's blade, taunted with the loss of his unborn child, had been more than she could bear.

"Oh, God, forgive me. I've taken a man's life." She let her tears fall freely into the water. "It was right. It was right. Oh, Lord, forgive me. Let it have been right."

She remembered the strength that had suddenly poured through her, not just physical strength but strength of will, courage to do what she must. It was a strength beyond her own. Her tears slowed, and she washed the last blood stain from her hands, all the while thanking God for giving her that strength and for sparing Philip's life and hers.

By the time the water began to cool, she smelled of soap instead of the stable, and her once-snarled hair hung smooth and sleek down her back. Her plate was nearly empty. There was a pleasing fullness in her stomach, and for the first time in days, she felt warm. It was good not to be afraid anymore.

She rinsed her face one last time, stepped out of the water, dried herself, and put on the borrowed shift. It was far too large, as Rafe had predicted, but it was clean. She pulled a ribbon from one sleeve and used it to tie back her wet hair.

Hearing Rafe still in the next room, she took a blanket from the bed and wrapped it around herself. Then she opened the door. Philip was already in bed again, but he had washed and been shaved and had eaten every bit of the food Rafe had brought him. Rafe was gathering up his clothes.

"I shall have to clean them as best I can, my lord. There's none of the squire's clothes will fit you by any stretch."

Philip burrowed farther down into the bed. "I may not need them for a long while yet," he said through a yawn. "This bed is too soft by far."

He turned his head and saw Rosalynde watching him from the doorway. A hint of a drowsy smile crept across his face.

"Do you have everything you need, my lady?"

She nodded. "I only wished to bid you good night."

Rafe cleared his throat. "Pardon me, my lord, if there is nothing more you or my lady want . . . "

"That is all, Rafe. Just see our host is treated with respect and find Her Majesty some fresh clothes for tomorrow."

"I will, my lord." He took away their dirty clothes and empty dishes and shut the door behind him.

Rosalynde came across the room and sat down on the edge of the bed. "Is there nothing I can get for you?"

Philip reached his hand out for hers and gave her fingers a gentle squeeze. "Stay with me, Rosalynde."

She put her arm across him and laid her head on his chest. "Philip."

"Stay with me," he murmured again, stroking his hand across her cheek to the nape of her neck, under the heavy dampness of her hair.

After a moment she sat up and let the blanket around her shoulders fall to the floor. Then she got under the coverlet and lay down close to him in the deep softness of the bed. For a long while he was very still, and she thought he had fallen asleep. But then he turned to his side and curled up against her with his cheek resting gingerly on her stomach.

"Tell me again. About the child."

"He will likely come in June."

"How do you know?"

Her mouth curved up in a secret little smile. "I know."

He spread one hand caressingly across her stomach. "Can you feel him kick?"

"Not yet. It is too soon yet for that."

"It does not show." He smoothed the loose smock flat against her. "You are to have a child, and I would never have known."

There was a touch of bewildered sadness in his voice, a grieving for the short time he might have known Katherine was to give him a child, for that little while he might have shared that deep joy with her. Even that brief moment had been denied him.

Rosalynde wanted to tell him she was sorry for the terrible things she had overheard in the barn, that she was sorry for the tragedy her own sister had helped bring him, but again she dared not. This, too, was past, and he had forbidden her to speak to him about the past.

"It will show soon enough," she said, putting her hand over his.

"I cannot imagine it yet. A child."

"Our child."

He wove his fingers into hers and accepted, without realizing, her silent comfort. "Our child."

They slept well into the next day, and when Rafe tapped on the door a short while before noon, only Philip woke. For a moment he lay there dazed. Then he slid his arm carefully from under Rosalynde's head and sat up. Rafe opened the door a hesitant crack.

"Shall I bring your breakfast, my lord?" he whispered.

Philip wiped the sleep out of his eyes and nodded.

"And Her Majesty?"

Philip looked at Rosalynde lying beside him, breathing slowly and deeply, her lips softly parted. "Later."

He was halfway through eating when she finally stirred. She looked puzzled for a moment. Then she wrinkled her nose and sat up.

"Eggs."

"They are wonderful," he said around a hearty mouthful, and he held out his spoon to her. "Want some?"

She took a choking breath and quickly turned her head.

"What? Oh, I am sorry."

He set the dish on the bedside table and called for Rafe.

"Take this away, Rafe, and bring Her Majesty some warm milk."

Rosalynde turned even whiter and put both hands over her mouth.

"Water?"

She nodded.

"Water, Rafe, and be quick."

"At once, my lord."

Philip held the cup for her as she drank, but she could only manage a few sips. Seeing his concern, she laughed weakly.

"I only feel a little queasy now and again, my lord. It will pass."

"It must have been dreadful for you these past few days." He took her hand lightly in his own. "I would have never expected such courage to be housed in such tender flesh."

He touched her fingers to his lips, a kiss of admiration and gratitude. She longed to tell him that everything she had done had been for love of him, but she could not.

"I told you I would watch over you," she said instead.

"I am only sorry you had to soil these fair hands on that swine. You should let me tell everyone that it was you who saved us."

Her stomach churned at the blood-fouled memory. "No, please, my lord. We are safe now—let it end. I just want to forget Dunois and all his evil. I want you to forget him, too."

He released her hand and lay back against the pillows, looking very tired and very far away. "I cannot forget. Too many things will not let me."

CHAPTER

THEY STAYED TWO MORE DAYS WITH THEIR SURLY HOST AND THEN made ready to go on to Treghatours. At first Philip insisted on returning to Winton, but they had news from there that Stephen had fled back to Cold Spring, and Tom's men were keeping watch over his movements. Philip's army was in Treghatours already upon Eastbrook's orders, expecting to winter there. There was nothing of any moment to keep him from joining them.

He had Rafe pay Keller generously for their food and shelter. Then he remembered another debt. He looked out over the squire's people until one of them caught his attention, a boy of about fifteen.

"You are Jerome, yes?"

The boy's eyes widened, and he bobbed his head.

"Come here."

Jerome came to him and knelt beside his horse, but Philip leaned down and pulled him to his feet.

"I owe you much, Jerome. What would you have as payment?"

A crooked grin appeared on the boy's face. "Why, nothing, Your Majesty," he said, tugging at the back of his hair. "I did no more than as I should, though I did never think I might be entertaining a king unawares."

Philip almost grinned, too. "Not quite as the Scripture puts it, but I am grateful to you none the less. What would you have?"

The boy glanced furtively at his scowling master and then shook his head. "I cannot ask payment, my lord, for Christian charity. I thank you just the same."

Philip also looked at the squire and knew the boy would surely be punished for the trouble he had brought his master.

"How much money do you have left, Rafe?" he asked in a low voice.

"Little now, my lord. Shall I give it to the boy?"

Philip shook his head and thought for a moment. "Is that ring precious to you, my lord Darlington?"

Darlington glanced at the emerald and diamonds on his finger, puzzled. "No, my lord, except that it cost me dearly."

"Will you trust me for the worth of it?" Philip asked, holding out his hand.

"Of course, my lord."

Philip took the ring from him and tossed it to the squire.

"I am taking this boy, too. That's six or seven times what he cost you, I am certain, though it could not be one-hundredth his worth."

"Take him and welcome," Keller said, examining his prize greedily. "You'll soon find you've made the worst of the bargain. I've no use for the scoundrel traitor."

"Am I to come with you now, Your Majesty?" Jerome asked incredulously.

"If you please to, or take your freedom if you had rather."

"N-no, my lord."

Rosalynde graced him with a warm smile. "We owe you more than we can think to repay, Jerome, and the more because it was given freely." She, too, looked at the squire. "And not without some danger to yourself."

"You have my service so long as it pleases you, my lady, so God make me faithful!"

As the party traveled to Treghatours, Jerome walked along at Philip's stirrup for hours, speaking with expert appreciation of the fine horse Rafe had brought him or of the bite to the winter air or the clouds that promised snow. He spoke to his king with friendly deference, and Philip found himself liking the boy, admiring the freeness in his spirit, a freeness he could only envy.

At midafternoon Rafe pulled his horse close to Rosalynde's carriage.

"Can you persuade His Majesty to ride with you, my lady? I fear he is not so strong yet as his pride would care to believe."

Rosalynde watched her husband for a moment. He was drooping in his saddle, and she saw by the tired, determined set of his mouth that Rafe had spoken truth. She scrambled for some plausible reason for him to rest awhile. Jerome grinned at her, and she smiled back. Then she heard him remark once more on the superiority of Philip's horse.

"Did they have such fine horses back at your master's, Jerome?" she asked casually.

"Never once, my lady. I cannot even hope ever to ride such a fine one, but it is a pleasure just to watch him walk."

"Perhaps my lord will let you ride him one day."

"Oh, no, my lady, I—"

"Perhaps you will favor me with riding him now," Philip said, as she had expected he would.

"Your Majesty, I could not take your horse and leave you to walk. It would not be seemly."

"You would be doing me a service, Jerome. I would like to ride with my lady awhile." He dismounted and leaned into the carriage window. "I hope you have no objections, my lady. He deserves a great deal more than that."

"I would be honored, my lord," she said. Behind him Rafe nodded at her in approval.

"He does well with horses," Philip observed as they went along. "I can tell he's learned much of them in keeping Keller's stables. He might do well apprenticed to my groomsman, not only for being suited to the place, but because he might go some way in easing Hawkins's grief for those he lost at Abbey."

"It would be a wise choice, my lord," she said quickly, before he began to remember too much of that tragedy. "He was of great comfort to me and never lost his good cheer all that time he looked after us."

"He's like Tom, I think."

There was a touch of satisfaction in his weary face as he leaned back in the carriage and shut his eyes. That same look was reflected in her own expression.

"Treghatours," Philip murmured, a longing light in his eyes. They had finally emerged from the forest, and the castle loomed before them, overawing the sloping meadow below. "Treghatours," he repeated as if to say guardian, refuge, home. All that and more it was to him, Rosalynde read in his face.

He was drawn and pale, and he tired too easily, but the tension that had been in his expression since they had married seemed to lessen, replaced by peace, as if the winter and this well-loved place had given him respite from the insatiable demands of war.

The conflict was not resolved. Stephen still was free, still king in the eyes of many, but nothing could change that until the two armies could meet again in the spring. For a brief time Philip could lay down his battered sword and his heavy, tarnished crown, and he could rest.

It was some while before they actually reached the castle, and even his eagerness could not keep him awake. Even the hollow rumble of the carriage wheels over the drawbridge did not disturb his sleep.

When they pulled up into the courtyard, Rosalynde saw a little, round middle-aged woman bustle down the great stone stairway leading from the hall.

"Have you brought him?" she asked anxiously. "Have you brought my Philip?"

Rosalynde was wondering who she might be to dare address the king so familiarly when the woman thrust her head into the carriage.

"Oh, my poor boy," she clucked, seeing him lying in the cushions asleep. Rosalynde looked at her, and, startled, the woman made a quick curtsey. "Pardon, my lady. Will you come inside now? There is a room ready for you."

Rosalynde put one hand gently on her husband's shoulder. "My lord."

He struggled to sit up. "I hadn't meant to fall asleep again. Are we home?" Then the most amazing smile dawned on his face. "Joan!"

Rosalynde saw at once the overwhelming affection this woman had for the boy she had raised and how she was struggling to treat him like her king and not her child.

"Your Majesty," Joan said with another curtsey, her voice holding that soft caressing sweetness that belonged to the north and especially to this place. Forgetting his dignity, she pulled him into her arms and kissed his forehead. "Philip, my honey-love."

For a moment he let her hold him there. Then he pulled back, ostensibly so he could look at her.

"You've not changed a bit in all this time, Joan."

"If I have aged, it's been in the last three days, since that ruffian you have keeping care of you came tearing in here with news of the danger you were in."

Rafe glowered at her from astride his horse, and Philip started to smile. Then he saw the tears in her eyes.

She pulled out a handkerchief. "If I was to lose another of you so soon, I do not know how I would keep my heart from breaking."

"You mustn't fret, Joan," Philip soothed as he climbed out of the carriage. "Tom is in Winton now and safe. And you see you've not lost me either, though I cannot vouch for that if supper is long in being served."

Immediately she was a flurry of action, ordering the servants to set out the huge meal she had had prepared.

"You, young man, shall have your supper in bed."

Philip scowled. "Now, Joan—"

"Not a word, my lord. Make yourself useful, sir," she said, turning to Rafe. "Take your master inside and see he lies down."

"Joan."

"My lord, I know what is best for you."

Rosalynde forced herself not to smile at her husband's exasperated expression.

"Joan, I am your king."

Joan calmly finished her instructions to her helpers. Then she turned to him and patted his cheek.

"Of course you are, my lord, and you'll be no less a king for a good meal and a day or two in your own bed. Now go along, and I will come in a bit to see you've been properly cared for."

"I'll not spend two more days in bed," he said in the most authoritative tone he could muster, the one that commanded vast armies.

But Joan paid him no heed. "A week would be better for you," she mused, "but I suppose we mustn't expect miracles."

"Joan."

"Well, go on now. Your lady will want settling in, too, and I cannot care for you both. Master Bonnechamp, see to His Majesty."

"At once, mistress," Bonnechamp said, only just managing to keep his expression dignified. "My lord, will you come?"

Philip frowned stubbornly. Then to Rosalynde's amazement, he smiled a little. "My lady," he said as he handed her down from the carriage, "you will find soon enough who is master here, if you cannot see it already. Come, Rafe, let us do as we are bidden, or we are both likely to have a switching."

Joan smiled, too. "I've still an arm for it, my lord, if you've a mind to cross me."

"Not for the whole kingdom." He turned to go but then looked back again. "You will see to my lady, Joan?"

"Of course, my lord," Joan assured him.

He and Rafe went inside.

"Will you come in, my lady?" she invited.

Rosalynde nodded gratefully.

"Are none of your gentlewomen with you, my lady?" Joan asked as they started up the steps.

Rosalynde shook her head, not wanting to remember. "Those I had with me were killed in Abbey."

"I am sorry for it. Still, I shall see you have all you need here. I may not know the courtly ways of your fine ladies, but I used to wait upon my lady Elaine when she was mistress here. Even she found little to complain of in me."

"My lord Philip never speaks of her, but I remember she was very beautiful."

"She was that, my lady. As fine and rare as diamonds and rubies."

"They say King Robert loved her above his own soul."

"He did. I can vouch for it."

"And she him?"

They were at the end of a long hallway now, and Joan quickly pushed open one of the doors.

"Here is your chamber, my lady. You will want to refresh yourself a moment before supper. Or would you prefer to have supper brought to you here?"

Rosalynde sat down on the plump bed. "I would like that best. Thank you, Mistress Joan."

Joan curtseyed. "I will fetch it at once. Then I will make you ready for bed."

She stepped into the corridor and started to close the door, but Rosalynde stopped her.

"Did you attend Lady Elaine when she was with child?"

"Oh, yes, always. And I helped birth all four of those boys. I remember it as clear as day still. If you are here when your child comes, you needn't worry. I will see it all goes well."

Rosalynde looked startled. "How did you know?"

Joan chuckled. "Why, it is written on you plain as day. I know the look. Have you reckoned the time? It should be early summer, I would say."

Again Rosalynde was amazed. "Yes. I think so. Do you know everything, Mistress Joan?"

"I had His Majesty convinced I did once," she said with another chuckle. "Perhaps he believes it still."

"To hear him speak of you, I daresay he does."

True to her word, Joan saw to Rosalynde's every need until Julia and Ursula and some of the other ladies-in-waiting were sent from Winton along with some clothing for her and for the king. It was decided that they would winter in Treghatours and let Tom keep Winton. Rosalynde knew Philip did not wholly approve of this idea, but she could see he loved this place too much to have to be coaxed into staying when there was no profit in leaving.

He flourished under Joan's nurturing. She fed him plenty of her good, plain cookery and ordered him to bed early at night. She even made so bold as to forbid him to discuss matters of state with Darlington and the others for very long at one time.

"There is nothing that has happened already that you can undo, my lord, and nothing that can be done now that will not be the better for waiting until spring. If you rest now, you'll be fit to see to things when the time comes."

Rosalynde was pleased to see him take her advice, to see him shake loose the bonds of kingship just a little. He began to spend less time with his councilors and more with Jerome and the other boys about the castle and from the village. He taught them the games he and his brothers had played here just a few years before and learned their games, too. They accepted him as one of their own, and he took pleasure in pretending that he was.

When he came in at dusk, cold and dirty, Joan always treated him as if he were still a boy of twelve, scolding and pampering him all at once. He would assume a dignified manner and remind her of her place, but she was long used to hearing his heart and not his words and knew he welcomed her meddling, whether he admitted it or not.

It was not long before he lost that hollow, hunted look, and Rosalynde was once more astonished by his deep beauty. She marveled again at how much he had changed since Westered. His lean face was still quite the most handsome she had ever seen, more handsome perhaps for the life that had been written on it, but it had lost the bland prettiness she had pined after in her girlhood. Only his mouth was the same. The inviting fullness of his lip still seemed to beg to be kissed, but she dared not.

His rare smiles came more frequently in this place of peace, and when custom forced them together, he did not seem so wary of her as he had once been. There was a wondering in his eyes, as if he were reassessing her and himself, sometimes an unexpected tenderness in a touch or a glance, an expression of concern for the child she carried and, yes, for her, as well. Yet still he held his distance and always left her to spend the nights alone. Christmas came and went, and still he never so much as kissed her, unless it was the formal kissing of her hand upon some brief parting that left her sighing disconsolately.

"Do not let it fret you, lady," Joan said once, seeing her wistful expression. "He'll not be gone from you long."

"Tell me about him, Joan, when he was a little boy."

"Why, he was just as he is now, lady . . . a trifle spoiled, softly spoken, sweet to look on, master of everything he set his hand to, and wanting everything just so. And stubborn. Oh, lady, stubborn as a snapping turtle! And he had a temper then, I'll warrant you, though I must say it was usually hard to get at. He'd sooner freeze you than burn you. He'd never budge an inch with his honor at stake, but he could be so sweet, too. In his own way, if he thought no one would know it, he could be as tender as a new fawn."

"I can see that in him," Rosalynde said, "but he's careful not to show it often."

"I could always see through him, all four of them, like rainwater—good or bad. Not that any of them was truly wicked. My husband, Nathaniel, God rest him, raised them to fear God and honor the king. Richard was rougher with his brothers than he might ought to have been, I'll grant, but John was pure angel, first to last, and Tom—" She laughed, and her laugh was oddly like Tom's. "Tom was ever at one mischief or another, but we could never fault him for it. He had us laughing too hard. Truly the good God planted sunshine in that child. I never saw one match him for it. My Philip has sun in him, too. Sun enough to dazzle when he chooses."

"When he chooses."

Rosalynde's mouth turned down, and Joan chucked her under the chin.

"Now, lady, no tears. You've the finest gentleman in all Christendom to love you and in a short while a fair babe to prove it."

"And an empty bed to mock it!"

She sobbed in spite of herself, and Joan gave her a motherly hug.

"Well, I wondered if it might not be so. I will tell you a thing, lady, about these foolish young men. Some of them think they must treat a woman with child as if she were made of window glass, and if I know my Philip, he'll deny himself forever before he'd risk that babe."

"He has no more use for me, that is all. Now that I am to give him an heir, he's done his duty, and he does not want me anymore."

"Oh, my lady, could you say so? Not want you? I think you do not know him well if you can believe that."

Rosalynde shook her head. "He loves another."

"I know you do not know him if you can believe he would be unfaithful to you, my lady."

"No, I know he would not be, not with his body. Still, without faithfulness of heart there is little value in all the rest."

"I'll not believe inconstancy of him, lady," Joan said, a little stiffness in her voice.

"Neither will I," Rosalynde admitted sadly, "and that is what makes me despair of him ever coming back to me."

"I do not understand you, my lady, but I can see you are grieved for love of him, and you need not be. You have a woman's fears, and he has a man's ignorance. No doubt he worries for the child, and it is no more than that."

Rosalynde knew she was ignorant in such matters. "Would it hurt the child if—"

Joan laughed. "Law, lambkin, so early on? Not a whit!"

"But would he truly fear so?" Rosalynde asked with a trembling hint of a smile.

"To judge from his glances, it's not lack of wanting you that's kept him alone these nights."

There was still a pretty flush in Rosalynde's cheek when she came upon him awhile later, straddling one of the braces that arched up to the ceiling in the great hall, swinging his legs some five or six feet above her head. There was a little gray and white cat stretched out on the heavy beam beside him, looking down upon Rosalynde with queenly hauteur. Rosalynde had grown used to seeing the creature about the castle, always when Philip was in sight. She seemed to have little use for anyone else except the cook who fed her.

Rosalynde craned her neck to see them better. "How ever did you get up there? You shall fall!"

"You sound like Joan," Philip said. "We've not fallen yet, have we, Grace?"

The cat's answer was a lazy yawn and a slow blink of her eyes.

Philip grinned at her and lowered himself to the length of his arms so his boots dangled in front of Rosalynde's face. She was surprised to see he wore no shirt, just a leather vest loosely laced in the front and a cut of the same lacing looped around his wrist. She let her eyes travel down the long length of him, covertly admiring the play of muscle in his bare arms and the way his boots fit to his well-turned legs.

"I shouldn't like Joan to catch me at this now," he said. "She always used to switch us for it."

"She might still, monkey!"

"Joan!" He dropped to the floor, a naughty little-boy look on his face that he knew his old nurse could never resist. "I was showing my lady where we used to play when we were boys."

"And where is your shirt? I could never keep him in clothes when it got cold, my lady! In dead winter he would go out in little more than his breeches if he thought I'd not catch him at it!"

Rosalynde smiled at that, remembering his delight in the snow that had fallen in Westered, how it had brought that same fresh eagerness to his face.

"Go out, rascal," Joan scolded with a twinkle in her eyes, "and take your lady, too, if you're minded to show her all the places you've made deviltry in!"

"It is the fairest place mere earth can boast, my lady," he said, offering his hand uncertainly. "Would you come see it with me?"

With a hopeful glance at Joan, she let him lead her away.

He took her through the castle, showing her the fine paneled rooms and intricately carved furniture, the age-darkened portraits of his royal ancestors from both his father and mother, the treasures of silver and gold and fine jewels that were but a portion of his family's wealth. He showed her the fine glass work in the windows of the room where his mother had done her sewing, and she found herself entranced by the view below.

"The view is better from here," he told her as they walked into a bedchamber off the other room.

"It is no wonder you love this place, my lord," she said after a long, long look. "The way the stream flows so fair from the mountains through those trees, it's as if an artist had set them there."

"I think He did." He drew a deep, slow breath as if to smell a memory. "In May that field will be so full of saint's rose you shall think it snowy December."

She smiled and looked up into his face and forgot to admire the view. "You are kind to show me all this."

"I was always happiest here of any place," he said unsteadily. "I was, uh—"

She tried to smile again, but her tremulous lips would not cooperate. "I want you to be happy."

She looked up at him still, knowing he could read the look in her eyes.

"My lady, I know I've not been what you have wanted. I am—I have too much I am bound to. I cannot—"

She moved closer to him and lifted her chin just enough to bring her lips within reach of his.

"Rosalynde—"

The kiss was urgent. Then she felt his hands around her waist, felt them pull her in tighter. She clung to him closer, expecting him to lift her up and carry her to the wide, soft bed, but he did not. Instead, feeling the tell-tale thickness in her middle, he tried to tear himself away from her.

"We mustn't," he urged between kisses. "The child."

"We'll not hurt the child."

He looked deep into her eyes. "No?"

"No."

He kissed her again until she thought she would drown in the taste and the feel of him. Then he swung her up into his arms. Her heart sank when she saw he was carrying her not to the bed but to the door.

"Philip—"

He stopped her protest with another kiss, hard and relentless. She heard the bolt clank into place. She closed her eyes.

"Kiss me that way again."

CHAPTER

SOMETHING DEEP INSIDE HER, SOMETHING THAT STILL FOUND THE strength to hope, had made her think that this morning she might wake still in his arms.

But he was gone.

"Is it to be as it was back in Winton, love?" She caressed the pillow where his head had lain. "After all this while, will you still not trust me with the tender side of your heart?"

There was a quick knock at the door. Joan came in with breakfast and wash water and a fresh dress.

"Good morning, my lady. I trust you've slept well."

"Joan!"

"My lord Philip sent me to help you dress. I'm to give you his good morning, too, and tell you he left early to hunt and did not wish to disturb your sleep. I told your ladyship he was but concerned for you."

Rosalynde somehow managed to smile. It was his usual message to satisfy his duty to her and yet free himself from further intimacy. Well, there was nothing new in this.

The day passed with unbearable tediousness. Rosalynde spent the time sewing tiny garments for the child that was to come and wondering how she was to bear a lifetime of being wrenched one way and then another by this love that would not let go of her, this love she would not let go. It tarnished the glory of the night before, of all such nights, to know that her fiery, expressive lover would be a distant stranger when next she saw him.

She prayed again for the strength to love him, come what may, to love him steadily and strongly, to love him as God did, with no thought for what love he might give in return. She had vowed to love him, and she was determined to show him that she, too, had a sense of honor.

Finally night fell. Just as she began to wonder when he would return, she heard his light step on the stairs to her chamber.

"Good evening, my lady," he said, his smile as uncertain as hers. "Did you have a pleasant day?" He sat down on the cushions at her feet and looked up at her. Then he put one hand on her stomach. "You are—you are well?"

She pressed her hand over his. "We are both of us very well."

With a light caress, he moved his hand away from her, but still he sat at her feet looking up at her, still searching her face. "I would you could have come, my lady. We had fine sport."

"And what did you bring in?" she asked, careful of her words, wondering at his awkward concern for her and his admission that he had wished her with him that day.

"Nothing at all." He laughed hesitantly. "But it was great sport."

The waiting women giggled, and Rosalynde could not help joining them.

"We sighted a doe at the west edge of the forest," he recounted, letting a little eagerness into his eyes, "and Sweetheart caught the scent at once and set after the animal. We had only her and Beauty and Blanche with us, but they bayed like a whole pack, and the doe bounded away into the forest. She led us a merry chase until she made a misstep and caught her hind foot in the branches of a fallen tree."

"You did not let the dogs get her!" Rosalynde cried.

"No, no," he reassured her. "I had the men hold off the dogs and freed her myself."

She smiled. "I am glad of it."

"So was I until the beast kicked me for thanks." His rueful expression made the women giggle again. "But it was a fine chase we had—all the clean winter air in our lungs and nipping our faces and the crunch of snow under our boots and the baying of the hounds. We hardly needed the deer at all. Still, I would we had taken something. If I had that doe here now, I'd be more apt to eat her than free her."

"Shall we go in to supper then, my lord?" she asked him, disappointed that this sweet meeting should be so brief.

But again he surprised her. "I doubt I could endure another of Darlington's tedious discussions about 'what ought to be done.' I am certain he can carry on that whole conversation without me even being there now." He leaned closer to her. "What do you say to sending one of your ladies to fetch our supper in here tonight? You have the musicians, and the rest of your ladies can sing for us." He watched her face, gauging her reaction. "Would that please you?"

"It would please me very well," she agreed, still astounded. She sent her waiting women as he had suggested. She did not want to share him tonight with all Treghatours.

They ate there before the blazing hearth fire to the accompaniment of gentle love songs.

"Sit down here," he invited, and she accepted, her voluminous skirt covering the cushioned floor, making a sea of blue brocade around her where she sat. He lay on his stomach beside her, propped up on his elbows, swinging one lazy foot to and fro.

He took the last of the pheasant from her plate, watching her still, an almost playfulness in his eyes. "It's hungry work, this hunting."

"It must take a great deal of food to fuel such brazenness," she agreed.

He smiled. "A hard day's work earns a man a good appetite."

She noticed that Grace had, as usual, mysteriously appeared along with the food. Philip offered her a piece of cheese, but she only sniffed the proffered morsel and turned her head haughtily away. Philip snatched her up, ignoring her vociferous protests.

"Too fine to eat from the queen's plate, are we?"

Giving her a kiss on the nose, he set her once more on her feet, but she was still not satisfied. She watched him intently as he pulled bits of pheasant from the bone. Her cries became insistent when he did not give her any, but he simply shook his head.

"From now on, when you beg, you should take what's offered you."

Rosalynde giggled as she watched Philip's stern attempts to ignore her. Grace was becoming more and more restless. Tantalized by the smell of pheasant, she began to pace back and forth, all the time following the movement of Philip's hand from his plate to his mouth. Finally overwhelmed, she stood up on her hind legs and seized his wrist with her forepaws in an effort to pull his hand and the pheasant down closer to the floor. At that, Philip laughed, and he set the plate down for her to finish.

"You'll not be denied, will you?" he said, scratching her behind the ears, but this time it was she who would not acknowledge him.

"You've spoiled her, my lord," Rosalynde observed smiling.

To her surprise, he lay his head in her lap, gazing up at her, again that searching, uncertain look in his eyes. "I could deny no one anything tonight."

The musicians began a sweet, lilting melody, and as it reached his ears, a slow smile crossed his face. He rolled onto his back, his head still pillowed against her.

"I've not heard this since I was a boy," he said.

She listened for a moment. "It is lovely, but I do not recognize it."

Grace came and nestled in the crook of his arm, and he stroked her absently. "I suppose it never got so far as Westered. It's an old, old ballad of the time when Treghatours was a kingdom of its own. You see, the king of Treghatours then was a good king, as kings go, and he had a long, happy reign. The song is really a hymn of thanksgiving to God for the peace and prosperity they had then. It's a very sweet song. Joan used to sing it to us as a lullaby. I thought I had forgotten it."

He listened for a moment, waiting for the music to repeat, then he sang softly, the exceptional low sweetness of his voice echoing the words of grateful praise. There was a contented, faraway look deep in his eyes. This memory was sweet.

"Did you ever feel you belonged to a place?" he asked after a moment. "As if you weren't quite whole outside of it?" She shook her head, and he took her hand and rested it over his heart. "This is my place."

The footman put more wood on the dwindling fire, and Rosalynde, dismissing him, told him to send her waiting women to bed, too, and leave the musicians to play on awhile longer. Philip drew her other arm around himself and closed his eyes.

"I could make a pleasant life out of days such as this one."

"And I, too," she agreed softly, wishing that the night could go on forever. The sweet harmony between them was as rare and precious to her as roses in the snow, made the sweeter for being so unexpected.

She held him a little tighter, savoring the nearness of him. Gathering her courage, she leaned down and whispered what was in her heart. "Philip, I love you."

He made no reply. He had already fallen asleep.

She brushed her lips against his hair. "Truly, I do."

The master of the musicians came to her half an hour before midnight. "Your Majesty—"

Rosalynde put one cautioning finger to her lips and then dismissed him and all of the musicians with a wave of her hand. Now she and Philip were truly alone.

She listened for a while to the night sounds—the crackle of the fire in the hearth, the rattle of the window glass as the moaning wind beat upon it, the cat purring in Philip's arm—sounds that spoke of comfort, security, and contentment.

"Twelve o'clock and all's well!" The voice of the town crier drifted up from the street below.

Waking, Philip yawned and stretched. Disgruntled at being disturbed, Grace went to the hearth and curled up near the fire. Philip smiled sleepily at her and then at Rosalynde.

"I remember when John first brought her home," he said. "He was soaking wet, and he had this little bedraggled kitten clutched against him, her eyes not even open yet. Faith, I never thought such a row could come from so tiny a thing. He'd rescued her from a sack in the millpond, and we all thought sure this one would die like the rest of the litter, but John kept her fed and warm, and by the time she was weaned, he'd even trained her to come to his whistle. I'd never seen the like of it." His smile turned wistful. "He had a gentle way with animals."

"I remember him so from Westered," she said. "I can remember nothing of him but good."

"There was nothing in him but good," Philip said softly, putting his hand on hers. "It pleases me that you should think so, too."

Drawn by the rare, gentle warmth in his eyes, Rosalynde bent slowly over him and touched her mouth to his, just enough for him to taste her softness. For a long while he merely looked at her, something deep and longing in his eyes. Then he brought her fingers to his lips, kissing each one tenderly, each kiss a lingering caress.

"Your eyes shine like sapphires in this light," she said, smoothing his hair back at the temple. He kissed the underside of her wrist. Then, sitting up, he pressed his lips in slow succession from her wrist to her elbow and then to her shoulder, drawing her closer as he did.

She felt his arm steal about her waist and found herself a willing captive in his embrace. In his eyes there was a fathomless depth of passion and an unmistakable question. In answer, she put her arms around his neck and laid her head on his shoulder.

The dawn light found them asleep there on the cushions, entwined in each other's arms for warmth. A violent clash of pots from the kitchen woke him. Carefully disentangling himself from her embrace, he got up and began to dress himself. It would do nothing for his kingly dignity for her maids to find him there as he was.

Once dressed, he went back to her side, intending to put her in bed and let her finish her sleep in comfort, but instead he stood for a moment watching her, thinking how innocently defenseless she looked, unaware of the tender expression on his own face.

Eventually, he took her again into his arms. She only sighed in her sleep and nuzzled closer to him, bringing to life once more the gentle protectiveness he had felt for Katherine. It was with reluctance that he finally set down his drowsy burden and covered her with his thick hunting cloak.

The fire had died out hours ago, and he began to make another, working as quietly as he could. He managed to complete the task without making a sound until, seeking to push two struggling embers together, he dropped the poker, and it clattered to the floor. She awoke with a start and then looked questioningly at him, as if she were unsure what his mood would be after so surprising an evening.

"Good morning, my lady," he said, a becoming shyness in his tone. "I am sorry to have wakened you."

A touch of relief in her sleepy smile, she huddled under his cloak. "It is very cold."

"It snowed again. My meadow will be beautiful today." He hesitated. "Will you come ride with me? I promise I'll not let you fall into the stream this time."

There was still that little remembrance between them, one that was all innocence and no pain. Her mouth turned up just a touch at the corners in answer to his.

"Show me all the places you love, so I may love them, too."

He nodded a little self-consciously. "I will go ready the horses. Wrap you up well. Then come down to the stables. Hurry."

"I will."

Soon they were riding through the forest, the horses fetlock-deep in snow. The air was cold, but the sky was as blue as May, and the sun was shining its winter best, reflecting warmth off the dazzling whiteness on the ground.

"This is my meadow," he told her, stopping at the crest of a low rise.

The meadow was wide and deep with snow, untouched as yet by man or beast. Only the faint tracks of birds embroidered the flawless surface. She thought she would never tire of looking at the frosted beauty of it.

"Oh, my lord, it is glorious!"

His eyes shone with eager love for the place. "Come, let's go down."

He dismounted and wrapped his reins and hers around a sturdy branch. Then he caught her carefully around the middle and set her on her feet.

"Come," he beckoned, plunging into the deep whiteness first to his ankles, then to his knees. She followed after him, finding it hard to keep up in her heavy skirts and with the unaccustomed bulk of her growing belly.

It startled her at first to see him so abandoned to joy, to see him roll in the snow like an unruly colt until, head to foot, he was white with it. He looked at her as if he had surprised himself. Then he grinned as if he did not care and plunged back into the drifts. His breath rose in wisps over his head as he drank down the air's icy freshness like the rarest of wines.

"Come," he beckoned again when she fell a little behind. Then he loped back to her and took her by the hand. "Come."

They spent a long joyous while playing in the snow, making pictures in the smooth drifts, pelting each other with snowballs. To Rosalynde it seemed that the years had fallen away, and he was again the boy she had lost her heart to in Westered. Of course, she had never dared to be so unconstrained with him then, and Westered had never seen such snow, but he seemed unchanged. There was a delighted boyishness in him just now that warmed her heart and made her forget her frozen feet.

When the shadows began to lengthen toward the east, he spread his cloak out over a sunny spot and invited her to sit by him, to again admire the beauty of his meadow. She began to feel the cold once she was still. Noticing her shiver, he put his arm around her.

"I love this place," she said, and he squeezed her closer.

"I had forgotten just how much I love it myself." He took a deep contented breath and watched it curl upwards when he slowly released it. Then he closed his eyes. "I could die here and ask nothing more."

He did not open his eyes when she touched her lips to his cheek, but he slid his hand from her shoulder to the back of her neck and lowered his face to hers. He kissed her lightly at first, then with more intensity. She felt his hand in her hair, tugging it loose from the clasp, and she pressed closer, losing herself in the kiss. Without warning, he stiffened and scrambled to his knees. "No. Not out here."

She sat up, reaching for him, but he drew back.

"We are alone, my lord. No one sees."

"Not out here," he repeated. "Merciful God, out in the woods like some cheap—"

He stopped and looked at her sitting there with her hair tumbling around her shoulders, her skin rosy with the wind's kisses and his own, her eyes round with innocent bewilderment. Still breathing hard, he stood up and looked away from her, out over the meadow, over the snow that was scarred and soiled now with their tracks. He clenched his teeth to steady himself.

"We ought to go in now," he said. "The wind is picking up, and you must have your rest."

Suddenly cold, she drew her cloak more closely around herself and stood up. "I do not want you to be angry, my lord," she said tentatively. "I only—"

He turned to her and took her arm brusquely, his expression stiff and sickened. She wondered what memory, what deep hurt had come back to him here in this place he so dearly loved, but she knew he would never say.

He led her back to the horses, and when he started to lift her to her saddle, she dared to drop a little kiss on his cheek. A shiver of pain ran through him, and she felt his hands tighten around her waist. He took a moment to steady himself once again. Then without a word he set her on her horse and led her away.

All that evening he took refuge in silence. Memories had yet again taken him unawares, the sharp edges cutting through the wadding he had packed around his heart, making him bleed inside. Rosalynde did not know how to reach him in his self-made prison. She wanted to weep in her helplessness, but instead, when he bid her a curt good night, she followed him into his chamber.

"Let me alone tonight." He wrapped himself in his arms and sagged against the casement, looking out into the blue-black night. "Do not think of me anymore at all. I cannot be what you want."

"But we've been happy—"

"I was a fool to think it might be different here. There is no place in this world that's not fouled already." He glanced back at her, deep condemnation in his eyes. "Let me alone tonight."

"I only wish to comfort whatever has grieved you, my lord."

"Comfort? A woman's comfort? I'd sooner have the comfort of fanged adders. Their poison works more quickly."

"Please, my lord."

She touched his shoulder, and he turned and seized her wrist. "I know you fair-faced devils, tempting and deceiving and killing us by inches. My mother was one such. She betrayed my father with his seneschal and then passed off the child of their adultery as a royal prince. And John was left to pay for their sin."

"Your brother John? He was not—He was—"

"A bastard! Say it! He died for that word, for a woman's fault."

"Adultery is not the sin of a woman alone, my lord."

His fingers tightened on her wrist. Then he released it.

"I grant you. Let us speak, then, of your own dear sister Margaret. How many died to feed her ambition? She did not hesitate to take the life of her own child."

"Oh, no, my lord," Rosalynde cried. "She was wicked to betray your father as she did, but she could never have—"

"Do not be such a fool. Do you think Stephen would have taken her still carrying my brother's child? True heir to the crown? She had a taste yet to be queen, and if the child stood in her way, well, that was easily remedied. She was a brave woman though, taking on so fierce an adversary as a child unborn."

His sarcasm stabbed through her. "I am sorry for it, my lord, but her wrongs do not prove all women false."

"No? Name me one you think was not, and I will prove to you she was."

"What of Katherine?"

She had never dared speak that name to him before, and it struck him like a blow. Then his eyes grew colder, cynical.

"You mean my harlot?"

"You were married. Dunois said—"

"Yes, we were married! Do you think I would cheapen the woman I love by making a harlot of her?"

"Can you prove her false, my lord?" Rosalynde asked.

He turned to the window and did not answer.

"If I could make it right, my lord—"

"No one can make it right," he said emptily, "and no one can take her place."

She put her arms around his waist, pressed her cheek and then her lips to his back.

"You needn't carry this alone, my lord," she said.

He took her by the wrists and put her away from him. "And do not think you can tease me again into satisfying your lust," he said, his tone brutally cold. "You are with child. My duty asks no more."

"I beg your pardon, my lord," she said, dignified, fighting tears. Head held high, she turned and walked to the door. Then for a moment she paused, hoping, praying he would call her back, but he was silent. She pulled open the door and stepped into the corridor. Still there was silence, silence she did not break when she shut the door behind her.

His breath shuddered out of him. "How is it she does not hate me?" he murmured. If only she would strike back at him, rail and accuse and spit, he could feel justified at his harshness instead of feeling as if he had just used his lash on a kitten. "I deserve that she should hate me. I could bear it better than all this patience."

He began to pace. Then he remembered his father's guilty pacing and stopped abruptly. Driven, he went into the chapel, hoping to find some peace, some absolution, glad to find it dark and empty.

He thought back on the fervent prayers he had prayed here so long ago. No, he realized, only four years ago. Only four years and he hardly remembered anymore how to pray, how to reach heaven with his heart. He knew that if the man he was now stood beside the boy he was then, there would be little more than a vague physical resemblance between them.

What have I become? he asked himself. Lifting his head, he caught sight of his moonlit reflection in the thick silver candlestick at the side of the altar.

"Father."

The word leapt to his tongue before he could check it, and the truth of it sent a shudder of revulsion through him. There was the same cold determination, the same haughty pride, the same cruel stubbornness. He had become what he had sworn never to be. He had given up himself, his heart, his emotions, his God for his self-righteousness, for his perfect honor, for his hate, just as surely as his father had given up himself for the crown.

"All either of us bought for our pains was remorse." He looked again into the polished silver and turned his head, the better to see his scarred cheek. "And hurt those we should have best loved in doing it."

Rosalynde. Why could he not let himself love her? She was not to blame for those things that had hurt him. She had never done him wrong, yet she had borne his reproach meekly, as only the innocent could do. He told himself he owed Kate his love, and it would be wrong to betray his pledge to her, but that argument was wearing thin. Kate was dead and could not feel his love anymore or give him hers.

Now and forever, I swear it.

"Oh, forgive me, Kate," he murmured as guiltily as a man

tempted from the true faith into idolatry. "I love you and you alone. I will keep my vow."

He had vowed, too, to Rosalynde. She had done nothing but love him patiently, stubbornly, unfailingly, and he had used that love to please himself, when it pleased himself, and had never given any in return. He could not, he reminded himself. He must not soil his honor.

His honor.

He remembered when he was a boy, fourteen, fifteen, sixteen, and his heart had burned with a passion for God. He had chosen then to walk in purity because he knew it would please his Lord. Now he knew his perfect righteousness came not from a heart of love but from a will of iron, a cold pride in his own perfection. Philip Chastelayne would lay down his life without a sound rather than soil his precious honor, his precious, worthless, suffocating honor.

He remembered Tom at his side in this very place, his voice rising above the others, strong and deep in God's praise. Stand him now beside the boy he had been, and the resemblance would have been close. There was still so much of that boy in Tom. It seemed there always would be.

Why did I let that go? Philip wondered, and always he came back to the truth—stubborn pride. He felt an urge to fall to his knees and beg God to break that pride out of him, to put himself into the hands of the living God in submission to His will.

Then fear overtook him. If he prayed that prayer, would not God take him at his word, his unimpeachable word, and humble him? Would He not remove His hand of protection and leave him to Satan's destruction as He had Job? Family and goods and even his own flesh destroyed? He shuddered at the thought, especially that last. Then once again he looked upon his reflection, recalling the scriptural indictment of the fairest of all the created, Lucifer.

Your heart was lifted up because of your beauty. . . .

Would not God cast him away as He had Satan for that father of all sins, pride?

Oh, he was proud—he knew it too well, proud and stiff-necked, stubborn and vain. Could such a miserable creature survive God's justice?

He wiped the candlestick with his hand, smudging it so it could no longer show him what he was. Then he crept up to his bed but did not sleep.

CHAPTER 16

BEFORE THE WINTER WAS PROPERLY OVER, WHEN THE COUNTRYSIDE was still covered with the slick, dirty look of snow that had frozen and thawed and frozen again, messengers began to come from Winton. Stephen was reportedly gathering a larger force than ever before, one that could rival Philip's army. Still graver was the news that Ellenshaw was negotiating with Grenaver for aid in his cause. Rosalynde knew Afton could not meet both enemies at once and hope to emerge victorious.

She watched her husband coming and going from meetings with Darlington and the others, that wary, burdened look again on his face. She prayed fervently for help, for guidance, for a way out for him and for them all.

"Please, my Father, my God," she prayed, seeing him sit silently beside her night after night at supper and as she lay night after night in her bed alone, "do not let his way be made more steep. Show him Your way."

She fell into the habit of wandering near the room where he and his men did their planning, listening to the low comments that passed between them when they came out, comments that did not put her mind at rest. She listened until she could bear no more. Then when she knew he was alone, she summoned her courage and went in to him.

He was sitting with his back to the door, studying a map of Lynaleigh, a map that had been marked and re-marked with the movements of Stephen's men and his own. The feathered end of the quill he clutched was chewed and ragged, and two more like it lay on the floor at his feet. She watched for a moment as he made a note and then another and then marked over each of them. He drew a deep breath and then with an oath slashed his pen across the map, ripping it clean through. It was only then that he caught sight of her.

"I still have my father's ring, my lord," she said hesitantly.

The bewildered frustration in his expression hardened into stern control. "I did not send for you."

"I still have the ring," she repeated, holding it out to him, but he would not take it.

"This is my fight, not his."

"But he will help you if you would but ask him. He told you he would."

Philip stood and began to pace.

"Who is king here, madam?" he asked finally, stopping in front of her. "I or your father?"

"You are, my lord."

"Then it is my duty to defend my kingdom, is it not?"

"Of course, but if he can help us to victory—"

"I told you I would see to it myself."

"Very well." She knew an argument would only make him more implacable. "I will leave it with you, should you change your mind."

She pressed it into his hand, and his fingers clenched around it. Drawing a hissing breath, he brought back his fist as if he would throw the ring into her face. She flinched.

"Never do that!" he commanded. "Do you think I would strike you? Do you think I am coward enough to strike any woman? By heaven, I would sooner rob an altar!" His grip tightened on the ring, and he shook it in her face. "But as to this, do you think I am a woman that I do not know my own mind? Or that I can have it changed for me? I will defend my kingdom. Myself."

Once more he drew back his fist, and this time he hurled the ring out the window with the whole force of his arm. She quickly stifled a cry of protest as he looked at her defiantly.

"Let me be king here, madam," he said, a glittering cold fire in his eyes. "I assure you, the moment I have need of your counsel, I shall send for you."

It was a dismissal, and she dared not object.

As the days passed, more reports came of Stephen and his plans, one after another. Philip's dark mood blackened with each one. Even Joan could not come near him, and it was a stranger she bid farewell when time came for him to leave Treghatours.

He stood on the wide stairway at the entrance to the castle looking over his men, giving instructions to Rafe. He still stood stiffly when Joan gave him a caressing hug.

"I shall hate to have you from me again, my Philip."

"I have my duty to do," he told her, looking steadily southward.

She traced her worn fingers over his stern brow. "Let there be more in your life than duty, child."

He had no answer to that, and after a moment she went up the steps to Rosalynde.

"I am sorry you'll not be here when the child comes, my lady, but you needn't fear. It's sure you'll be well tended."

Rosalynde threw her arms around her. "I wish you would come to Winton with us. He needs you so."

"You know I must see to things here, lady," Joan said. Then she glanced toward Philip. "I can no longer reach him. He's shut himself away from us all."

"I need you," Rosalynde cried, and Joan shushed her as she would a child.

"Go along now, girl. Love him well and be vigilant in praying for him. That is the only good you can do him. God will bless you for it."

She kissed Rosalynde's cheek. Then she moved back down to Philip and laid one hand lightly on his head. "Heaven bless you, my sweet boy."

His eyes still fixed on the road before him, he walked away with no hint of acknowledgment. "Come along, my lady."

Joan sighed, almost a sob, and he turned. His eyes met hers, and she read the look in them. He wanted to run back to her as he had so often when he was a child, to kneel before her and ask her blessing, to bury his face against her and beg her forgiveness, but he could not. Here before his men, before his queen, he could not. Perhaps it was enough that he wanted to.

He turned away again, and she watched him as he helped Rosalynde into the carriage. She was puzzled to see him stoop down and pluck something from the ground before he mounted his horse. Then he said something quietly to the boy, Jerome. In another moment he was gone.

"Mistress Joan?"

Surprised, she turned to find Jerome at her side.

"What, not gone yet?" she asked, trying to blink away the tears that threatened.

"The king sends you this."

He pressed something into her hand. Then he, too, was gone. Astonished, Joan opened her fingers, and the tears came. Philip had sent her a tiny saint's rose, newly sprung up, the first of the year.

"My sweet Philip."

When they returned to Winton, spring had made its presence felt. Green had finally overcome the winter's brown and white, and the birds had come back to nest. Tom strode out to meet the king and queen, followed by the nobility and the people of the town in as hearty a welcome as the grim times could afford.

With all due ceremony, Tom returned rule of the city to the king. Philip made a gracious speech, speaking of the justice of the Afton cause and promising swift victory in the battles to come, with prosperity afterwards. His words almost drowned out by the approving shouts of the people, he spoke of the kingdom's heir that his queen carried and the kingdom's lasting peace he had sworn to for the child's sake. After he had praised the valor of his soldiers, the wisdom of his councilors, and the loyalty of his people, he took Rosalynde's hand, kissed it with all the gallant flourish of which he was so amply possessed, and led her into the palace. Even the heavy doors could not entirely muffle the cheers of the townspeople.

"Can they truly believe it?" he asked.

He had left Rosalynde with her ladies-in-waiting and was sitting alone with Tom in the council chamber.

"They need to believe it," Tom said, dismayed by the cynical tone of his brother's voice. "You of all people must believe it, or we are lost."

"No. I only must make them believe it. My duty requires no more of me."

"Then you do not believe our cause is just?"

"Is it? Is it right that so many should suffer just to keep an Afton king on the throne?"

Tom shook his head. "When Father was alive, perhaps we fought for that because it was our duty. Even though his claim was lawful, I think he was in the wrong to rip Lynaleigh's belly open with civil war. This is different. Stephen is a butcher, and it can only be right to defend the kingdom from him. Have you forgotten Abbey?"

Philip had believed it then, that his cause was just. Standing among the slaughtered, listening to the howls of the bereaved, he could believe nothing else.

"It was our father's cursed ambition that bred that tragedy."

"They found his body."

Philip started. "What?"

"They found his body, what the wolves had not carried off, in a shallow ditch along the road to Cold Spring. I've sent men to bring it back here for burial." There was a tremor in Tom's voice. "I shall never forget the terror in his eyes that day in Breebonne."

Philip thought of his father, of the magnificent knight he had once served, trusted, worshiped, and of the rotten stench of what would remain of the once-golden idol. The thought left him cold.

"I am sorry you had to see it."

"Is that all? He was your father, Philip. They cut his throat in the street! He had not even a moment to make himself right with God before he went to meet Him!"

"He lived by murder, Tom. Have you forgotten? Have you forgotten King Edward and Kate and John? Have you? I've not, and I shall burn in hell before I forgive him."

"And burn in hell if you do not!"

The two glared at each other. Then Tom softened his tone. "But you can repent still. He cannot. He has nothing now but a forever in torment, in gnawing agony. Can that sit easily in that cold heart of yours?"

"He chose death for others," Philip said with a careless shrug. "It is only right he should taste of it himself."

"Do you realize you spent so much time blaming him and hating him that you never noticed Dunois's hand in those deaths? He played upon our father's weaknesses to promote himself, even pushed him to do things he could not bear afterwards."

"Father need not have listened. He could have been strong enough to do right. There are some things I could never be pushed to do and should never expect to be forgiven if I were."

"I hope then, as you say, you never have need of such forgiveness," Tom said, "but I pray, should you need it, you would have it freely given you."

"I shall never need it, and he shall never have it. Not of me."

"Philip, you must—"

"He struck me when I was wounded and vulnerable, for speaking plain truth. It was past forgiveness. He could have chosen to do right."

"He could have. It was his choice for himself though, not for anyone else. There is no one in this wide world can choose destruction for us save ourselves, and no one save ourselves can choose life for us either. We can wound one another, bruise and cut deep, deceive and abuse, or we can comfort and cherish and lead truly, but we cannot choose for anyone to live or die. You say our father chose death for them, for Katherine and for John."

"He did."

Tom shook his head. "I say they chose. Long before Father ordered their natural deaths, they chose to live. They chose Christ. I cannot truly mourn for them. I mourn the emptiness they've left us, the pain of their loss. I mourn that their deaths weighed so heavily upon our father that he felt he must condemn himself to eternal death for taking their lives. I most mourn that you have let his wrongs destroy you."

"I loved him!" Philip swore. "I believed in him! Even after he foreswore his loyalty and destroyed King Edward, I fought for him! But it is too late now if you expect me to pity him. All the love that was in me burned at Bakersfield with Kate; every bit of faith trickled into the dust at Tanglewood with John's blood. I've no more to give." The passion in his expression turned to contempt. "And you can take that look off your face. There's no one here to applaud your filial piety."

"You know I grieve for him," Tom said, his voice soft. "I know you loved him once. He loved you a great deal, though I know he did not always act on that."

"He never loved me. I was nothing to him but boot for his bargains, another bauble for the bartering table. Once Richard was gone, he needed an heir, someone to leave his ill-gotten kingdom to. Well, here I am, heir to a bloody usurper with a questionable title to a broken kingdom. My only question is, who shall take my kingdom and my life from me? There seems to be no other course for the kings of Lynaleigh. King Edward learned it from our father, and Father learned it from Stephen. Now if we are fortunate, Stephen shall learn it from me." There was a bitter gleam in his crystal eyes. "Whom shall I learn it from then? You and I are the last of the true Chastelaynes once Stephen is dead. Will it be you who comes to take my place?"

"You do me wrong, Philip."

"Assure me of your loyalty, Tom," Philip insisted, his voice seething with sarcasm. "King Edward told me our father did that, and Richard, too."

"You know I am loyal to you," Tom said patiently.

"I do, in faith, as surely as I know John is safe and well."

That brought a grimace of pain to Tom's face. "I suppose I should have let you die in Tanglewood rather than tell you that. You might have forgiven me then."

A dangerous fire flashed in Philip's eyes, but it was quickly quenched in regret.

"Faith, Tom, forgive me. I do not know what devil torments me into saying such things and will not let me believe good of anyone. Truly, you should have let me die. It would have been a kindness."

Tom shook his head. "God Himself gave you back your life in Tanglewood. Surely He meant more for you than this desperate hopelessness."

"Granted, I was hurt badly—"

"You were dead! Livrette had given you up! Were it not that God has a merciful ear for prayer, you would be dead still."

"He should have let me die then. Hell holds no terror for me, having lived it already here on earth. He would have done better to spare John, but I suppose God has no more mercy on bastards than our father did."

"Philip!"

"He was a bastard, you know. That's why Father let him die."

"I know."

"How?" Philip demanded in disbelief. "How could you know?"

"John told me himself not long after he came to Winton."

"He told you? Why did he never tell me?"

"He was afraid of you. He was afraid you would hate him, too, if you knew."

"Did he think my love such a light thing?" Philip asked, stung.

"How could he know but that your honor might not bear with a bastard brother? You've not been known for great tolerance of the faults of others."

"That was no fault of his." Philip covered his eyes with his hand so Tom could not see into the shame and grief that was there. "Poor John. How did he know of it?"

"Our lady mother, God forgive her. He told me she used that knowledge of him to shut his mouth from telling anyone about her association with Albright. That whole while we were gone from Treghatours, John had to bear her brazenness in silence."

Philip did not respond, and there was a sudden sick revulsion on his face.

"Philip?"

"I came upon them together once in the forest, her and Albright. It was a very long time ago."

"You never told me of it."

Philip wiped his forehead with the back of his hand. "I—I must have wanted to forget it. I never remembered until this winter when I was in Treghatours."

The memory flashed back to him again, swift and hard and clear. His mother—fine, beautiful madonna of virtue—lying in the autumn leaves in Albright's adulterate embrace. He remembered jerking frantically at his horse's reins, desperate to escape back into the forest, and Albright ordering him to stop. He remembered the jolting flashes of light behind his eyes as Albright dragged him to the hard ground.

"I shall tell my father!"

He remembered more flashes with every blow of Albright's hard fist and the taste of blood.

"Speak one word of this, boy, and I'll crush every one of those fine bones!"

He remembered his mother hurrying toward them. "You would break your father's heart."

"You betrayed him!"

"She could burn for this, boy, and you've heard the duke say he cannot live without her."

"Your father's death would be on your head, Philip, as well as mine." He remembered her sharp nails digging into his cheek as she forced him to look up at her. "Your own mother. Can you be so cruel?"

He remembered the smell of damp fall earth mixed with tears and blood as he turned from them.

"I did not remember it until I was in the meadow this winter. I must have told Nathaniel I was unhorsed in the forest." He looked at Tom with the eyes of a wounded twelve-year-old. "But it was Albright who left those marks on me."

"Then Samson never did throw you."

"No."

Philip sat there forcing back the pain, reading the aching pity in Tom's eyes. He and his brothers all had different wounds that they had for shame kept hidden, painful incidents that they had agreed among themselves not to remember. But he knew too well how such hurts festered under the silence.

"You must forgive them," Tom urged. "All of them. Not just for their sakes, but for the peace of your own soul."

"I will surely forget it again in time," Philip said, dismissing Tom's earnest counsel with a shrug. "There must be many more important matters we ought to discuss."

King Robert was buried in Winterbrooke Cathedral four days later, laid forever beside his faithless queen. Philip thought it fit, almost smiled as the solemn final words were spoken over the tomb. But then late that night as he lay sleepless and alone, he remembered Tom's words. "You must forgive them, Philip. All of them."

He slipped into his boots and breeches and, wary of observers, padded into the darkness, through the castle, into the street, and to the cathedral. Once there, he passed swiftly through the nave and down to the crypt, down the narrow stone steps that were worn in the middle from four hundred years of palmers' feet.

The silence here among the sepulchers seemed a part of the rock, imbedded and unbreakable, the marble effigies guardians of the dark stillness. He lit a candle. Then he whispered a prayer to dispel his fears and muffle his footsteps as he walked toward his father's tomb.

The marble likeness that lay on top of the crypt was stiff and staring, surrounded by blank-faced angels and smirking stone cherubs who presided over the tormented damned and their gleeful demonic persecutors closer to the floor.

One of the demons in particular caught Philip's attention with its bulging eyes and protruding tongue, too-high cheekbones, and hooked nose. It leered wickedly down at him from where it had wound itself around a column at his father's foot, its bony, clawed fingers gripping into the stone. What had possessed the stone carver to put it up there by itself above the angels?

Philip laughed at his own foreboding. As the sound echoed back to him, he felt a chill. Why had he come here? Forgiveness. He had to forgive.

He looked again at his father's effigy. The king's likeness lay with its head on a fierce stone lion. He was dressed in carved semblance of the battle armor that had seen so much victory. The stone legs were crossed, but the angle was unnatural, giving the figure a strained appearance.

Robert's sword had been buried with him, but its replica lay across the stone chest, gripped in marble fingers as cold as those that had been bent around the true weapon and entombed below.

With one finger Philip traced the stately letters carved along the edge of the tomb. Then he spoke them aloud. "'Robert, King of Lynaleigh, third of that name.' You have done me wrong, yet in holy justice, I must forgive you and those fair, faithless bones that lie beside you. Well, then, if it must be, for all those wrongs you have done me—" He knit his brow and felt each pain over again, undulled by the passage of time. He touched the effigy's marble cheek and then his own scarred one. "For all those wrongs you have done me—"

He could not say the words, could not relinquish the pain that was his by right.

"God, I know You'll not hear my prayer if I hold unforgiveness in my heart," he said into the darkness, "so I'll not waste my time. I know I am wrong not to forgive, but I have tried, and I cannot. If You cannot forgive me for that, then there is nothing for it but that I must be damned."

He stood there desolate, certain that his words had gone no farther than the sound of his hushed voice. He was sure that God Himself had turned away His face and left him to struggle through a miserable life that would be only a prelude to hell itself. Was there no more?

"Oh, God!" he cried out in anguish, and he felt his knees bending under him. He would beg God's mercy and forgiveness. He would humble his pride and ask pardon. God was merciful. God would hear a plea for help. God would—

God would not forgive unless he, too, forgave.

Philip lifted his head and forced himself to stand straight.

"I am a Chastelayne. I can do what I must alone."

He snuffed out the candle with his fingertips and felt his way back through the darkness.

As spring warmed into summer, Philip immersed himself in ruling his kingdom, pouring his energies and abilities into every detail of government, demanding of his nobles and councilors a dedication to match his own. Some of them began to call him Philip Ice-Heart again among themselves, seeing his single-mindedness that admitted no joy or pleasure. Rosalynde watched him from a distance, the distance he enforced, and prayed for the peace he so obviously lacked.

As her belly grew rounder and the time for delivery grew near, it was Tom rather than Philip who looked after her and saw that she was kept comfortable. She was grateful for his kindnesses, grateful for his brief attentions, but that only put starker emphasis on her own husband's neglect.

How she needed Philip now, but he was in council early and late or receiving messengers from the battles or making heartening speeches to his soldiers and to his people. She knew Philip Chastelayne would win this war for the sake of his honor, even if he had to fight every battle alone. No one could ever fault his diligence if Afton did not have victory.

She was half a day in labor before anyone dared interrupt his council to bring him word.

Philip waited in the corridor for what seemed hours. Then he stole uneasily into the room, not knowing what to expect. He could no longer stand listening to Rosalynde's cries, and he could not bear to put himself out of hearing when he knew she suffered so.

Half a dozen women attended her, but Rosalynde was oblivious to them.

"Philip. Philip," she moaned. "Philip."

He crept closer, unnoticed until he was at her bedside.

"This is no place for you, my lord," the midwife said sternly. "No place for any man."

"Rosalynde," he whispered, ignoring the woman.

Rosalynde opened her eyes. "Philip."

He took her hand. "I am here."

"Stay with me, Phil—ip!"

His name stretched into a scream as the pain wracked her again, and her once-limp hand clutched his, bruising in its sudden strength. Her body stiffened, and she arched her back, panting.

"Can you do nothing?" he snapped at the waiting women, fearing she could not long survive such pain.

"It is the penalty of Eve, my lord," said the midwife calmly, wiping Rosalynde's face with a damp cloth. "They have it one and all."

Philip snatched the cloth from her. "Leave us," he ordered, blotting the sweat from his wife's face himself.

"My lord, you do not know what you say!" cried the midwife. "We must tend your lady and the child."

"Is it time yet?"

"No, but—"

"Then leave us. Come every hour or every half hour or what you will to check, but leave us now."

"My lord—"

"Go and be hanged!" he raged, stepping toward her as if he would put her out himself, but Rosalynde murmured his name again and clutched his hand tighter, refusing to let him leave her side.

"Be it upon your head then," the midwife said with a look of foreboding. Calling her assistants, she left the room.

Philip filled a cup with lukewarm water from the pitcher and gulped it down. Then he filled it again and held it to Rosalynde's parched lips. She swallowed once weakly and then let the water run out of the corners of her mouth, too weary to swallow again.

"Is there anything you want?" he asked as he wiped her face once more. Her hand tightened slightly on his, but she made no other answer.

"Do you want the women back?"

"No," she whimpered. Then she gasped again at the sudden pain and dug her nails into his arm, drawing blood. He clenched his teeth and held her close until the contraction passed, leaving her spent and panting. Gently he stroked her cheek and pulled her tangled hair away from her face, wondering if he would know when it was time to call back the midwife.

"Forgive me," she sobbed after a little while. "I did not mean to hurt you."

For the first time he noticed the blood that had soaked into his sleeve, and he laughed faintly at her concern for such a trifle.

"Never mind." He pulled her up to a sitting position and sat down at the head of the bed, settling her back against him. "I have long been a soldier, and this—"

He grimaced and gritted his teeth again as another spasm hit her and she clawed his arm once more, raking the first wounds afresh. Yet she did not cry out. She had not but once since he had entered the room.

"I am sorry," she said once the pain had ebbed. "I know a queen should show more courage. I fear I have made you ashamed of me."

He smoothed her damp hair and tried to comfort her, feeling inadequate to the task. Then he held her a little closer, remembering all they had been through together.

"You have more courage than any woman I know," he told her, only just realizing it himself, "and there is no shame in crying now. Do not spare for my sake. Even I am not so selfish as that."

She said nothing, but nestled closer to him, a grateful tear running down the side of her face. For a moment all was still. Then another contraction wrenched her, and though she tried to hold back, the pain was too much, and her moans grew once more into screams. She clung to him as if for her life. He wrapped his arms around her, wishing desperately that he could bear some of the pain himself.

"Oh, God, help her," he pled. The contraction passed, leaving them both bathed in sweat. The pain had grown so fierce, he began to be afraid. "Shall I call the midwife back?"

"If that is what you wish," she said brokenly, holding more tightly to him. He shook his head.

"No, no," he soothed. "It is what *you* want that is important. I know nothing of these matters, but I will stay as long as you will have me."

"Please, please stay," she begged. Another contraction began, and she wrung his bruised hands again, writhing as the pain gripped her.

So the night went on, hour after slow hour, the pain coming and going relentlessly. It seemed that the child was no nearer to being born than it had been at nightfall. Philip talked to her ceaselessly, trying to distract her and himself with the old tales Joan had told when he was a boy. She took in few of the words but rested easier to hear his voice and feel his arms about her. The midwife came and went, and each time Philip asked her if the child would come soon.

"Not yet. Not yet," the old woman would answer. Rosalynde would sigh wearily and cling closer to him.

In the hour after midnight, the midwife brought her attendants back into the room along with basins of cool water and fresh linens for the bed.

"Now?" Philip asked her tensely.

"I do not think so yet, my lord," the old woman said, "but for your own comfort and hers, let us change the bed and her shift and cool her with this fresh water."

He looked uncertain for a moment. "You will not be long?"

The midwife shook her head. "Not long."

He squeezed Rosalynde's hand. "My lady—"

"Come back to me soon," she told him weakly.

The women lifted her off his lap, and he slid out from under her, his back stiff and his legs half numb. "I swear it, my lady, the very minute I may."

He limped out into the corridor where Tom was waiting for news.

"How is she?"

Philip paced, trying to bring feeling into his legs again, holding himself back when he heard Rosalynde cry out.

"It is torture for her, and so hot."

"Here, drink this." Tom handed him a cup of cool water. "Rest awhile."

"I promised I would go back. I cannot let her suffer alone. It is my child, too."

The women soon came out of the chamber, bringing the crumpled sheets and empty basins with them. Philip went to the door.

"Can I do nothing?" Tom asked.

Philip returned only a weary shake of the head. "Pray for a breeze."

Shutting the door, Philip came and sat as he had before at the head of the bed holding Rosalynde against him. She seemed to be resting easier now that the women had changed the sweat-drenched linens and pulled her hair back away from her face.

"When will it be?" she asked later, helpless and tired. "When will it be?"

"Soon," he promised, not knowing whether or not he lied. "It cannot be much longer."

"Oh, for a breath of air," she moaned. At her words a breeze drifted through the east windows, and a strain of soft music came from the corridor.

"Tom," Philip breathed. "No doubt he's set people outside to fan the air in to us and brought the musicians, too."

"Dear Tom." Rosalynde drew a grateful breath and put her hands on her swollen stomach. "Won't you come, little one?"

As if in answer, it began again, worse than before, the pain, the brief respite, and again the pain. He talked on and on, trying to fill the hours and distract her from the pain and fear. When the pain became continuous, the midwife and her attendants came back into the room and hurried Philip out into the corridor. He stood staring at the door, and Tom had to draw him away.

"I did not know it would be like this," Philip said. "I would have never left her so alone."

"Let the women take care of her. They know what's to be done."

"They say many of them die of this, Tom. I could not bear it, not after—"

"Rest now," Tom said, pulling up a chair. "It may be hours yet."

Shrugging, Philip began to pace again, too tense to rest. How could a child be worth such suffering? How could a woman survive it?

The minutes passed like days, and Philip fought the urge to bolt each time he heard her cry out. Once, after a particularly terrible scream, there were several minutes of silence. At first Philip thought nothing of it, but soon the quiet began to worry him.

"Tom," he began uncertainly.

"Maybe it has been born," Tom said, forcing hope into his voice.

"Then we should have heard it cry," Philip insisted. He listened again, straining to hear, but still there was nothing.

"Tom, no!" he cried, springing to the door. Only Rosalynde's weary moan stopped him. Suddenly unable to stand, he dropped into the chair Tom had offered it seemed days ago.

"I should have left the midwife to her work," he said. "If anything were to happen—"

"No, believe me. They could do nothing until the time came. No doubt you comforted her more to stay with her as you did."

Philip leaned back in his chair exhausted. "If anything happens please . . . " He drifted into sleep.

It seemed he had just closed his eyes when he heard someone call his name. He started awake, blinking in the flood of morning sunlight. Tom was holding a squirming bundle out to him.

"You have a son," Tom said, supporting Philip's arms around the child so Philip would not drop him.

"It—it's tiny," he stammered finally, and Tom's laughter rang through the corridor.

"The queen?" Philip asked with an anxious look toward the door.

The midwife smiled. "Very well, my lord."

With a relieved sigh, Philip looked again at the baby lying in his arms, the tiny fists curled up against his chest, his little mouth puckered and quivering, his eyes closed. This was his own son and heir, his firstborn, one day to be king. This child would be raised in his royalty, not brought to it later when he was old enough to know the shock of the newness of it, not brought to it in shame, but bred to it as his right. Lynaleigh would be a kingdom of peace as well when this child was made king. Philip had already promised that, and he would keep it so.

He touched the soft mouth, and the baby opened his eyes and began to cry angrily.

"Faith, he has your temper," Tom said, laughing again.

Philip smiled. "It is a wondrous thing, Tom."

"Here, my lord," said the midwife, holding out her arms. "I will take him to the nurse."

"No. His mother will nurse him."

"Now, my lord, it is not fit that the queen of Lynaleigh should suckle the child herself. Only the common—"

"I said no." He turned his attention to the still-crying child and shifted him gingerly in his arms, quieting him. "Shh. You shall have your breakfast."

Rosalynde smiled through her exhaustion when Philip pushed the door open with his foot and carried the baby in to her, smiled to see the two she loved best.

"Good morning, my lord."

He dismissed her waiting women and sat on the edge of the bed. "You have done well, my lady," he told her, keeping his gaze fixed on the baby. "I am sorry it was such grief to you."

"Oh, no. It was a small price to pay for such a precious treasure. Look at him. Is he not beautiful? He is so like you."

Philip looked up at her suddenly. "Do you love him?" he asked urgently. "Truly?"

"Yes, of course—"

"Truly?" he insisted.

"My lord, you know I do. You must know."

"I need you to love him. A child needs his mother's love."

"His father's as well," she added gently.

"Faith, he does. Let me stand for that. Swear that he will know your love and be secure in it. Swear."

She had never seen such insistence in him before. "I do swear it, my lord, but you had as well make me swear to eat and sleep, to worship my God, or to please you. All these things I do without any thought not to."

She ventured to touch the baby's velvet cheek, and Philip's expression softened.

"He is too small to be left in this world alone," he said. "The midwife was going to take him to the nurse, and I—"

"Oh, my lord, forgive me, but may I not have him? At least at first?"

"You want to nurse him yourself?"

"I know it is not the fashion, but, my lord, he is my baby. A nurse could not love him as his own mother would. I beg you, let me nurse him, if it does not displease you."

"It pleases me very much," he said, handing the child to her. "If you love him."

She cradled the baby lovingly to her breast. "I love him better than all the world." *Next to you alone, my love*, she added in her heart.

Philip's eyes took on a warm tenderness that she had rarely seen there. He settled her against him as he had during the night and watched his son greedily taking his first meal.

Rosalynde studied him as he did. His hands were bruised, his sleeve torn and bloodied as she remembered. His face was tired and unshaven, his hair tousled and in disarray, but to her he was more beautiful at that moment than ever she had seen him.

How she had longed for this. How she had missed this closeness after that brief bit of heaven they had shared in Treghatours. Surely for the sake of the child he would remember now that there was more to this life than duty and honor.

She remembered little of her labor save the pain and his soothing presence. He had been faithful to her all through the night, heart and soul, as if there were nothing in the world but the two of them alone. Truly this child was theirs together. More than compounding their flesh, they had brought him together into the world, and together they would raise him to manhood. Philip had promised.

CHAPTER

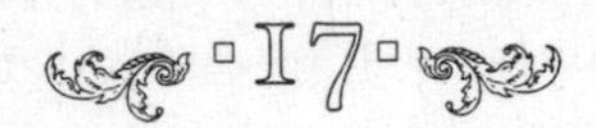

17

FOR A WHILE PHILIP SEEMED TO LOSE HIS OBSESSION WITH THE WAR and let Rosalynde nearer to him. He had told her that their son would be named Robert, another of his duties, a promise he had made his father a long while ago. There had been a touch of fear in her eyes when he made his grim announcement, fear that the obligation would sour his pleasure in the child. But then he had cooed at the baby and called him "little summer Robin," and she had smiled again.

It is only for the sake of the child, Philip told himself, but he found he could not so easily push her away from him now with so tangible a bond between them. Still, he would take care that it never grew to be something more. He had told her from the beginning that he would not love her and had made sure she knew he would never break his word. So long as she remembered that, so long as she did not try to press close into his heart, into the deep places he had reserved for Katherine, they would have peace enough.

Tranquillity ended with the news that Stephen had amassed an army at the Grenaven border and begun marching to Winton, leaving a wide path of destruction behind him. The council chose Tom to lead the force against him. Philip was set on going himself, but Tom reasoned him out of that.

"You are more needed here," he said, glancing at Rosalynde as she sat with some of her ladies across the great hall.

Philip followed his glance and frowned. "My duty is first and always to Lynaleigh."

"Your duty to Lynaleigh lies here. I know you had rather be in the midst of the fight, but it is part of your duty as king to direct rather than do."

"You are right, of course. Well, take my men then. I trust you with them over anyone."

"You can trust my diligence if nothing else." Tom grinned at him. "I've a wife waiting, and no amount of letters between us will content me until I have her with me always, and that cannot be until this war is won."

How often he forgot that Tom had a wife. Had and did not have. Would he be content when they were reunited?

"I pray she proves worth the winning, Tom."

"God's grace upon us, we shall have peace soon, and then I will prove to you what great return a little investment of love will bring." Tom looked again at Rosalynde. "You might find it so yourself if you cared to."

They exchanged farewells, and Philip watched him go to Rosalynde's side and speak something cheerful to her, something that made her smile. He scooped up the baby that lay kicking and cooing at her feet and kissed his pink cheek. Then he touched his lips to Rosalynde's hand and was gone.

What great return a little investment of love will bring, Philip reflected. *I know you have not found it so with me, my lady.*

But he could not ignore the pull that endless love of hers had upon his heart.

The news of the battles was grave in the weeks that followed. Messengers came and went, and the council seemed forever in session. Then late one night, word came that Tom's army had been pushed back to Chrisdale. The nobility debated long about what must be done next, and afterwards, exhausted with their bickering, Philip made his way up to the nursery.

Duty and nature and affection all demanded he love this child of his, just as he would have loved Katherine's child. There was nothing in that innocence that had ever wronged him. Although he had little time these days to demonstrate that love, the tiny speck of softness in his heart, that little bit he still admitted to, longed for it. He wanted just a moment to hold the baby, to know tangibly that he was not alone in the world, before he went to the empty sleeplessness of his bed.

"Good evening, my lord."

He was startled to see Rosalynde in the nursery so late. "I had thought you would be asleep long ago, my lady."

"I was," she said, "but our little Robin decided he was hungry again. I've only just settled him back in bed."

He came up beside her as she leaned over the cradle, and they both looked fondly on the sleeping child.

"It pleases me to see you caring for him yourself. He will grow to be a good man with such a mother."

"And such a father."

She turned to him with that unquenchable adoration in her eyes. Taken unawares, he felt everything in him fighting to answer it, everything but his pride. Before that could be overmastered, they heard a furtive knock.

"My lord?"

Philip recognized Rafe's voice and opened the chamber door.

"Lord Tom is coming back into Winton, my lord," Rafe said. "He and his men are not half a mile away."

"Tom?"

Rosalynde clutched Philip's arm. "My lord—"

"Pardon me, my lady, but if they are coming in so late at night, it will not be in triumph. You must excuse me."

He briefly kissed her hand. Then he hurried out of the chamber with Rafe scurrying behind him.

Tom's soldiers poured into the city, wounded, dirty, dying. One demoralizing defeat had crowded onto another, and Tom brought with him the blackest news of all. "Stephen's hot behind us, Philip, and King William with him."

"So Grenaver is backing him as we heard. But why? Stephen hates Grenaver. And we both know what small love Grenaver holds for Lynaleigh."

"Stephen's promised them all the Riverlands in exchange for their aid," Tom informed him, "and they've not forgotten our father's triumph over them not so long ago. They'd love to pay Afton for that."

"So how far off is our loving cousin?" Philip asked tightly.

"His main force will likely be at Winton's walls by tomorrow afternoon. Next morning latest."

"Can we not meet them before then? The garrison here and all your men—"

"All my men? Philip, I've perhaps a quarter of those I left with if I count the wounded, and many of those'll not likely last the night. Why do you think we came to shelter here? There are simply too many of them now. We must consider another way to defeat them. Winton will keep us safe for some while if we are wise. In that time, we can devise a plan."

"We've no choice but to try," Philip agreed slowly, "though with your men here, drawing on our supplies too, we'll not last long."

"Long enough, I pray."

Tom's prediction proved true. The combined armies of Ellenshaw and Grenaver surrounded Winton at sunset the next day, a formidable host of foot soldiers and horsemen with colorful banners held high. Tom and Philip watched from the walls as Stephen himself came to the city gate with a great show of heralds and footmen and other bright trappings to give legitimacy to his claim.

"Good evening, Cousin Philip," he called confidently.

Tom watched his brother's reaction, but Philip merely looked down on the would-be king, not deigning to speak.

"Still proud, cousin?" Stephen demanded, needing no provocation to spoil his temper.

"Still king, cousin."

Stephen smiled. "King of Winton perhaps. For a while."

"That is yet to be tried. Despite your armies, and whatever the outcome of this battle or this war, I am king of Lynaleigh. By the acclaim of the people, by right of blood, by my father's holy anointing, I am king."

"Not so, cousin," Stephen said with a bland smile. "My father, the one you had murdered, was king. Who but his only son and heir should be king after him?"

"My father," Philip shot back, "the one *you* had murdered, was rightful king, leaving me rightful king now."

Stephen laughed outright. "I suppose we are even then regarding fathers. Let us speak of kingdoms. I've no wish to bandy pedigrees with you."

"No, you'd hardly want that."

"I'd not feel so secure, cousin, were I you. Who can tell how many bastards your mother passed off as Chastelaynes. Rounchaux may not have been the only one."

"John was worth a hundred of you!" Tom spat. Then he stopped himself and matched his cousin's sardonic grin. "Better a bastard by birth than by disposition."

Stephen's expression blackened. "I'll have that insolent tongue—"

"Your informants know their duty well," Philip interrupted icily.

Abruptly Stephen was smiling again. "Dunois was a veritable fountain of information. Still, I have meant to thank you for disposing of him for me. He was too clever and ambitious for my tastes. He betrayed my father; then he betrayed yours. I could hardly trust him. Besides, I believe he had some fancy that I would marry his daughter and put his grandson on the throne. Ha! A yeoman's son grandsire to Lynaleighan royalty? Indeed."

"I believe you came to speak of kingdoms, cousin," Philip reminded him, his cold voice cutting through the growing darkness. "Pray you, keep to that."

"I did not come to speak of kingdoms, cousin, but to take mine."

"Hell is the only kingdom you have due you."

"Then let the devil look to his crown. Until I come there, though, you had best look to yours."

"I do, cousin, and shall. Winton has never been taken by force and is not likely to be."

"You cannot stay sheltered there forever. We will breach the walls, or you will starve. Either way," Stephen gloated, "I will take back my city and my throne. Return them both to me now and save your people from the destruction I will bring them if I must take what is mine by force."

"Take them, cousin," Philip said, "if you can. I'll not give them to you."

"The slaughter is on your head then. I wash my hands of it."

Tom's eyes turned hard. "Any blood you shed here will join with the seas of blood you have shed already and cry out to God for His vengeance."

"If this God of yours is so great and mighty, why are you who claim to be His people driven into hiding here? Why does He not strike me dead now and my armies too and give you victory?" Stephen looked up at the silent sky. Then he laughed, an evil mirth that deepened Tom's anger.

"He is merciful and not willing that even you should perish." There was no godly charity in Tom's tone.

Philip shook his head. "Do not waste your words on him, Tom."

Tom studied him for a moment and then looked down at Stephen. They were so alike in their proud disdain. He realized he was himself no better, speaking of God's mercy without love.

"Please, cousin," he said to Stephen, his tone gentler. "It is not too late even now for you to come to Him and make peace."

"Do you think I will give up everything that is mine to follow your helpless God? I'll not submit myself to anyone—God or man!"

Stephen raked his horse's flanks with his cruel spurs, making the beast rear up as he turned. "Call on your God. Let Him save you if He can. I do not fear Him or you."

He signaled his men, and in a moment they were gone. Philip stared after them long after they had disappeared into the darkness.

The days of siege wore into weeks, and with every day that passed, the tension grew. Philip's soldiers became restless and quarrelsome as they wasted the time away inside the city walls, eager for action and spoiling for trouble. Philip himself was as restless as they and spent his time in endless meetings with Darlington and the others, trying to find some way to end the siege.

Stephen had them. For all the years Philip had led armies, for all the wisdom and experience of his councilors, he could see no way out. Stephen would breach the wall, or Philip and his people would starve. Already the shortages that were too common throughout the city had reached the royal palace.

Philip took a bite of heavily spiced meat, horse by now he suspected, and watched Tom and Rosalynde in animated conversation a short way away. They seemed to be together a great deal since the siege.

Since she first came here, he thought sourly.

A melodious cascade of her laughter reached Philip's ears, backed by Tom's throaty chuckle. He felt a stab of jealousy. The emotion surprised him.

What should I care if she enjoys herself? There is little enough opportunity for that these days, and it is kind of Tom to show her some attention. God knows I've not.

It occurred to him that Tom had been given only a week with his bride, just enough, doubtless, to sharpen his natural desire for her before she was taken away from him, and now Tom had been a long while without her. It occurred to him, too, that Rosalynde was very, very beautiful and he had left her too often alone.

My father made that mistake.

She turned suddenly in his direction and saw him staring darkly at her. In an instant the sparkle died in her eyes, and all merriment left her face.

"Is anything wrong, my lady?" Tom asked.

"Pray excuse me to my lord," Rosalynde murmured, and she escaped out onto the balcony.

Tom turned and gave Philip a reproachful glance, but Philip only returned a cold stare until Tom looked away.

"I am sorry," Rosalynde said to the pale-faced moon as she stood letting the night air cool her burning cheeks. She realized she had again somehow transgressed. Again she could not fathom in what. "I am sorry."

"For what, my lady?"

She turned to see Philip standing in the dark archway just out of the moonlight.

"You left your supper uneaten," he said. "Was it not to your liking? Or perhaps it was I who was not to your liking. I think I have let this siege make me very poor company for you."

"You have a great many things to see to, my lord," she said, unable to read his mood in his half-shadowed face, wondering if he were trying to make amends. "I understand."

"I'll not admit that as an excuse. You should be angry."

"Never, my lord. Not with you."

He stepped a little way out of the darkness, and for a moment they stood in awkward silence, searching each other's eyes. Then she looked away and sat down on the rough-hewn bench the sentries sometimes used.

"They are quiet tonight out there," she ventured finally.

He sat down beside her. "I pray it bodes peace both inside the wall and out."

She lifted her eyes to his, still searching. "Surely if peace were offered, both sides would put aside their grievances and embrace it."

"If it could be done with no compromise of honor. If it could, I would open my arms wide to it." He gently twisted a lock of her hair around his finger and then released it, letting it spring back into place. "But honor is not so easily kept, and such differences cannot be always so easily mended."

"But they can be mended," she said, hearing something like regret in his tone, and she moved closer to him. "Both sides being willing."

"I would it could be so." He leaned back against the wall. "I want nothing now more than peace."

"As I do, my lord."

He rested his cheek against her hair. "Only peace."

She felt the breath of his words against her ear and nestled closer to him. The night was quiet.

For several minutes he sat holding her, considering what she had said.

. . . both sides being willing.

Being willing, he thought. Then he felt her hand at the back of his neck, felt her gentle fingers easing away the tension. He had had nothing from those hands save soothing tenderness, sweet comfort. He pressed his face into the curve of her shoulder, his breathing slow and deep, and felt all the tightness melt out of him. She held him closer.

He had not meant even to touch her. That was never his intent in coming out to her, but she smelled so intoxicatingly of saint's rose. Her skin was softer than its petals and fairer, too, and when he pressed a tentative kiss against the sweet whiteness of her throat, her sigh, soft and low in his ear, made his heart quicken. He tightened his arms around her, and she offered her lips in wordless invitation. Wordlessly, he accepted, holding her with an endless kiss, until finally he dragged his mouth away from hers.

"God have mercy," he gasped with sudden fear. "What are you that you draw me so?"

Frustrated tears welled into her eyes. "What are you then, my lord?" she cried, throwing his hands off her and getting unsteadily to her feet. "You madden me, Philip! Either ice or fire always and never a warning which!"

He looked at her for what seemed eternity. "I suppose you wish you'd not married me. Have you learned to regret that yet?"

"No, my lord."

"You might have had someone who makes you laugh and not cry." His eyes narrowed, and there was a sudden edge to his voice. "Tom makes you laugh, does he not? He makes you laugh and soothes your hurts and bids you trust in God to set things right and never says a wrong word."

"My lord—"

"Oh, I know it well enough. He can always smile. He has no past to bind him, no memories to rot him, no scars to hide. He need do nothing more than smile and talk sweetly."

"Just because he is kind, my lord, that does not—"

"I daresay you think he would have made you a better husband."

"I think no such thing, my lord," she said with a weary sigh. Again there was a long silence between them.

"Forgive me, lady," he said finally. "Your patience deserves better than I have been able to give you. Give me time, and I will make amends."

She looked up at him in astonishment. Then the hope faded from her eyes. "I know that look in you, my lord, that dutiful emptiness that is as far from your heart as heaven is from hell. Why do you say such things when we both know how little you mean them?"

"Because I do mean them," he said impassively.

"You told me you would not lie to me, my lord."

He clenched his jaw. "Because I promised your father I would—"

"Because you promised my father?" Tears sprang into her eyes. "Because you promised my father!"

She turned away, and he tried to make her face him.

"My lady—"

"Do not touch me. Save your charity for the almshouse."

Instantly, he released her, and his expression turned cold. "As you please."

Before he could stand, she caught his face in her hands and pressed a gentle, loving kiss on his lips.

"Why did you do that?" he breathed, that mistrustful fear once more flooding through him.

"I am not made of stone, my lord, as it seems you are."

"No," he murmured, "not stone." He caressed her cheek with the back of his hand. "Not stone, but too much flesh."

She clutched his hand and held it there. "Philip—"

He leapt to his feet and shook her by the shoulders. "Stop! Stop trying to make me what I cannot be! What I must not be!" He pushed her away from him. "Go back inside. No doubt my brother is missing you by now."

With a quickly muffled sob, she went back into the great hall. A few minutes later, Tom came out onto the balcony.

"I would have a word with you, Philip."

"Now is not the time. Come to me tomorrow."

"Shall I bring this up before the council, my liege?" Tom said, keeping his expression pleasant. "I hardly believe you want all of your nobles to hear what I have to say. You know how they talk already."

Philip could feel his temper tightening around his self-control, straining it, ready to snap it at any moment. With effort, he nodded calmly. "As you say. What is it you want of me?"

"I have tried very hard to hold my tongue since I've come back to Winton, but I just—"

"You just could not resist an opportunity to meddle in things that do not concern you."

"Please, Philip, for your lady's sake and your own, be kind to her if you can manage nothing more."

"You're quick in her defense," Philip observed, a trace of acid in his tone.

Tom studied him for a moment. Then he laughed abruptly. "Oh, spare me your jealousy. What—jealous of me?"

"I am not!"

"You are," Tom said, "else why are you so angry over nothing? Why do you care unless you love her?"

"And why are you so bent upon pushing her at me? You are worse than Father ever was."

"I am not trying to push you, Philip. It just pains me to see you so cruel to her when she loves you so."

Philip's eyes were cold crystal. "What does she know of love? She is a woman, a creature of appetite. She does not love me; she needs me. She needs me to see she is well kept, to make her queen, to deck her with jewels and fine silks, to keep her safe. Love me? Use me rather. Can you call that love?"

"I call it love when she weeps for your pain and pleads with God for your happiness, when she lives and dies by your smiles and frowns."

"I never professed to love her, Tom. She is the one who claims there is something nobler than lust between us. Still, for all her words, I am nothing more than a moment's pleasure to her."

"I daresay she would thank God, fasting, for even a moment's pleasure with you," Tom retorted. "Can you be so blind? She wants your heart, not just that fine flesh you are so vain about. It's certain she wants you, and it is right that she should, being your wife, but she knows too well that that is not enough. I've seen the heartache in her eyes when you treat her as if you can scarcely endure her presence or, worse, when you do not even acknowledge it. If you are determined to be miserable, must you make her miserable as well?"

Philip lifted his chin. "I never asked to marry her."

"Has it never occurred to you that perhaps your marriage is not the most pleasant thing to her either?"

"She wanted it."

"She wanted you because she loves you. Can you ask more of love and devotion than she has already given? Put aside the past, Philip, and take the happiness that is even now in your hands. Do not turn away the love and comfort God has sent to help you through this trouble."

"What love and comfort?"

"Rosalynde. Love her. God's own Word says you ought to take pleasure in the wife of your youth."

"Kate was the wife of my youth. I ceased to be young when they burnt her."

"Do not waste your life in grieving for her. She would never have wanted that for you, not if she loved you as deeply as you claim. Let go of the past. Love Rosalynde."

"It could never be the same."

"True, it could not possibly, but it could be as good, better, if only you would let it be so. Give up that pride that makes you cling to what has hurt you. Give up your grief and live."

"It is more than I can do after all that has happened," Philip said, his voice expressionless. "I would not know how."

"Give it to the Lord. He will carry sorrow's burden for you if you will let Him. He surely knows what it is to grieve, watching over this poor world. You think you loved John? You think you loved Katherine? He loves them more than you could ever hope to know."

"Then why did He not love them enough to save them?"

"What did you do when they were taking Katherine to be burnt? Did you pray?"

Philip looked away, and Tom forced him to turn back.

"Did you? Did you pray? I was told you cursed everyone from the peasants to the king himself. How was God to answer that?"

"What about you then, Saint Thomas?" Philip wrenched away from him. "When John lay bleeding to death, did you pray? Did you ask God for his life?"

Tom winced. "No. God forgive me. I came too late for that."

There was deep pain in his face, and Philip wished he could take back the words. He knew Tom's prayers at Tanglewood had saved his own life.

"Tom, I—"

There was a thick silence between them until Tom finally spoke again. "All that is past, but Rosalynde is now. You needn't fear to trust your love to her."

Philip laughed harshly. "Rosalynde again? What would she need with my love so long as she has you to pet her and remind her how ill-used she is."

"Yes, well, I am certain it must be easier by far for you to be angry with us both than to admit to yourself that you love her."

"Take care, Tom."

There was a fierce spark of anger between them. Then Tom bowed. "If you will pardon me, my liege, I have better things to occupy me than to try to coax you into loving your wife."

"See to them then."

I do not love her, Philip told himself once Tom was gone. *I do not. I am merely drawn by my pleasure in her*.

He knew that was a lie, and he cursed his weakness. There were other women who would have willingly satisfied his desires and asked nothing else, but he was familiar with that feeling—lust and no more. He was long used to mastering that.

With Rosalynde, there was a difference. If there had not been, he could have kept that distance between them without effort. He could have gone to her bed and found it easy to leave and not think of her until he wanted her again, easy to use her as he deemed necessary and feel no remorse if he should hurt her. If there had not been a difference, he would not have this torture inside him now.

He had found something healing in her embrace, something that satisfied more than his body. He told himself the desire he felt for her was weakness. No, not his desire for her—that was his right and duty as her husband, as natural as eating and sleeping. The weakness was in his need for her to hold him close, to fill the emptiness in his heart that Katherine had left, an emptiness he should not want anyone but Katherine to fill. Could it be that Rosalynde loved him as deeply as her every word and deed cried out she did? That if he went to her, even now she would not turn him away?

He knew she had a tender heart, despite all the blows he had dealt it. Doubtless she was weeping even now, and he could not bear to hear her cry. She was fortunate to be a woman, to have the sweet release of tears. He was a man—more, a king. Tears were not allowed him; he could not allow them to himself. But he knew she would allow them to him, her with her tender heart.

He berated himself again with his vows to Katherine and realized that her image was fading from his mind. He struggled to recall it, to see again the golden hair, the soft, fresh-blooming cheeks, the innocent fawn-brown eyes, but he could not form the pieces into a coherent whole. All he could see was Rosalynde, her emerald eyes crying out the devotion he had forbidden her to speak aloud and her soft, trembling lips pressed to his in a kiss that held nothing of lust and everything of tender love.

With a groan, he leaned against the wall and buried his face in his arms, trying to obliterate the image. Had he inherited his constancy from his inconstant mother?

I'll not love her, Kate. Did he love her? He must not. What had he heard about a double-minded man? Unstable in all his ways? *If I lose all else, Kate, I will keep my honor and keep my vows*.

"My liege?"

Philip straightened with a jerk and then at once was all dignity. "My lord Darlington. What news?"

"Ellenshaw has brought his siege guns to our walls, my liege. They are bound to begin using them come morning."

"It was sure to come. Go and tell the rest of the council. I will find Tom."

When she left the great hall, Rosalynde went into the nursery to visit Robin. She could not just go sit down at supper the rest of the evening, not with Tom looking at her, reading the distress in her eyes, his own filled with knowing pity. She could not bear that tonight. Besides, it comforted her to hold the baby, to know that at least this much of Philip was hers. She did not cry anymore. There was little to cry about, she knew, unless it was the months of seeing her husband slip farther and farther away from her.

She often wondered why she let him hurt her at all any more, why she still cared, why she did not let her pain sour into hatred. Then she would remember the sweetness of their winter together at Treghatours or his tender care of her the night the baby was born or the searching lost look that was sometimes in his eyes when he did not know she could see him, and she would remember that he was wounded still. Inside. Those times she knew that everything else did not matter. He belonged to her, he needed her, and she would always love him.

She stayed with Robin until he fell asleep with most of one chubby fist in his mouth. Then she crept quietly back to her own chamber, glad that her ladies would not return for some while yet. Not bothering to light the candles, she loosened her bodice and began to unbind her hair, hoping that would ease the throbbing in her head. Things ought to look better in the morning. At least with a sound night's sleep, she would be better able to face them.

She pushed off her shoes and ran her fingers through her thick locks, glad to feel her headache ease. Closing her eyes, she rolled her head to one side and then dropped it forward.

"Oh, God, please—"

There was a knock at the door, and her prayer went unfinished.

"Yes?"

Tom pushed the door open. "Stephen has brought his siege guns to Winton, my lady. The council is looking for the king. He is not here?"

She almost laughed, thinking how unlikely it would be these days to find her husband in her bedchamber. Instead, she burst into tears.

"Oh, my lady, please do not cry." Tom lit a taper from the hearth and came to her. "I am sorry."

"Can I never reach out to him without touching a raw place?"

"Do not blame yourself, my lady," he said, pity in his eyes. "He is his own chief torturer. Until he bends that stubborn will to God's, he will never be free. Until then, you will never be able to love him enough to make him happy."

"I thought I could, but he always has his memories to poison any happiness I try to give him. He is sworn to his Katherine, and she had one chief charm that I cannot hope to defeat. He loved her."

"He did," Tom agreed. "I know it. And with him it is impossible to love by halves."

"They were married," she said. "He loved her as much as that."

"Yes, I know."

"You do? Of course you do. He would have told you."

"No, he never told me. He never told anyone."

"Then how—"

"I heard the gossip, saw them together, and knew with him it could be no less than marriage. If you know nothing else of him, my lady, you must know how strictly he holds his honor. Sometimes beyond reason. That is why he fights so hard to keep you away from him. Not because he does not want you, but because he wants you too much. He considers his vows to her binding yet."

"But she is dead."

"That does not matter," Tom said. "To him any thoughts of you are lust and adultery."

"Why did he never tell anyone she was his wife? She was a princess. Would that not have protected her from your father?"

"Philip feared that if Father knew they were married, he would do just as he did and make away with her for it, because he did not think her fit to be queen."

"But surely for her child's sake, he could not—"

"You knew there was to be a child?" Tom asked.

"So Dunois said. He said your father knew it as well."

Tom nodded, his mouth grim. "Does Philip know?"

"Yes. I think that has only bound him more closely to his Katherine. What was she, my lord? What was in her that made him so forever tied to her love?"

"Nothing but a pure heart and a love for him he was sure would never prove false. That was all in all to him. It is still."

"He longs for her even now," she murmured.

He shook his head. "He longs for you."

"For me?"

"There is a fineness in him and a love well worth having if you could but reach it," Tom said, taking her hand. "Even if he denies it to himself, he loves you. I've seen it in him all along, but he is so bound in his pride I fear he would die before he would surrender to you. He'll not even yield himself to God."

"He is grinding his heart into dust," she sobbed, "and I do not know how to stop him."

Tom sat down and put his arm around her, and she clung to him, taking comfort from his strength, from his soothing calmness, from just the touch of kindness. He held her a little tighter.

"Love him. Pray for him. I can only believe that in time he will see—"

"See what? My brother and my wife whoring behind my back?"

Rosalynde sprang to her feet.

"No, my lord," she cried, trembling at the implacable contempt on her husband's face as he slammed the door shut behind him. "No, never!"

"You do your lady great wrong," Tom said, standing too. "I do not think you know what you say."

"No," Philip said. "No more than I know what I see."

Tom nodded. "Precisely."

Philip's slap caught him off guard and knocked him to his knees. Before he could defend himself, Philip took him by the throat and slammed him against the wall.

Rosalynde watched, horrified. "No!"

"You want him?" Philip demanded, and she shrank away from him, tears streaming down her face.

Tom grabbed his brother's wrists and tried to free himself.

"Philip," he said thickly, tasting his own blood, "you cannot think—"

With cool deliberateness, Philip increased the pressure, silencing his protests. Tom's grip tightened convulsively, but then suddenly relaxed as Philip slammed him into the stone wall again and again and again.

"You want him?"

Rosalynde tried in vain to pull his hands away. "Please! I beg you, stop!"

Philip pushed her aside with a sweep of his arm, using the other to keep Tom from sagging to the floor, but Rosalynde went straight back to him, dragging at his sleeve.

"You mustn't!"

"Mustn't, strumpet? Mustn't think you've betrayed me with my brother here? You with your hair down your back and your bodice unlaced? What would I have found here in a quarter of an hour?"

"Oh, no, my lord!"

"My mother was a strumpet. Why should my wife prove any better? She used to look at my father as you do me, all demure chastity, all devoted adoration, as if she would die out of his presence, and yet she was as false as the devil himself."

"I cannot help but look at you so, my lord. If your mother's love was counterfeit, still mine cannot dissemble and look like anything but love."

"She would have said so, too. My fine, virtuous mother would have said no less, though she might have been more convincing at it." He dropped Tom down senseless at her feet. "I'll spare both of you the justice I might have for this. Stephen's brought his siege guns to our walls. No doubt he will prove a fine executioner."

"Please," she sobbed, "you mistake—"

"No, madam, you mistake if you think I will let my brother supply my place in my wife's bed or let that fault go unpunished."

"You cannot believe that! My lord, you must hear me!"

"Must I?" he mocked.

"You must. If for nothing more than the justice you profess as king, you must."

She saw she had struck a responsive chord, calling his honor into question.

"Well?"

"Please, my lord, I do not know what I should say," she cried, wondering how a look so cold could burn straight through her. "I do not know how you could think such a thing."

"I think there was only one woman on this earth who could keep faith, and they burnt her."

Rosalynde knelt beside Tom and wiped the trickle of blood from the corner of his mouth. "Whatever it is that has made you so blind to truth, I swear you wrong me and him and yourself in this."

"I almost believed you," Philip said with sudden, fierce earnestness. "I almost believed you loved me."

"Philip! Please, Philip!" she sobbed, reaching her hands up to him, but he was gone.

CHAPTER

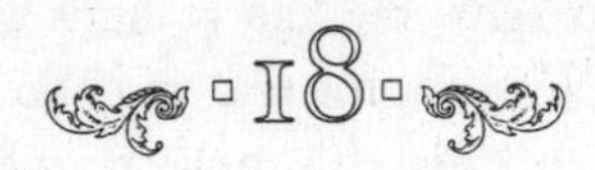

18

THE BOMBARDMENT CAME AT DAWN AND DID NOT STOP THROUGHout the day. Philip stood up on the wall listening as the sounds of war raged around him—deafening, maddening, ceaseless. The enemy was hammering at the walls of Winton, Winton that had never fallen—Winton that had survived siege after siege, attacks of fire and pestilence, merciless famine. Despite their efforts at defense, Winton's walls would soon be breached.

There would be no help and no mercy for them now. Philip tried to encourage his men, tried to maintain calm in the terror, but he could not. Fear ruled his kingdom now, not he, and he knew no way to regain his authority, no way to save his people and himself from certain disaster.

"I must do something," he said, watching the continuing flash and boom of Stephen's siege engines. Suddenly the wall beneath him shuddered, and he leapt to the ground just as it collapsed upon itself. Another crack and flash brought down the side of a nearby house, showering him with debris. Again the guns fired, and a large beam crashed down, grazing his shoulder. He had to get out of the street.

He ran up the stone steps and pushed his way into the shelter of Winterbrooke Cathedral. The quiet reverence of the place had been shattered. People huddled everywhere, peasants and nobles alike.

Few even noticed their king, and none cared. It was for their own safety they now prayed.

"What can I do? What can I do?" Philip muttered. He had to gather his troops and make them once more into an army, an army with heart enough to fight. He had to fight to his last man, to his own last breath, for Winton, for the oath he had made as king. It was all he had left. If only this hellish bombardment could be stopped—

"'Do not forsake me, oh, Lord,'" one of the priests quoted. "'Oh, my God, do not be afar off. Hasten to help me, oh, Lord, my salvation. Oh, Lord—'"

A shriek rose from the cowering refugees as another ball shook the building, shattering the multicolored glass in the cathedral's huge windows. Shaken, Philip stumbled to his knees at the foot of the marble statue of Christ that stood behind the altar, its arms outstretched in welcome.

"Where are You?" he demanded. "Can You not hear them crying out to You? Will You do nothing?"

Yet again the guns roared, and Philip ducked his head as the ceiling began to fall around him. He heard the groan of the heavy beams as they began to split. He heard the terrifying thud of the huge stones as they cracked apart on the marble floor. He heard the agonized screams of the people who were pinned under them, the sickening sound of bones crushed and flesh mangled beyond repair.

"Jesus," he whispered, looking up. To his horror the heavy statue began toppling toward him. Trapped where he was, he could do nothing but duck his head and uselessly shield himself with his arms.

Tom bounded up the steps into the cathedral. Inside, people were trying to free themselves from the ruins, aiding the wounded and carrying off the dead. The bombardment had stopped for the night.

"Where is the king?" Tom asked. "Is he here?"

One of the men shook his head. "He was at the east window when I last saw him, my lord, but it's all fallen in over there now."

Tom looked where he was pointing. There was only an enormous pile of rubble where the magnificent window had been, and no sign of Philip.

Tom began pulling pieces of stone and wood from the pile. "Philip! Philip, can you hear me? Philip?"

Philip's voice was faint. "I cannot move."

"Philip!" Tom began to work faster. "Some of you men, help me. The king is trapped under here."

With their aid, he was soon able to see Philip's grimy face.

"I can finish here, men. Go tend to the wounded." They were quick to obey him, and he leaned down to Philip. "Are you hurt?"

"No, but I still cannot get out."

"Nothing short of a miracle," Tom marveled as he moved a few more stones. Philip did not have even a scratch on him, only a dusting of fine powder from the crumbling marble. Tom reached his hand toward him to help him stand, but Philip would not take it.

"A pity that one of those stones did not dash out my brains," Philip said sullenly. "Then I would not have to see Winton in Stephen's hands."

"You've given her up for lost then."

"We've no chance now. We're hopelessly overmatched."

"Have faith!" Tom insisted. "God can make a way when there is none. We've seen that time and again, too many times to doubt now."

"Open your eyes, Tom. God has turned His back on me. He'll not send me His help again."

"Open *your* eyes, Philip," Tom said, pointing.

Philip looked up. Above him, shielding him from the murderous stones, was the statue of Christ, fallen with its hands and forehead wedged firmly against the wall, making a perfect shelter for him beneath it.

"Has He truly forsaken you?" Tom asked.

Philip pulled himself uneasily from the rubble, his eyes fixed on the gentle marble face.

"Do not be more of a fool than you are already, Tom," he said, his voice gruff as he turned away. "He has forsaken me. Kate and John and Father, this whole unholy war, everything that has happened is proof enough of that."

"Those things are Satan's doing because we oppose Stephen's evil in Lynaleigh, because we stand for the Lord."

"Then Satan is stronger than God, and we should worship him."

Tom was stunned by these blasphemous words and the deep bitterness in his brother's voice. "Oh, Philip, no. How can you say so?"

"Because otherwise we would not be in this strait."

"That was your doing as much as anyone's," Tom said. "You were too proud to send to Westered while there was yet time, and now it is too late. Is God to blame for that? We choose our own pain or happiness."

"You can easily say so," Philip said. "You have always been fortune's pet, her darling. No wonder you can always smile. She has left you unscathed."

"Has she, Philip? Has she truly?" Tom shook his head. "You forget, brother, I too have had cause to mourn. John and Richard were my brothers as much as they were yours. If your mother was an adulteress, so was mine. It was my father as well as yours who was a traitor and a murderer. I saw his throat cut in the street, not you. Granted, Katherine was not my wife, but her death broke a heart as dear to me as my own. Do you think I am not touched by that? By all of this? That this war does not grieve me, to see such a poor waste of life for so little? And even had I no cause of my own, Philip, what grieves you grieves me. You must know that."

"Let me alone," Philip replied with a surly frown. "Why are you even here?"

"To find out why I am free."

Philip's frown deepened. "I did not want to see you trapped and defenseless when Stephen takes this city. Even you deserve better than that. I was wrong to strike you in anger, whatever you've done."

"I thought perhaps it was because you had a chance to realize that your accusations were not true, that you had wronged your poor lady."

"I was the one wronged," Philip said, his voice low and fierce.

"Not by her and not by me. Rosalynde would never betray you. You've hurt her, Philip, too many times, but she loves you. She loves you near to idolatry. And even if she would betray you, do you think that I would? That I would be false to my Elizabeth and to God and damn myself for a moment's pleasure?"

"Stephen will take this city tomorrow. It does not matter now what I think."

"Do you truly think that I could do you wrong? I can bear anything from you but that."

Philip looked away. "Go on. None of this matters now."

"Please, Philip, do not leave it at this. We were never false to you."

"I said it does not matter."

"It matters to me. You are a stubborn-hearted idiot, but whatever you do, you are my brother. I would give you my life if it would stop the hurt you've been nursing. How long can you live in this hell you've made, turned by every wind of doubt and suspicion, believing God does not care for you? The proof of His love is all around you."

"All around?" Philip looked at the cathedral's destruction. "Proof, indeed."

"Not in this rubble," Tom insisted, "but in this." He gestured toward the statue. "He's protected you throughout this long conflict. He's chosen you to bear His light in this darkness. He's given you charge over this kingdom in His name, to defend His people from Stephen and the destruction he brings, and He's graced you with every gift of man and nature to help you do it. Beyond that, He's given you someone who loves you as He does, no matter what you do or how cruelly you use her. Do you think you've earned her love any more than you can earn His? She loves you."

"Yes, she loves me, and you love me, and this faithlessness is how you demonstrate your love."

"We did not wrong you! You know in your heart we did not! You know Rosalynde loves only you. Not your name or your title, not your wealth or any other trappings of nobility, but you. You know she loves you, and you are afraid because you love her, too. Do you think that if you make her hate you that it will be easier for you not to love her? Philip, Katherine is dead. It is no sin for you to love Rosalynde now."

"You talk like a fool, Tom. What difference does it make now who was false or who was not, whether I love her or she me? We've fallen into Stephen's hands, and there there is no mercy."

"Put yourself into God's hands, brother, and there you will find great mercy. He'll not forsake you."

"He *has* forsaken me."

"You've forsaken Him! Are you so enamored of destruction that you rush to it with open arms? Make it right with Him, Philip, and make it right with Rosalynde before tomorrow. It is not too late yet. Go into the battle with faith, not fear. Do not let your pride destroy you and pull all Lynaleigh down with you. Please, Philip."

"You are a fool, Tom." Philip shook his head and walked deliberately out into the street.

Out of Tom's sight, Philip began to run. When he reached the city wall, he climbed the steps near the east gate. He knew as he stood there panting that he should call together his lieutenants to plan for the coming battle, but he also knew that planning would be no use. He could see the enemy camped around the town, the glow of their fires, the grim silhouettes of their siege guns. There was no hope against so mighty an adversary. He would no longer waste his time in planning—or in prayer.

Rosalynde would never betray you. She loves you.

Tom's words had come too near not to cut, as much as he denied their truth to himself. "Why should she love me?" he whispered into the darkness. "I've hurt her too many times. Tom was right in that much."

Do you truly think that I could do you wrong? I can bear anything from you but that.

He saw again the unfeigned hurt in his brother's eyes, the silent reproof of the bruises his fury had left on Tom's throat, and had to steel himself against the shame he felt.

"I've hurt him, too," he murmured. Then he looked up at the starless sky. "I've done nothing to make You love me either. Well, You will have Your justice tomorrow."

Wearily he walked the top of the wall toward the castle. He was tired, but he knew there would be no sleep, no comfort for him tonight and surely none tomorrow. He would wait out the night alone. Let the day come and bring with it what it would, he was tired and had run out of answers.

"Are you hurt, my lord?" Rafe asked as Philip came up to him in the corridor outside the nursery, covered with dust and grit from the cathedral. Rafe had been given special charge to guard the baby prince since the bombardment had begun, so he knew little of the siege beyond the sound of the guns. "Have they broken through yet?"

"Not yet, but soon." Philip looked with great intensity into his face. "Rafe, my lady and my son—"

He broke off, struggling to resign himself to their loss.

"I will guard them with my life, my lord, until you release me of that charge."

Philip nodded and padded silently into the nursery, startling the nurse.

"I want a moment with my son," he told her. With a clumsy, sleepy curtsey she left them alone.

Robin started to whimper when he took him from the cradle, and Philip held him close in farewell.

"Better a life too short than one too long," he murmured. "We'll not meet again in this world, little summer Robin." Nor, he feared, in the next.

Robin quieted against him and was soon asleep again. Philip laid him back in the cradle with a final caress and turned to see Rosalynde in the doorway. She curtseyed low.

"Your Majesty."

"Madam," he said with a cool bow.

She seized his arm as he passed by her. "Please, my lord, a word."

"Well?"

The nurse had come back to tend the baby, and Rosalynde looked apprehensively at her. "Please, not here, my lord. I must speak with you."

"Very well."

She took him to her chamber and dismissed her fretful ladies.

"They are all afraid. It is said that tomorrow Stephen will take the city."

"Yes."

"We must fight them then!"

"We will, but I'll not lie to you, madam. Not now. We cannot match them. We are lost."

"No, please, never say so."

"It is true," he said dispassionately. "I shall meet my judgment tomorrow. I only pray God will end it there with me."

"Oh, no, Philip, please. Ask His pardon and favor for tomorrow. Do not surrender before the battle can even begin. Put your trust in Him and in His mercy. He'll not fail you. He loves you. I know He does."

Philip shook his head. "Why should He? What have I ever done to make Him love me?"

There was pity in her eyes as she took his hand, pity for all the needless ache in his heart. "You still do not understand, do you? It is His goodness, not yours, that makes Him love you. All you have to do is accept it and be thankful. How can you say He does not love you? He has blessed you with everything a man could wish for."

He looked at her as if he desperately wanted to believe her. Then the old anger came again to his eyes.

"This *blessing* you claim I have—what is it? If I have my crown from God, it is a curse, not a blessing. It drains my strength and eats away my life until I have none left. If He gave it, then it was punishment for my pride."

She held tightly to his hand, and, surprised, he stopped trying to pull away from her.

"Do not go like this," she pled. "I could not bear to lose you."

"You mean you could not bear for me to lose. You know Stephen will have no mercy on anyone belonging to Afton. Not women, not children. He might spare you for Margaret's sake, but never Robin. Heir to Afton? Never."

"Please, Philip, for Robin's sake and for your own, do not go into the battle this way. Stephen would not have to kill me if you were lost. I would die."

"Why should you care?" he asked bitterly. "After last night, after what I said to you, why should you care? I know I was unjust. I beat Tom half to death! You should be well rid of such a wretch."

She caressed his cheek. "Do you not know yet that you take my life with you into every battle? That my heart does not beat until I see you safely home? Will you never understand? How much more plainly can I say it? I love you. With my whole heart, I love you."

Stiffening, he pushed her away and stood quivering like some wild thing at bay. "Don't."

"But I do love you. Perhaps at first when I said that, I did not know what I meant. Maybe then I did only love the image of you I had created for myself, but you have surely destroyed that. You cannot say I have any romantic notions about who and what you are. But just as surely as I have learned to know you, I have learned to love you. As difficult as you have made it, I know you, Philip, and I love you still."

"Don't force me."

"It was my choice, not yours. If you cannot return my love, well, let it be so. My love will be as silent and as invisible as you wish, but I will love you."

"Never say that."

"Whatever you do, I will love you."

"I said, never say that!"

He cracked his palm fiercely across her face, making her stumble backwards. They both gasped, and his hand went instinctively to his own scarred cheek.

"Oh, Rosalynde," he stammered, backing away, his eyes wide. "I never—I could not—"

There are some things I could never be pushed to do . . .

The print of his hand was livid on her white face, but she did not lash back at him. She had not even cried out. Her tear-filled eyes held nothing but compassion and deep love.

. . . and should never expect to be forgiven if I did.

He lowered his head in shame. "Rosalynde, I—"

She slipped her fingers around his and gently pulled his hand from his face. Then she pressed her lips to the fine white scar on his cheek.

"I still love you, Philip."

The realization pierced through his heart. She still loved him. After all he had done to wrong that love, after all he had done to kill it, she still loved him. No matter what he did or whether he ever loved her in return, she still loved him.

As God loved him.

He was still for a moment. Then he shuddered, feeling the pain of ice cracking in an unexpected thaw. He exhaled twice, deep hurting rushes of air. Suddenly he was on his knees before her, his arms tight around her waist. She held him against her as the sobs wracked him.

"Oh, Rosalynde, what have I done?"

"Shh. It will all be well."

"I cannot—" He clenched his teeth and turned his face away. "I cannot do it anymore. I cannot do it alone."

"Shh," she soothed, her own tears falling into his hair as she pressed her cheek against it, "you are not alone."

She had never before seen him cry, never before seen him anything but strong and so in control, but she did not turn him away.

He pressed closer to her, straining to hold her tighter and tighter, shielding himself from the flood of memories that assaulted him—

his own doubt, bitterness, unforgiveness, ingratitude, faithlessness, vainglory, wrath, blasphemy, stubborn pride—more, an endless litany of sins against a gracious, openhanded God who was, in the very face of them, still holding out His arms in loving welcome. How could he have been so blind?

"Forgive me, please forgive me, God. Dear Lord, my God, forgive me."

He looked up at Rosalynde, remembering also his sins against her, and touched her wounded cheek with trembling fingers. "Can you forgive me, too?"

"Yes. I love you," she said simply.

He stood up and took her into his arms. "Then love me, Rosalynde. I need you to love me. I swear before God and all heaven that I love you."

After Philip left him, Tom knelt alone in Winterbrooke's ruins, pleading for peace and deliverance for the town and for his brother. It was not long before the moon broke the heavy clouds and shone through the shattered roof, bathing his earnest, upturned face in pale silver. He felt an almost-physical release and a gratitude that defied words. He had no answers yet, only peace.

CHAPTER

ROSALYNDE LAY IN PHILIP'S ARMS, BASKING IN THE DEEP JOY SHE felt. This time he had given her himself, all of himself, openly, freely, without reservation. There were tears in her eyes because she had never before known such love.

There were tears in his eyes because he had known and had thought never to know again.

She sighed his name and stroked his hair as he rested his head against her shoulder. Then he began to tell her everything. She wept with him and for him as he struggled with the painful words and the agonizing emotions behind them, the merciless torrent of feeling he had kept so long chained up inside himself. He told her everything, forced himself to feel the pain he had denied, until at last he lay in her arms, his ribs aching from sobbing, nothing binding him but deep love.

She held him tightly and prayed with him as he asked God once more to forgive him and then forgave all who had wronged him—his faithless mother, his ambitious father, Margaret, Dunois, Stephen himself. "Give me the grace, dear God, to forgive them as You have forgiven me. In Your strength, Lord, I do forgive them."

Again he asked Rosalynde's forgiveness, and again she gave it, this time in exchange for his—for all the times she had in her ignorance rubbed his bruises with gravel. She had known so little about the hurt he had suffered, the cruel losses and crueler betrayals, the memories and fears that had tortured him. Now she understood him better and loved him better still. He told her again how much he loved her, and she could read the clear truth of it in the crystal depths of his eyes.

❧

Palmer came to Tom before true dawn and found him sprawled out on the cracked marble floor, sound asleep.

"My lord," he said, waking him. "You choose a strange bed, my lord."

Tom stretched and stood up, shaking back his tousled hair and straightening his clothes. He knew Palmer was looking him over, questioning his battered appearance, but Tom made no explanation beyond a wry grin. "Could a man ask for sounder sleep than when in the hand of God Himself?"

"Best pray He will use that hand on Afton's part today," Palmer said with a grim, set expression. "Ellenshaw has sent his terms."

Tom was instantly alert. "Has the king read them?"

Palmer shook his head. "The lords sent me for you. They think it best if all of you go together to him."

"Do you know where he is now?"

"With the queen yet, I expect."

Tom was surprised. "So early?"

"So late, my lord. Her ladies said she did not call for them last night or yet this morning, so he must be with her still. Shall I take this to him?"

There was the tiniest hint of a smile on Tom's face. "No. Let me see what our good cousin proposes first." He read the paper and whistled low between his teeth. "He does not ask much!"

"Shall I send word to the king?"

Tom looked up through the ruined wall to the window of Rosalynde's tower chamber. It was still dark.

"No. Let him have peace awhile longer. We have a few hours yet to answer this. I will go to the lords, and we will make what preparation we can without him."

Philip woke with his head cradled against Rosalynde's bosom. She was still whispering endearments into his hair, toying with the soft, damp wisps at the nape of his neck. He wondered again at the resilient depth of her love, remembering how they had talked during the night—more perhaps than during all their marriage before.

He remembered laughter, too, among the tears—his own laughter at his proud, foolish self that had fallen further and further from truth, clinging to his stubbornness, imagining that it was strength and only now seeing it for the blind weakness it was. He felt now as he had while he was recovering from his wounds in Tanglewood, when he had almost had to learn to walk again. Only this time he need not face the struggle alone.

He smiled at Rosalynde, his eyes as warm and blue as the summer sea, and pressed a tender kiss on her lips. He knew that the battle would begin today and end today, too, but he did not allow worry to darken his contentment or hurry him from her arms. The fate of Winton, of all Lynaleigh, no longer rested on his shoulders.

He had been too proud to send to Westered while there was yet time, and now he had no choice but to trust in the mercy God had already shown him, but there was a curious freedom in that. He had been so tied to duty. Now his only duty was to trust and obey. How could he do any less for the One who had shown him so much love undeserved? So desperately undeserved.

He looked into Rosalynde's loving eyes, and a shadow passed over his face. She was at risk now and the baby, too, all because of his pride, but she had already forgiven him that. There was only one confession left for him to make.

"Will you forgive me, love, for lying to you?"

"Lying?"

"When I swore I would not love you."

She pressed one finger to his lips, smiling a little to think that the long-ago pain could now be so sweet. "I could never think you a liar."

"I was then. Oh, believe me."

"You have never lied to me, sweet love."

"But—"

"Philip Ice-Heart made that oath—not you, and so long as I have you instead, he may keep his word."

He kissed her again, still astonished by the reality of her love. "I love you," he said. Then he pulled her head to his shoulder and held her against his heart. "I could stay here and tell you so a year together."

"And I would not think it enough."

"I do not think my dear cousin will wait so long," he said lightly.

She was suddenly apprehensive. "Must you go down to him?"

"I promised Robin a kingdom," he said. Then he squeezed her tighter. "And should I not defend the treasure I have so lately discovered?"

She did not return his smile. "Oh, Philip, if anything should happen now—"

"Do not fear, love. God will dispose the day as pleases Him. You told me to trust Him. Now you must also."

"I do. Truly, I do. But we've had so little time."

"I do not know God's will for this battle, only that I must go to it in faith and obedience to Him."

"Can your soldiers match Stephen's in the field?" Her voice sounded very small.

"No. There aren't enough of us to last an hour against his forces." He felt her tremble, and he turned her face up to his. "But there aren't enough of them on earth or in hell to last an instant against God."

Her eyes were suddenly bright with tears, but she smiled, too, and nodded, trying to hide her fear from him.

"It will be all right, love," he soothed.

Seeing a hint of dawn in the east window, he kissed her once more and started to get up, but she held on to him.

"Not yet," she pleaded. "I cannot let you go."

"You must," he said. "I must." Slipping his hands out of hers, he got up. "Pray God's mercy on us today, but more that His will would be done."

She held tightly to one of the pillows and wept quietly as he pulled on his boots and breeches. Finally unable to bear more, he knelt beside the bed and put his arms around her.

"We'll not be parted long, sweet," he said, holding her close and closer still. Then his voice dropped to a husky whisper. "Just do not ever stop loving me."

She held her breath as if she could hold the moment, and for a little while there was no sound but the beating of their hearts. Then he gently took her arms from around his neck. Her breath came back in a painful sob.

"Shh," he murmured. "If I do not come back to you today, then you shall one day come to me." With one sweet kiss he stood up and somehow managed a brave smile. "Do not be afraid."

"I do love you, Philip. Truly, truly."

That brought the tears to his eyes, and his smile was suddenly not so steady.

"I know." He touched his fingers to her cheek. "Truly."

He stood for a moment outside her chamber once he had left it, waiting until his breath came more evenly and some of the pain of parting diminished. She loved him *truly, truly,* and he took strength from his certainty in it, but he felt like such a fool recalling all the time he had wasted not loving her, the pain he had brought them both, and now their time together might be ending.

"Oh, Jesus."

The very sound of the name fell like a healing balm on his soul. Here was another love he held as a certainty, this one beyond the human capacity to fail. Whatever happened, he knew he could trust in that love.

"Show me Your way," he prayed. Then he went to ready himself for battle.

Clad in chain mail, wearing the proud symbols of his royalty, Philip went down the steps into the courtyard. He slowed as he saw Tom, also fully armed, tightening the cinch on his saddle.

"Tom?"

Tom turned to him, an expectant hopefulness in his expression, as if he knew already of the peace Philip had made and was glad of it. But there were those bruises, too, still on his throat.

"I've been so wrong," Philip said, feeling a keen pang of shame. "Will you forgive me?"

"I did that long ago," Tom assured him.

Philip felt his uncertainty melt into nothingness. He grasped the hand Tom offered him. "I haven't time to say what I would say to you, Tom. Only that I've been every bit the stubborn fool you said I was."

"That is a common enough trait in mankind," Tom allowed, "though I've not seen many who've worked so hard at it." He grinned. "Perhaps it was your diligence that made God choose you to rule this kingdom."

"Perhaps it was," Philip agreed with a rueful smile. Then his expression sobered. "Whatever it was, whatever my failings, I know He chose me for this, just as you said, to bear His light in this darkness. His light, not mine. There would be no honor in me if I did not uphold that charge with my life." Catching himself, he smiled again and added, "By His grace."

"By His grace," Tom repeated. "We need nothing else."

Philip looked him steadily in the face. "You've stood by me all this while, Tom. Will you once more?"

"You know my answer. My sword is yours, now and for so long as you have need of it."

"Ellenshaw has sent terms, my lord," Darlington interrupted, and Philip looked over the paper he was given.

"So we are to have peace. That is, if we will surrender all Afton claims to the crown, forfeit all our lands and goods, and be brought to trial in the death of King Edward and, no doubt, face the full penalty the law allows for that. What say you, my lords?"

"It is more than we would have Your Majesty answer to," Darlington replied. The other lords nodded their agreement.

"We must go out to meet them then," Philip said calmly.

Darlington gaped at him, certain he had misheard. "My lord, you cannot think so! They outnumber us five for one! They've had food these past weeks! They've got cannon! They've—"

"They've breached the wall, my lord," Philip reminded him matter-of-factly. "If we do not go out to them, they shall merely come in to us."

"Suicide," spat one of the soldiers.

Philip turned to him. "With the men we have? With no reinforcements? Suicide," he agreed. "But with help . . . " A sly, knowing smile hovered at his lips, and the others looked at him as if his reason had been shaken loose along with the ceiling beams at Winterbrooke Cathedral.

"There is no help, my lord," Darlington said, holding his voice down with effort. "If we cannot stay here, we've nothing to do but go out and fight for your right and God's truth until our last man goes down. I say there is nothing better than to die for the right."

"And I say it is better to live for the right!" Philip turned to his soldiers, determined to replace the fear in their eyes with faith. "Hear me. Fight now, and we do not fight alone. If we stand in faith, our God will send us help. He's promised us that, and I will believe in Him though I stand alone."

"You do not stand alone," Tom said, and Philip warmly clasped his shoulder.

"All you who believe, who'll stand true to the Lord, to trust in

His mercy, pray with me." Halfheartedly, the men knelt, and Philip closed his eyes and prayed, "Holy Father, we have no wisdom but in You. We have no strength but in You. We have no hope but in You. I do not know how Your deliverance will come, only that it will come. Because of Your mercy and grace, it will come. God, You know my men are too few and too worn to face so mighty an enemy alone, but Your grace is enough to make a way for us. For Jesus' sake, I ask Your help and mercy today. Spare the blood of Your servants and of those who, seeing Your holy power, might come to call You Lord. Let Your will alone be done today, in the name of Your Son, Jesus. Amen."

"Amen," Tom echoed firmly. A few more low responses came from among the soldiers.

Philip lifted his head, a purposed fire in his eyes. "Come, we've a battle to fight."

He leapt onto his horse and, with Tom riding beside him, led his army out onto the field.

Rosalynde looked down from her window, watching the soldiers form a ragged line before Winton's gate. At the sight of them, a great shout arose from the armies amassed at the bottom of the hill. Line after line of men on sleek horses, their fresh banners snapping arrogantly in the wind, waited for Philip's tattered army, waited for the morning sport to begin.

"Our men are so few!" Rosalynde cried. "God! God, help them!"

She could see Philip riding before them, and the faint, confident sound of his voice was borne up to her on the morning breeze. Deep sobs shook her, and tears coursed down her cheeks. Her heart ached to see him there—free and strong, shining with faith, fearless—and utterly doomed.

"Please, Lord God, not now."

She would have grieved without consolation to lose Philip as he had been, Philip Ice-Heart. But now that he was finally her own, now that he was free from his bitter prison, now that she had at last been given one glorious taste of the love she had so long craved—

"God, please, I cannot lose him now!"

She had been so brave, so full of faith the night before. Now the reality of the enemy filled her with fear. She could no longer see down to the battlefield, her eyes were so dimmed with tears, and she reached for something to dry them with. It took her a moment to realize that it was Philip's shirt she had snatched up from the floor.

She held it caressingly against her as if he were still wearing it. Then, crying out in desperation, she buried her face in it. It still carried the delicious faint scent of leather and saint's rose and man's sweat—his scent.

"God," she mourned, "God, what can I do? I cannot lose him now that he's mine."

He is not yours. He is Mine.

Startled by the still voice inside her, she lifted her head and choked down a sob.

You must give him to Me.

"Lord—"

If I require him of you today, will you give him to Me?

"But, Lord—"

You must have no gods before Me.

She lowered her head for an agonized moment. Then she went back to the window and took one last longing look at the god of her idolatry. Resolutely she turned her back and went into the tiny chapel just off Philip's chamber. Realizing she still held his shirt, she pressed it briefly against her heart. Then she laid it upon the altar and sank to her knees.

CHAPTER

20

COURAGE, MY MEN!" PHILIP SHOUTED WITH A FLASHING SMILE. HE could see the fear on his soldiers' faces as they silently compared the size of the enemy forces to their own. Only Tom at his right hand seemed unafraid.

"Let us begin it," Tom suggested.

"Wait!" One of the captains pointed to a small party of horsemen coming toward them under a flag of truce. "It's Ellenshaw himself and King William as well!"

Tom looked hopefully at his brother. "Perhaps God has answered our prayers already, and they have come to make peace."

"Have you come to make peace, my lords?" Philip asked when they halted before him.

Stephen only laughed. "We come once again to ask you to surrender, cousin, before you and all that are yours are destroyed. Give me back what's mine, and I will give you mercy. Otherwise you and all these fools who follow you will sleep in hell tonight."

"You know my answer, cousin. I have seen your mercy before—at Grant, at Abbey, at Breebonne—and I will give my life and all I have, if that is God's will, to keep you from selling off Lynaleigh to those who hate her and to keep you from destroying her people."

"God's will? You and your God!" Stephen jeered. "Where is your mighty God who sets you here with too few men to even bury your dead? Where is this God of yours? He is as helpless as you are!"

"God is not mocked," Philip said solemnly. "You will see His hand, if not today, then someday and soon enough. There will be no denying Him then."

For a moment there was ominous silence, silence finally broken by Stephen's high laughter. King William glanced uneasily at Philip and Tom, unnerved by the unshakable certainty on their faces.

"We waste the day," he said gruffly.

Stephen sneered at him. "Afraid?"

Still laughing, Ellenshaw spurred his horse, and, relief on his face, William followed him back to their own men.

"No, God," Philip promised between clenched teeth, watching them go, "I will not doubt You. You will deliver us in Your own time and in Your own way."

"Be ready, men," one of the captains ordered. "They've almost reached their lines."

The men drew their swords and stoically awaited the signal to move forward.

"Have faith, for the Lord is with us!" Philip called to them. "This is His battle!"

"My lord, they are coming!" Darlington exclaimed. "We must go down now!" He stopped and looked down the hill. "We are lost if we hesitate!"

Philip shook his head and closed his eyes, fervently twisting the reins in his hands. "God, this battle is Yours. Show me Your way."

"My lord, they are coming!" Darlington warned. "For God's sake, begin it! Open your eyes!"

Philip did as he was urged and saw scores of fiercely armed soldiers swarming up the hillside. "Stand fast, men," he ordered. "No one is to move without my command."

His soldiers fidgeted where they stood, desperate to fight or flee, hoping they had not pledged their lives and honor to a madman.

Philip sat quietly before them, waiting for Stephen to move up the hill.

"Will you stand there like sheep?" came the taunting voice. "My army was meant to go against men, not old women! And where is the power of this God you promised I would see? Are these all the ranks He could muster?"

Philip did not acknowledge Stephen's words or budge from where he was. He merely waited, watching the enemy draw nearer and bunch closer together so each of them would have an opportunity to strike at least one blow against the city's meager defense. He closed his eyes again.

"Show me Your way, Lord."

Now, something inside him prompted. He looked up to see Stephen's ranks slowing, the neat lines blurring into disorder as the soldiers heard a rumble like thunder behind them. It was the sound of an army coming from the forest at their backs, from the west.

"It is Westered!" Tom cried.

Philip looked at him in astonishment, and then he saw another troop of soldiers riding up from the forest at his right with his father-in-law leading them.

"May we be of assistance, Your Majesty?" Westered called, pulling his spirited mount up beside Philip as his men began to array themselves behind the enemy. "Your guests were so certain of victory that they left three sides of the city lightly guarded. It was easy to dispatch the sentries here on the north side and then wait until my men were ready to come at them from behind.

The armies of Ellenshaw and Grenaver faltered to a standstill.

Stephen's generals halted beside him. "We cannot fight so many, my lord," one of them said to Ellenshaw, "and we cannot retreat. They will cut us down. We must surrender."

Dismissing him with a look of contempt, Stephen spurred his mount up the hill until he and Philip were face to face. Then he lifted his visor. "Come, cousin, we have still a kingdom to decide for."

Philip looked at his father-in-law, then back at Stephen.

"Spare the lives of your men, cousin," Philip said. "Surrender."

"I will not surrender! Not to a coward who'll not even fight for himself. You men who follow after this milk-livered whelp, is this the king you would have rule you? If you be a king, cousin, if you think yourself worthy the name, you will settle this between us now. Just you and I alone to see who best merits the throne here."

"You have nothing to prove, boy," Westered told Philip. "You needn't take the risk."

"Then we shall fight to our last man," Stephen sneered. "And you will have this blood, too, on your hands."

Philip looked into his rival's pale eyes and realized it was meant to be so between them. He had prayed God would spare the blood on both sides, and here was his answer.

He dismounted and dropped to one knee. "God," he said softly, his head bowed, "however You would have this battle end, end it here, and let my sword strike only as You would have it so."

"Yes, pray for your soul, cousin," Stephen taunted, dismounting, too. "Your life already is mine."

Philip lifted his head. "Not yours, cousin, nor yet mine either, but come on." He drew his sword and kissed the hilt of it. "Come on."

"Never do it, son," Westered urged. "He has nothing to lose from it, and you have nothing to gain. He cannot win against us both together."

"This is between us, my lord," Philip replied. "Not for my pride nor for my honor, but because it must be so. Either I am king, or he is. There can be no more doubt. Tom, if he should win, Winton is his. Take Rosalynde and Robin and keep them safe. My lord of Westered, I trust they will have shelter in your lands."

Westered nodded, and Philip turned back to Stephen.

"Cousin, if you are victor, as I said, Winton is yours as if we had matched our armies for it, and none of my people will oppose you. Be warned though. If you touch my family, my army and the army of Westered will cut you down and take it all back. Is that not so, my lord?"

Westered nodded gravely.

"Tom?"

Tom took him in a quick, fierce embrace. "End it here, Philip."

Philip nodded. "This will be the last," he said. Then he put on his helmet. "Come, let us settle this thing."

Stephen smiled blandly and lowered his visor. Then without a pause, he made a savage cut toward Philip's head. Philip parried the blow and redoubled it back to him with such swift power that Stephen sprang backwards in surprise.

"I did not half believe the tales of your prowess in battle, cousin," he said as if he were amused. Then he slashed at Philip again, a blow that would have easily taken off Philip's head had it not been deflected.

He struck once more, his blade and Philip's meeting between the two of them, wedged together. The faces of both combatants strained with effort, each pressing harder, determined to take the advantage. Then the impasse ended. Stephen's sword slipped up higher on Philip's with a metallic shriek, and both of them pulled back.

"I am going to kill you, cousin," Stephen panted. "I will see you in hell if I must accompany you there myself."

He raised his sword as if to strike again at Philip's head and then dropped his arm, catching Philip's leg just at the knee, forcing him down to the ground. But Philip, lighter and swifter in his chain mail than Stephen in his plate armor, rolled away from the next blow and scrambled to his feet.

"If you are bent upon visiting hell, cousin, you must go alone. I've come already as near that place as I care to."

Stephen lunged at him again, driving him a few steps up the hill, then gradually to one side and down again, his blows falling hard and heavy. Philip repaid each one with interest, but he was not so surefooted as before. Stephen's strike had left his knee deeply bruised and made him just a shade slower than usual. He was being forced farther and farther down toward the enemy army, slipping in the trampled grasses that had once been lush and green on the hillside.

"Hold him, Philip!" Tom called, moving with the rest of the men alongside the combatants.

"Retake the high ground, boy!" Westered shouted. "The high ground!"

Philip was almost to the forest now, unable to force Stephen back up toward the city. He was surrounded by the soldiers of both his enemies, but they cleared the way around him, and Philip was driven into the trees.

"God," he gasped under his breath, "show me."

Stephen's blade fell again and again and again, but Philip found that here where the land was level, he was no longer losing ground. He backed still farther into the forest, forcing his opponent to follow him.

"Will you run, puppy?" Stephen demanded.

Philip drove him back a step or two. "Only toward you, cousin."

Stephen swore and lunged at him, but Philip met the blow and turned him sideways so each of them had one shoulder to the forest and one to the city. Soldiers from both sides circled around them now, shouting, straining, feeling each blow, adding to the ringing din of metal on metal.

"You shall win, Philip!" Tom cried. "He is falling back!"

"Come on, man!" William of Grenaver urged, seeing his ally's plight. "Do something!"

"Hold, cousin!" Stephen panted, holding up his hands, and Philip slowed his stroke.

That instant of hesitation was all Stephen needed. He struck again at Philip's leg where he knew he was vulnerable, again forcing him down. Philip met his next blow from his knees, bent backwards almost to the ground, stopping Stephen's blade not inches from splitting his skull. Again their swords were wedged together at the hilts, neither of them able to move.

"You cannot defeat me, cousin," Stephen grated. "It is over."

Gradually, Philip pushed upwards, rising by main force to his feet, bracing his legs apart to keep his knee from giving way. Stephen swore again and pressed harder against him, trying to force him back down.

Philip increased the pressure, then abruptly released it, throwing Stephen off balance. In an instant he wrenched the blade from

Stephen's hand and drove him back against a tree. The impact forced the air from Stephen's lungs with a whoosh.

"That is enough, cousin," Philip said, his tone leaving little doubt who was true king in Lynaleigh. "*Now* it is over."

There was a long pause as Stephen stood there, glaring defiantly, wheezing and gasping for breath with Philip's well-muscled forearm shoved against his windpipe.

"I—I yield."

A cheer rose from the armies of Westered and Afton, and Philip dropped his weary arm. Tom was instantly at his side, taking his helmet from him, pounding his back in congratulation.

"My lord Darlington," Philip commanded as he pushed Stephen forward, "take my dear cousin here to our most secure cell."

"At once, Your Majesty," Darlington said. He grabbed the would-be king by the arm, unceremoniously dragging off his helmet before he led him up the hillside.

Philip watched for a moment. Then he looked at the men surrounding him.

"As for the rest of you rebels—"

"Philip! Philip!"

He turned to see Rosalynde running along the top of the wall above them, still in her shift and robe, still with her hair cascading down her back. Looking up at her, he smiled, that same radiant smile that had won her so long ago in Westered. He did not know it was the same. He only knew the nightmare was over, and he was free.

"Rosalynde!"

He lifted his sword above his head in triumph. Then he flung it to the ground and started up the hill. She disappeared for a moment, then reappeared inside the gate and ran across the drawbridge, her bare feet pattering lightly on the planks.

"Philip!"

His soldiers began to cheer again as he held his arms out to her, and she ran through their ranks, past their captains, past Darlington and Stephen—Stephen!

"Philip!" Tom warned, but it was too late.

Stephen broke Darlington's hold and snatched his dagger. In another instant that dagger was at Rosalynde's throat, and Stephen was dragging her backwards, his left hand wound fast in her hair.

"No closer," he cautioned.

Philip halted midstride, holding up his hands to show he was unarmed. "What do you mean to do?"

"I only wish to become better acquainted with my fair sister, Lady Rosalynde."

He pressed familiarly against her, and Westered swore. "Before God I'll tear him to pieces myself!"

Philip stilled him, his eyes never leaving the white terror on Rosalynde's face. "What do you mean to do?"

"Not to be taken," Stephen answered. "Not today. Not if you hold your lady dear."

"I need not tell you the value of your life if she is harmed," Philip warned.

"No, nor the value of hers if I am hindered."

Stephen began to back toward his men, pulling Rosalynde along with him, and her eyes widened in a silent plea.

"Have faith, love," Philip called to her, tensing forward.

Stephen held her closer. "Have a care, cousin. Such a little, little force would leave you with nothing but a pretty corpse."

Philip and Tom exchanged a covert glance, and Tom took a step toward Stephen.

"Stay back, Brenden," Stephen said. "I am watching you."

"Never do this, cousin," Tom said, stopping where he was.

As they spoke, Philip moved back slightly, just in front of one of his men, and reached backwards out of Stephen's sight. Soon he felt the press of something heavy in his hands. Stephen was at his horse now, Rosalynde still shielding him, and Philip tightened his fingers, waiting.

"Ellenshaw, you'll pay dearly!" Westered threatened, and Tom came to stand beside him.

"Let him alone, my lord," Tom advised. "He knows we cannot move against him now."

"Very wise, cousin," Stephen said. Then he pulled Rosalynde up into his saddle with him and turned to Westered with a self-confident sneer. "My dear father-in-law, I—"

His body stiffened, and the dagger thudded to the ground. Then he pitched backwards, a bolt from Philip's crossbow squarely between his startled eyes. In that same instant, a hundred of Westered's archers aimed their weapons at the rest of the enemy leaders, daring them to make a move in revenge.

Philip tossed down his bow and in a few long strides was at Rosalynde's side, lifting her from the saddle, cradling her in his arms against his racing heart.

"Thank God, thank God," he murmured, rocking her gently, his eyes squeezed shut, his cheek pressed to hers. "Oh, Rosalynde, thank God."

A moment passed before he remembered that there was a host of enemy forces still surrounding him. With Rosalynde still clinging to him, he lifted his head, a stern look of kingly displeasure on his face.

"Have Lynaleigh and Grenaver any further quarrel, my lord?" he asked King William.

Westered moved to stand behind him. "My army is still at your disposal, Your Majesty," he reminded Philip.

The King of Grenaver quickly shook his head. "No, Your Majesty. We cannot hope to stand against you now. We are at your mercy."

"Very well," Philip said. Then he raised his voice for all to hear. "Ellenshaw is dead, and King William has surrendered. You who have come here to challenge my right as king, leave your arms, and I shall leave you your lives."

All around him soldiers laid down their weapons.

"Now leave my sight."

"I will see to it," Tom said. "Your lady needs you."

Philip looked down into Rosalynde's face, his eyes full of tenderness. "He did not harm you, did he, love?"

She shook her head. Cuddling her to him again, he carried her up the hill back into the city. As they came to the cathedral, he halted and looked up at the ruins, feeling as if he could not pass the holy place with her safe in his arms and not pause to give thanks.

Reading the thought in his eyes, she smiled her assent, and he carried her through the rubble to the altar. Then, careful of her bare feet, he set her down. Hearing the clatter of armor, they both turned.

"You should never frighten my old heart as you did down there, child," Westered said, coming up to them.

Rosalynde stood on tiptoe to kiss him. "Oh, Father, I am so glad you've come."

"You look as if you were not expecting me, girl," Westered said, the release of victory making his booming laugh come easily. "Does this husband of yours not keep you in his confidence? The two of you look as close as bees and honey."

He laughed again, and she looked up into Philip's face, her eyes questioning. Philip shook his head, equally puzzled.

"You looked surprised to see me, my liege," Westered said.

"I *am* surprised, my lord."

"Did you think I would not keep my word when you had need of me, son? I told you I would come when you sent for me."

Again Philip shook his head. "I never sent for you, my lord. We've been weeks under siege. I could not send."

"Then what is this?"

Westered slipped something from his finger and dropped it into Philip's hand. It was his ring, scarred and encrusted with dirt, the only bright spot the engraved lion that Westered had rubbed clean in order to identify it. Now Philip rubbed it, too.

"How? I never sent it."

"I've asked Darlington to escort King William back to the border," Tom said as he came in from the street. "He and his men will—" He broke off at the bewildered look on Philip's face.

"I thought it was gone forever, Tom. I threw it away last winter in Treghatours. I thought—" Philip struggled for words, rubbing the ring again, amazed at its very tangibility in his hand. "I thought—"

"You thought God would not know just when you would need Him?" Tom asked softly.

"I thought—" Philip clutched the ring against his chest and stared past his brother's face at the gentle-eyed statue still wedged into the corner. "I never stooped to ask His help before last night. The journey to Westered and back at best takes at least—Oh, God," he whispered, lifting his face to heaven, trembling as he gulped down the crisp morning air. "Great God, my Lord."

Rosalynde nestled against him, and he stood for a long moment holding her.

"You never sent this to me?" Westered asked Philip finally.

"No, my lord. How did you get it?"

"One of my lieutenants brought it. Are you certain none of your people—"

Philip shook his head, and Tom looked at the older man keenly. "How did your man come by it, my lord?"

Westered chuckled. "I never thought to ask. We merely set out for Winton at once. I could have it traced down—"

"No," Philip said quickly. "Whomever He used to bring it, I know who meant you to have it. I need know nothing more." There was a reverent wonder on his face, coupled with utter humility and thankfulness. "God has delivered us without a drop of blood shed, save Stephen's, and I can only think that his death was a move of God's sovereignty." He pulled Rosalynde closer and drew a deep, shaky breath. "May He judge me so, too, if ever I doubt His love for me again."

He bowed his head, and for a moment there was silence. Then behind him came the sound of singing, starting softly and then growing to rich resonance. He turned to see the cathedral filling with people, his people, all joined together in thanksgiving.

"*Non nobis, Domine,*" they sang, "*non nobis, sed nomine tuo da gloriam . . .*"

It was a psalm in the language of the old church. "*Not unto us, oh Lord, not unto us but unto Your name do we give glory . . .*"

The great Bible that had once graced the pulpit now rested on a pile of shattered stones, but the archbishop stood before it as if he were at High Mass and began reading words of mercy and deliverance, his usually droning voice cracked and beautified with emotion.

Philip closed his eyes and listened. Then he came to stand beside the clergyman.

"My lord Archbishop, please you to let me read from the Holy Scriptures."

The archbishop backed away from the great book with a graceful bow, and Philip stood in his place, turning the stiff illuminated pages. Then he looked up, haloed in the shaft of sunlight that broke through the ruined roof, his face earnest and solemn.

"Is there one of you who'll not say that God's grace alone delivered us today?"

"No!" came a thunder of soldiers' voices, augmented with many others, old and young, peasant and noble, all who had seen that day's victory.

"'Not unto us, oh Lord,'" Philip read, the words of the Scripture flowing from his heart. "'Not unto us but unto Your name do we give glory, for Your mercy and for the sake of Your truth. Why should the unbeliever say, Where is now their God? Our God is in the heavens, and has done whatsoever He has pleased.'" He shut the book. "He has pleased to show us His mercy today. He has given me—" He pulled Rosalynde to his side. "He has given me more than I could imagine to ask, forgiveness when I deserved judgment and deliverance in a way I have yet to comprehend. If you are my subjects, then you are His, for I am His, and I pledge that He, not I, shall rule sovereign here in Lynaleigh."

He pledged it over again a few days later at the long-neglected coronation, kneeling before the altar in the midst of the cathedral's reconstruction, under the serene gaze of the statue of Christ that had been set back in its proper place. The archbishop anointed him with holy oil and then set the crown, hallowed and blessed, upon his head. Then Philip stood, meeting Rosalynde's radiant gaze.

God fashioned you for such a time, she had told him earlier, that same light shining in her eyes. *I imagine the warrior angels seen by the saints of old must have looked just as you do now, strong and resolute, clad in royal white and so very beautiful.*

He had laughed at the comparison, but she had only smiled and caressed his cheek.

A king made of legend and fancy could never have shone finer, my lord, she had said. Then she had smiled again. *My love*.

She knelt to him now, and he gave her formal welcome as his queen, adding a quick warm kiss on her lips to the kiss on each cheek that the ceremony required. He lifted her to her feet, thanking God as he did for the profound steadfastness of her love. He knew Katherine would always be a part of his heart, but the pain was leaving the memory of her, and he knew in time he would be able to do as she had once asked—remember her love and forget all the rest.

He counted himself greatly blessed. He had been given a second love, as true and as pure as the first, a love he would cherish and thank heaven for so long as God lent him life. He took Rosalynde's hand and stood her at his side as once again the nobility came to pledge their loyalty.

Tom swore first, as nearest in blood, and as he knelt to seal his vow, Philip leaned down to him, clasped his shoulders, and murmured a low, fervent thank you in his ear. There was a look of deep understanding between them. Then Tom smiled at him and at Rosalynde, happy in their happiness, doubtless feeling his own drawing nearer. Peace was come at last, and his Elizabeth would be with him soon. There was contentment in his eyes as he, too, stood at Philip's side while the rest, one by one, great and small, came to acknowledge Philip as true king.

Even Margaret, again in widow's black, knelt before the throne and swore her allegiance, an unrepentant gleam in her eye. For Rosalynde's sake and for the great mercy God had shown him, Philip had sent for his sister-in-law and pardoned her. She was accounted little threat now. Stephen was dead and with him the Ellenshaw aspirations. He had no heir, and there was no one now who dared stand against Philip. Heaven's approval was clearly upon his reign.

Even King William of Grenaver had sent his humbled emissaries to Winton, pleading peace between the long-time foes and surrendering all claim to the Riverlands, acknowledging his utter inability to stand against Lynaleigh united under God. Still awed himself by God's deliverance, still humbled by His majestic graciousness, Philip had felt compelled to be gracious in turn.

"From my enemies I take the spoils," he had written, "but with my friends I share. If it will keep peace between us, through brotherhood and not fear, then take the southern half of the Riverlands. Leave me the north, and let us be in accord. The only surrender I ask of you is to God and His will. Then we shall be brothers indeed."

Tom had read it over his shoulder as he put his signature and seal to it.

"There will be grumbling over this, you know, if you give away half of what Lynaleigh's fought for for so long."

"Let them grumble," Philip had said, knowing his brother supported his decision. "I believe it pleases God for it to be so. It is just."

King William was in the cathedral now, coming last after all of Philip's nobles to bring his greetings and offer public assurance of lasting peace and goodwill. That done, Philip knelt once more, and the archbishop laid his hands on his dark hair, blessing him in the name of the Father and of the Son and of the Holy Spirit.

"Great God of heaven and earth, merciful and mighty God, look graciously upon this Your servant. Keep his eyes ever upon You, and teach him to reign in Your strength and in Your wisdom that Your kingdom might be seen here in our land."

To that, Philip answered a fervent amen, and the archbishop raised him to his feet.

"Behold His Majesty, King Philip of Lynaleigh, of that name the fifth. Long may he rule over us in peace and justice, leading us before God in the way of faith and truth."

"Long live King Philip! God save the king!"

Philip drew Rosalynde to his side where she belonged and listened to the growing anthem of praise that rose up through the cathedral.

"*Non nobis, Domine, non nobis, sed nomine tuo da gloriam . . .*"

He closed his eyes and joined in the song.